HER HEART WAS TORN IN TWO

"Jeffrey," she pleaded. "Give me time . . . I don't have answers yet . . . but I promise . . . I'll let you know . . . I promise!"

His hands dropped from her shoulders, his fists clenched. "I can't believe any of this is happening." He looked at her, his chest heaving. "Catherine!" He called her name and she came into his arms for the last time, unable to resist, unable to fight her own need and longing. Time passed and still they could not leave each other, clinging with a fierce desperation which wracked them both. Catherine found the strength to pull away, finally. Jeffrey cradled her head in his hands and examined every flawless detail of her face. "Make the right decision, my love," he begged and hungrily kissed her lips once more.

Her eyes shone as she looked up at him. "I love you and Michael . . . and I always will. Remember that . . . whatever happens." She wrenched free of his embrace and ran through the thicket.

Her last statement raised pure terror in his heart.

BY LOVE DIVIDED

Rebecca Burton

LEISURE BOOKS • NEW YORK CITY

A LEISURE BOOK

Published by

Nordon Publications, Inc.
Two Park Avenue
New York, N.Y. 10016

I

The curtain at the upstairs window parted and a face peered out into the darkness. The quiet April night was still tinged with winter's bite and though Jens had dutifully kept the grate fire alive in the drawing room below, the slight woman did not move from her vigil. For some time, she'd been watching the headlights of a car making its way along the road which would eventually lead to the house. It was Jeffrey . . . she could tell by the low, purring sound of the motor.

The small, immaculately groomed woman continued to wait for the car to make the final turn at the gate before entering the courtyard. In the moonlight, large staring eyes dominated the square face. The mouth was a touch too pencil thin, but all in all, she was not unattractive, for her dark blond hair piled neatly on top of her head, secured with mother-of-pearl combs, was streaked with ash which picked up the gray flecks of her eyes in certain lights. At first glance, one might be tempted to say she was a handsome young matron.

A figure got out of the parked car and began walking swiftly toward the house. The only sign of agitation visible on her otherwise placid facade was the way her perfectly manicured nails dug into the velvet drape which was clenched in her hands. The front door opened and closed, and voices drifted up the stairs and into the suite of rooms which were hers and Philip's, temporarily.

She turned from the window and headed for the door, leaving the moss green plush drape streaked with moisture from her palms. Philip hadn't come back from London yet . . . he had never been this late before. This would give her some time alone with Jeffrey. Her cool exterior, so long accustomed to waiting for just such moments, betrayed nothing of her feverish desire, her almost insatiable need for Jeffrey to notice her. It was ironic that she'd fallen in love with the man she had orders from German Intelligence to keep under surveillance. For six long years she'd come and gone freely in his home, yet she'd never been as close to him as she was now. She'd finally won his confidence and trust. In time, she planned to win much more . . . in fact, it wasn't inconceivable that she'd give up espionage all together if she were sure of being loved in return.

Instead of finding him stretched out in his favorite lounging chair, absorbed with the mail and the newspaper, he was standing in front of the fire, his head buried in his hands. There was a tragic air about him.

"Jeffrey?" she called to him from the threshold. "What has happened?"

The lean figure turned around, his face a mask of anguish. "Elinore, I didn't hear you come in. I thought you'd be asleep by now."

"Never mind me. What's wrong?"

He sighed and put his hands in the pockets of his gray trousers, turning to the fire once more. "There's a possibility that Michael isn't going to make it!" The last part of his sentence was practically inaudible. Elinore moved closer, unsure of his meaning.

"What did you say?" she whispered.

He suddenly banged his fist against the mantel. " Elinore," his voice cried in pain, "Michael is

6

much worse tonight! Hugh says a few more days like this could mean . . ." and he fell silent, but she saw his shoulders heaving and heard the sobs that came from deep within the man.

"Jeffrey," she mouthed his name, moved with an irresistible desire to comfort and love him, as she had longed to do when Connie had been killed, but this time she acted on that impulse. Without hesitation, she crossed the floor and put an arm around his waist. His arm went around her shoulder and applied gentle pressure. He looked down at her with a tear-stained face, the tortured eyes staring through her, as they had always done, never really seeing her at all. The fire crackled and spit on the enormous hearth, but its warmth could not permeate the icy chill in her heart when she realized that she was as far away from his thoughts as Philip was from hers.

"Thanks for being here, Elinore. I don't know how I would have managed this last week without you. You're wonderful." He kissed her forehead lightly, before releasing her to sit down in the rose colored chair near the fire. She had to be content with their relationship the way it was, for a while longer anyway. She turned to him.

"Hasn't the fever dropped at all?"

"No," came the low, flat reply.

"I'll go over to the hospital now. Jens can drive me in. You haven't had any relief for the last two days."

"It doesn't matter," he responded without emotion, running his hands through his hair, pacing the floor in a kind of quiet rage.

"What more can be done for Michael than we're doing?" came her cry.

"I don't know. If he doesn't get well . . ." Jeffrey had stopped in the middle of the room, the trauma

7

exaggerating the lines of his face. There was a pallor beneath the bronzed skin. He'd come back from his last mission to the Mediterranean tanned and fit, but now . . . Elinore had to remember that this was the time to be strong for him.

"Of course he is going to get well," she masked her concern with a quick smile. "Stop talking like that. Your problem is that you need some dinner and rest. If you're not careful, there will be two patients to care for instead of one." He expelled a sigh and slumped into the chair.

"You're right," was the distant reply, "but I couldn't tolerate food right now."

"Let me fix you a drink."

"No . . . thank you . . . Elinore?" the detached voice called her name. "How does a thing like this happen? All Michael had was a simple case of influenza, and now . . . pneumonia."

"Stop brooding about it, Jeff. It won't do any good, you know. I'm going to ring for Jens. He can serve dinner in here."

"At this hour? Heaven forbid," he shook his head vigorously. Then, as an afterthought, "Were there any messages for me today?"

"Yes. Lord Wyngate called this morning and left word for you to get back to him, but he made it clear it was not urgent. Oh, and Lord Harley phoned this afternoon, but when I told him Michael was no better, he said it could wait till your return to London. He sent his regards and said he'd cover for you at the meeting with the Prime Minister tomorrow."

"He's a good friend. I should have gone back to London yesterday . . . things are really piling up, but that's out of the question now."

"Is it an important meeting?" He nodded. "Is there

anything I can do for you? I used to be a pretty good legal secretary. I could type up any notes or go through your correspondence if you'd like. I want to be of help."

Jeffrey sighed. "I know that, but the nature of my business is highly confidential. I'm the only one who can take care of it."

"Except that right now you're preoccupied with other worries. For once, why don't you let someone else share the burden? It would be no trouble, I assure you."

Jeffrey shook his head. "Thanks, Elinore, but I can't discuss my work with anyone, not even you."

She stiffened. "Then I wish you'd take my advice and go up to bed. I can spend the rest of the night with Michael."

"No . . . I'm going right back to the hospital. I only came home long enough to change clothes." Elinore could see it would be no use to try to change his mind.

"I had Millie do up your shirts. I folded them in your drawer myself, the way you like them." Jeffrey looked over at his efficient sister-in-law, amazed that she would be so devoted to him and his work.

"Elinore, I appreciate all you do . . . thank you, again. I know I'm not much good at expressing myself. It appears I'm always using your shoulder to cry on. Maybe some day I can return the favor. This can't be easy for you, being separated from Philip so much." A tiny smile crept into her face. He would never know how glad she was to be away from Philip for a while.

"Jeff, that's what family is for. Don't ever forget that."

"Phil's a lucky chap to have you. How come the solid, reliable women are always the married ones? It's a pity Mother and Father never had the opportunity to

9

meet you. Father, particularly, would have approved."

"Thank you for the compliment," she whispered and the blood drained from her cheeks, but the distance between them was too great for Jeffrey to have noticed how pale she had become. Suddenly a distinguished looking man appeared in the doorway.

"Did I hear my name mentioned? Good evening, my love," Philip said and walked briskly into the room, bending over his wife, giving her a peck on the cheek. She remained motionless and he drew back, aware of the cold aloofness to which he had grown accustomed during the past year. He stood up and caught sight of his younger brother seated near the fire. Philip was immediately stirred with compassion as he beheld the gaunt face and the deep furrows of anxiety there. Philip had always had a soft spot in his heart for his slightly headstrong brother, and felt responsible for him in a way, now that Jeffrey was alone. He walked over and put a hand on his shoulder. "Hey, old chap? I take it something is really wrong."

Jeffrey was out of his seat, pacing the floor once more. "He's much worse, Phil. Hugh says his chances for recovery are very slim."

The older brother was aghast. "Is he still asking for Sister Catherine?"

Jeffrey nodded. "Yes . . . he's obsessed with the notion that she will come. It means everything to him. In fact, he's spoken of nothing else since he left the convent. This evening he was delirious. Phil, he thought I was Sister Catherine, and he talked a blue streak. I don't know what to make of it anymore. That old insecurity is back, just as it was right after Connie died. You remember what that was like, except that this time, according to Hugh, we're fighting an affliction of the spirit as well as the body. He's homesick for Sister

10

Catherine.''

"That's only natural," Elinore broke in, upset that the child was dependent on a woman other than herself. Jeffrey worshiped his son. If Elinore could win over the boy, if she could be the replacement for his dead mother, then it was just a matter of time till Jeffrey would start regarding her in a new light. "After all," she continued, "he was there almost nine months. The sisters were bound to make an impression on him, but he'll get over it. He just hasn't had enough time. Illness always brings out insecurities in children."

Jeffrey listened attentively. Elinore's opinion usually carried weight with him, but this time he remained unconvinced and shook his head. "It's more than a mere insecurity with him, Elinore. He loves Sister Catherine. His feelings for her far outweigh the usual show of affection a child might display for a nurse or a teacher. He hasn't been himself since I brought him back. Physically he seemed fine, and we got along splendidly, but he kept telling me that Sister Catherine was going to come . . . that we had to arrange it. He was almost frantic about it. Then he caught the grippe, and now . . . it has gone way beyond that. This new withdrawal is allowing the infection to spread. He's not fighting any longer," and his voice trembled with emotion.

Philip stared into the fire, wondering if it would be wise to discuss an idea that had been forming in his mind for the last few days, but seeing his brother so distraught prompted him to bring it to light.

"Jeff, there could be a solution to this . . . at least, I think there could be." Elinore looked at her husband with curiosity, and Jeffrey's head raised up. "Think back to what Michael was like after Connie died. He retreated within himself, as he is doing now. Elinore

11

couldn't draw him out, yet he'd known her since he was born.'' Elinore bit her lip, but remained silent. ''Michael couldn't accept the reality that Connie was gone, until you put him in the convent school, and through some miracle, he became attached to Sister Catherine. Did you notice how Michael never brooded about Connie after you brought him back last month? He spoke only of the nun.''

Jeffrey nodded, pondering his brother's every word. Oh, yes, he'd noticed the change in Michael. He had wondered right away how this sister had managed to have such a far reaching effect on his son in so short a period of time. He even had to admit to a streak of jealousy, that a stranger had been able to succeed where he had not. For the life of him, he could not understand Michael's preoccupation with her. He never stopped chattering about how kind she was, how much fun . . . why couldn't she be his new mummy? The last question had shaken him . . .

''It's just a hunch,'' Philip continued, ''but maybe Michael has transferred his feelings for Connie to this nun, so that in his eyes, she has become the mother he lost. Do you follow me?''

Jeffrey had been concentrating on Philip's words and suddenly a look of excitement washed over his face. He grabbed Philip's arm. ''My feelings exactly . . . and . . . Sister Catherine is still very much alive! Phil, that's it. Why have I waited so long?'' and he gave Philip a brotherly hug. The look on both their faces was more than Elinore could tolerate, for sheer jealousy raged through her. Jeffrey was practically out the door before she could stop him. ''I'm going to call the Mother Superior right now and persuade her to let Sister Catherine come to the hospital as soon as possible and visit Michael . . . stay with him if necessary. She

12

brought him back to life once before. Let's pray she has the power to do it again!"

Philip smiled encouragingly at his impetuous brother and nodded. When Jeffrey had an idea, he ran with it. That was part of his genius. "Jeff . . . hold on just a minute. You didn't get a chance to meet this Sister Catherine when you went for Michael a month ago, did you?"

"No," he responded. "I've never met anyone but the Mother Superior. Why?"

Elinore got up from the chair and in an agitated state, walked over to Jeffrey. "Because if she is a professed nun, rather than a postulant, it is very likely that there are rules about her going outside the convent, no matter how pressing the circumstances." Elinore voiced Philip's mind with an almost triumphant ring. He glared at his wife. She was very shrewd but definitely lacking in tact. It was for this very reason that Philip had hesitated broaching the subject in the first place. It was true that nuns had strict rules about such matters.

Jeffrey's face had a determined expression. "The Holy Mother is a very remarkable woman, Elinore . . . a friend of the family. She took Michael in when the convent was already filled to capacity. I can't believe she would deny this favor under the circumstances," he spoke with optimism.

"I think you're jumping to conclusions. A nun's life runs by a different logic. Be reasonable, Jeff, and give me a little more time to work with Michael. I want to take care of him and nurse him back to health. I've made so many plans for us. I know Connie would have wanted it this way."

"Elinore," Philip's voice cajoled. "Michael cares for you, but right now he needs someone he is really close to. He requires something at this point that none of us is

13

capable of giving him. Think a minute . . . if Jeff can't provide the impetus now you can see—" his voice trailed off.

"Of course," she responded coolly, fists clenched behind the folds of her dress. "I just don't like to see you get your hopes up, Jeff, and then have them dashed to pieces because your need may be beyond the Mother Superior's power to fulfill."

He was already out in the hall. "She's got to," he fired back. "It's a matter of life and death!"

Elinore went to the sideboard and poured herself a drink. She sipped it and walked back and forth, working on her self control, running tapered fingers lightly along the keys of the grand piano in the corner of the room, watching Philip through veiled eyes. Who could guess that he was only forty-two? The extra layer of fat around the middle and the graying at the temples had only recently come—signs of the War—she mused. He was a darker blond than Jeffrey, and shorter, but reasonably attractive when she first met him. Now he was beginning to repulse her. He had an annoying habit of catching on to her games when she least expected it. If Philip were to discover her plans now, it could ruin everything. Later on, it wouldn't matter, since she intended to divorce him . . . but the time was not right . . . not yet . . .

"Philip, you're wrong to have raised Jeffrey's hopes that way. A man of law like you knows very well that convent life owes its allegiance to a government above temporal law."

She was sounding very smug. Philip put the poker to rest. His wife could be sorely trying at times. There was a selfish, ruthless streak in her. She was relentless in pursuing her own way, but right now he was not in the mood to indulge her jealousy nor put up with her sarcas-

14

tic attitude. He knew how much she suffered over her inability to relate like a mother to Michael, but for once she must consider someone besides herself. "Elinore, you're intelligent enough to realize that Michael's life is at stake. For his sake, let's pray Jeff can succeed with the Holy Mother." Philip wasn't usually as direct and cutting. She finished her drink and said no more. Always where Jeffrey was concerned, Philip was there to protect. Suddenly everything was going wrong, and she wasn't about to let some nanny of a nun usurp her rightful place with Michael. It was her one sure link to Jeffrey.

"Damn the war, anyway! The lines are down somewhere and I can't get through to Castle Combe," Jeffrey spoke loudly upon entering the room. "I'm going to drive there tonight!"

Elinore almost dropped her glass. Her large eyes were cavernous. "You can't go off to the convent in the middle of the night, and certainly not in your condition. You'd fall asleep at the wheel and be killed . . . what would become of Michael if he lost you, too? Philip, talk some sense to him!" But her husband wasn't listening to her.

"I'll go with you, Jeff. We can be there at dawn if we take turns driving."

"Right. Phil, I won't forget this."

"Have you both gone mad?" she cried out.

Philip turned. "What choice do we have, Elinore? You know how much the boy wants to see Sister Catherine again."

"I can't believe either one of you. You desperately need a good night's sleep, and it would be proper if you were to speak to the Holy Mother before tearing off into the country in the dead of night, arriving on her doorstep unexpectedly."

15

Jeffrey was already pulling on his overcoat. "We can't wait. I'm going to take you up on your offer to stay with Michael tonight. There's a cot in his room. You can sleep there, if you'd like. Tell Dr. Endicott that we've gone to Castle Combe to bring back Sister Catherine . . . he'll understand. If all goes well, we should be at the hospital before noon."

She fought to control the hysteria in her voice. "Very well . . . but you have absolutely no idea what you're up against, and even if she could come, what makes you think she'll be able to perform this miracle you're alluding to?"

Jeffrey's eyes turned to flint. "She'll come . . . dammit . . . and he'll get well!"

Elinore had gone too far, incurring his wrath. She'd never known him to be angry with her and it hurt. He opened the front door. "I've given Jens the exchange. He will keep trying to get through to the convent to forewarn the Holy Mother. If there is any change in Michael, you can reach us there, if the lines are repaired in time," he added and slipped out into the night.

Philip put a firm hand on her arm. "Why are you doing this?" he demanded, but she would not look at him, and yanked her arm from his grasp. He followed his brother out the door, at a loss for explanations. She remained frozen near the piano until the sound of the car died away, then unwillingly followed through with the plans to have Jens drive her to the hospital.

Philip drove for the first few hours while Jeffrey slept in the back of the car. Elinore's behavior was a complete mystery to him. Why in heaven's name wouldn't she want their plan to succeed?

The stars were finally fading when Jeffrey awoke with a start and insisted on driving the rest of the way, eager to channel his energy into something physical.

They spoke briefly about the latest Nazi offensives and got into a discussion of aerodynamics having to do with one of Britain's new fighter planes, but presently, Philip was asleep and Jeffrey was alone with his thoughts, maneuvering his car through the turns and twists with the same speed and accuracy with which he flew a plane, slowing down momentarily to check road signs. They'd just passed through Chippenham, so Castle Combe couldn't be more than five miles away now. Was Elinore right about the Holy Mother? Was this too much to ask of her? But the image of the sick child, struggling for breath, calling for Sister Catherine in the night, haunted him endlessly and drove him closer to the holy sanctuary. The world had turned upside down and nothing was the same for anybody since bombs had been ruthlessly dropped on London fifty-seven nights in succession, killing the rich and the poor, the important, the unimportant, mother, father, friend, child . . . and wife without mercy or discrimination.

Suddenly the sun appeared above the horizon and he was brought back to Michael. He had to recover! What irony that his fate lay once more in the hands of the Holy Mother and an unseen nun.

II

The Mother Superior of the Benedictine convent of Our Lord of the Lamb had started out her day in the usual way with morning prayers and a quick stroll about the grounds. Dew blanketed the white petals of the dogwood trees. The atmosphere was conducive to meditation and it was with reluctance that she had to step quickly inside her office to answer the telephone which sounded like a distress signal at the early hour of 5:30 a.m.

She lifted the receiver in her plump hands and was out of breath as she strained to hear the other voice, but the connection was poor. The call was coming from Norwood . . . and immediately a worried expression broke out on her round face. It appeared she would be expecting visitors shortly, and she hung up the receiver with apprehension. She realized this sudden visit had to do with young Michael, sensing that it could only bring more suffering and torment to Sister Catherine, the nun who had literally saved the boy's life.

Sister Catherine loved little Michael Norwood. The Holy Mother had seen the signs from the very beginning and had ferreted out the truth. It was a good love, a healing love for the terror stricken child, and love could never be wrong . . . but it did mean that Catherine had formed an attachment which went beyond the Christlike compassion a nun was to feel for others, and had

18

entered into the bounds of earthly love, such as a mother would feel for her own son. The Holy Mother understood the reason for this special attachment. Michael had undergone a shock to his system which had caused such severe emotional damage that the doctors feared he would be affected for the rest of his life . . . but from the very moment that Catherine saw the dear child, the devoted nun was drawn to his angelic face and spirit, and looked after his wants and needs, day and night, slowly, carefully, working the miracle the father had prayed for, and she had reversed the prognosis. In the process, however, she had learned to love the child.

After months of love and attention, the boy and the nun had become inseparable and could be seen most afternoons in the early spring, playing on the green, lying on the grass at the water's edge, picking out shapes in the clouds, or holding hands as they walked through the fields and woods, alive with pink and white rhodedendrons. They were as close as any mother and child could possibly be. Perhaps too close . . .

When Catherine first became aware that she was seeking his company too often, preferring to tend to him rather than carry on some of her other duties, she had come to the Holy Mother seeking help and advice. The Holy Mother was pleased that the sister recognized what was happening. Unfortunately, Catherine had not had enough time, was not sufficiently strengthened to detach herself before Michael's father had taken him away. Jeffrey Norwood had kept in constant touch over those first critical months, inquiring about the progress of his son. When the Holy Mother felt the boy was recovered enough to be reunited with his father, the little boy, normal and happy once again, went back to London, and both were obviously delighted to resume the family relationship. But Catherine was devastated

19

by an ache which could not be soothed.

The nun said nothing, did nothing outwardly to show her distress, but the Holy Mother could see things beyond the naked eye and she knew of the nun's struggle, her suffering. Michael had been gone from the convent for a month now, and each day Catherine's complexion paled a little more. If Mr. Norwood were bringing bad news about Michael, the Holy Mother was tempted to keep it from Catherine, for it would break her fragile heart. The situation was precarious.

The Holy Mother could never remember a time when a sister had experienced this particular problem, but then, the circumstances in this case were highly unusual. There was a war on, and Michael was one of its casualties. He had watched his mother's body blown to bits before his very eyes, the result of an explosion which shattered the dining room of the Mayfair mansion, the city home of the Norwoods for many generations. She had died immediately in the rash of bombings which had demolished the kitchen at Number 10 Downing Street, and had crumbled the House of Commons. The Holy Mother remembered the incident with horror, not only because of that monster, Hitler, but because the Norwood family was a noble institution and had been patrons of Our Lord of the Lamb for generations. The death of Constance Norwood had been given extended publicity in Lord Wyngate's paper, causing a furor among friends and relatives of the famous family.

She was the wife of one of England's young heros, Jeffrey Norwood, an aviator and engineer, who had been awarded the coveted Distinguished Flying Cross for valor over and over again beyond the call of duty, during those bloody days in September. All England would remember his name for his daring air-sea rescues in the icy waters of the North Atlantic.

German submarines had been patrolling the waters and had torpedoed merchant and military ships carrying officers, men and children to America. It was Jeffrey Norwood and a crew of incredibly brave men who rescued hundreds of drowning victims in the high seas and roaring winds. His name was synonymous with the flying boats which he helped to improve in design, and both were associated with bravery; therefore, when the news revealed that he had been widowed and his little son left without a mother, Londoners particularly mourned the loss and were shocked to their very roots.

The Holy Mother had kept news articles about the prominent members of the family over the years. Constance Norwood was the daughter-in-law of the late Lord Edmond Norwood, former ambassador to Japan. The elder son, Philip, was one of London's leading barristers and retained his father's seat in the House. More recently it appeared Jeffrey Norwood was destined for great things as well since he had recently been made Commander over the Mediterranean Forces of the Air Command in Africa, and, because of his genius with planes, was consultant to the minister of air craft production, and met frequently with England's beloved Churchill, almost a saint in the Holy Mother's eyes.

When Michael was brought to the convent by his desperate father, the Holy Mother vowed that she would do all in her power, relying on God, to see Michael cured. It was a debt she wished to pay his father, for many reasons. The day of his arrival, however, the Holy Mother doubted seriously that anything could be done for the boy. He was barely five years old and catatonic, suffering complete withdrawal. The child had not responded to anyone; not his loving aunt, not even the father he idolized. No doctor or friend could bring the child around.

And it was no wonder with one so innocent and small: one minute he had been playing contentedly with his mother; the next minute, bombs screamed overhead, destroying the room and his mother at the same time. The shock of losing her in such a brutal manner was too much. In utter despair, Jeffrey Norwood had turned to the Holy Mother for help, hoping that in the solitude of Castle Combe, away from the long arm of Nazi tyranny, the boy could be rehabilitated, along with many other shell-shocked children housed in the convent. If at all possible, it was her desire that no child be denied at the Motherhouse. When it was verified that Michael would be coming, the Holy Mother spent many long hours in fervent prayer and fasting that God would intervene in the boy's behalf.

After a few difficult months, Sister Catherine was able to win his confidence and trust, and it came as no surprise that Michael ended up loving her with all his heart. There was something especially endearing about the cherubic smile of the boy, something which touched all the sisters, but in particular, Sister Catherine, and there was no question that the nun's appealing qualities found their way to the child's heart. Loving little ones came as naturally to her as living and breathing. She could create happiness out of desolation with one story, bring a smile to the face of a grief stricken child with a word or a song . . . the children worshipped her.

Yes . . . Catherine had many attributes. She was a selfless spirit, and had that inborn quality of guileless-ness which was desired above all else in a good nun. Catherine's make up ensured her becoming a model sister, for she had been a gentle, unselfish child by nature, blessed with an exceptional musical talent and a brilliant mind . . . but it was her love of children which set her apart from the others. Through her the boy began to regain his emotional health, and the old woman rejoiced for him as well as his father. She also became increasingly aware of the love developing between the nun and the boy. The child adored her.

The Holy Mother began to worry about this relationship. When she saw him playing hide and seek behind Catherine's voluminous skirts, darting about as children have done from the beginning of time, with the hearty laughter of a happy, carefree child, the Mother Superior knew it was time to direct his attention elsewhere. He needed to develop relationships with children of his own age. The Holy Mother drew closer and called to the boy.

"You will be late for your supper again, Michael, if you don't hurry back to the refectory right now." The admonition caused the child's eyes to fill with tears.

"I—I want to stay with Sister . . . she hasn't finished singing my song," he answered with a trembling lower lip. Without hesitation, Catherine knelt before him and swept him in her arms, pressing the blond, curly head to her shoulder, rocking him back and forth to give comfort. That one gesture of pure love verified once and for all what the Holy Mother had suspected. It meant that Catherine, also, must return to meditation, even to semi-seclusion, to get back into perspective the measures of self-discipline necessary for a bride of Christ. The Holy Mother had always been fond of Catherine and was particularly pleased that the girl had such deep religious inclinations. It would be a tragedy if her attachment to Michael grew so great that it rendered her incapable of giving the valuable service she was born to. There was no question in her mind that it was best to keep any news of Michael from her, good or bad.

Jeffrey pressed on the gas but the never-ending dips

and round-abouts prevented the car from taking flight and it wasn't till the Cotswold stone walls of the convent came into sight that his taut body relaxed. "Phil," he called over his shoulder. "We're here!"

Philip sat up and blinked. "What time is it?"

"Six-thirty."

"Why didn't you waken me sooner? I could have driven. You're the one who needed the rest."

"No . . . I'm feeling better than I've felt in a week. I hope Jens got through."

Both men directed their attention to the serene and picturesque setting of the ancient citadel. Two geese bobbed complacently on the waters of the meandering brook which ran lazily near the motherhouse. Michael had been insistent on his first day home that his father see the drawings of the geese which swam there daily. He and Sister Catherine had made many of them, and there were other pictures of rabbits and fawns, as well, some of them extraordinarily good, and Jeffrey's mouth turned up at the corners. Michael also told him of the high wall which he could see now, enclosing the courtyard, and how Sister Catherine ran below him as he pretended he was a plane in flight . . . and just in case he should crash, she would be there to save him. The smile disappeared and the grim expression returned. Save him . . . that was the whole reason for this sudden nocturnal trip into Wiltshire, one he had never supposed to make again.

Jeffrey brought the car to a halt, and the two brothers jumped out and pulled at the cord of the bell at the side of the locked gate. After a minute it was opened by the caretaker, a thin old man with a stooped back. They followed him to the double wooden doors of the immense convent. Presently a portly, middle aged sister cautiously opened the door and bowed. "I'm Sister

24

Margaret."

Jeffrey inclined his head. "Sister, excuse this untimely intrusion, please. Allow me to introduce myself. I'm Jeffrey Norwood and this is my brother, Philip Norwood."

"We've been expecting you. Come in, please." Jeffrey smiled with relief at Philip and they followed her into a dimly lighted entrance hall. "Sit down, please," and she indicated several chairs near a statue of the Holy Virgin. "I'll tell the Holy Mother you've arrived," and she lumbered across the bare hallway and knocked at a large, paneled door. They were at once aware of women's high, pure voices singing from a little distance off. Philip turned around, straining to hear more.

"Pretty, isn't it?"

Jeffrey nodded. "The Holy Mother told me the sisters sing the Holy Office every morning. I asked her about it when I was here before. What a terrible waste that no one hears them."

"To us, perhaps," Philip mused, "but they're singing for God. You can hear the fervency in their voices."

Jeffrey was pensive. "To me, a nun has always been a mystery. She hovers between being a half-woman, and a sexual nonentity, if you know what I mean. I used to feel sorry for them. Remember when Father would take us to church in Hammersmith and how the sisters could be seen behind the grilled gate? I used to press my face against the bars and watch them as they walked in the garden. I couldn't imagine a life like theirs . . . one in which one had no freedom to go where one wanted, to accomplish what had to be done. Now, I sometimes wonder who is free and who is the prisoner . . ."

Philip nodded in quiet understanding. His brother had been in Hell for the last year. The Holy Mother had

25

to come through for him now. Philip could read his brother's mind. He knew it hadn't really occurred to Jeffrey that the Holy Mother might refuse his request. When Jeffrey wanted something, he went after it with zeal. If the Holy Mother denied his request, Philip didn't want to think of the consequences.

"It's a whole other world, here," Jeffrey continued. "You'd never guess a ghastly war was raging out there. Thank God for this sanctuary of refuge! I can't forget that in the scheme of things, the sisters were here for Michael when he needed help."

"Nor I. The change in Michael when you brought him home was unbelieveable. I'm very curious to meet this Sister Catherine."

"No more than I," Jeffrey murmured, then stood up as Sister Margaret approached, indicating they could see the Holy Mother now.

The office was fairly large and the furnishings simple; the Holy Mother at the desk stood up and smiled. "Come closer, my sons." They walked to the desk and sat down.

"Holy Mother," Jeffrey began, "Allow me to introduce my brother, Philip Norwood."

"How do you do, Sir. You look like your father . . . a fine man."

Philip smiled. "Holy Mother . . . I'm pleased to meet you at last."

Jeffrey was impatient to get on with matters. Philip could feel his unrest, but the Holy Mother had set the pace of the interview and it was best to let her lead. She looked from one to the other with searching eyes. "About an hour ago, we received a call from your manservant, indicating we could expect you some time this morning. Obviously this visit has something to do with little Michael," she conjectured, and the withered

26

face showed genuine concern. Her eyes probed Jeffrey's. The Commander had aged in the last month. There was a tightness about his eyes.

"Yes," he nodded, stood up and began pacing the floor, unable to contain his nervous energy. "Holy Mother," he began, and leaned over her desk, his hands gripping the solid oak for support, "Michael is seriously ill in a hospital in Norwood. When I took him back home a month ago, he was perfectly well and happy . . . but two weeks ago he came down with the grippe and has gone downhill steadily. It has developed into pneumonia and he grows weaker every day." The face of the Mother Superior sobered instantly.

"What a tragedy, my son! We will say special prayers for him."

"Holy Mother," Jeffrey went on, "when Michael drove home with me, he began talking about a certain sister. At first I didn't pay much attention . . . he was chattering incessantly about everything and I had a hard time keeping up with him, but it became clear before we ever reached home that Michael had formed a special attachment for one sister in particular. He refers to her as Sister Catherine."

Philip couldn't fail to notice how the Holy Mother blanched at the mention of the sister's name. He also saw the veined hands clasp the crucifix suspended around her neck. He looked up at Jeffrey, but his brother was deep in his own thoughts.

"Can you tell me anything at all about this amazing sister?" he pleaded. "She was the one responsible for his remarkable recovery, wasn't she?"

"Yes," she nodded, almost unwillingly, Philip thought.

Jeffrey's hands dug deep into his pockets, and he straightened up. "Michael has never stopped hoping, not for one second, that Sister Catherine would come to see him. She has become an obsession, Holy Mother. He loves her.''

The Head nun stood up, her five foot figure seeming bigger than life. ''Mr. Norwood,'' she smiled, ''all the children who come here form attachments to the sisters. These are not ordinary times, with the war on. We have over three hundred children to take care of here, from all over England as well as the continent—victims of shock—like Michael, and it is a normal thing for them to find security among the convent dwellers. Michael was a more challenging child than most because of his deep withdrawal, and though Sister Catherine was most definitely the one responsible for the good done, many other sisters were instrumental in helping him recover from the loss of his mother.''

''But I'm not talking about a temporary attachment, Holy Mother. The love Michael feels for this sister is all consuming!''

The Holy Mother was perplexed. Jeffrey turned to Philip. ''Tell her about the night Elinore tried to get Michael to sleep.'' She looked at the older brother, more confused and worried as the seconds passed. Philip cleared his throat, a habit left over from presenting depositions in court.

''Holy Mother . . . Jeff and I share the theory that Michael has transferred the love he felt for his own mother, to this sister. The child is inconsolable without her. My wife has tried to comfort the boy, without success. Several weeks ago, he began being very hostile toward her, crying out that Sister Catherine was the only one who could get him to sleep. It was an evening none of us will ever forget. The boy obviously misses Sister Catherine much more than anyone had guessed.''

''Michael doesn't even talk about his mother any-

28

more," Jeffrey added in a low voice. "He adores Sister Catherine now, and since this illness, he has called for her over and over again. At the hospital yesterday, he was delirious for a while and began talking to me as if I were she, crying hysterically. His world has caved in again, without her. That is why we're here. If something isn't done right away to make that boy secure . . . he's not going to make it."

"My son," there was alarm in her voice, "this is shocking news, but what can I do?"

"Phil and I both feel that if Sister Catherine could be allowed to come back to Norwood and visit Michael in the hospital, it would be the medicine he needs to fight the infection. I honestly believe Michael has given up." Philip lowered his head. "He doesn't care if he lives or dies while the light of his life is here, inside these cloistered walls. I'm begging you, Holy Mother, to allow this sister to go to him and make him well. I know he will recover if he can see her and talk to her again. He's homesick for her. If you could hear the things he has told me. He's even gone so far as to ask me why she can't be his mother."

The Holy Mother gasped, very quietly, but both men heard and Jeffrey began to doubt, for the first time, that the Mother Superior would grant his request. It was as if in that one intake of breath, she had revealed her shock and wonder over such a request . . . as if it were out of the question.

His energy spent, Jeffrey sank back into the chair and Philip put a reassuring hand on his shoulder. It was the Holy Mother's turn to pace the floor. She turned, clutching the rosary in her hand, and the heaviness in her breast was almost more than she could bear. His wet eyes, pleading for help, haunted her like a spectre. She was not unaware that he had risked his life many

29

times over for others' children. She bowed her head and prayed for Divine guidance. This was a crucial moment in the lives of three people. No decision could be made in haste, and there would be consequences either way.

"Holy Mother," a tremulous voice called out, "I know this request is highly unusual, but I don't want my son to die." The plea was uttered more like a prayer, and it reached the old woman's heart. She turned around and returned to her desk, staring at the crucifix above the door. God did move in mysterious ways, she thought. This turn of events was the kind of thing she'd hoped would never come to pass. Given enough time away from the Norwood child, Catherine would learn detachment; but now, to see him again in his sick condition, so soon after their painful parting . . . she closed her weary eyes. And there was Michael's father . . . Catherine had not been out in the world since she was fifteen. What would such a drastic change of scene and surroundings do to the sister under these circumstances? Yet, how could she ignore the plea of a grief-stricken father whose child was on the verge of death?

The silence was unbearable. Even Philip, who was long-suffering in the courtroom awaiting a judge's verdict in a trial, was anxious.

"Commander Norwood," she began quietly. "I, too, want everything possible to be done for the child. Sister Catherine has my permission to leave Our Lord of the Lamb and attend to your son. If anyone can bring the will to live back to that sweet child, it is she. But," and she raised a finger of warning, "it must be her decision to accompany you. This sister will have to search her heart to decide what is the will of God in this instance . . . and you must be prepared to abide by that decision."

"Of course, Holy Mother," Jeffrey's voice cracked

with emotion and a sigh of gratitude escaped his lips. "Bless you, Holy Mother!"

"I will go to Sister Catherine now, and then send her to you. You can explain why you are here. Repeat to her what you have just told me and then let God work His will in whatever way best suits His purposes. Wait here, please," she commanded and left the room. The brothers faced each other and both pairs of eyes were wet.

Catherine had been kneeling in prayer, petitioning the Holy Virgin to remove the agonizing sense of loss she'd felt since Michael's departure. For weeks now, there was an emptiness inside which cried out to be filled. The nights were the worst . . . she could not sleep . . . her skin burned with fever. The face of the precious boy followed her everywhere . . . his smile, his eyes— so trusting, the sound of his sobbing ringing in her ears when he knew he was going to leave her. She could still feel the round arms tightly clasped about her neck, the tear-stained cheeks pressed to hers, the little body inconsolable.

But she'd been able to assuage the pain of parting by making Michael a promise that they would see each other again. He could make a visit to see her later in the summer. Michael had brightened somewhat at the thought and then naively made the suggestion that she could go to Norwood on a holiday. He had pressed the issue, insisting that his daddy would love her, too. His childish desires, so out of the question, tormented her unceasingly. Michael's was a persistent, determined nature. He was a fighter. She loved him more now than ever. How could it be that she cared so much, after a whole month of not seeing him, not laughing at his clever antics? Would she never find peace? Would God forgive her for harboring this uncharitable resentment against his father, for taking him away from her?

Catherine made the sign of the cross, arose and went out a side door of the chapel into the hallway which connected the chapel with the classrooms. It was time for her to begin the children's morning lessons . . . later she would practice on the organ and then take a walk. The walls of the convent seemed to be closing in on her this morning. She turned the corner and felt a pull on her sleeve. She turned to stare into the eyes of the Mother Superior, sensing an urgency in her demeanor. At this time of morning, the Holy Mother rarely left the sanctuary of her private chapel, for it was her allotted time for meditation before the altar. Only a matter of the gravest importance would deter her from her prayers, and for that very reason, Catherine grew alarmed. Some poor child had probably arrived at the convent . . . another victim of this ghastly, horrible war.

"Sister," the Holy Mother began, but hesitated, her courage almost failing her. "There are two gentlemen here to see you . . . Michael Norwood's father, and his brother, Lord Philip Norwood."

Catherine's eyes widened in astonishment. "Michael's father . . . here?" she mouthed the question silently, wondering what all this could possibly mean, but the discipline of a nun had taken hold and she checked herself. She continued to stare at the Holy Mother.

"They are in my office, Sister, and Michael's father has a request to make of us. I told him to speak to you . . . when you have heard him out, search your heart to discover God's will in this matter, then come to me in the chapel and tell me of your decision."

Catherine had known the Holy Mother for many years, and she'd never seen her behave in such a manner. She was secretive . . . and there were shadows under her eyes. What could be going on? Michael had to be involved, and the thought that there might be something wrong with him caused beads of perspiration to form on her brow. The Holy Mother watched the nun's reaction and the gravest misgivings welled up inside of her. Every nun had to face tests . . . they came at odd hours . . . at different moments in life, in various manners and ways. Every nun had to pass through Gethsemane some time in her life. The Holy Mother had the premonition Catherine had already stepped through the gate of that unfathomable garden of sorrow . . . it would not be a pleasant sojourn.

"Very well, Holy Mother," Catherine answered almost inaudibly, and walked slowly toward the office, her willowy figure moving regally along the hallway lined with stained glass windows which filtered the early morning light, projecting colors of red, gold and blue across the inlaid wood floors. Her queenly deportment gave her an air of dignity which belied her youth. Only around the Norwood child had the girl within manifested herself. The Holy Mother went along to her private chapel to pray for three souls, hoping each would find peace, but she knew deep within her soul that Catherine's unrest was just beginning. . . .

Jeffrey stopped pacing when he heard footsteps stop outside the door. He glanced back at Philip who was seated at the opposite end of the room, thumbing through a Bible. He admired his brother's ability to remain calm under this kind of stress . . . unlike himself, who found relief through action. He had wondered for a long time what Sister Catherine was really like. She would have to be special to replace Connie in his son's affections. He shifted his weight. War was no respector of persons, but why did it have to touch children? Michael was an innocent victim, and now his life was hovering in the balance because of some stranger . . . an old woman, most likely, who was important to Michael in the same way his mother had been important.

Jeffrey knew the separation from Michael the past year had not been a good thing, as far as their relationship was concerned. He'd missed his son terribly, but he had no recourse at the time. Thank God for his work at the Ministry! It filled a gaping hole in his life, leaving him no time to ponder his half-alive state, few moments to remember what it was like having a wife share his bed. War left scars and he was not alone in his miserable state . . . still, when he thought of Michael . . . he became angry and understood why men killed, almost eagerly at times. He longed to feel that satisfaction, deep inside, as he chased a Nazi plane out of the sky into oblivion. His eyes wandered to the framed maxim hanging on the frescoed wall near the desk. "Prayer—twenty-four hours a day. Saint Francis de Sales," was the inscription. He did not find the thought extreme in the least, not now that his only child was slipping away as the hours passed.

Catherine stood outside the office for a long moment, fighting the uneasiness in her breast. Michael had talked so much about his father, she felt she knew him intimately, yet now she was frightened to actually meet him face to face and hear news about the boy which had to be of a serious nature. Why else would he be here at such an early hour, accompanied by his brother? Fear was overtaking her good sense. Finally, she turned the handle and opened the door.

The room was always somber, for there was only one stained glass window beneath the arch of the ceiling. It had been designed this way to provide peace and tranquility, to shut out worldly distractions . . . to allow for reflective meditation.

Catherine stepped quietly inside and noticed immediately the adult version of her precious Michael, standing in deep thought before a painting of the Madonna and Child. The man's head was bent in concentration, exactly like Michael's when he was pondering something important, and the likeness was so startling, a slight cry escaped her throat. Jeffrey heard her and turned his head.

In the shadowy light, he was aware of a fairly tall nun, shrouded in a white robe, a cross at her breast, a rosary and missal in her hands. He drew closer. She was staring at him in guarded fascination, focusing on the dark blond hair which curled about his aristocratic head, several careless tendrils boyishly spilling over the tanned forehead. She had to resist the impulse to brush them back, as she so often had Michael's silken curls. The wide mouth was almost arrogant and would not smile without provocation, she surmised, as opposed to Michael's, whose dimpled smile would appear spontaneously. She took a step closer to peer into the brilliant blue eyes, as penetrating as the Channel breezes, and of the same hue as the water churning around the rocks at Land's End in summer. Michael had inherited their color, but not their dazzling intensity. His features were strongly defined . . . he gave one a feeling of security, that he could handle anything. He was standing in such a position that the sun, shifting higher in the morning sky, sent a shaft of light from the window above, bathing his handsome head in golden light. He reminded her a little of the painting of Saint John which hung in the chapel.

Jeffrey blinked. The face beneath the wimple was surprisingly young. Lord . . . she couldn't be more than twenty or so! Yet the majesty of her carriage, the white

35

material draped about her slender figure, made her seem older somehow . . . and she was beautiful! Michael had never mentioned her looks. He was momentarily at a loss for words. So this was the sister dearly loved by his young son! He had expected some-one like the Holy Mother, or Sister Margaret. Someone motherly . . . jovial . . . it never occurred to him . . .

"Sister Catherine," he finally cleared his throat. "I'm Michael's father, Jeffrey Norwood, and this is my brother, Philip." The older brother crossed the room and smiled. Catherine inclined her head to both of them, observing the strong family resemblance. Michael's uncle was older, with softer features . . . his was a gentle face with warm, gray-blue eyes. Michael was very fond of his Uncle Philip.

"How do you do, Sister," Philip responded, equally surprised at her youth and striking beauty. It wasn't difficult to see why Michael was so attached to her.

Jeffrey felt a new wave of fear wash over him. He had no way to gauge this young nun's feelings. It was possi-ble she would not understand the urgency of his re-quest, that she would refuse to accompany them to Norwood. Generally he had felt on safe ground with the Holy Mother. Now, he wasn't sure of anything. "Sis-ter, has the Holy Mother told you why we are here?"

"No," she responded in a soft, low voice, unaccus-tomed to the timbre of the masculine voice addressing her. "But I presume it has to do with Michael. How is he?" she tried to ask calmly. She couldn't let him know how much she loved Michael. No one could know.

"He's very ill, Sister . . . in a hospital . . . losing a battle with pneumonia." She jerked her head up and gazed at him, holding on to the table to steady herself. Jeffrey stepped closer, realizing that the news had really shaken her. The color had left her cheeks.

36

"How is that possible?" she cried out softly, forgetting her self-imposed discipline. Jeffrey thought she was going to faint. Not once had he considered the nun's feelings. It was always with Michael's needs he had been concerned. It hadn't dawned on him that Sister Catherine might have cared for the boy as much as he cared for her; but he had heard anguish in her cry just now and it tugged at him.

"He caught the grippe, Sister, and never recovered. That's why I am here. Michael has been calling for you. He has spoken of nothing but you since I took him back home. He loves you very very much." His voice was husky.

A sob escaped and a trembling hand went to her throat. Through the long, black lashes, her deep-set blue eyes seemed pools of liquid light. She turned her head to hide her anguish, but she had revealed her true feelings and Jeffrey rejoiced. He knew she loved his son as deeply as the boy loved her. That was all he needed to know. He felt braver.

"Sister, if you would come back to Norwood and see Michael in the hospital, talk to him, tell him those funny stories he's missed hearing, sing him the French songs he has tried to teach me, then I know he'll get well!" Jeffrey was purposely driving the point home. Sister Catherine was shaking and he could see it as well as feel it. "When he came back home a month ago, he was my Michael again . . . thanks to you," the low voice seemed to penetrate her being and touch her heart. "You performed a miracle, Sister." There was a catch in his throat. Catherine was afraid to turn around and reveal the raw emotion she knew was exposed in her face.

"It's true," Philip found his voice at last. "The boy was himself once again."

37

"Thank the Good Shepherd, Mr. Norwood. It was his divine intervention which brought Michael back to you."

"Yes, I believe that, Sister, but it's not the Lord he is calling for now," Jeffrey appealed to her with deliberateness. She turned and looked at him. "It's you he wants to kiss him goodnight," his words beseeched her. "Will you come? The Holy Mother has given her permission, but she said the decision would have to be yours. I love my son," he whispered, "I don't want to lose him."

Dear Father in Heaven, she didn't want to lose him either! A man's soul was reaching out to her, and Michael truly was on the brink of death, for the Holy Mother had already granted permission for Catherine to go to him. Was this the way God was answering her prayers, at last? To think that she could feast her eyes on her adorable Michael again. The boy couldn't die!

Jeffrey watched her as she went through all the steps in her mind before reaching a decision, and he already knew what it would be.

"Of course, I will come," she finally whispered with a haunting, wistful smile that betrayed her deep concern. "I will go immediately and tell the Holy Mother of my decision."

At that moment Jeffrey thought he'd never seen a face so lovely, nor heard words so beautiful. He blinked away the mist. "Thank you, Sister." Words were inadequate at a time like this. The smile he returned to her was reward enough, erasing the lines on his worried face. So much happiness had depended upon her simple answer.

"Bless you, Sister," Philip blurted out. "It could make all the difference," he offered.

"We would like to leave for Norwood as soon as

possible, Sister," Jeffrey added. They both stared expectantly at her. Catherine knew Jeffrey Norwood was an important man. The Holy Mother had told her many things about him, and she inferred from his manner that he was accustomed to giving orders and having them obeyed. She couldn't blame him for wanting to rush back to Michael. She was every bit as anxious to see the child and hold him close. She bowed graciously to him, then his brother.

"Wait here, please." She put up her hand as a sign they should not follow. There was an air of the Holy Mother about her, despite her youth. Jeffrey was mystified by the combination. Philip was tremendously relieved and grateful that she was actually going to be traveling back to Norwood with them. Somehow, Jeffrey was able to make things work out. As he was about to congratulate him on his good fortune, he realized he wasn't looking at the same exhausted man, who, on a thread of hope, had frantically driven to Castle Combe in the dead of night. The expression on his brother's face was one of complete relief, even awe, but he'd known Jeffrey all his life and wondered if there wasn't something else mingled in that look as his brother's eyes followed the graceful figure of the retreating nun.

Catherine walked slowly down the hall to find the Holy Mother, but she felt like picking up her skirts and running . . . she had a suffocating feeling in her chest. The Mother Superior was just leaving the chapel when Catherine approached. She looked up and saw an expression on the young nun's face which had not been there before. She knew Catherine had agreed to go to Michael and suspected this filled the girl's heart with great joy; but there was a new restlessness about her and the Holy Mother sighed, feeling the full weight of her eighty years. She had had to experience those painful, early years of the refiner's fire and had done so with eagerness . . . coming to a new peace with God which transcended the worldly, and now . . . it was Catherine's turn, and the older woman knew exactly what the girl was experiencing. It wasn't difficult to understand. Mr. Norwood was an imposing, exciting figure of a man . . . and he was Michael's father. The resemblance of father to son was uncanny, and with his son so ill, the combination was too much for young Catherine to handle in just one meeting. There were many forces that would start pulling the nun apart in the next while. It would be a testing period . . . and for once in her life, the Holy Mother was not confident of the outcome.

"Sister, I perceive that you plan to go to Michael's aid. It is the right decision, my child. You will be on God's errand . . . make no mistake." Catherine stood in awe of the Holy Mother. "Trust in the Lord always, and you will be guided in the right direction. I know of the turmoil that has been going on inside of you. I've seen it festering for months. Catherine, I know how much you love the boy." The young nun's face was pained. Had she been so transparent? "Don't be ashamed my child. Do not worry about detaching yourself from him again. This is a unique case . . . God has sent you this test . . . and I'm sure you're aware that He is answering many prayers at the same time." Catherine nodded. "Right now your mission is one of an administering angel to a sick child who wants nothing more than to see you again."

Catherine listened to the Holy Mother's words, marveling at the wisdom and faith demonstrated. Her words struck a haunting chord. Honesty and love had always been the Holy Mother's way. Catherine remembered something the Mother Superior had said when she entered the novitiate: "A nun is not an un-happy spinster, but an eager, joyful bride of Christ. Anything less offered to the Bridegroom would not be sufficient, nor would it make for a good nun."

"Thank you, Holy Mother," she murmured, kissing her hand. Then she raised her head. "Mother, Commander Norwood wants to get back to Michael right away."

"Of course . . . and we mustn't be responsible for more delays. I wish I could spare a sister to go with you, but the convent is severely understaffed with all the children here right now. I've given the matter some thought, and since the drive back to Norwood is reasonably short, I see no reason why you can't go with the Norwoods as soon as you have packed the necessary items. You're going to be on your own for a time, and no one knows how long that will be. But you will never be alone, my child . . . not if you pray for the Holy Spirit to attend you. You will be in my prayers, day and night. There will be a chapel in the hospital there. Attend to your Holy Office whenever it is possible. I trust in your basic goodness and wisdom, your instincts. There are no precedents to follow in this situation, Catherine. Do you understand that?"

"Yes," she nodded once more, suddenly frightened.

"Remember—you can call here, day or night, if you should need anything. Don't forget . . . this mission of yours is holy. Treat it with respect and reverence, and you can never doubt that God approves. Go along now, Catherine, and prepare for your journey."

"Bless you," Catherine sank to her knees and kissed the ring on the holy woman's finger a second time. The Mother Superior felt the cold hand tremble, and smiled down at the innocent face, blessing her. Then she went to her office to talk over certain matters with the Norwoods, while Catherine ran to the dormitory to assemble the few items she would need. She made a detour into Michael's old room and pulled something from the drawer which had been left as an oversight. She put it in the large pocket of her habit, to be given back at a later date.

With satchel in hand, Catherine stepped out from the somber passageway into the courtyard, the warm rays of the sun falling on her face, stinging her eyes, blurring her vision of the Holy Mother and the two men who stood conversing near the red automobile.

"Sister," the Holy Mother said, taking Catherine in her arms for a brief embrace, "Godspeed and a safe journey. Michael will recover. Never fear," she smiled with great solemnity. The woman's prophecy gave Catherine new faith, though she felt small and alone momentarily, and thought how easy it would be to run back inside and shun the world, but the moment passed as Jeffrey Norwood climbed into the car and started the motor. She couldn't look at him without seeing Michael's precious face and that was all it took to strengthen her resolve. His father was impatient to be on his way.

Philip stood on the other side, holding the door open for her so she could climb into the back seat. Catherine seated herself on the plush upholstery. How incongruous she appeared against such a backdrop! In seconds they were off.

III

Once they reached the open road, Jeffrey pressed on the accelerator and it was apparent to Catherine that Michael's father was very adept at handling a car at high speeds. She knew that skilled, experienced hands were on the wheel. He was a brave man to have gone after all those helpless men and children, floating about in storm tossed seas. Holy Mother had allowed her to read the news clippings concerning the rescues. Michael was proud of his father as well, even if he didn't quite understand the magnitude of the circumstances. It was strange to be riding in the car with this man, after hearing about him for so many months.

Jeffrey chanced a look at her in the rear view mirror, as if to insure her reality. Their eyes met and he smiled, still amazed that he was actually bringing her back to Michael.

"Michael is going to be one surprised, happy little boy when he finds out what I've brought back with me," he said. Catherine couldn't help smiling back, and finally left his gaze to stare out the window, oblivious to the passing landscape.

Philip half turned to talk to her. "Sister, have you been to London before?"

"I passed through once, when I was a child."

"Well, Norwood is a small village to the northwest. We should be there before noon." The mention of noon reminded him they hadn't eaten anything and he was starved. Jeffrey was probably famished as well. "Are you hungry, Sister? We can stop some place along the way."

"No, thank you, Mr. Norwood. We only eat two meals at the convent and I don't plan to sup before evening." After she had explained herself, she realized that the two men were probably anxious to eat, but were too polite to mention it. They'd been driving all night. "Please . . . stop if there is something you want. It was thoughtless of us not to have offered you food at the convent. It's just that everything happened so fast."

"Please, Sister," Jeffrey responded, "we imposed on you, but I have to admit I would like a little something. How about it, Phil?" He nodded and when they came to Chippenham, Jeffrey pulled over in front of a small shop. In a few minutes he had purchased some meat pies which both men devoured with relish. It took her back to the time when her father was still alive. He'd always had a big appetite, after farming in the fields till sundown.

"Michael says you're part French, Sister," Jeffrey started up the conversation once the men had eaten and were on their way again. He spoke as casually as if they were all good friends out in the country for a lazy afternoon drive. This was something she was going to have to get used to, being in the company of men—it was inevitable . . . and he wouldn't be normal if Michael's father weren't curious about her. There was little casual conversation at the convent except around the children, of course. And if there weren't a war on, there would be no children at Our Lord of the Lamb, and life would be austere and quiet. To be suddenly engaged in conversation with someone like Commander Norwood was no small matter, but she found it stimulating and it eased her nervousness. She presumed it was a release for his pent-up emotions as well, so she tried not to react as if she were timid.

Jeffrey noticed a faraway look in her eyes and wondered if she had heard his question. "Sister?" he repeated, "are you part French?"

"Actually, my father was Belgian."

"And your mother?"

"English."

He smiled. "An interesting combination. Where were you born?"

"In Bruges."

"That explains why you have taught Michael so many French songs. I think his pronunciation is quite remarkable for a child."

"Michael is an excellent student, even if he is only five," she volunteered.

"Six," he corrected her. "We had a birthday party for him the second day he was home. Needless to say, his great wish before blowing out his candles was that you would come to see him." Catherine closed her eyes.

"He loved parties," she admitted. "There are birthdays almost every day of the year with all the children we house at the convent. It helps to pretend that there is some normality in the world. The children play the game much better than do some of the rest of us." The brothers eyed one another. Philip realized that this nun was no backward farm girl.

"Michael told me you lost a brother in the war last year, Sister. I'm very sorry."

She paused before answering, a bit surprised Michael had revealed so much information to his father. "Yes . . . he lost his life in the trenches."

"Don't you have another brother as well? It seems to

45

me Michael said something to that effect."

"Yes . . . my oldest brother died of a liver ailment when I was thirteen. His death killed my father who suffered from a bad heart. After that, my mother brought me and my other brother back to England, to Castle Combe . . . and when she knew she was going to die, she asked the sisters to look after us."

"You've been through a great deal of suffering in your young life, Sister," Philip said softly.

"Hasn't everyone?" she answered abstractedly, her thoughts on Michael. If he died . . . but the Holy Mother had said Michael would recover . . . she had to believe that now.

Everyone was pensive after that last statement, and the three sat in silence for a long while, each absorbed in his own thoughts. Catherine had been so keyed up emotionally that the purr of the motor seemed to be the soothing balm she needed to relax and soon she was feeling drowsy. After a few minutes, she was lulled into slumber and soon was asleep, totally exhausted from the strain and worry of the morning's unexpected activities.

Philip glanced over at Jeffrey, but his brother was not in a talkative mood. In fact, both of them were much more quiet than usual. Philip stretched out and put his hand behind his head, closing his eyes. He'd rather have looked at her . . . she was quite breathtaking. Philip had no way of judging one nun from another, but he had the impression she was no ordinary oblate, and this premonition hadn't come purely because of Michael's attachment to her. It was something else . . . her demeanor, the way she spoke with such authority and poise, her native intelligence, the way she carried herself. There was depth of character here . . . he knew this, despite the fact he'd only been in her company part of a morning. Jeffrey sensed these things as well, Philip could tell. The whole situation of Michael and Sister Catherine was remarkable. There was more here than was apparent at the outset.

Another hour and the car pulled up in front of the Sacred Heart Hospital in Norwood. It was made over from a municipal building which had been erected before the turn of the century, and looked more like a government building than a medical center. Jeffrey turned off the motor and jumped out of the car, quickly opening the back door for Catherine who had awakened from her sleep. Philip preceded them into the hospital.

"Michael has a room on the second floor, Sister. Before we go in, I want to find Hugh," Jeffrey explained, "and let him know we're here. Phil, wait with Sister Catherine for a moment, will you?" Philip nodded and Jeffrey practically ran down to the end of the hall and disappeared.

Catherine gazed around at the high ceilings and the well worn linoleum floors. There were sisters from the Dominican Order serving the hospital and she was thankful that some of her kind were on the premises. Catherine had never done hospital work. She had little taste for it, much preferring the life of the children and the school room. Her thoughts were interrupted, for Jeffrey was approaching, his arm around the shoulders of a small, balding man. Jeffrey's tired face was excited and eager as the two of them conversed and the old man looked with fresh interest into the face of the lovely nun before him. In all his years of work with the sisters, he'd never seen one like her.

"Sister," Jeffrey offered, "this is Dr. Endicott."

"Doctor," Catherine smiled, inclining her head in a graceful bow which was more natural to her than shaking hands.

"How do you do, Sister," he responded with warmth. "Frankly, when Elinore told me the boys had gone to fetch you, I shook my head . . . but I hoped! Now you are here, and not a moment too soon." He became serious. "Come with me, please. Michael is in a very weak condition. I don't have to tell you how much it will mean to the boy to see you. He's been asking for you continually. I respect the field of medicine, but there comes a time when a case is in the hands of God. Michael requires a miracle, Sister. I presume that is why you are here."

"I'll do whatever I can," Catherine answered faintly. Her fear increased. The four of them went up the stairs and down the hall to the end door. Jeffrey turned the handle.

"I want to go in first and tell him you're here," he said to Catherine. She folded her arms tightly, hands tucked in her sleeves, and waited, growing more anxious by the second. Jeffrey finally reappeared, his face wearing the haggard expression once more. His skin was the color of paste and Catherine groaned inwardly. He raised pained eyes to hers and motioned for her to come into the room with a weak wave of his hand. She stepped inside and shuddered at the thought of seeing Michael under these conditions. The day he'd left Castle Combe, he'd been a strong, healthy child, with sparkling eyes that spread sunshine. Dear Father in Heaven, to think that it had come to this . . . she tiptoed past the curtain which had been pulled aside. She was hesitant to go any closer to the bed. There was a little body lying there, propped so his head was higher than his feet, but a croup tent had been erected about his chest and head, so she could not see him. The blinds were shut and the room was dark. Several chairs and a bedside table were the only furnishings of the sterile, green room.

"That couldn't be Michael lying there," she cried to herself. "Not the energetic child who kept all the sisters alert with his vitality!" His father went to the side of the bed and lifted the flap of the tent so she could see him. Catherine finally found the strength to cross over to him. One pale hand lay palm down on the sheet, seemingly lifeless. She slipped her hand into his. There was no response. Her heart pounded painfully. She leaned over to look beneath the tent cover and beheld the white, pinched face of the dear child. His red-rimmed eyes were half opened and the golden locks which hugged his scalp in straggly, wet tendrils were dark, and had lost their lustre. He was much thinner and there were hollows beneath his eyes and under the cheek bones where once there had been firm, rosy flesh. A distinct rattle came from deep inside his chest each time he took a breath and he was fighting for every bit of air he could get.

Her pain grew. She shook her head unconsciously. "Michael," she whispered. "My little love," she cried out softly and bent over to kiss the sunken cheek which bore the telltale red spots of high fever. His head did not move but the eyes opened a little wider at the sound of her voice, their color more gray than blue. They were dull and lifeless. "Not his eyes . . . not his eyes," she murmured, and fought for control. "Michael," she called to him. He stared and finally recognized her. She smiled. "Yes, darling," and sobbed in spite of her efforts not to show emotion. "It's Sister Catherine. I've come to take care of you." He closed his eyes and the little lids looked like dried parchment . . . then he opened them again, turning his head a trifle this time, as if to get a better look. The hot little hand pressed her fingers.

"Sister," he whispered. "I knew you'd come. It took so long. Sister," he sobbed and the thin chest heaved, forcing a deep, rasping cough which she felt through her being. Her heart lurched and her arms went around his shrunken form. He tried to sit up and put his arms about her neck, but his strength failed and she held him against her breast. Catherine put her face against his burning cheeks, letting him feel her coolness for a long moment. The boy was crying, the tears soaking the scapular of her habit. "My precious one," she wept along with him. "I love you, my darling . . . I'm here now," she assured him over and over again. "Go ahead and cry, precious. It's all right . . . I won't leave you . . ." she murmured and rocked him back and forth in her arms.

Jeffrey stood spellbound, watching in wonderment the love that flowed between them. He raised his head, blinking back tears. Such deep affection emanated from her face as she held the boy close to her, that Jeffrey knew he'd done the right thing. Dear God, if only he'd realized! He could have gone for her a week ago . . . before it had reached this point. He noticed how the boy clung to her . . . there was a desperation about the way he whispered her name repeatedly. They were like mother and son.

Michael finally fell into a light sleep, and Catherine reluctantly lay his head back against the pillow. His hand was still holding tightly to hers. She raised a tear-stained face to Jeffrey as he replaced the flap. Unspoken words passed between them . . . both their hearts were on the verge of breaking. Finally Catherine bowed her head in prayer, never letting go of the limp hand. Jeffrey moved over to the window to pray for his son's recovery. He'd done everything he could do now. Sister Catherine was here. The rest was up to God.

Catherine shifted position in the hard chair and he moved back over to the bed. "How long has he had this difficulty breathing?" she asked.

"Since yesterday."

"He's burning with fever," she spoke quietly. "Do you think we could ask a sister for a basin of cold water and a cloth? I could at least keep his lips moist. He's dehydrated."

Jeffrey nodded and went into the hall, bringing the items she had requested and together they took turns wetting his lips and face. By late afternoon, the boy stirred and Catherine removed the cover. "Hello," she smiled at him.

"Did you go away while I was asleep?" His voice was a mere whisper.

"No—I sat right here."

"Where's Daddy?"

"I'm here, son." Jeffrey leaned over the other side. "How do you feel?"

"It hurts," he put his hand on his chest, then reached for his father.

"I know," Jeffrey's voice broke as he let the boy cry, tenderly kissing him. "It will go away soon." Michael kept his eyes on his father.

"You said Sister couldn't come, but she did."

"Yes," Catherine interjected. "It has all been arranged. You see how important you are?"

"And you won't go away?" he coughed painfully.

"No, darling. I plan to stay right here with you."

"At night, too?"

"If you want me to," she smiled.

"You can use the cot they've kept here for me," Jeffrey whispered.

"Aunt Ellie came last night," he spoke without feeling.

"I know," Jeffrey nodded. "I asked her to stay with you while I went for Sister Catherine."

"Daddy, will you and Sister stay with me all the time, now?" His breathing was heavy. Jeffrey looked at Catherine and sighed heavily.

"Yes, son . . . for as long as you like."

"That's good," Michael whispered and closed his eyes. He doubled up to reduce a coughing spasm which started once again. Catherine wished to God she could spare the boy. When the coughing subsided, he spoke once more. "Sister," he called out, his eyes still closed. "I've missed you."

"I've missed you, too," she assured him, wiping away more tears from her cheeks. Jeffrey handed her a handkerchief. "I've brought you a present." His eyelids fluttered. "What is it?"

"Something you left behind," and she reached into her pocket. Jeffrey watched with curiosity. "Here," she said, putting it into his hand.

"My whistle," he sounded surprised.

"The one Peter whittled for you. Holy Mother says she's missed hearing you play it in the afternoons."

Michael tried to hold it up to his lips but the effort was too much. He coughed and it slipped out of his hands, on to the sheet. "I'll put your whistle here in the drawer by the bed. It will be here when you want it. Now, go to sleep," and she placed her hand on his forehead, stroking it gently. Then she began singing a charming French tune which apparently was familiar to the boy for his mouth curled up at the corners. "Ecoutez tous, écoutez, tous . . . l'écho, l'écho, il dit, il dit, soyons toujours amis." She had a rich, mellow voice, soothing to the ear. Michael felt for her hand and fell sound asleep. She sat back in the chair. Fatigue was taking over. Presently her weary eyelids closed. Jeffrey slipped out of the room. Dr. Endicott was filling out reports at the nurse's station.

"Oh, Hugh . . . I was just coming to find you."

Dr. Endicott took one look at Jeffrey and put a hand on his arm. "Jeff, you've got to get some rest. There's a bed down in the doctor's lounge. I want you to lie down for a while, and no buts," he admonished.

"I will . . . Sister Catherine has gotten him back to sleep, now."

"Good . . . just what the boy needs."

"Wake me if there's the slightest change?"

The doctor licked his lower lip. "Jeff . . . he's going to reach the crisis sometime tonight, I suspect. We should know before morning. You get some sleep now, later Michael will need you."

Jeffrey felt ill. "Thanks, Hugh."

"No thanks necessary. By the way, Elinore phoned. I told her you'd brought Sister Catherine back with you. I presumed you'd both be staying the night and told her so. She wanted to come back to the hospital but I told her that now that the Sister had come, it really wasn't necessary."

"Good . . . she should be with Philip. I told him to take the car home and get some sleep."

"And you do the same . . . now!"

Jeffrey nodded wearily and went down the hall to the doctors' quarters.

Catherine stirred when she heard the rattle of trays outside the door. An aide brought in her dinner. She had been dozing on and off and hadn't realized the lateness of the hour. Michael was still asleep but his breathing was more labored. A new wave of fear seized her and she couldn't touch the food, preferring to sponge Michael down as the fever raged through him. Several hours passed and he began babbling incoherently. His sleep was fitful. Catherine was beside herself and ran out into the hall in search of his father. Dr. Endicott had just left a patient's room and saw her frantic expression. He hurried into the room and pulled the tent away, examining the boy. First he listened to the chest, then the boy's back. Even Catherine, untrained in medical matters, could tell that the child's breathing was too shallow. He glanced at her for a second and the worried look on his face left nothing to the imagination. He gave the boy another injection and propped him on his side once more, raising the bed till the boy was almost in a sitting position. Then he replaced the tent. "Sister—all we can do now is wait and pray."

She nodded, immobilized with despair. Dr. Endicott hurried out of the room to get Jeffrey. "It's not fair," she cried out to the Lord, in her first rebellion against the Divine order. "Don't let this child die," she pleaded, and slowly sank to her knees, pouring out her heart to the Creator. Jeffrey rushed into the room, but stopped immediately when he saw her kneeling. She hadn't heard him enter the room. Tears streamed from Jeffrey's eyes as he heard the last few words of her prayer.

"Take my life, if Thou wilt, but don't take this boy from his father. This man has already lost his wife . . . and he has saved so many other lives. Father, if it be Thy will, spare his son. He needs him. And Father, if it is not Thy will, then let this man find peace . . . ease his grief . . . be with him in this hour of travail."

It touched him that she had prayed for him as well as for Michael. There was great sweetness in her. It was no wonder his little boy worshipped her. Dear God, Michael had to get well! Jeffrey hurried over to the opposite side of the bed and knelt down. With a prayer in his heart, he reached out and took the boy's other hand. For a long time afterward, he remained in that position.

Elinore had insisted that she and Philip go right over to the hospital. Dr. Endicott had tried to discourage her from coming, saying it wasn't necessary, but she had to be near Jeffrey. Philip agreed to go as soon as he had eaten and slept. They arrived at the hospital shortly before eleven p.m. Philip knocked on the door very quietly. There was no answer. He pushed it open. There, on their knees, were the two people who loved Michael most in the world. Philip felt he was intruding on a sacred moment and shut the door again.

"What's the matter?" Elinore questioned. Philip was very subdued.

"We shouldn't go in right now, Elinore. I don't want to disturb them."

"But Jeffrey doesn't know we're here. What kind of family are we if we can't be at his side when he needs us?"

"He has someone at his side right now. He needs her much more. Believe me, this is no time to go in. We can stay out here in the hall. If the worst happens, then we can help . . . but not now!" Philip's voice was shaking. Elinore had never seen him so disturbed. It was best not to press the issue.

"I don't see Hugh about. I'd like to talk to him and find out how things really are," she muttered.

"Elinore—let's just be patient. He's been here around the clock. He's probably resting."

They sat down on chairs near the nurses' station and stared numbly into space, waiting, until Elinore could stand no more and went over to the door to Michael's room. She pushed it gently to look inside. Philip put out an arm to restrain her, but it was too late. From the doorway she could see the white-clad back of the nun plainly. Only Jeffrey's blond hair was visible from the other side of the bed. Both were kneeling, oblivious to everything. The scene was so poignant that even Elinore was deeply moved. She fought tears, not so much for Michael as for herself . . . she should be the one in there with Michael at this crucial moment. She found herself resenting the fact that Jeffrey was relying on the Sister, now. Philip was right! It would do no good to disturb Jeffrey. There'd be time later. She shut the door and sat down, feeling very bitter.

Philip sighed with relief that for once, she had not tried to take charge. He gave her a wan smile, but she ignored it, staring past him. He wanted to understand her, but she'd become detached of late. For the last few years, things had started to go wrong for them. He couldn't put his finger on it, but there was no kindness or gentleness in her nature. Elinore had turned cold. It had been months since they'd slept together. It was Elinore who was uninterested, always excusing herself with a headache or being too tired. And Philip wanted to start a family. He ached for it. Philip put his face in his hands and his thoughts strayed back to the tender scene in the next room. He could only imagine what his brother was going through, not being a father himself, but he was terribly fond of the boy. Michael was a sweet little chap . . . bright and well behaved. His death would be an inconsolable loss to all of them . . .

Dr. Endicott suddenly appeared in the corridor. "Phil, I didn't know you'd come back. I'm just going in."

Elinore jumped up. "Hugh, how is Michael, really?"

"I'll know when I've examined him. Wait out here. I'll let you know." They sat down again and he disappeared through the door. Catherine heard footsteps and rose from the floor to make room for the doctor. Jeffrey also stood up and helped him pull the tent away. After a thorough examination, he turned to Jeffrey. "His fever is down a little."

"Hugh," the father's heart leaped.

"Wait a minute, Jeff . . . it's much too soon to tell, but let's be thankful for that much improvement." Catherine's face broke into a tender smile which she flashed at Jeffrey. It spoke of hope and love. They looked down at the boy and seated themselves in chairs on either side of his bed. The doctor replaced the tent and left. Several hours passed, the two of them deeply absorbed in the boy. Suddenly Catherine was aware that she couldn't hear the rasping noise. She sat up and strained to listen for any sign of life. Jeffrey was alert to her sudden movement and jumped as she called softly to him.

"What is it?" he asked.

"I don't think I can hear him breathing!"

Jeffrey paled and hurriedly threw back the tent as Catherine leaned over the child. He was lying perfectly still . . . but his chest was rising and falling at regular intervals. She realized that he was sleeping soundly . . . and quietly.

"Oh," she sighed. "He's breathing normally! He's going to be all right. I know it!" She raised her head and they shared each other's happiness. "He's going to be all right," she cried in a rapturous voice, and the tears poured forth, unashamedly. Michael was resting comfortably and the flush of fever was slowly leaving his hollow cheeks.

"Thank God," Jeffrey whispered, and Catherine fell to her knees once more, thanking the Lord with all her heart for this great blessing He had bestowed upon them.

IV

A feeling of peace washed over Jeffrey as he gazed tenderly at his little boy. He couldn't take his eyes from Michael's face, so precious it was to him. Another hour passed and it was growing light outside. Catherine still knelt on the floor, her head bowed, her cheek against the bed. Suddenly she felt something pat her wimple. She sat up. Michael's eyes were open. They were still red-rimmed, but a spark of life was present which had not been there before. She took his hand and held it between both of hers. He turned to his father. "Daddy, I'm thirsty," he managed, in a cracked little voice. Jeffrey held a glass of water to his lips, attentive to his every need. "Could I have some juice?" Michael coughed, and though it was grating, it was not as sustained as before and the boy no longer struggled for breath.

"You can have whatever you want," he smiled and walked swiftly from the room. Catherine couldn't resist the urge to kiss his cheek.

"Do you know what? You're getting better already!" she beamed.

"It doesn't hurt as much, Sister."

Jeffrey came in followed by Dr. Endicott. The physician was obviously pleased at the change in Michael's condition. He came over to the bed and made another check. Then he nodded his head at Jeffrey. "He's defi-

nitely improved. Of course, the recovery will be slow
. . . things will take time, but Jeff, I think I'm safe in
saying you've got your son back. Congratulations!"
Pure elation dominated Jeffrey's tired, pale face. He
went over to Michael and kissed him on the forehead.

"Sister," the doctor whispered, drawing her aside,
"Michael is still very sick. He is going to need rest and
watching. As you know, children always bounce back
more quickly than do adults . . . but he is very weak.
I'm depending on you to make sure he doesn't overdo.
You can let him sip the grape juice now . . . later on, if
he has some appetite, we'll send in some broth. He
needs sleep, lots of it. And now that you are here, that
should be no problem."

"Very good, doctor, and thank you," Catherine
smiled warmly at the kind man.

"Don't thank me, Sister. I wouldn't have given the
boy a chance if you hadn't come when you did. You've
saved his life . . . I take no credit."

"God saved his life, doctor."

"Let's compromise and say both of you played a
part," he winked and turned to leave. "Philip and Elinore are outside, anxious to see Michael. I'll give you
and Jeff a few more minutes alone with the boy, then I'll
let them come in, but only for a minute. I'm leaving you
strictly in charge," and he walked out.

Catherine went back to Michael's bed. He had drifted
off to sleep and there were traces of grape juice on his
upper lip. He was beginning to look like a typical little
boy again. She smiled and wiped away the purple
moustache. Suddenly weak from the ordeal, she
brushed the perspiration from her forehead with the
sleeve of her habit and sat down in the chair, closing her
eyes with a deep sigh. Jeffrey was so exhausted he felt
as though his body weighed a thousand pounds. He

couldn't move from the chair, but still he didn't feel like sleeping. He was watching Catherine, in absolute awe over what had transpired. He would never forget the words of her prayer . . . they were indelibly impressed in his memory, there to remain. She seemed to him a kind of saint. For the first time, he really looked at her.

Her face was white with fatigue, but the translucent quality of her skin only enhanced her inner radiance. How could he ever repay her? This sister emanated goodness and purity, qualities which were rare in most people, even in most nuns, he surmised. Not once had she thought of herself or her own comfort. She'd left Our Lord of the Lamb on a moment's notice and her every thought and prayer had been for Michael . . . and for him. He wondered by what miracle Sister Catherine had been there for the two of them. Twice, she had saved Michael's life. Jeffrey had often seen the hand of God reach down and change the outcome of a desperate situation during the war . . . and as he studied the lovely nun who sat across from him, a strengthened belief in the Diety filled his soul.

Catherine wakened with a start. She'd been dreaming. She couldn't remember the details, but she'd felt sad. Then she looked at the child, slumbering peacefully, and sighed aloud, reaching out to touch his hand which lay on top of the sheet. How she loved him! Jeffrey was still looking at her. Slowly she raised her eyes to his and the two gazed at each other for a long moment. A brilliant smile slowly illuminated her face. For Jeffrey it was as if the black clouds of despair and heartache had suddenly dispersed and glorious sunshine filled his universe once more. Without realizing what he was doing, his hand reached out and covered hers, applying gentle pressure, as if to communicate by touch his deep emotion. She felt the warmth of his

61

fingers as they twined around hers. She knew he was trying to express his gratitude. There was a bond between them, for they had shared in the love of his little son at the critical hour of his life. The love Jeffrey had for Michael was special, and it filled her with joy to know that one day soon he would be walking again at his father's side. His happiness was hers. When Catherine finally lowered her eyes, she discovered that Philip had come into the room and a blond woman stood at his side, both faces staring at the two of them. Catherine realized Jeffrey's hand was still firmly clasped over hers across Michael's small figure. She pulled her hand gently away and stood as Jeffrey quickly got to his feet. Philip watched the scarlet blush creep over the nun's face. The look on his brother's face was almost one of worship.

"Jeff . . . Hugh says Michael is going to be fine."

"Yes," came the emotion-packed reply. Jeffrey was still looking at Catherine. Elinore was tongue-tied. She appraised Jeffrey, then the Sister, but could see only a partial profile, due to the white wimple.

"It's wonderful, Jeff," she mouthed the words, then abruptly left the room. Philip was ill at ease, wondering if it would be best to leave as Elinore had done. He had walked in on a deeply private moment and there was no mistaking the look in Jeffrey's eyes this time. "I'll come back later when Michael is awake."

"Stay with me, Phil," Jeffrey implored, with a new, excited quality in his voice. "Sister, you need to eat and then rest. Please feel free to leave Michael for a while. Phil will watch him with me." Catherine bowed and left the room. Jeffrey had just excused her from a potentially embarrassing situation and she appreciated his sensitivity. She hoped Philip was sensitive enough to accept what he saw as a handclasp of thanksgiving. As for his wife, Catherine knew little about her. Once, at the convent, Michael had talked about his Aunt Ellie. He had told her that the reason he didn't want to go back to Norwood was because he didn't want his aunt taking care of him. She wasn't his mum and he didn't like her—and sometimes she talked like Sister Anna, and it scared him. Catherine couldn't imagine what he meant, for Sister Anna was a dear, sweet woman of German extraction whom all the children adored. Still, Michael was very serious about his feelings and Catherine had to respect them.

Catherine went first to the nursing station to inquire about the location of the chapel. One of the sisters said she would accompany her as soon as she finished her morning rounds. Catherine then went to freshen up and eat some food. She was feeling shaky and had lost all sense of time . . . and then there was the Holy Mother. She must phone her the wonderful news, just as soon as she had given thanks in the sanctuary.

Long after she disappeared around the corner of the corridor leading to the chapel, eyes of suspicion and envy stared after her. Elinore watched the figure of the nun with great interest. She still hadn't had a good look at this Sister who had once again accomplished the impossible, but she would never forget the look of adoration on Jeffrey's face when she walked into that room with Philip. It would haunt her to the grave.

Elinore could no longer remain in the hospital under the circumstances. Without a moment's hesitation she left the floor, walked out the front doors and drove back to Norwood. She would send Jens back with the car for Philip, when he was ready. In her frame of mind, she didn't care if Philip ever came back. As for Jeffrey, she would have to find another way to reach him. Using Michael's illness as a bridge would not bring them closer together now. She would have to wait till Michael was fully recovered and home from the hospital. With the Sister around, she couldn't get near Jeffrey. That much was obvious! No, she'd wait till Sister Catherine returned to her cloister and life returned to normal once more. There were other ways to make a man interested . . . she just had to be patient for a while longer . . .

The crisis was over and Catherine slept through the late morning and part of the afternoon in the nurses' quarters. It was a deep sleep, without dreams, for her exhaustion had reached its peak. Once rested and fortified with a late lunch, she returned to Michael's room. His father was sound asleep on the cot by the bed where Michael lay. Both father and son were sprawled over their beds in much the same position. Catherine tiptoed in and smiled. Michael's father looked younger now, despite the day's growth of beard. He seemed almost helpless . . . not at all the way she first thought of him back at the convent. The lines had gone from his forehead.

She went to the closet and found a blanket which she quietly put over him. It was cool in the room. He opened his eyes briefly, saw her face close to his as she tucked in the sides, and smiling, he settled back to sleep, obviously enjoying his new found warmth. Since both were sleeping, she left the room and inquired about some books at the nursing station . . . something a little boy would like to read. The sister said there was reading material in the children's wing on the main floor. Catherine went downstairs and was shown into a playroom which was a make-shift nursery for the convalescents. There were blocks and toys, tables, chairs, a piano, and over on a corner table were several stacks of books, well worn. She looked through them but nothing appealed to her. Then she saw a book on the floor, behind the table. It was an old edition of *Robin Hood*. She leafed through the pages. The drawings captured her fancy. It was her favorite book as a child. Michael had wanted to hear this famous tale. She put it under her arm and returned upstairs.

Michael and his father were still asleep as she crept in, so she sat quietly in a chair near the window and for want of anything else to do, opened the first page of the book. It wasn't long before she was immersed in the enchanting story. She had always been interested in history. When she wasn't practicing the piano or organ, she often had her nose buried in a history book. Holy Mother had said on more than one occasion, that when the war ended, Catherine could begin advanced studies at the Theological Institute in Leicestershire. She could continue her studies of Latin and Greek, and pursue her interests in history and literature at the same time. It would prepare her for her work as a teacher. Many of the sisters preferred hospital work and wanted to be nurses, but Catherine tended to enjoy more intellectual pursuits. There was so much good literature to read, so many ideas to implant in young minds about God and Life . . . so many lessons to be learned from the rise and fall of civilizations and dynasties. To be able to put this across to children was very appealing to her. To shape a mind! That was a supreme challenge!

As the Sheriff of Nottingham was about to dismount, Jeffrey stirred. She looked over at him. He yawned and then sat up, staring at her as if she were an apparition.

"Sister, how long have you been here?"

"For an hour or more."

He felt his beard and was embarrassed. "I didn't hear you come in. Where did the blanket come from?"

"It felt cool in here, so I put it over you."

"Thank you," he smiled. "What time is it?"

"Almost five o'clock."

"I've been asleep all day," he muttered, a bit surprised.

"So has Michael," she explained. "It has been good for both of you."

"Did you get any rest?" he asked a bit sheepishly.

"Yes . . . I, too, slept all morning and part of the afternoon."

Jeffrey got up and folded the blanket and cot, placing them in a corner, out of the way. "I'll see if they can't bring us some tea and biscuits," he suggested. He left the room momentarily, and came back with a tray. Catherine was looking at the drawings in the book. Jeffrey poured the tea and took a cup over to her, bending down to see what held her captive. "*Robin Hood*—where did you manage to find that?"

"In the nursery. I'm anxious to read to Michael when he awakens."

"He'll love it. There are books at home that I can bring, Sister."

Her eyes sparkled. "You wouldn't happen to have *The Count of Monte Cristo*? or *The Black Tulip*?"

He smiled broadly. Those were two of his old favorites. "I have those and more in the library back at Norwood. When I go home tonight, I'll pack a bundle and bring them to the hospital in the morning."

"That would be wonderful. He's a fortunate child to be surrounded by good books. Most of the children at Our Lord of the Lamb are sorely lacking in that department. I'm afraid the library there has little to offer. I've had to rely on memories from my own childhood to keep the children entertained." It suddenly occurred to her she was talking too much.

"I wish I had known," Jeffrey was thoughtful. "I'll

66

have Jens pack a box and we'll see that your library is enriched right away.''

"Oh,'' she sighed. "You can't imagine how happy that will make the children! You are very kind.''

"Not at all. It's the least I can do after everything you have done for Michael and me,'' and he stared at her. Lord, she was beautiful! Catherine averted her eyes.

"I've discovered that when a child is frightened or sick, a book can do wonders to alleviate the stress . . . they escape for a while. You can tell they are starving for good literature by the way they hang on your every word. It is a type of therapy which benefits them for years to come.'' There was a pause. "What other books do you have?'' Her face was hopeful. He paced the floor for a moment, digesting what she'd just said.

"Like what, for instance?''

"Oh . . . historical novels, anything to do with the Plantagenets, or something from the French revolution . . . Russia.''

"Aren't those a little steep for Michael?''

"I—I was asking for myself . . . I enjoy good books. When Michael is asleep, I can study. I like to read everything I possibly can.''

He stroked his chin, impressed. "Well,'' he cleared his throat. "I'll see what I can find. I know we have *Les Miserables*.''

"I read that years ago,'' she remarked. "That is one book I'd like to be reading again for the first time.''

"I know what you mean,'' he answered softly. "Sister, I'll go through our books and bring anything that I think you'd like.''

"Thank you,'' she answered. Michael began coughing, announcing his return to the world. They went over to the bed. He opened crusty lids and looked at them.

"Sister, I'm hungry. Can I have something to eat

now?"

Catherine was delighted. "Of course! What would you like? How about some broth and a little egg custard?"

He nodded. "That sounds good."

"All right. I'll go down the hall and get it. Commander Norwood," she called to him, "he can have those biscuits I haven't eaten." Jeffrey nodded and handed them to Michael. The boy took a tiny first bite, then devoured them between coughs. It was so wonderful to see the boy's appetite back, Jeffrey felt giddy. Catherine returned and began feeding him the custard, spoonful by spoonful, like a mother with her baby, Jeffrey thought. They were so natural together, he sighed with contentment. When Michael pulled a face, she knew he was full.

"Now," she said, "you lie back and I'll read you a story you've been wanting to hear for a long time."

"*Ivanhoe*?" he asked eagerly. Jeffrey realized Michael had been exposed to good books while he was at Our Lord of the Lamb.

"No, another one that you wished we had in our library."

"King Arthur?"

"No . . . *Robin Hood*!"

"Goody," he clapped his hands and began to cough violently. Catherine held her breath till it was over. Jeffrey found a chair and sat back, putting his hands behind his head to listen as she started one of his favorite tales. When the different speaking parts were introduced, she changed her voice to suit the characters. Michael was living the adventure. So was he for that matter! The lovely Sister was enchanting. She came to the part where King Richard was returning from the crusades.

68

"Sister?" Michael stopped her in a wheezing voice. "What's a crusade?" Jeffrey was also waiting for the answer.

"Well, it was a religious war . . . you see, the place of Christianity, where Jesus was born, had been overrun by infidels . . . men who did not believe in God, and so, many knights went to that country to free it and make it God's country once more. King Richard went for England."

"I wish I could have gone." Jeffrey glanced at her and they both smiled at Michael.

"Michael . . . did you know that there was a whole army of little children from France who went on a crusade? If you'd been alive then, maybe you would have been among them."

"Really?" They could see the wheels turning. Then, "Did they die?" he asked soberly.

"Yes . . . some of them."

"They were brave."

"Yes . . . very."

He was quiet, then said, "Will you keep reading now?" Catherine resumed the story. Jeffrey said nothing, continuing to listen and enjoy the interchange between his son and the Sister. It gave him a great deal of satisfaction to know that Michael had been in her stimulating company for such a long period of time. The boy was even more fortunate than Jeffrey had realized.

The child's eyelids closed just as King Richard knighted Robin Hood, Sir Robin of Loxley. Catherine closed the book. She turned to Jeffrey and noted the pleased expression on his face. It made her happy to see that he was no longer burdened with worry. "Commander Norwood, until Michael has recovered, I will stay here at the hospital. I can sleep on that cot."

"Thank you, Sister. I was hoping you were going to

say that. I'm more than grateful. Michael will rest easier if you are here at night; however, that cot is not the most comfortable bed I've ever slept on. Perhaps you can use one of the beds in the nurses' quarters. I'll inquire."

"That's not necessary. I want to be right here with Michael till he's on his feet. The cot will be fine. At the convent—" she stopped talking. She shouldn't be telling him about her life at Our Lord of the Lamb. It just slipped out. He was easy to talk to. In the future she would have to be more careful. Jeffrey understood her momentary plight. He knew she'd almost said something she shouldn't have. It made her seem more human and he was glad of it.

"Very well, Sister. Would you join me for a little dinner?" He wanted to continue their conversation.

"I think not . . . I'll stay here with Michael until you come back. Then I will eat and go to chapel."

He nodded and left the room. There was a pub around the corner from the hospital where they served fish and chips. He would go there. It wouldn't take long, and he could get back quickly. The thought occurred to him that fish might taste good to Sister Catherine, and so he placed two orders and purchased a bottle of ale. On an impulse, he also picked up a light wine. While he waited for the order, he telephoned Jens and instructed him to bring the car to the hospital, later.

Catherine was still reading when Jeffrey slipped back into the room. His arms were loaded. Michael's eyes opened wide. "Daddy, are we going to have a party?"

"Well," he chuckled, "why not?" Catherine was curious and stood up to watch as he put the things on the table. The odor of fish permeated the room. She hadn't eaten flounder in newspaper since she was twelve. It brought back many memories. Jeffrey watched her eyes sparkle. "I've brought some wine for you, too, Sister.

70

Shall we eat?" he invited her, having distributed every-thing on the bedside table. He pulled a chair near his, indicating she should sit down. He was a very thought-ful man, Catherine noted. She did his bidding. Jeffrey sat beside her, opened up the fish and chips, then poured some wine into a cup and offered it to her. She seemed hesitant. "Aren't you hungry, Sister?"

"Sister always blesses the food before she eats, Daddy," Michael blurted out in his raspy voice. A smile raised the corners of Jeffrey's mouth. What else did his son know about this delightful creature? He put the wine down.

"I'm sorry, Sister. I'm afraid I've gotten into some bad habits this past year. That is what comes from not having a woman around. Would you say grace?" He smiled so cordially at her, she felt at ease. He was a gentleman. Catherine bowed her head.

"Please, Dear Lord, may we be thankful for this food . . . may it help us to remember Thee and to do good in Thy sight. Amen."

"And thank you for letting Sister come," Michael's little voice cracked. "Amen."

Catherine's eyes opened wide with surprise. "Amen," Jeffrey offered in a deep, rich voice. Then he offered the wine once more. "Is it against the rules of your order to have this, Sister?"

"No," she smiled charmingly and sipped it. "It's delicious, just right."

"I think it is a good companion to a salty dish. I, however, prefer ale," and he proceeded to swallow the contents of his cup without stopping for a breath. Her father had loved English ale . . . had said on more than one occasion it was England's most outstanding contri-bution to mankind.

Her eyes told him she found it all very entertaining.

71

There was something so natural and refreshing about her . . . a naiveté . . . he was charmed by her. "All right," he said after they had finished eating, realizing food had never tasted so good before. "What will it be now?" He looked over at Michael who lay quietly on the bed watching them. "Another story or a game, maybe?"

"A game, please," he whispered. "Sister?" the boy looked at her with an eager expression. Jeffrey didn't know what was coming next. No doubt she had some new idea up her sleeve which Michael wanted her to share with him. His curiosity was piqued.

"Charades?" she suggested. He nodded his curly head.

"Daddy," he began, but coughed for a full minute. It was a horrible reminder of his illness. Catherine and Jeffrey exchanged worried glances. Finally the spasm subsided. "You and Sister have to find out which nursery rhyme I'm doing," and he pretended he was a bleating sheep. He did it with such feeling, despite his illness, both of them were laughing.

"Baa, baa, black sheep," Jeffrey finally answered. The little face looked crestfallen.

"He guessed it, Sister. It was too easy." Again they laughed. He was so dear. "Your turn, Sister," the feeble voice spoke once more.

"All right, let's see . . ." and she rolled her eyes in a mock pretense of concentration. Jeffrey had thought of them as being clear blue, but now he saw a tinge of violet which shone like a rare amythyst through the thick, black lashes. She stood up, and put her hands to her full, wide mouth, the lips as red as the wine which had touched them. She pretended to blow on a horn. Jeffrey had forgotten the game for the moment as he fixed his attention on her. He had to rack his brain to think of the answer, but it would not come.

"Daddy, don't you know? It's Little Boy Blue," Michael said animatedly.

"Yes," she cried and gave him a kiss. He turned to his father. "It's your turn now, Daddy."

"I'm not quite up to this," he apologized. "Let's see . . ." Finally he ran about the room knocking on the door and window.

"Wee Willie Winkie," Michael laughed and quietly clapped his hands.

"Couldn't fool you, could I?" he pinched the boy's cheek. They played several rounds of charades and then Michael wanted to go to sleep. Catherine and Jeffrey heard his prayers and soon he was asleep. She pulled the covers up over his chin and gave him one last kiss on the forehead. "I love you," she whispered.

Jeffrey heard her. How could the boy help but love her, too? He thought of the other children back at the convent and wagered that she was sorely missed. In fact, he began to realize how remarkable it was that she had come to Norwood at all . . . that she was here with Michael, taking care of him as only she could do.

"Sister, thank you for what you're doing for Michael. I'll go back to the house now and I'll see you both in the morning. I won't forget the books."

"Thank you, Commander Norwood . . . and I appreciated the delicious dinner. It was kind of you. Good night." They clasped hands briefly.

"Call me if Michael should need anything, no matter the hour. Good night."

Jens was waiting as he stepped out of the hospital doors. The air was soft and sweet. Jeffrey took a deep breath, exhaling slowly. He felt as if the terrible episodes of Connie's death and Michael's illness were things of the past. He hadn't had this feeling of well-being for a long time. When he thought of Michael now, he knew his son was in the best of hands and a feeling of sweet relief flooded through him. Tonight he would sleep as he hadn't done for over a year. He leaned his head back against the seat. A smile still played on his lips as he recalled the various events of the evening. Like a montage, Catherine's face appeared—animated, thoughtful, happy, sad, haunting, radiant, spiritual. Sister Catherine was resourceful as well as intelligent. He couldn't remember the last time he'd spent such an enjoyable evening.

Catherine prepared for bed after a period of prayer in the chapel. The hospital was quiet. Dr. Endicott had made his nightly rounds and it was time to sleep, but she could not turn off her mind. So much had happened in the last twenty-four hours, sleep was impossible. Michael was going to get well . . . what a great blessing! But she found herself thinking other thoughts as well. Michael's father was on her mind. He had left the room so happy and relaxed. He wasn't at all difficult to talk to. In the car, on the way to Norwood, she had feared that being in his company would prove to be uncomfortable, but on the contrary, she could chat with him as easily as with the Holy Mother. It had been a very pleasant evening . . . and it was especially thoughtful of him to bring the fish and wine . . . in fact, he was a very generous man. He had even planned on sending books to the library back at the convent. She smiled when she thought about the game they had played. He probably hadn't said nursery rhymes since his childhood. Michael was a sweet child. He obviously received his good nature from his father . . . and she permitted her thoughts to drift until she was no longer aware of anything.

V

Jeffrey arrived at the hospital the next morning just as Catherine and Michael had finished breakfast. Catherine had been up early, saying Holy Office in the chapel, and now she was ready to entertain Michael for the day. He seemed much more chipper and ate a substantial amount of oatmeal. Color was reappearing in his cheeks and a smile brightened his face. The two of them were going over a list of items Michael wanted when Jeffrey walked in, with a load of books beneath his arm. Catherine stared for a moment. He was clean shaven, and sportily dressed in a brown jersey and trousers. A heathery frágrance entered the room with him. He looked different somehow, even dashing. He radiated health and vigor. His smile was dazzling. She looked away quickly.

"Good morning. I see you two are already hard at work." Michael reached for his father and gave him a big hug. "Daddy, can you get the things Sister and I need?"

"What things?" She handed him a list: pencils, paper, charcoals, pastels. "Of course. If I'd known, I could have brought them with me. It looks as though you're going to do some sketching." She nodded. "I recall those geese drawings. I want the truth now," he looked around with a half smile. "Michael—did you do them all by yourself?" He put down the books.

"Sister helped me," he answered honestly.

"I thought so . . . Sister?" he turned to her. "They were very good. I have them in my study. I'd like to see more of your work."

"I'm afraid you would be very disappointed. I'm not an artist."

"Yes you are, Sister," Michael challenged her. "And my daddy is good at drawing, too."

"Really?" her eyes probed Jeffrey's, interested in this new aspect. He shook his head.

"Yes he is . . . draw her a picture of a plane, Daddy. He can draw anything, Sister—just like you."

The two adults exchanged glances. Catherine spoke first. "Well . . . when we get some paper, we'll have you draw something special for us. Maybe you could sketch a Sunderland?"

Jeffrey blinked in amazement. "How would you know about that?"

She bit her lip in a teasing manner, totally unaware of the saucy picture she made. "I know a great deal about you, Commander." She placed the emphasis on his title and lowered her voice. "Your son is a veritable encyclopedia."

He laughed quietly. "I hope he hasn't let all the skeletons out of the closet."

"Oh," she smiled, "not too many."

"I'll get the things you need and be right back." He left the room, excited, but he didn't know why. Catherine looked through the stack of books. There were some familiar ones for Michael and a few for her: *The Silver Chalice*, Charles Dickens, *Bonaparte*, *Elizabeth the Queen*. She looked forward to the moments she could spend reading while Michael was recuperating. Michael found the books he wanted and settled back, trying to pronounce some of the words.

Catherine opened *Elizabeth the Queen* and became so engrossed that when Jeffrey returned, she wasn't aware of his presence till he addressed her. "Did I bring something to interest you?"

"Oh," she cried, startled. "Yes, thank you so much. I didn't hear you come in." He had already started to sketch something on paper, sitting next to Michael so the boy could watch. Both heads were bent in concentration and it caught at her heart to see them so happy.

Catherine continued to read, but occasionally went over to see how things were progressing. He drew with rapid, swift strokes, decisive and clear. A two-decked plane was emerging from the pencil.

"You really are good," she remarked and stepped closer to observe his work.

"It's just part of my job," he replied modestly. The plane was coming to life now. It was fascinating to watch him work.

"It's a very large plane, isn't it?" She leaned over to see better, and her face was so close that he could see the fine down on her cheeks.

"Yes . . . the biggest one in the air command. It seats a crew of seven, but we've had as many as forty-three in it on some rescue missions."

She was thoughtful. This man, sitting here sketching, was the same man who had risked his life to save others, and received a medal for bravery during the early days of the war, but he was too modest to ever talk about it. He really was quite extraordinary, she decided, in many ways. Michael would have a lot to live up to.

Jeffrey sketched for a while longer and Michael drew right along with him. They were all happily occupied until lunch time, when Michael ate most of his stew and settled back for another nap. Catherine returned to her novel and Jeffrey began a new sketch. She glanced up after a while and discovered his eyes upon her, studying her carefully. She put the book down. "Don't move, Sister." She was so startled, she couldn't budge. He made a few quick strokes with his pencil. "There," he sighed and put the picture on the table. She walked over to take a look. It was a sketch of her and Michael. She was kneeling at his bed, with one hand holding his as he lay asleep. There was something very beautiful about the expression on the child's face. Jeffrey had drawn her as he had seen her when he entered the room the night of the crisis. It was a lovely picture. Tears gathered in her eyes and she blinked hard to keep them from falling.

"You're a very gifted artist," she said softly. "You've captured Michael's sweetness."

"Maybe," he answered slowly, "but I couldn't do justice to you." His eyes were misty as he looked up into her face. She turned from him. There was something about the way he spoke to her just now . . .

"If you are going to stay for a while, I would like to go to the chapel." She felt the need to be alone, to commune with God.

"Of course. Please feel free to do what ever you wish," but his heart was not in the reply. He wanted her to stay.

Catherine went back to the room at the dinner hour. "We've been waiting for you, Sister," Michael called out. "Daddy has made a spot for you." Indeed, everything had been set up. She sat down at her appointed place. Tonight, cabbage rolls were on the menu. This time Jeffrey said grace. "This is fun," Michael commented as they ate. "Can we do this every night?"

"If you like," his father answered automatically. Catherine said nothing. Michael's illness had forced both of them to throw discipline aside, temporarily.

Eventually the boy would have to face a normal life once more. And so would she. This fairy tale could not go on indefinitely, but she refused to think about that just yet. An orderly cleared away the dishes and the three of them faced another evening together. "I brought some cards, Michael. Shall we teach Sister to play Duck Duck?"

"Duck, what?" she questioned, looking first at Michael, then his father. "Do you think I can learn?" her mouth turned up.

"Sister, you're silly," the child responded and watched while his father shuffled the cards, placing them in two stacks on the table. Jeffrey was amused at Michael's comment. Even his son wasn't fooled by her attempt to appear humble, though he admired her for it. He wondered how she would be at a game of chess? He'd have to find out later. They played the game till the boy fell asleep with the cards still in his hands. Jeffrey was glad. He was looking forward to spending the rest of the evening with Catherine.

"Sister, have you ever played chess?"

"Yes. There's a fourteen-year-old boy at the convent named Christian Leeds. He taught me a few fundamentals. He used to play with his father until the man was killed in a bombing raid over Sussex. The boy is disturbed and the game relaxes him. It helped him pass the empty afternoons last winter." Again she realized she had said too much. A simple, "yes," would have sufficed.

"Well," he eyed her intently. "Let's see if you've done your homework. I'll be right back." He'd seen a chess set in the doctor's lounge and asked an orderly to fetch it. Soon he was back in the room and had the board set up. Catherine wondered that he did not return to Norwood now that Michael was asleep, but he made no

79

move to leave, and she was anxious to find out just how well she'd measure up. She'd never played chess with anyone besides Christian. There was no doubt Michael's father was an expert, so she determined to play her best. A friendly spirit of competition always enticed her. They began their moves and there was no time to talk. She was entirely caught up in the game. It was the most stimulating activity she'd engaged in for a long time. She was no longer aware of her surroundings.

Jeffrey found her a worthy opponent and as time passed, he had to start taxing his brain to stay in the game; but he could not refrain from watching the various expressions on her face as she planned her strategy, and he enjoyed it to such an extent that he failed to pay proper attention to the play at hand.

"I have your king in check," she called out triumphantly. Her eyes flashed and she was obviously delighted. He sat back to think this one over. She was right! His fingers drummed the table top and he looked at her. She watched him very carefully. He couldn't allow her to become too confident of herself. She'd have to ask forgiveness for succumbing to the sin of pride, he mused, and moved a knight in front of his king. Her face fell. His move had upset her whole plan. He could see that she was disappointed. Her fingers shook as she moved her queen. He then proceeded to move his rook into position.

"Check mate, Sister . . ." She relaxed and finally smiled at him engagingly across the board. "Christian should have you around to coach him." She was even a gracious loser.

"I'll tell you a secret," he winked, "you almost had me . . . and I've had many more hours than you to develop skill at this game."

She imagined he was referring to his spare time during flights in the coastal command. "Does it get lonely when you're out on a mission?"

"Yes," he nodded with a far away look, amazed she could read his mind. "Terribly at times . . . not when we're in the air so much. With seven of us, there's a great deal of camraderie . . . we get to know each other extremely well. We're close, like brothers. But during the hours on the ground, while we wait to go out on sorties, there are times when thoughts of home and loved ones are almost unbearable." He sounded sad. She shouldn't have asked. His eyes were half veiled as he ventured another comment. "Don't you ever get lonely for relationships with other people?"

She stared at him. "You mean, outside the Order?" His question came from out of the blue.

"Yes."

"But we do mix with people from the outside. I'm with hundreds of children every day . . . it is very fulfilling. Some day I plan to be a teacher and I will always be surrounded with children, and of course, my sisters. My life is rich."

He was listening, carefully. "And do you sisters care about each other, the way the men of my crew do, for example? You're always in each other's company as well, aren't you?"

"We care," Catherine said quietly. "But it isn't a demonstrative kind of love. We lead an active life; we are very busy with our various duties. Close relationships with one another are not encouraged. It would interfere with our work, which is the service of God."

"Does that apply to the children as well?"

She sat straighter in her chair. "What do you mean?"

"Are relationships with them discouraged?"

"We try to remain objective with all people so that we can render the greatest possible service to everyone who needs our help," she answered quietly.

He saw the becoming red blush tint her cheeks. "Do you love all the children with the same intensity you love my son?" By her silence he knew he'd hit a nerve. She loved Michael as a mother loves a child, and that was not in the rules. He was still waiting for an answer. For some reason, it was vitally important to him.

"Michael," she started, "Michael is a special case . . . he's—he's very precious," she said the words haltingly. It thrilled him that she cared so much. She was still a saint in his eyes, but seated across from him was a very exciting woman of flesh and blood and heart.

"You missed him when I brought him back here, didn't you?" he questioned further. She bowed her head.

"Yes," came the muffled reply.

"When you go back, will you be lonely for him again?"

She clasped the crucifix in her hands tightly. "Yes." There was pain in her tone and expression. He hadn't meant to hurt her. He felt ashamed to have caused her any discomfort, but he couldn't help himself. His thoughts were darting hither and yon. "Will you stay at Our Lord of the Lamb indefinitely?" He decided to steer the conversation in another direction, and besides, he wanted to know her future plans—for Michael's sake, he told himself.

"No," she asserted. "There are missions in Tahiti and French Guiana. I will do my life's work at one of those two locations, but that won't be for some time . . . till the war is over." She looked up and their eyes held. He couldn't imagine her so far away. It bothered him.

"Are you a nurse, too?" he asked quickly, to cover his distress.

"No . . . many of the sisters have chosen that area to

82

serve, but I prefer to deal with concepts and philosophies, rather than disease, though there is ample need for both fields. The war has been an education in itself. There are many children in the world who need enlightenment desperately. Their minds are eager to soak up knowledge. If the wrong people get there first, it is a tragedy. I grew up believing we are born to do some service for mankind . . . even before I entered the sisterhood. Now my vocation will enable me to do such work. Children are the hope of the world, as it has been stated, and I believe it. I'd like to be able to have a part in their education."

"That is a very lofty ideal for one so young," he smiled, deeply impressed.

"I don't believe age has anything to do with it. Many of the sisters come to the convent at an early age, their lives already set on a particular path. It is not remarkable, Commander Norwood."

Jeffrey remembered that nuns did not take credit for the good they accomplished. Sister Catherine had a difficult time accepting praise graciously. "Sister—why did you become a nun?" The question was out. All evening he'd wanted to ask her. Maybe he had gone too far, but something had come over him. He found himself wanting to know everything about her. Catherine's eyes remained fixed on him. She didn't know if she should tell him anything more. The Holy Mother was right! There was no precedent to follow; yet, the man seated across from her had asked a very simple question, really, in all sincerity. Was it wrong? She didn't know. "You don't have to answer that question," Jeffrey said, noticing her perplexed look. "I've no right. Forgive me."

"It—it's all right," she stammered. "When my brother, Paul, died years ago, I became quite despondent. It seemed such a waste. He was my dear friend. We were very close, like you and your brother. Paul had always wanted to become a priest. Even as a youngster, he wasn't like the other boys. He had a more serious nature. Anyway, the priesthood was a dream for him, and I was inconsolable after his death, knowing it could never be a reality for him."

"He must have loved you very much," Jeffrey added quietly.

She paused. "As the years went by, I found myself turning more and more to the Lord for comfort, and one night, the thought came to me that I could serve God in Paul's place . . . and that idea began to dwell in my heart." Jeffrey listened, haunted by the depth of her religious zeal. "Later, when my mother was ailing, I told her of my desire to live the life of a religious. It shocked her deeply and she didn't want me to do this. She did everything in her power to persuade me otherwise. I believe it was because she and my father had been very happy together, and I suppose she wanted me to have that same fulfillment."

"You can't really blame her, can you?" he questioned.

"No . . . of course not, and it was because of her that I went through a long period of self analysis to decide if I were doing it to fulfill my brother's dreams, or if I was committing myself to God for *me*. Do you understand what I mean?"

Jeffrey nodded. She had great wisdom and maturity for one so young. Again, it baffled him.

"Then my mother died. John, my older brother, and I went to the convent to live. After a year, John went to live with my mother's sister in Liverpool. I could have gone and been raised by her, but I loved the spiritual life at Our Lord of the Lamb, and I made the decision to

84

stay. I've never regretted it," she spoke with fervor. Jeffrey shifted position in his chair, completely engrossed. "In my eighteenth year, I became a postulant . . . it's a time period in which you learn about the life of an oblate, and a period of testing, to see if you are ready to make vows to God, and to see if God wants you. During that year, I began to find joy in my service to the Lord, and when the time came for me to enter the novitiate, I did so willingly. After that year, the war broke out, and the children began to arrive. It was then I knew beyond a shadow of a doubt that I had chosen the right vocation. It was indeed the right choice for me. Children need so much love and comfort."

"Thank God you were there for Michael! I thank Him for you, Sister." They were both quiet for a long while. He reflected on their conversation. She was completely sincere and honest in everything she said. There was nothing artificial about her . . . a pearl beyond price. He couldn't take his eyes off her. Then, forcing himself against his will, he stood up, and put the chess set away. "Good night, Sister," he said soberly. "Thank you for indulging me in the chess game. Thank you for everything," his voice broke. "I will see you tomorrow," and he quickly left the room.

Catherine stood in the same spot for many minutes after, not understanding why she was in turmoil. When she was with him, another dimension of life unfolded, and she had to admit that she enjoyed it . . . so much so, in fact, that she really hadn't wanted him to leave just now. He had many fine qualities . . . he was exciting! Catherine had no idea it could be like this. She recalled times spent with her brothers, but this was different somehow. The room seemed dim without his vital presence. She looked at Michael. Holy Mother of God . . . even his father realized that her attachment to the boy was not accepted by the rules of the sisterhood. Her love for him was obvious to all. She would have to go back to the convent as soon as Michael was able to leave the hospital. Everything was becoming much too complicated!

The next day Jeffrey came so the three of them could have breakfast together. He seemed to bring the sunshine with him. She immediately lowered her eyes, determined to keep from looking at him. The doctor said Michael could go for a ride in the wheel chair, just around the floor and back. Dr. Endicott felt that at the rate he was recovering, he'd be able to go home in another week. It was marvelous news, but the good doctor was totally unaware of its impact on Jeffrey and the Sister. Catherine couldn't bear to think about leaving Michael, and Jeffrey just refused to think.

That afternoon, after a short nap, Michael had visitors. Philip and Elinore had come to spend some time with their nephew. It was the opportunity Catherine needed to be relieved from responsibilities . . . but it was their presence, Michael's and his father's, from which she needed a vacation. They'd been together constantly. Catherine planned to go for a walk in the fresh air. There would be time for meditation in new surroundings.

"Sister?" Jeffrey called to her in the hall. He had just stepped out of Michael's room, afraid she'd already left. She turned in his direction. "Yes?"

"I thought that since Phil and Elinore are here to be with Michael for a while, I'd drive you over to Shepherd's Cross. There is a cathedral there. I realize after our conversation last night how much you must miss your life at Our Lord of the Lamb. I have to go over there on a personal matter anyway."

He was always so considerate, she mused. How did

he know she wanted to go to church right now? To surround herself with the religious life, if only for a while? "Thank you . . . if you're sure it won't put you out."

He shook his head, as if what she'd said was absurd. "I want to. One of the fellows of an old crew was shot down last week. His wife lives right around the corner from the church. I would like to look in on her and the children . . . see if there is anything I can do."

Her face sobered instantly. Death was everywhere, yet again, she was touched with his compassion for others, his decency. She followed him outside the hospital and they were off. She felt self-conscious in the front seat with him and kept her face straight ahead, clasping her hands rigidly in her lap. Jeffrey stole a look at the woman seated so demurely beside him. The haunting profile just barely appeared from the edge of her wimple. Her nose turned up a bit, and the curve of her cheek was noticeable. "I must stop admiring her like this," he thought, and fastened his attention on the road once more.

The sun had made an appearance earlier in the day, but now dark clouds had gathered overhead and drops of rain were pelting the windshield before they arrived at Shepherd's Cross. When he finally pulled up in front of the cathedral, a solid sheet of rain fell from an angry sky. Catherine searched the heavens for some sign of clearing, but the driving wind and rain had no intention of stopping. Jeffrey hadn't said anything for some time, but she felt his eyes on her. It was disturbing. Even if she were drenched by the time she entered the cathedral, she couldn't bear his nearness any longer. "Thank you for bringing me here, Commander Norwood."

"You're entirely welcome, but I think we should wait a few minutes before going inside. You'll be soaked to the skin if you go now." He was enjoying sitting with her. Lord, what was happening to him?

"I don't mind the rain," she blurted and opened the car door. Jeffrey was at her side in an instant and together they dashed up the steps of the cathedral, dodging pools of water on their way to the foyer inside the massive doors. Catherine shook out her skirt and turned to him. "I'll be ready when you return from your visit."

He didn't move. His eyes searched hers with an intensity she'd never felt before. "I'd like to stay with you, if you don't mind," he whispered. His tone was solemn. "I haven't thanked the Lord properly."

After a pause, she nodded and side by side they entered the gothic interior. No one was about and their footsteps reverberated in the huge nave. This was her domain, her sanctuary of refuge . . . but this time, a man was at her side. It was a very strange feeling. Jeffrey knelt and made the sign of the cross at the first pew. Catherine studied the tall, dashing figure which had retreated from her momentarily. His head was bowed in prayer. She'd always thought it a lovely sight to see the sisters at prayer, but as she continued to gaze at Jeffrey, she realized there was nothing more beautiful than a man subjecting himself to God, kneeling in reverence before the Lord. Michael's father was one of God's finest creations. Suddenly she felt overcome with a strong emotion, an intense feeling of admiration, even affection for him. He sensed her eyes on him, and like a magnet, they drew his gaze. A feeling of love for her all but consumed him as they looked at each other. Perhaps she belonged to God's kingdom, but she had touched his life and it could never be the same again.

Catherine finally found the strength to continue down the aisle, where she knelt before the shrine of the

Blessed Virgin and focused all her attention on the Mother of God. She closed her eyes, making the sign of the cross, but she could not concentrate. She tried to pray and repeated the words of the Holy Office, but she kept seeing Commander Norwood's eyes and captivating smile. She tried to block him from her mind, but the more she tried, the more she felt his presence. She could not forget that he was there with her . . . it began to haunt her. She could find no peace before the sacred altar and finally came to the conclusion that worship and communion here were impossible. He was coming between her and Diety. It wasn't his fault. He'd brought her here as a kindness; yet her feelings were anything but tranquil. Sweet Jesus, what was happening to her? Never in her life had she ever found it impossible to put herself in total communion with her Savior!

A half hour passed, and she rose to leave. As she walked down the aisle, she noticed he was no longer there . . . he had probably gone out to the car to leave her alone. He always knew the right thing to do. Why was she so terribly disturbed? She hurried out to the car and Jeffrey helped her inside.

"Betty's house is right around the next corner. It won't take long." She nodded but said nothing. She couldn't speak right now. They pulled up in front of a row house which looked like all the other houses in the village, their exteriors of dull red brick. Jeffrey climbed out of the car once more and came around to her side. She didn't understand when he opened the door for her.

"I can stay here, Commander Norwood."

"Sister," his voice pleaded, "would you come in with me, please? This is difficult for me to do alone. I need you at my side." Hesitantly, she got out of the car and walked up to the door with him. He knocked and pulled the collar of his dark coat up around his ears to keep out the rain which was still coming down, though not as heavily as before. The door opened. The wife's face was a picture of misery. She recognized Jeffrey and threw her arms around his neck.

"Jeff," she sobbed against his chest. "Andy's gone," the forlorn voice cried out. He comforted her for several minutes. Finally the woman raised her head and looked at Catherine. "I'm sorry, Sister. Please forgive me. Won't you both come in?" They stepped inside the humble house which looked as if it needed a thorough cleaning. "I haven't been up to keeping things the way I usually do. You'll have to forgive the way the house looks," she apologized. "Just a minute . . . I have to check on little Andy," and she hurried to a back room. They looked at each other. Here was the real tragedy of the war, an awful reminder of what life was really all about. . . .

"Come on, Andy," the mother coaxed a two-year-old into the room. "Come and see Commander Norwood . . . come on, that's a love," and she picked him up. The child had bright red hair like a copper penny and ruddy cheeks. Their roundness half hid the large eyes. Catherine smiled and reached for him. "May I?" she asked.

"By all means . . . please do . . . there, Andy. Go to Sister," and the boy hesitantly went into her arms. He pulled his head away from her face and stared, examining everything.

"I guess I'm something of a curiosity, aren't I, Andy?" Catherine laughed and cuddled him. After a moment, when she no longer seemed suspect, the child showed her a block he held tightly in his fist. There were more on the floor. She bent down and put the boy next to them. "Shall we build something?" she asked and the child started to put one on top of the other, the way

90

she was doing.

"Sister, you have a way," the mother sighed. Yes, Jeffrey thought as he watched the two of them. She had a way . . .

"Come on, Jeff. Sit down and tell me about Michael."

"Betty," he put a hand on her shoulder. "I'm sorry. Andy was the best. I wish I knew the words to say to you right now."

"You've been through it yourself, Jeff. There isn't anything anyone can say. You just have to go on."

"How well I know. Is there anything I can do for you? Please . . . name it. Andy and I always looked out for each other."

"Nothing, Jeff . . . just be my friend."

"Do you have enough money?"

"Does anyone? Oh, I'm all right. I have a job at the factory. It's enough, and Roger has a job after school. It all helps." She sniffed again. "Is Michael better?"

"He's coming along splendidly." His eyes wandered to the nun's face, but Catherine was unaware of his glance.

"That's wonderful, Jeff. If I didn't have the kids, I don't know what I'd do," and she sobbed. Catherine was listening. "Why did it have to happen, Jeff? I love him. God, how it hurts! I reach out for him in bed . . . nothing. I lie awake all night, pretending I'll wake up and find it's not real. But it is . . . and he was my whole life. The sun rose and set with him, even if he was an old grouch before his first cup a tea in the morning," she choked.

"I know, Betty," he whispered.

"But I thank God for one thing. I had fourteen wonderful years with him," she rambled on, "and I've his children. Florence's daughter down the street just lost her fiancé yesterday . . . she didn't even get to the altar. She's worse off than I am. At least I have memories." She straightened up and wiped her eyes.

Catherine played with the little boy but she had been deeply moved by the mother's words. She had never thought about marriage in terms of herself. She arose and patted the child's head. This red-haired boy was a product of love. She found herself wondering what it would be like to lie in a man's arms and experience the intimacy which could result in a beautiful baby like Andy. She was not naive to the mechanics, but it never occurred to her to wonder . . . till now.

Jeffrey noticed how reflective Catherine had become. Something about his conversation with Betty had caused a reaction in her. "Betty, Sister and I have to get back to Michael. Phil and Elinore won't be able to stay with him much longer."

"Sure, Jeff. You're a love for coming," and she kissed his cheek. They went to the door and Catherine followed. "Thank you for coming, Sister. Andy has taken a liking to you, I can tell."

"He's adorable. I'm so sorry about your husband. I pray you will eventually find peace."

"I doubt it, Sister. Once you love a man, there is no peace. Maybe you sisters have the answer after all . . . but thanks anyway for the thought. God bless you."

Catherine nodded and hurried out to the car, her mind in utter confusion, as if she'd been dealt a blow. Her life at the convent had not prepared her for all this. She felt as if she were drowning in reality. Jeffrey got in beside her. Neither of them spoke.

VI

Jeffrey waited before starting the motor. Catherine's face was buried in her hands. "Sister?"

"Yes?"

"Are you all right?"

"Yes," she replied and raised up, staring straight ahead.

"Then before we go back to Norwood, I'd like to stop at the Emporium down the street and pick up a little present for Michael. I was hoping you could help me think of something."

"Well," she thought aloud, "he loved the puppet shows we put on at the convent. They were a regular occurrence. Of course, the puppets were all made by the children and I'm afraid they were a bit makeshift," she smiled in remembrance. "If we could find a real puppet, something to be worked with the hand, I have no doubt Michael would be delighted."

"What a wonderful idea! Let's go looking," and he started the car, happy to see she did not seem as distressed as before. They went into the Emporium but the woman said they did not carry puppets . . . perhaps down the street. After five stops, they found a small shop on a quaint, narrow street which handled antiques, used furniture, old clothes and toys.

"You say you want a puppet?" the old man peered through thick glasses at them. "Yes," Catherine grew animated. "A person or an animal . . . it doesn't matter."

"I'll look in the back. Just a moment," and he shuffled to the rear of the store. Catherine wandered through the aisles, amazed at the collection of merchandise. There was literally everything imaginable hanging from the ceiling and cluttering the tables and display counters.

"How does one make up his mind in a shop like this?" she asked.

"I'm sure I don't know," Jeffrey chuckled. Then something caught his eye. "Come over here, Sister. Look at this!" She drew closer and was immediately taken with the superb marble replica of the Pieta.

"Oh," she sighed and picked it up, admiring the detail. "It's the Michelangelo from Saint Peter's. Isn't it exquisite?" she exclaimed, turning it over. The bottom was marked fifty pounds. She quickly put it back on the table. "When I think of the Son of God, it is that likeness I see. Look at the expression on his face, and the way his mother smiles down at him! Love radiates from her eyes. It's incredible that a mortal could have captured that special glow which must have enveloped them. I'm certain she was as lovely as he portrayed her here."

Jeffrey was standing close to her, watching in rapt attention as she spoke. "It's a remarkable piece, but even her beauty couldn't compare to yours, Sister." Once again, he had spoken his mind without thinking. Her eyes opened wide as she looked up at him. A blush suffused her face. There was a noise and Catherine turned quickly in the direction of the back of the shop. Jeffrey looked away reluctantly.

"I have two puppets but they're not the marionette type. You work these with the hand."

94

"That's perfect," it came out in a whisper. He handed her the first one. It was a country bumpkin with freckles and several teeth missing. She slipped a trembling hand inside and wiggled her fingers, but she wasn't very taken with it. "Here is the other one."

Jeffrey's face lit up. "May I see it, please." It was a dog—a spaniel. He smiled at Catherine. "You're not going to believe it, but this face looks a lot like Michael's dog at home. It has a little too much red in the fur, but the expression around the eyes and nose is very much like ours."

"He's delightful," she smiled and put it on. "Michael will love it." The shop keeper seemed pleased. "We'll take it," Jeffrey said. The man nodded. "Can I interest you in anything else?"

As Jeffrey spoke quietly with the shopkeeper, Catherine walked to the entrance and gazed out the windows. The rain had stopped. In a few minutes Jeffrey had his packages and they were on their way back to Norwood. They went a different route this time. She didn't recognize the scenery. He drove through several villages and into a park which was a veritable forest. The road wound deeper and farther into the trees. Finally he pulled the car to a stop and turned off the motor.

"Sister, before we get back to the hospital, I want to give you this as a token of my—my appreciation for all you've done for Michael," he stammered, floundering for the right words. Catherine was deeply touched as she opened the parcel and found the lovely Pieta. "I know you don't take any credit for his recovery. You're too modest for that, but it is true! Michael would not be alive if it weren't for you," his voice cracked. "You're a wonderful woman, Sister. I've never known anyone like you. Please accept this present. It can't begin to

95

demonstrate what I feel, but since you admired it, I want you to have it."

She couldn't get the words out, her heart was too full. Finally she said, "Thank you, Mr. Norwood. You are very kind, but we are not allowed to accept personal gifts." A shadow crossed his face and his disappointment was apparent. She didn't want to hurt him. He had never treated her with anything but the greatest respect. "Commander Norwood, I will always remember the thought. I will cherish the memory of you and Michael for as long as I live." Her head lowered. "Michael has always been a perfect gentleman. I used to think he was born with that exceptional characteristic, but now I know he acquired it from you."

Jeffrey stirred. He realized she was actually paying him a compliment, and it was probably difficult for her. And she'd made it clear that he would soon only be a memory to her. He couldn't accept that. She grew uneasy because he wasn't saying anything, and turned to him. He was staring into space, then started to speak. "You give me too much credit, Sister. Michael is his mother's child."

"I'm sure that's true. It takes both parents to raise a child as remarkable as Michael."

"Connie was a good mother and completely devoted to him."

"She must have been wonderful, otherwise Michael would never have suffered as he did."

"Yes . . . we both loved her very much, and I'll never forget her, but," he turned to Catherine and his face blazed with emotion, "she is part of the past now, for Michael and for me. There is still a lifetime ahead of us. This past week has opened my eyes to many things. Michael is going to get well and that erases the grief and sadness of this past year. That is why I am so grateful to

96

you. Your coming to Norwood has put hope and meaning into both our lives. I find that it is a great thrill just to be alive, despite the war, despite everything. My life seems filled with purpose again. You can't imagine how good it feels, to come back from such emptiness. I have you to thank, Sister.''

He started the motor and they returned to Norwood in silence. The young nun was overwhelmed at his admissions. His honesty and goodness reached an inner chamber of her heart. She was happy that he found life worth living again. He was too fine a man to waste away from emotional scars. She would never forget him.

They reached the hospital at the dinner hour, and Philip and Elinore returned to the house. Michael had had an exhausting day and was fast asleep as soon as dinner was over, but he had been overjoyed with the puppet. He fell asleep with it still on his hand. Catherine disappeared from the room for a long while, then came back and began reading, as if Jeffrey were not in the room at all. He wanted to talk to her, but she was detached, preoccupied. He'd probably said too much earlier. She was not in the habit of being constantly in a man's company. He didn't know what to say or do in front of her anymore. Much against his will, he decided to go back to the house. He sensed she wanted him to leave.

"Sister . . . since Michael is so much better, I think I will try to put in a few hours work in London tomorrow. I've been away from everything much too long.''

Catherine nodded. Naturally he had work to do. She had marveled that he had been able to spend all this time at the hospital. Yet, she could not understand why she felt so disturbed at his words.

"I'll be back for dinner, and tonight Elinore told me she would come and sit with Michael whenever you wanted to be relieved. You've been so unselfish with your time. I've imposed on you. Thank you again, for everything."

"It's my life, taking care of children. It's a great blessing. You don't need to thank me."

"Then I'll see you tomorrow at dinner."

She inclined her head. Jeffrey didn't want to go, but apparently there was no more to be said.

Catherine read for a while, but the book really didn't interest her. Tomorrow she and Michael would have a whole day together without the company of his father. Wasn't that the way it should be? Life was getting back to normal, bit by bit. It was right. She should be relieved! She'd had practically no time to study or meditate. Soon, Michael would go back home and she—she would return to Our Lord of the Lamb. There was always a great deal of work to be done at the convent. It was a place of refuge, her only home. Why was it so hard for her to imagine herself back there now? The convent had always been her whole life. . . .

The following day Catherine organized the morning into a workshop for Michael. He had lessons in spelling, printing and sums. After lunch she took him for a walk and then they joined some of the other young patients in the nursery, and she played a few pieces for them on the piano. It passed the time and seemed to give Michael pleasure. Presently it was time for dinner. She had been watching the clock rather anxiously. Michael eagerly awaited the arrival of his father as well. The trays were brought in and the two of them ate their meal without him for it appeared he wouldn't be coming after all. At seven o'clock, a sister told Catherine she was wanted on the phone. She went out to the nursing station and took the receiver.

"Yes?"

"Hello, Sister . . ." It was Commander Norwood.

"Hello."

"I'm sorry I didn't get back to Norwood this evening. When I went to work today, Lord Wyngate called a meeting. I had to be in attendance and we're still going strong. Please tell Michael I'll make it up to him tomorrow." There was an appreciable pause. "I really would prefer being with the two of you to anything else I can think of."

"I'll tell Michael," she spoke softly.

"Then I'll see you tomorrow and I hope to interest you in another game of chess. You have from now till four o'clock to sharpen your wits," and he clicked off.

Michael was asleep when she returned to the room. All was quiet and peaceful. The long hours of the evening seemed to stretch endlessly before her. A restlessness had come over her. She paced the floor, then sat down to read, but didn't even open the book. She got up again and went to the window. The sun was below the horizon but she could still see the oranges and pinks of the roses in the garden across the street.

Several hours passed and she had to face the truth about her inner turmoil. She was disappointed. There was no way around it. She'd spent almost an entire week with Commander Norwood, and she missed him . . . it was that simple. He brought life into the dingy hospital room. Aghast, she hurried from the room and went directly to the chapel. An hour's contemplation before the altar did little to drive away the pangs of emptiness she felt whenever she thought of returning to the convent, away from Michael . . . and from his father. When she went to bed, she resolved that from then on, she would avoid Commander Norwood's company as much as possible. She must!

Jeffrey was good as his word and breezed into

Michael's room the next day, a few minutes before four. The time spent away from the two of them seemed much too long. He hadn't been able to get back to the hospital fast enough, and was breathless when he finally pulled up to the curb, but his eager expression faded when he discovered that Sister Catherine was unavailable for the next few hours. She had purposely decided to be in the chapel. Father and son needed to be alone, and she needed to calm her troubled spirit. She stayed away till after the dinner hour, thinking that perhaps Michael was asleep and his father had gone home. But Jeffrey was reading to his son when she stepped inside. He looked up and gave her the special smile she'd learned to look forward to. A warm feeling passed through her body in spite of herself.

"Sister," Michael blurted out. "Why didn't you come to dinner? Daddy brought us a special treat. Look!" Her eyes strayed to the bedside table. He had brought them some delectable looking pastry, probably purchased somewhere in London. Sugar was hard to come by during the war. She wondered how he managed it. He never ceased to amaze her with his thoughtfulness.

"It looks delicious. I'm sorry, I didn't know."

"It doesn't matter, now that you're here," Jeffrey beamed. She wouldn't look at him, for when she did it caused troubling sensations she'd never felt before. "Michael, when I finish this story, Sister and I are going to show you how to play chess."

The evening progressed and Catherine was immersed once again in a battle of wits. This time, she won. It pleased her but she had the impression it had all been pre-arranged. His presence was very disturbing. She fiddled with the chess pieces and kept her eyes on the board.

100

Jeffrey studied her during the game, but she would not meet his gaze. He had an idea it was intentional. It maddened him now that he could not see her hair which he imagined to be dark like her arched brows but the blasted wimple hid such allurements from view. He tried to picture her without her habit—in a dress, perhaps, her hair long and flowing; or perhaps in a skirt and blouse with short, curly locks like Michael's. He was keenly aware of feelings he had thought never to experience again, and knew he should be repressing now. He wanted to feel her mouth on his . . . he wanted to feel the softness of her cheek against his . . . he wanted . . .

"Commander Norwood," she repeated. She had been asking him about a particular move and what she could have done differently, but he had not responded. She looked up, forgetting her earlier promise to herself. The longing in his eyes forced her to leave the room.

After that night, Jeffrey went to London on a regular basis and spent every evening with Michael and Catherine. She tried to find other things to do while he was there, but inevitably, he and Michael coaxed her into some game or activity which she could not refuse. In truth, she didn't want to.

Two weeks passed and Michael was getting stronger every day. One Thursday afternoon, at tea time, Dr. Endicott came into Michael's room and found the three of them busily engaged in putting a puzzle together. He thought it curious that Jeff had left London early enough to have tea with the boy. He knew Jeff loved his son very much, but he was surprised at the amount of time the usually busy father spent at the hospital. He'd taken care of Phil and Jeff since they were infants and it wasn't like Jeff to take so much time off from his work. His was a serious nature, dedicated to his work. Now he

101

found Jeff to be constantly at the nun's side, wearing a look of absolute worship on his face. The man was in love—deeply in love, there was no doubt about it. What a pity that she was a professed nun. They would have make a striking couple if things had been different. He wondered . . .

"Good afternoon, everyone. It seems I'm not needed around here anymore."

"Hugh," Jeffrey stood and shook hands.

"Well, Michael," he put a hand on the boy's shoulder. "I came to tell you that I'm letting you go home in the morning. What do you say to that?"

"Really?" he clapped his hands, his blue eyes sparkling as he turned to his father; Dr. Endicott's gaze was fastened on the Sister, for the color had drained from her face. Apparently the news was causing her a great deal of pain. Catherine felt as though someone had just taken the floor from under her.

"Sweet Jesus, no," she cried out inside. "Not yet!" It was as if a steel knife were cutting through her. Michael turned to her. She couldn't break down now! He put out his arms and she reached for him, holding him tightly. The room began to spin. Michael pulled away.

"Sister, why are you crying?" She bowed her head. "It's because I am so happy for you, darling. Now you can leave the hospital and go home. You've been a perfect little patient, but I know how much home means to you."

Jeffrey glowed with the wonderful news. "That's splendid, Hugh," he patted his shoulder, then walked around and swung Michael up in the air above his head. "Hey, Tiger . . . we're going home!"

The boy giggled and finally was lowered so they could hug each other. Catherine could stand it no longer and rose to leave. The time had finally come. The boy and his father were going back to their life. Her mission had drawn to a close. After tonight, her services would be required elsewhere. She would have to inform the Holy Mother. She'd been on God's errand, and now God was calling her back home. The circle of love which bound the boy and his father did not include her . . . indeed, it could not; yet, as she watched them, she felt as though her heart were literally being wrenched from her body, and the torment was excruciating. She traversed the room and reached for the door handle. Jeffrey's eyes followed her. "Sister, where are you going?"

"I'm going to telephone the Holy Mother, Commander Norwood. Now that Michael is well enough to go home with you, I must return to Our Lord of the Lamb. I must make arrangements to leave for Castle Combe in the morning." She shut the door behind her and walked swiftly toward the chapel as if pursued by demons—as indeed she felt she was. She would have to get a grip on herself before she could place the call.

Hugh Endicott watched Jeff's face turn ashen. Michael's countenance had changed as well. Jeff put the boy down and asked Hugh to stay with him, then hurriedly followed Catherine from the room. Catherine hastened her pace, but as she reached for the chapel door a hand darted out to detain her. "Sister . . . wait!"

It took every ounce of strength she possessed to appear calm. "Yes?"

"Don't go into the chapel yet. I need to talk to you, please. This is very important," he pleaded in a low voice. "Can we take a walk outside for a moment? There's a park across the street . . ." He looked so upset, she had no choice but to go with him. They crossed the street and entered the rose garden. There were benches for the strollers, but neither of them could sit. He began pacing back and forth across the gravel as she leaned over to inhale the fragrance of the flowers.

"Michael isn't completely well yet, Sister. You know that as well as I do. Just because Hugh is allowing him to go home doesn't mean he is out of the woods. If you should leave before he recovers totally, we could be right back where we started. He loves you too much. Don't go yet! Stay another week, at least. If necessary, I'll phone the Holy Mother myself, right now, and explain the circumstances. I don't want to take any chances where Michael is concerned."

His words permeated her being and a feeling of such intense joy leaped inside she had to fight to keep her control. It was true . . . Michael wasn't well, yet. And God knew she wasn't ready to go back to the convent. But if she gave in now, she knew it would be that much harder to leave in another seven days. What should she do? The Holy Mother said she had faith in Catherine's instincts, but her instincts told her that another week in this man's company would make the inevitable parting even more unbearable.

Jeffrey was on the verge of panic. "Sister—I've planned to take the next week off to really spend time with Michael. I want to be free from all my work. Phil and Elinore are going to stay at the house with us. I need to re-establish a routine with my son. I need you to help me . . . please."

As before, his soul was reaching out to her. How could she refuse?

"Sister?" his voice was frantic. "Say something!" An inestimable period of time passed before she dared look at him.

"I'll stay another week, Commander Norwood. I realize Michael still isn't fully recovered, but then I will have to get back to the convent. I've been gone too long already."

He heaved a sigh and relief washed over him, leaving him drained and weak. One more week, that was all . . . "Thank you. I know it's asking a great deal. Forgive me . . . but I couldn't let you go just yet." Their eyes held. He knew she was thankful for a little more time with Michael. If only he dared hope she didn't want to leave him, either. If only she weren't a nun!

Friday came. Michael was living for it. He was going home! Catherine packed all his belongings, but he wouldn't let her touch the whistle or the puppet. Those two precious items stayed with him at all times. In two weeks the room had become littered with paraphenalia—puzzles, books, charcoals, sketches. Catherine very carefully placed the drawings on top of each other. Jeffrey had done dozens of sketches of many subjects other than airplanes. He'd done a drawing of a new American model, called a Hudson. He had taught her a great deal about aviation and airplanes. It had been fascinating. His field was engineering and design, and he was an excellent teacher. Catherine put everything in readiness and an orderly came for the luggage.

Other than a hacking cough which seemed to burst out of nowhere at odd hours, the boy seemed perfectly well as he ran out of the hospital into his father's arms. Jeffrey had come to pick them up. A sun-filled morning greeted Catherine as she shut the hospital doors behind her. Surely the grass was greener! How different were the circumstances from two weeks before! She was no longer the same person. She had entered into a new realm of existence, and she had to face a frightening truth about herself. She loved this new dimension of life with an intensity that terrified her!

VII

The grandfather clock in the hall chimed eleven times. Elinore got up from the chesterfield and went over to the window, expecting Jeffrey to pull up in front of the house at any minute. Philip had long since left for London and Millie was upstairs making up another bedroom. Elinore had had all night to ponder the new turn of events. It shouldn't have come as such a tremendous shock to be told that Sister Catherine would be staying at the house with them for the next week. After all, Elinore hadn't seen Jeffrey for two minutes since the Sister had come to the hospital to be with Michael. It was apparent that Jeffrey was infatuated with the beautiful nun, but Elinore had not counted on Sister Catherine's extended stay. She thought of course that the nun would be on her way back to the convent this morning.

When Jeffrey had informed her last night that Michael was still too ill for Sister to leave him, Elinore began to understand the depth of his feelings and her jealousy was bordering on hatred. The chance of Jeffrey's falling in love with her was growing more and more remote. But that wouldn't stop her from divorcing Philip. Whether she won Jeffrey or not, her marriage to Philip was over. He would never stand in her way, she could give Philip that much credit. He really was a very nice person, but nice people bored Elinore.

The car finally made an appearance and Elinore opened the front door, anxious to meet Sister Catherine, face to face . . . they'd never been formally introduced. She couldn't help but be curious about this nun who had accomplished the impossible once again and had Jeffrey wrapped around her little finger.

The child seemed perfectly spry to her as she saw him scamper out of the car and disappear around the back of the house. She noticed immediately how solicitous Jeffrey was of the young nun's needs.

Catherine got out of the car and looked about. She knew the Norwoods were a wealthy, well established English family, and their home was as Michael had described it to her. The house was Elizabethan, Jeffrey had told her, very old and stately. It was set graciously amid rolling parklands.

"Elinore," Jeffrey beamed, putting an arm around her shoulder. Catherine approached and Elinore took a swift inventory. How beautiful she was! Even in the simple habit and wimple, she would make most women look drab and artificial. Jeffrey would have to be blind not to notice that gorgeous, spiritual face. On the same footing, Elinore had to look up to the graceful Sister, who stood with poise and dignity. This woman, nun or no, had everything a man could desire, and Elinore was sick with envy. She'd noticed reverence in Philip's voice when he spoke of Sister Catherine. Now she knew why, and it explained everything.

Elinore forced a smile. "Sister Catherine, I've wanted to meet you for a long time. I haven't had an opportunity to tell you how grateful we all are that you came when Michael needed you."

Catherine bowed and smiled sweetly. "How do you do, Mrs. Norwood."

"Sister," Jeffrey interjected, "Elinore is my sister-in-law and my good friend. She's helped me through some very difficult times," and he gave Elinore an extra hug. "Say, where's Phil?"

"He had to go to London. He'll try to get back early this evening." She looked around. "Where is Michael? I'm anxious to see him."

Catherine and Jeffrey both started to answer at the same time. He smiled broadly at her but she lowered her eyes. "He ran around the back to find Francis, I think."

"Well then . . . let me show you to your room, Sister." They stepped inside the hall, but the noisy patter of small feet caused them to pause.

"Sister," Michael ran past his aunt and grabbed Catherine's hand. "Come up to my room."

"Say hello to Aunt Ellie first, son," Jeffrey admonished, to Catherine's relief. She'd seen the hurt look on the other woman's face when Michael had brushed past her.

"Hello, Aunt Ellie."

"Well, Michael! It's so good to have you home, dear. Come, give me a kiss." She leaned over and he planted one sterile kiss on her rouged cheek. Then his hand slipped right back into Catherine's.

"My room has two beds so we can sleep together, Sister."

"No, Michael dear," Elinore reproved, a bit too sharply. "Sister Catherine must sleep in her own room now that you're out of the hospital."

"Is hers the green one?"

"No . . . Philip and I are using that room. The red room has been prepared for her."

"But Grandmama's old room is clear around the other side of the house from mine."

"Michael," Jeffrey warned, "your aunt has everything arranged. Come on, tiger. Let's go up to your room," and he lifted Michael up over his head, piggyback style. The two started up the stairs. "Sister?" Michael called out. "We'll show you the way. Just follow us."

Catherine turned to Elinore. "Thank you for preparing a room for me. I hope it didn't put you to too much trouble. I had planned on returning to Castle Combe today, but Michael's father felt one more week with the boy was advisable."

The gray eyes glittered. "It's no trouble, Sister . . . but I should imagine you are greatly missed at the convent. Jeff tells me there are several hundred children you take care of."

"Yes," was the soft reply. Catherine felt hostility from Michael's aunt and could not account for it. She started up the stairs, puzzled, but the two ahead of her were having so much fun, she gave no more thought to the cool welcome she'd received. Jeffrey had never seemed so relaxed and carefree.

"Watch your head now," Jeffrey warned the boy as they entered his room.

"Daddy, bring me in for a landing."

"All right," his father said and headed for the four poster bed, lowering his head so Michael could jump off his shoulders and dive into the middle of the counterpane. When Catherine saw the little boy go flying, she cried out in alarm and hurried to his side.

"Are you all right?" she asked as he rolled over, but his shriek of laughter answered her question. Out of habit, she hugged him to her. She had to remember that men roughhoused. Her father had played with her like that when she was little, come to think of it. She'd almost forgotten. Lately, however, too many memories, supposedly locked safely away in the past, seemed to come back to her, unbidden. She let him go.

109

Michael sat up.

"Sister, what's the matter?" His eyes were large, and he was just as sensitive to her changes of mood as was his observant father.

"Nothing, Michael."

"How come you stopped smiling?"

"Did I?" She bowed her head.

"I think Sister is tired and should have a chance to see her room. And you, young man, are to change your clothes and get right into bed. This afternoon, after your nap, we'll go down to the stable and say hello to Toby. What do you say to that?"

"I love you, Daddy," the boy replied. Jeffrey tousled his shiny locks. "I kind of love you, too." His voice was husky. "I'll be right back, now, and I want to find you in bed."

"Okay." Michael pretended to pout, but Catherine knew the bed would feel good to him.

"Your room is around this corner, Sister. There is a sitting room with a telephone. I'm sure you'll find the bed more comfortable than that cot." He opened the door and let her pass through.

"I'm sure I will be most comfortable. Thank you." She walked into the room but did not hear the door close. She turned. He was looking at her in such a strange way. "Is there something wrong?" she inquired.

"No . . . I was just about to say that Michael and I would deem it an honor if you would accompany us to the stable . . . shall we say two o'clock?"

"Perhaps you should be alone with Michael this afternoon, Commander Norwood. This is his first day home from hospital and you've taken this time to be with your son. He needs to spend as much time as possible with you alone."

110

"Do you honestly think he would step outside this house for one instant without you?"

She contemplated her clasped hands. "Very well . . . but the boy is progressing so beautifully that I think it is time he stopped depending on me. The longer I stay away from the convent, the harder it will become," she hesitated, "for Michael." She bit her lip. "I must return shortly."

Jeffrey stiffened. "I'm aware of that, Sister. We went over that whole business yesterday." There was an edge in his tone. "But may we worry about it on another day? As you said yourself, it is his first day home," and after another long pause, he quietly shut the door.

Catherine was frozen to the spot. She felt weary . . . but it wasn't of a physical nature. She was alarmed over the way he had spoken to her just now. He seemed to resent any mention of her return to the convent. Perhaps she hadn't given it enough time. Michael was just barely out of hospital, and she couldn't forget the way he scrambled from the front seat and into her arms on the drive back home because she mentioned that she'd have to leave him soon, nor could she erase from her memory the way Jeffrey spoke to her in the car after Michael was upset. "You're not going to leave us, are you, Sister!" He'd said it more like a demand and she groaned inside. What was it going to be like when she really had to say goodby?

Catherine sank down on the edge of the bed. Maybe in a few days, when Michael had adjusted to life at home with his father, she could begin to talk about leaving, but her relationship with Commander Norwood had undergone a change. He had seemed like a stranger to her just now. It confused her. He had always been so gentle, almost painfully tender, in fact. She'd seen inside the man during those crucial hours in the hospital.

111

Possibly it was a side no one else had ever seen, nor would again.

She knew he was an active man with tremendous responsibilities in the coastal command. He'd faced many dangers . . . his whole life was an adventure. For the first time she could see the cool aloofness which probably manifested itself when he was out in the world. Yet, it didn't seem like him to be so cold. Was he still insecure about the boy? Michael seemed so normal and happy, she could not imagine that his world would ever crumble again. He worshipped his father. But could she really be sure he was emotionally well? There didn't seem to be any answers.

Things could not go on much longer this way. She was losing her perspective. Was she losing her vocation as well? Michael was more a part of her life than ever, as was his father. Should she call the Holy Mother? But it was something she could not discuss over the telephone. She turned once more to the Holy Virgin for help, but as she knelt and tried to express the anguish in her heart, she trembled. The words would not come. She cried out and sobbed aloud as she realized that the reason she could not ask God for help in weaning Michael and his father away from her was because there was a part of her which did not want to let them go. "Blessed Savior," she wept and lay prostrate on the bed, finally giving in to welcome sleep.

At that very moment, many kilometers away, the Holy Mother was kneeling in prayer before the altar of her private chapel, petitioning God on Sister Catherine's behalf, praying that the girl was finding peace and direction. A dark, heavy sensation weighed the old woman down and she grew alarmed. Catherine was in trouble. She could feel it!

112

"Sister?" Michael called out, rapping on the door. "Are you ready?" Catherine had barely had time to freshen herself after her sleep. It was time to go look at the horses. Elinore was chatting with Jeffrey as Michael led Catherine out the front doors. Elinore was wearing a brown riding habit and it suited her. Jeffrey had also changed into sport clothes. "I've brought Sister," Michael shouted. "Now we can go!" Elinore glanced fleetingly at Catherine, without warmth, before linking her arm through Jeffrey's. The two of them walked with their heads close together as they discussed matters which had nothing to do with Catherine. She watched the casual way Elinore looked up at Michael's father, the ease with which she hung on his arm, almost possessively, Catherine thought; but these matters were none of her affair. Still, she felt for the first time like an outsider and chastised herself for such an unworthy reaction.

The grounds were extensive. They walked across the lawn, past the west wing of the house and followed a path down to the stables at the bottom of a hill. The familiar odor of horses, hay and manure wafted past her nostrils, conjuring up memories of her early childhood in Belgium. Catherine's family had been very poor and what little fun she and her brothers did have was usually out in the barn or taking rides on the plow horses. She hadn't grown up doing the things little girls were supposed to do—playing with tea sets and dolls. Her interests had always paralleled those of her brothers and she was generally in competition with them. Now the smell filled her with nostalgia.

Michael ran ahead and opened the stable door. She could hear him running about. After a moment, a gelding and a pony trotted out into the paddock, Michael

113

following after. "Guess which one is mine, Sister?" he shouted to her and Jeffrey broke into a hearty laugh which was contagious. Catherine couldn't refrain from smiling broadly. "Toby," the boy called out, "have you missed me?" The pony stood still but swished his tail back and forth. His eyes blinked in acknowledgement. "Daddy, I think he knows me!"

"I wouldn't be at all surprised, son." Jeffrey walked over and put a hand on his shoulder. "I'll have the horses saddled. We can ride as far as Longview. That shouldn't tire you." Jeffrey went into the barn. "That will be fine," Michael called after him. Then he turned to Catherine. "Sister, will you ride with us, please?"

"I can't Michael, I'm sorry. But I would like very much to watch you. If I were on a horse, then I wouldn't be able to see you to best advantage, would I?"

"I guess not," he frowned.

"Come on, Michael," Elinore interjected. "Sister will be here when you get back. Come inside with me. I have a surprise for you," and she took his hand firmly, leading him into the stable.

Jeffrey emerged, throwing a saddle on the gelding's back as if it were weightless. He worked quickly, tightening the girth, adjusting the stirrups. He was watching Catherine out of the corner of his eye. She looked wistful. It occurred to him that this must be hard for her, constantly being exposed to the world she had given up in preference for the religious life. He sensed her unrest and was savagely glad. He knew she loved Michael more than life itself. He was counting on that love to make it difficult, if not impossible, for her to go back to the convent. If he had to, he would exert even more pressure to force her to stay on.

Elinore reappeared with Michael at her side. They were carrying a new leather saddle which gleamed in

114

the sun. Catherine had never seen anything so fine. Jeffrey saddled the pony, picked Michael up and seated him. Elinore mounted her horse and the two started to move away. Elinore rode with the fluid grace of an expert equestrian. Catherine's gaze strayed to Jeffrey. He stood there, eyeing his son with fatherly pride. His hands were on his hips. There was something about his stance . . . his natural male grace . . . Michael was calling to her but she was oblivious to all except the man before her. Jeffrey turned and caught her staring at him.

"Look at me," Michael shouted. Catherine focused her gaze on the boy.

"You never told me you could ride so well, Michael! I'm very impressed."

Elinore pulled in the reins. She was a handsome woman, Catherine thought. "Jeff, Michael and I will walk the horses till you catch up." Michael waved to Catherine and they were off.

"I'll be right with you," Jeffrey called after them, his eyes still fastened on Catherine. Then he disappeared into the barn. Momentarily he was out in the sun carrying his saddle. Catherine decided this was an excellent opportunity for Michael to be alone with his family, so she started back to the house. From here on out, she would find more and more excuses to wean the boy from her, to free herself from the hold Jeffrey had on her.

"Sister?" he called out. She turned.

"I'm going back to the house, now, Commander Norwood. There are things I must do."

This was one time when he couldn't ask her to join him, much as he wanted to. What else could he expect? "Of course," he muttered, and mounted. He walked for a moment, then pressed the horse to a gallop. They moved like lightning, the horse and rider as one. For a moment Catherine could not catch her breath, for she saw herself suddenly at his side, racing her mount madly up that grassy hill, the wind in her long hair, riding harder and faster till horse and rider were spent. She groaned and turned abruptly from the scene.

Jeffrey raced to catch up with the others, but the outing had lost its appeal because Catherine was not there. It didn't seem right without her. He'd grown accustomed to her company.

Elinore and Michael were waiting as he reined in near the top of the hill. He couldn't resist the urge to turn around for one last glimpse, but she wasn't in sight. A terrible emptiness stole through him. He spurred his horse on to the summit, his thoughts in turmoil.

Catherine went back to her room and there she remained for the afternoon. She wanted to meditate, but her soul was anything but peaceful. She heard the telephone ring. A moment later there was a knock on the door. Jens, the man servant, wanted to know if Sister Catherine would take a call from Castle Combe. Catherine reached eagerly for the receiver in her room. "Yes?"

"Sister . . . it's Mother Angela. I called the hospital and they gave me this number. I felt you might be in some trouble. How are you, my child?"

Catherine wondered how she knew. "Holy Mother—" there was a pause. "I am well."

"Something *is* wrong. Is there anything I can do?"

"Pray for me, Mother—for all of us!"

"Isn't the child improving?"

"Oh, yes! He's wonderful. I think another week, possibly two, and he will be completely recovered."

"Sister . . . will it be difficult for you to leave Norwood? And the child?"

Catherine was shaking violently. "I don't know,"

she whispered, trembling. "I don't know."

"Perhaps you have been there long enough, Sister."

"Michael just left hospital this morning, Holy Mother. I had planned to leave for Castle Combe today, but his father insisted that I stay another week. Michael isn't completely well. I, too, question the wisdom of a separation just yet . . . but it is very complicated," she quavered.

"Yes . . . I understand." The Mother Superior could read between the lines. "I have given this matter serious thought. Under the circumstances, you might propose to Commander Norwood that Michael be allowed to make occasional visits to the convent during this year, to help him to adjust gradually to the separation. In that way, he would know you were not lost to him completely."

As always, the Holy Mother's words brought light out of the darkness. "Your wisdom is inspired, Holy Mother. I will discuss it with Michael's father. It sounds the perfect solution."

"I'm relieved then, my child. You are sorely missed at Our Lord of the Lamb. I trust you will come back to us soon."

"I will telephone when I know the date of my return."

"Sister? Don't stay away too long. The Mother General from Rome has just paid the convent an unprecedented visit. She has come on orders from the Holy Father himself. There is other work for you to do upon completion of your mission at Norwood." There was a long silence.

"Very well, Holy Mother."

"Bless you, Sister Catherine."

Catherine replaced the receiver in a stupor. "Other work?" she muttered under her breath. What did the

Holy Mother mean? Why had the Mother General come to England in the first place, with a war on? Catherine paced the floor. Under ordinary circumstances, she would be eager, would look forward to a new assignment . . . but she was no longer the same Sister who left Our Lord of the Lamb two weeks ago.

After her prayers, she left the room and went downstairs. The house was spacious and tastefully furnished. She wandered from room to room, until she came to the drawing room. The piano drew her attention. Michael and his father had not yet returned and she needed an outlet for her emotions so she sat down at the keyboard and began to play. Music to Catherine was an integral part of worship. She could pour out her love to the Lord as much with the piano as with the voice.

From the first days of her arrival at the convent, she was encouraged to study the piano and the organ. Holy Mother insisted that all the children who made their home permanently at Our Lord of the Lamb improve upon a talent, or find one. Catherine loved to hear Sister Anna play the organ for mass. Catherine soon learned to play and did very well. As the years went by, her technique matured until she was able to play the service herself. At the moment, she was playing a fugue of Handel. Handel gave the mind, as well as the fingers, a thorough exercising. It forced her to concentrate. Then, when she was warmed up, she turned to Beethoven and finally Tchaikowsky. The latter was passionate, romantic and deeply moving.

As she reveled in the music, Philip walked through the front door, fresh from a momentous day at the House. Lloyd George and the Prime Minister had met in debate and Philip was still mulling over Churchill's stirring address when his ears picked up the strains of music. He walked over to the door and peered in. No one had ever played the piano like that before. Whoever it was, was good, very good. He stepped inside and saw Catherine. Her back was toward him. She had no idea he was standing there and he had no intention of letting her know. He quietly sat down in a chair near the door. A few minutes later Michael came in the house, but went straight upstairs. Then Elinore and Jeffrey were in the hall and came immediately to the drawing room to discover the source of the music. Philip watched them approach and put a finger to his lips. He had a feeling she would stop if she knew an audience had gathered. She was much too modest to flaunt such talent.

Jeffrey, hot and exhilarated from the ride, leaned against the door jamb and closed his eyes. She was playing Tchaikovsky. He had never liked practicing the piano, though he and Phil had been forced to take lessons when they were young, but he loved the Russian composers and Catherine was playing with great depth of feeling. There was fire in her. A whole new dimension of her personality was revealed in her playing.

Elinore could scarcely believe her ears. It didn't seem possible that an obscure convent in Wiltshire could produce such talent. Was there anything Sister Catherine couldn't do? She turned on her heel and marched up the stairs to change, and the music followed her to her room, even after she had slammed the door.

Catherine finished the piece and stopped. She sat before the piano with her head bowed for a few minutes, then closed the lid and moved off the bench.

"That was beautiful, Sister."

She gasped and turned around, shocked to hear a voice. Philip was standing by his chair, smiling. Then she saw Jeffrey leaning against the door.

"I'm sorry," she searched for words. "I thought it might be all right if I played the piano. No one was

119

here."

"Sister," Philip rushed to reassure her. "I've never heard lovlier music."

"Oh," she sighed, at a loss for words. A flush washed over the fair face, intensifying her beauty.

"Michael never told me about your extraordinary talent," Jeffrey said.

"Maybe that is because it is *not* very extraordinary and because he has never heard me play anything but simple tunes for the children. I practice in a room above the chapel and the children are not allowed in that part of the convent."

"Do the sisters get to hear you play?" Jeffrey questioned further.

"I accompany the mass."

"Did you learn to play like that early in life?" Jeffrey had forgotten that Philip was in the room with them.

"No . . . my parents were very poor. A piano would have been an impossible luxury. No . . . when I went to Our Lord of the Lamb, the Holy Mother started me on the piano. . . ." The way he looked at her only made further explanations more difficult. "To me, music is as sacred as prayer . . . it feeds my soul."

"Perhaps after dinner, you would feed the rest of us," Philip broke in.

"I think not," she shook her head.

"Please, Sister," Jeffrey pressed. "After all those years of practice, and Phil and I know a little about that," he smiled at his brother, "it would be wrong if you didn't share your gift with the rest of us. I, for one, could listen to you play indefinitely." He paused. "God has been especially kind to you, Sister, in many ways." He turned and left the room before she had a chance to answer.

"Jeff is right. You are special," and Philip also left to

freshen up before dinner.

Catherine hurried out of the room. Where could she go? If she stayed in this house much longer, she would lose her perspective altogether. Without a conscious thought she went outside and started walking. The evening breeze was rustling the leaves of the trees. There was magic in the air, and perfume from the blossoming fruit trees. Her body felt a wonderful pain, even to the palms of her hands.

"Sister," Michael was madly waving to her from the threshold. "We are going to have dinner!" he shouted loudly.

"I'll be along later, Michael. Go ahead without me." She couldn't go in just yet. There were things to be sorted out. She walked aimlessly about the grounds. After a while, she went back to the house. Tonight she must begin to build up her spiritual strength, and abstinence from food was the first step.

Jens saw her in the hall. He was short and plump and moved with surprising grace as he escorted her to the dining room at the back of the house. The family was seated around a rectangular table, eating dessert. Catherine was glad to see that dinner was almost over.

"Why didn't you come in, Sister? Millie cooked steak and kidney pie." Jens pulled a chair out from the table so she could be seated. All eyes were upon her.

"I needed to be alone, Michael."

Jeffrey sensed an aloofness about her, but it was Philip who spoke his mind.

"Is something wrong?"

Catherine's head was bowed. "In the Holy Scriptures," she began quietly, "the Lord says, My ways are not your ways." Her head came up. "Forgive me if my ways seem strange to you." Philip didn't know what to say. Jeffrey swallowed hard. Something *was*

121

wrong! Catherine was removed from him, tonight, and it hurt, yet it endeared her to him more.

"*I* don't think you're strange, Sister," Michael's cheerful comment broke the silence. He had a way . . . she smiled sadly to herself.

Elinore resented the fact that everyone was so involved in the Sister's display of whatever . . . and her entrance had been very ill timed. The conversation was just getting interesting, if not informative.

"Finish telling us about the debate, Philip. You've left me hanging." Catherine had interrupted Philip's conversation.

"Well, the Prime Minister really let George have it. It was something to hear." Philip turned to Jeffrey. "I'm sure you're aware that some of the staff officers opposed the Greek operation . . . felt it cost us the reverses in Libya. Well, Churchill has received the brunt of the blame . . . and today, he put his critics down royally. By Jove, it was a good show," Philip grinned. "Only three votes against him. The lot of us cheered him to the rafters. I say, let him run the whole damn business. The man is a genius. I'd march into hell with him, cheering."

Catherine smiled at Philip. He expressed her sentiments exactly. Catherine had followed Churchill's career with total admiration. She couldn't refrain from comment. "He is a prophet in tailored clothing, and every Englishman and woman should pledge him undying homage!"

Jeffrey's spoon dropped to his plate and he stared at her, wondering where that remark had come from, for he, too, felt the head of England was an inspired man. Elinore looked positively shocked. Her face had paled.

"Do you follow the war so closely at the convent, Sister? I thought your allegiance to God precluded all

122

else."

Catherine did not miss the note of sarcasm, nor did the two brothers. "Christianity has always been at war with evil, Mrs. Norwood," Catherine stated, staring Elinore down. "As Mr. Churchill has so aptly pointed out, Hitler is the devil incarnate." Jeffrey sat straighter in his chair, intrigued with her tone of superiority and righteous indignation. Her remarks seemed to jolt Elinore.

"Aren't those words a little strong for a bride of Christ?" Both Jeffrey and Philip raised questioning glances at Elinore.

"They're not strong enough," Catherine replied with ice in her usually mellow voice, and her eyes narrowed. "My order has priories all over the continent, even in South America. Some of our sisters in Poland, France and Belgium were paraded through the streets with their heads shaved when the Nazis invaded their helpless lands, sacking and pillaging even the holy sanctuaries. In Poland, a contingent of Nazis raided a monastery and shot the bretheren as they chanted the Holy Office." Catherine paused to allow the words to sink in. "We must always stay informed, Mrs. Norwood. The same thing could have happened in England," and her voice grew bolder, "but, by the grace of God, and Mr. Churchill, so far it has not! Let us all be thankful for that."

There was silence in the room for a minute. "Amen," Jeffrey affirmed, shaking his head at this remarkable woman. Her eyes were filled with violet fire, and her face radiated a glow which came from her very soul. She would make a formidable adversary. He'd never seen her more beautiful than she was just now. The candle light flickered on her face, showing to advantage the proud tilt of her chin, her exquisite facial structure.

Her nostrils flared as she spoke and her eyes . . . her eyes . . . he could not get enough of them! Lord, she was more than a woman at times, he muttered to himself.

Philip nodded his approbation. "Well said, Sister. Bravo! No one has ever put it better. We could use someone like you on our ticket, and I mean that as a supreme compliment."

Catherine flushed and expelled a sigh which seemed immediately to change her back into the submissive, sweet Sister she always appeared to be. "I'm afraid my habit wouldn't get me very far, Mr. Norwood," she smiled.

"On the contrary, Sister," Jeffrey broke in. "It might be just the thing to shake up a few old fogies, eh Phil? How could they possibly argue about your sources of inspiration?"

Catherine spoke to him from across the table. Is there anyone on this island who doesn't recognize from Whom the Prime Minister receives *his* inspiration?" Jeffrey nodded and the two of them communicated in silence.

"Well . . . if they could hear you talking, they'd be believers soon enough, I should imagine," Philip reiterated with a voice full of emotion. He had eyes only for Catherine. Jeffrey realized his brother was fascinated by her, as well. He was feeling possession of Catherine, but he couldn't help himself.

At this point, Elinore was seething. "You sound as if you have a personal interest in the war, Sister. May I ask why?" Philip glanced at his wife. She was unusually persistent tonight.

"Yes, Mrs. Norwood. When my brother died last year, I was bitter. I had supposed that it was in vain. Now I know better. The bitterness is gone. It is our duty to check tyranny. Throughout all of history, beginning with the death of Abel, the Devil has wreaked havoc upon humanity, yet there has never been anything more devastating than the Blitzkrieg, in my opinion." Her eyes flashed with an intensity which held them all spellbound. "Hitler would wage war upon the entire world, Mrs. Norwood. I firmly believe he will destroy civilization if given the chance. We mustn't let that happen," she almost whispered, but her voice still held an awesome power.

Jeffrey felt a lump in his throat. "I agree, Sister. The man is a lunatic. Last month they marched on Greece. There's no predicting what he will do next."

For once, Elinore had no retort. Never in her life had she felt such animosity for another human being. She would have to be careful that her dislike for Sister Catherine did not become apparent to all. She would have to deal with Sister Catherine in her own way and in her own time.

In the midst of the silence, Millie, the nursemaid, came into the room. "Michael, let's go up to bed now. The adults want to talk and you must get your sleep." The little boy raised his head from the table top where he'd been dozing. Millie's entrance brought them all back to reality. Michael looked at Catherine beseechingly. "Will you read me a story before I go to sleep, Sister?"

"Yes, Michael."

"I want to hear some more about Goupil and Chanticleer." He disappeared with Millie, his chatter lost as they went up the stairs.

"Who is Goopy?" Jeffrey demanded in a laughing voice, his eyes fixed on her.

"*Goupil*," she corrected. "A very clever fox! It's a story of French origin. The events and characters are

125

taken from the little town of Senlis. All children love it."

"I believe you could make them love anything," Philip muttered, more to himself than anyone else, but everyone at the table heard him. Elinore was the first one up from the table. It was all too much. Philip and Jeffrey were both acting like schoolboys. Sister Catherine's display of innocence did not fool Elinore. That nun-knew exactly the effect she was having on them. "Let's go into the drawing room and see if there is something on the wireless, Philip," Elinore suggested.

"Splendid idea, my love." Philip arose with more vigor than Jeffrey had noticed in a long time. Jeffrey helped Catherine from her chair and held the door open for her. As she passed in front of him, she smiled. He was always in tune with her feelings and tonight she felt a special bond with him. It was when her lips turned up at the corners that it happened. He suddenly knew that he loved her more than life . . . and he wanted her more than anything he had ever wanted in his whole life. The desire to take her in his arms was so intense, he had to look away.

Elinore had switched on the wireless and picked up some music. She turned up the volume. Catherine hadn't heard music like that for a decade. It sounded as foreign to her as if it were being piped in from another planet. It was the kind of music her parents used to dance to. In her whole life, Catherine had never danced with a man. Jeffrey had seated himself on the sofa to read the newspaper. She looked in his direction, wondering what it would be like . . . to dance with him. At the thought, she felt shame.

Philip picked up a candy dish from the table and passed it around. "Sister, try these mints. They are

126

very good."

"No, thank you."

"You didn't eat dinner, either," Jeffrey commented, alert to her every move."

"N—no," she stammered.

"You're not ill are you? Do you need a doctor?" Philip asked with a worried expression. Jeffrey put the paper down and stared at her. Was she sick?

"I hope not," she smiled. "Fasting is supposed to strengthen the spirit, Mr. Norwood."

Philip pressed his lips. "I'm sorry, forgive me."

"It's perfectly all right." She was seated on a chair near the fireplace. Jeffrey watched her over the newspaper. He found himself wishing for the intimacy they had enjoyed in the hospital room. He didn't want to share her with anyone else. There was a great gap, both physically and mentally, between them here at the house. Tonight she was more like the Holy Mother . . . somehow removed from the rest of them.

Another song floated over the air. This time it was sung by a female vocalist. "Who is that singer?" Philip asked, putting down a magazine. "I've heard her before."

"It's a new Edith Piaf recording," Elinore called over her shoulder. "It's all the rage right now. She's that singer from Paris."

"That's right. She's good. I wish I understood French."

Catherine had been listening to the love song. "Sister? What is she saying?" Philip asked.

"She's telling a very sad story about a boy who was killed in the war. All his friends had come back to the home town, but he was not among them. The girl who loved him searched the crowds, but he was not there. She asked each one if he had seen her man, but no one

127

knew of his whereabouts. Then, the last soldier she met told her that her lover was dead on the field of battle. She went home to cry for the man who would never hold her again." Catherine finished the story and sat very still.

Catherine stood up. "I'll say goodnight. I promised Michael a story before retiring."

"We were hoping you would play for us. Just one piece before you go up," Philip asked.

"Please," Jeffrey added.

"I'm sorry, but it has been a long day. Good night."

"I'll come up with you," Jeffrey said and fairly leaped out of his chair. She turned and walked slowly up the stairs with Jeffrey in quiet pursuit. It was all he could do not to reach out and touch her. Catherine walked into Michael's bedroom and found him tucked in bed, looking at a large book. He looked up.

"Sister . . . Daddy . . . Look what Millie found for me! My picture album."

They went over to the side of the bed. Catherine sat down and Jeffrey went around to the other side, placing an arm lovingly around his son as he sat back. "See, Sister. That's the plane Daddy used to fly when he was little." Catherine smiled at the remark. By "little" he meant when Jeffrey was about her age now—twenty-two. He was dressed as an aviator, and the grin on his face was all encompassing. Even in the faded photo, his eyes sparkled with life. She wished she had known him then. Michael turned the page. "And that's a picture of the Sunderland . . . and the crew."

Jeffrey peered closer. "See that fellow in the back?" Catherine nodded.

"Yes. He looks just like his little red haired boy." The page turned again. This time she saw a somewhat older Jeffrey, around thirty, in an officer's uniform, his

128

arm around his wife. She was blond like Jeffrey and Michael and fairly small. Michael was just a toddler.

"Look, Sister! That's me when I was really little . . . and that's my mum."

"Yes, darling." Catherine's eyes smarted. "She's very lovely." How painful this must be for Jeffrey! Michael turned the page again, to her great relief. There were pictures of Michael in every conceiveable pose and more of Jeffrey. "Now, Sister. This is my favorite picture," and he turned the next page. It was Jeffrey being hoisted on the shoulders of the men of his crew, probably the rescue group. He obviously was fighting to get down and the men wouldn't let him. The looks on their faces needed no translation. Someone had signed it, "In remembrance of one great moment in time. We'd do it again, Commander. The forty-second squadron. Speed, Conway, Trucker, Barry, Al and Deuce."

Jeffrey reached out and closed the book. Catherine had never seen him blush before. "That's enough, Michael. We don't want to bore Sister." Catherine knew there were still more pictures to be seen, probably one of him receiving the Flying Cross. She'd peek later, when he wasn't in the room. She looked at him and their eyes held.

"It couldn't bore me. I've wondered what you looked like in uniform. Her face went hot, "I—I mean, Michael has told me so many things about your life in the coastal command . . . now I have a better picture- . . ." She lowered her head, embarrassed.

A strange smile suffused Jeffrey's face. He rubbed his hand in Michael's curly hair. "Come on, son. It's time to go to sleep."

"One story, first?"

Catherine looked at Jeffrey for his permission. How could he refuse? "All right . . . one story, and after that, to bed!'' Catherine recounted another exciting episode in the life of the naughty fox, Goupil. Jeffrey could have listened to her tell a hundred tales, but it finally ended and Michael was asleep. She bent over to bestow a kiss on his son as he turned out the light. The door was slightly ajar and there was just enough light for him to distinguish her silhouette in the darkness. She walked slowly toward him. He didn't want the evening to end. He didn't ever want any of it to end. She aroused desires in him he never thought possible.

"Good night," she murmured as she brushed past him and hurried down the corridor.

"Goodnight," he whispered.

VIII

The morning after her arrival at the Norwood house, Catherine stayed close to her room, her religious observances keeping her occupied. Last night she had felt things for Jeffrey that she refused to acknowledge. It was best to avoid him; however, Michael would not let her hide from them all day. Jeffrey was taking him to a puppet show in the afternoon, and then to dinner in London. As Michael wouldn't go without her, she acquiesced in order to keep him happy.

The show was very entertaining and the dinner a gourmet treat the like of which she had never before experienced. Catherine did not know what to choose and left the decisions up to Jeffrey.

"Two châteaubriands, and a wine you would recommend with the dish," he spoke to the waiter. "My son will have the chicken."

"Very good, sir," and the waiter went off. Catherine felt conspicuous in the dining room among crowds of people, all elegantly dressed or in uniform. She felt many eyes on her, but nothing was as unsettling as the way Jeffrey would smile whenever she chanced a look at him. Her attraction to him was becoming too much for her to handle. She knew in her heart of hearts she should not be out alone with him like this, but she couldn't help herself. She enjoyed being with him more and more . . .

"Sister?" Michael piped up. "Why don't you tell the Holy Mother that you are going to stay with us all summer? Daddy said it would be all right." She stared at his father, then looked away. Michael's question had come from out of the blue.

"What would Peter and Brock and Marty and all the others think if I didn't go back? Who would teach them their sums?"

"Sister Margaret."

"But Sister Margaret has to help in the infirmary. We each have our duties, you know that, Michael."

"Would God be angry if you didn't go back?" He was totally serious. She shifted in her chair, disconcerted by his questions. His father was doing nothing to stop him.

"No, darling. He wouldn't be angry, but He would be disappointed. I've promised Him that I would do His work. You wouldn't want me to break a promise, would you?"

He thought about it and then shook his head. "But do you love your work more than me?"

"No, darling," she choked, unable to look at his father. "But you have your daddy and the rest of the family, and the children at the convent don't have anyone except the sisters."

"But I want *you*," he cried and tears gushed forth. Michael suddenly slid out of his chair and crawled up on her lap, hugging her tightly. She bit her lip and looked in Jeffrey's direction for help but his tender expression only added to her consternation. She wiped Michael's tears and pulled his chair right next to hers so the boy would consent to be seated.

The waiter brought the main course and they ate in silence. When it was over, and no one could force down another bite of the delectable food, Jeffrey rose from the table. "I think we should see a bit of London before

132

going home. How about it, Michael? Shall we go past Buckingham Palace on our way?''

''Can we?'' he jumped up and down and ran ahead of them out of the restaurant. Catherine hurried after him while Jeffrey took care of the check.

They drove around the buildings and monuments which Michael was anxious for Catherine to see, then started back to Norwood. Michael fell asleep on her lap. His body was completely relaxed. She studied the precious face, the soft round cheeks which had started to fill out again. The golden curls swirled about his head once more. She couldn't keep herself from bending down to kiss him. She traced the outline of his nose and lips with her finger. How could she leave him?

Catherine sighed aloud. ''I want to talk to you about Michael,'' she began in a low voice. ''I think it would be best if you and he were to spend more time together, without me, so he can have a normal life. He ought to be put in school when your vacation is over. He needs to occupy his mind and find other children to play with. The adult world has made him much too serious.''

Jeffrey listened attentively. ''I agree, and when I return to London, I'll look into it; however, there are only five days of my vacation left, and Michael wants us all to spend them together. He and I will have a lifetime together, after you leave,'' he whispered. She could hear the tremor in his voice. She felt his emptiness for she was suffering the same torment.

Jeffrey was obsessed with thoughts of her. She was an extremely intelligent woman, and she was talented in so many areas. He understood completely the attachment Michael had formed for her at the convent. The lucky chap had been in her presence for nine whole months. He'd only been privileged to have a little over two weeks with her. There was a growing ache inside of

133

him. Life would never be the same without her. When he took Michael back to London with him, Millie would help him raise the boy. There were schools in Mayfair where he could enroll Michael. Then he could be with his son in the evenings. But the two of them without Catherine was unthinkable. He glanced over and saw her face. Her eyes were closed and her head was resting against the window. He needed her tonight. He wanted to tell her how he felt. He wanted to make love to her. A woman as lovely as she was, was made for love, not fasting and prayer!

He drew the car into the drive and turned off the motor, then gently lifted Michael from her lap and carried him into the house. Millie was waiting to put him to bed. Catherine paused on the stairway before going up.

"Thank you for a lovely evening, Commander Norwood. It was sheer luxury," and she turned to go.

"Don't go yet," he blurted out. Her eyes opened wide. He took a step closer to her, one hand resting on the bannister. "It's still early. We could take a walk outside."

"I think not," she responded. "Goodnight."

"I don't want to say goodnight, Catherine."

She stood perfectly still. He'd just addressed her by her given name. He shouldn't have done that! "Commander Norwood," she stammered, "Have you forgotten I'm here on a holy mission?"

"No," he answered, undaunted. "That still doesn't prevent me from wanting you to be with me tonight."

He wasn't easily put off. She didn't know what to say. "But it prevents me," she finally whispered, her jaw set. Jeffrey stared into her half-veiled eyes. She wanted to go with him, he knew it. No matter that her soul belonged to God—her heart and her body could be, must be his! If he could just break down that will of iron.

"It's a beautiful night, Catherine. You and I don't have many left. Please. I beg you. There is something I have to say to you."

A dizziness came over her, and she thought she would faint. "Goodnight," she managed to say at last, and hurried up the stairs to her room, locking the door behind her. She fell back against it, completely out of breath. Blessed Mother, she didn't want that! He'd never treated her with anything but the greatest respect, but now, he was asking something of her that was impossible. If she went with him . . . Heaven help her! She flung herself across the bed and sobbed till she sank into oblivion.

It was the middle of the night when she awoke feeling nauseated. She went to the bathroom and lost her dinner. Then she lay on her bed, weak and listless, staring at the ceiling, unable to think or to pray. The ticking of the clock on the wall caused her head to ache. She could feel the presence of the Adversary and fell to her knees. She waited for the comfort of the Holy Spirit to enter her ravaged soul, but no help came. She could not pray.

She was still on her knees when morning came and her aching heart was still torn in two. She had not been comforted. There was no peace to be found in this place. The answer lay in returning to the convent. Another night like last night and she would not have the strength to resist him. Every vow she had made was in danger of being broken. Her mind and heart were so far removed from the Bridegroom she shuddered in abject terror.

Catherine remained in her room for the day and night. She complained of a headache and asked to be excused from any activities. Jeffrey did not believe for one minute that the headache was real, but he could do nothing about it. She took her meals in her room and avoided any contact with the family. He had to respect her wishes and kept Michael away from her as well, but it was all Jeffrey could do to restrain him from running up to her room. Jeffrey too had spent a sleepless night and vowed to himself that at the next opportunity, he would not let Catherine escape till he'd told her everything.

Catherine rested on the bed most of the day, her thoughts on Michael and Jeffrey. They belonged to one world, and she—she belonged—she didn't know to which world she belonged anymore, and the loss of her former serene assurance filled her with despair. A veil of darkness descended upon her spirit, and she awakened the following morning more tormented and distraught then ever. She went downstairs, but the thought of food was repulsive to her. Jeffrey had had another restless night and was trying to make some plans with Michael for the day when he saw her pale face appear in the hallway. Her look of anguish smote him. Michael flew over to her and hugged her about the waist. She bent over to clasp him tightly. She had decided to leave Norwood. This would be her last day. She would have to tell Michael and his father. She lifted Michael from the floor and felt eager arms encircle her neck. She buried her face in the golden hair and stifled her sobs. Jeffrey walked over to them. There was an intensity about the way she clung to his son. Dear God . . . he knew she was going to leave. . . .

"Sister," Michael pulled his head back. "Today Daddy and I have something planned. We're going to go on a picnic. Please, will you come? Don't be sick again." Catherine couldn't speak. "Sister, please?"

"All right, Michael . . . since it means so much to you." He hugged her again and said enthusiastically, "Meet us in front of the house at noon."

"Where are we going?" she asked in a daze.

"That's a surprise," Michael replied. She smiled sadly and put him down. Jeffrey was standing near her, but she could not acknowledge his presence. She didn't dare, and turned to go back to her room until the appointed hour. One last picnic . . . then she would be out of their lives forever! Jeffrey watched her go up the stairs. She hadn't even said good morning to him. He thought he was going to lose his mind.

Michael and his father were waiting in the courtyard when Catherine stepped out the front door two hours later. The boy carried a blanket and his father held the hamper of food. For the first time in two days she looked at Jeffrey directly. She wanted to remember him and his son, standing there with the sunshine on their smiling faces . . . like fair gods, eager and happy. She planned to tell them during the picnic she was leaving. The time had come. Hadn't Christ bled from every pore for all mankind? Could she not offer the Bridegroom this small sacrifice? But in her weak moments, it did not seem small. They had become part of her, Michael and his father. They were inseparable in her mind now. These two men had wound their way into her heart. They had taught her so much about life, about love . . . in the end she would be the stronger for it, even if at this moment she shrank from the bitter cup . . . such a bitter cup . . . Nevertheless, Thy will be done, she murmured to herself.

She answered Jeffrey's gaze with a brilliant smile which seemed to transfigure her. It was a farewell smile. He didn't want her to look at him that way. It spoke of goodbye, of eternal parting. He could never say goodbye to her!

The path to the picnic spot wound behind the house, through the trees. The three of them followed it for half

137

an hour, singing rounds most of the way. It was another experience Catherine would treasure.

The path finally led to a small clearing; and a brook, no wider than Jeffrey's stride, rippled through the tall grass. Jeffrey spread the blanket over the cushiony tufts and put the basket down.

"Daddy, shall we tell Sister?" Michael rolled his eyes mysteriously.

"But I thought it was just between us men," Jeffrey teased.

"But Sister is a *woman*, not a dumb girl. That's different."

Jeffrey didn't dare look at Catherine. The boy's comment was very astute. She most decidedly was a woman. Even in her habit, the superb mold of her body was quite apparent. "You're right, Michael," he muttered, almost forgetting that he was not alone. "Sister Catherine is definitely not a dumb girl."

"Well, Michael . . . aren't you going to tell me?"

Michael flashed a conspiratorial glance at his father. "This is our special place, our hideout. No one knows this about it except you. We've never brought anyone else here before."

"Well, I'm deeply honored, sir, and I promise I won't tell anyone . . . not even the Holy Mother." Jeffrey flinched visibly at the mention of the Holy woman's name. Catherine noticed immediately the shadow cross over his face.

"Really?" Michael's eyes were wide open. "I thought you told her everything."

She sucked in her breath. "Well, this is one thing I will keep a secret forever."

"I believe you," he stated. Catherine could not repress a smile, he had said it so seriously. Michael's father laughed as well. The boy was utterly adorable.

138

For a moment, the darkness lifted and she shared the bond which united them. She realized how natural it had all become . . . the three of them together . . . as though they were a family.

"Oh," Michael cried out in delight as a small furry animal scurried through the clearing. "A rabbit," and he darted after it, crouching low, reaching for it with his arms. It ran underneath a sprawling bush and he burrowed his way through the leaves in hot pursuit.

Jeffrey had seated himself beneath a large tree, his back up against the trunk. He was chewing on a blade of grass, watching Catherine. She could feel his eyes. Now was the time to broach the subject of her leaving, but it would be easier if she said it in front of both of them. She walked about the clearing, enjoying the sweet smell of damp earth and foliage, but inwardly she was trembling. "Should Michael be out there alone?"

"These woods have been his domain since he was born. Don't worry about him. Sit down and relax. Today, none of us should have a care in the world."

Catherine obeyed and seated herself on one end of the blanket, lifting her face to the gentle breeze. If she did not shut out the world, she would be looking at Jeffrey's handsome profile. Sweet Jesus, how she loved him! She could no longer deny it. She was supposed to be in the world, not of it. Where was Michael right now to help the conversation? She had never been so aware of his father's presence. It was overpowering. She didn't know how to begin what needed to be said. Michael was calling after the rabbit, shouting for it to stop, and his voice was growing fainter. Back at Our Lord of the Lamb, she would be at meditation in the chapel . . . that is where she needed to be this minute. Not out in the woods with a man and his son . . . but Michael's father was not just any man. She stood up quickly. It startled Jeffrey.

"I feel like walking . . . perhaps I can catch up with Michael." She couldn't talk to him alone. She didn't have the courage.

"I'll come with you. These woods are ripe to be explored," he smiled at her and had to endure the pain of her silence. He followed behind her as she set out in the direction of Michael's cries. She wouldn't get away from him this time. Presently, after having to pull at her cumbersome skirts to clear the underbrush, she came upon the boy, who was totally dissolved in tears.

"Michael," she ran to him. "What is it, darling?"

"Look!" he sobbed, showing her a dead bird he'd discovered beneath a fern. One wing was distended. Catherine knelt down and rubbed its feathers gently with the back of her fingers. "Oh . . . its neck and wing are broken!"

"Daddy, can't you do something?" the boy implored. Jeffrey was down on one knee, inspecting it carefully. "I'm afraid not, son." Michael shuddered. "Why does everything have to die?" he moaned, tears pouring down his cheeks. Catherine wanted to rush to him and hold him, but it was no longer her place. She let Jeffrey reach out. "Michael," he pulled the boy close. "Son," he pressed the wet face to his breast.

"Michael . . . everything has a season," she began. "We are born, we live, and we die. It happens to all God's creatures." Michael wiped his eyes and listened to her. "It's sad, I know—very hard to understand sometimes, but, my love, that is why it is so important that we learn to love life for the time we have it." Her voice caught. "We must each find our place and fulfill ourselves the way God intended," her words died on her lips. Jeffrey hoped she was listening to what she was saying. Michael was shedding new tears . . . she had lost him.

"If anything happened to you or daddy, I'd die."
There was silence. Jeffrey felt as if someone had just
struck him. No one moved. The little boy wriggled out
of his father's arms and returned to stare at the dead
bird. Then he craned his neck and looked at both of
them with soberness. "My mummy died . . . why can't
you be my new mummy, Sister?"

For a moment she was speechless and Jeffrey bowed
his head, fighting the heaviness in his heart. "Because
I'm already married," came the low reply. She was
actually saying the words and he couldn't bear it.

"Where's your daddy?"

Catherine made a noise between a laugh and a sob.
"Nuns are married to Christ, Michael."

"But I've never seen him."

"No," Catherine choked on her own words and sank
to her knees. Jeffrey wanted to stop his son, now. He
didn't want her to remind him again, who he was, what
she was. . . .

"Do you love Him?" the boy asked earnestly.

"Very, very much," her voice broke.

"More than my daddy?" There was an interminable
silence. She groped . . . she felt lightheaded, but she
could not honestly answer Michael's question.

Jeffrey waited for her to say the words he knew would
answer the question . . . but there was no explanation.
The moment of truth had arrived. He waited . . . still no
answer.

"Daddy loves you, Sister. I know he does . . ." Jeffrey stood up.

"Michael, why don't you run back to the clearing and
find something good to eat in the basket." His hands
were shaking as he urged the boy on. "I'll be there in a
while. I want to talk to Sister Catherine alone. Be a good

141

little chap." Michael went off, obedient to his father's wishes and Jeffrey turned around. Her face was buried in her hands. She would not look at him. "Catherine," he began.

Her words were muffled. "I've made arrangements to return to Castle Combe in the morning . . . I was going to tell you and Michael while we ate our picnic."

"I'm in love with you, Catherine."

"No," she cried out. "Please don't say anything!"

"Are you afraid to hear the truth?"

"You don't know what you're saying. Everything is out of perspective right now. When I leave . . ."

"Why couldn't you answer Michael just now?"

"I don't know what you mean!"

"He asked if you loved Christ more than you loved me, and you didn't say anything."

Her shoulders shook. "I must go back to the house. I'm sorry." She started on the path.

"What are you afraid of?" he followed her. She stopped.

"When I was nineteen," she began, "I pledged my life to God. I made a vow. I chose that vocation of my own free will, entering the marriage with joy and happiness. In doing so, I renounced worldly pleasures . . . that was the sacrifice I offered to Him. It was not difficult to give up the world. I rejoiced in the offering. I wanted to serve him."

"I believe you, Catherine . . . but do your vows and covenants prevent you from telling me the truth now? I thought one of the tenets of your faith was honesty."

"It is," she answered in a muffled cry.

"Would you tell me the truth if I asked you a question?" She did not answer. "Do you love me?" She didn't move. There was no sound uttered. "Catherine . . . look at me!"

142

"I mustn't."

"Why? Because it would offend God?"

"Yes," she cried out.

"Then you do love me," he cried aloud.

"I—I don't know," she struggled. "Yes . . . I love you. I—love—you," she whispered.

"Is love between a woman and man offensive to God?" His voice was softly compelling.

"No . . . how could it be?"

"Will you marry me, Catherine?"

She finally looked at him. Sheer astonishment crossed her face. She opened her mouth, but the words would not come. As she shook her head, her astonishment changed to fear. He thought she was going to lose consciousness and drew closer. "You don't think I'm going to let you walk out of my life now, do you? Not after what you've just confessed to me . . . and God is our witness."

Her voice was almost inaudible. "You don't know what you're asking. I've already made my vows to God . . . and when I leave Norwood, I will do penance . . . while there is still time!"

"Penance? For what?" he cried out angrily. "For restoring a child to life, for filling my life with hope and love? No, Catherine! That would be a mockery to God as well. He knows what is in your heart and mine." He swiftly covered the distance between them and drew her into his arms before she knew what was happening.

"No, Jeffrey, we mustn't," she cried, and struggled to escape from his grasp, but he held her almost cruelly tight, till she ceased to offer resistance. Then he bent down and found her trembling mouth. She gasped and her lips parted as his mouth covered hers. They were caught up in a whirling rapture which sent a voluptuous warmth through her body. She had no sense of time or

143

place. His arms tightened to support her as he felt her supple body go limp from emotion.

"I love you," he whispered, kissing her till neither of them could draw breath.

"Jeffrey," she cried, tearing her lips from his, reeling from the passion he brought to life in her.

"Catherine, darling," he murmured, "don't pull away from me," and he found her lips once more, unable to curb the desire she aroused in him. He was shaken by the greatest passion he had ever known. He wanted her beyond caution. Finally, she pulled back and buried her head in his neck, sobbing uncontrollably.

He crushed her to him and they clung together for a long time. "How can Michael and I live without you?" he murmured against her hot cheek. "You are our very heart. How can you walk out of our lives after what we've had together? It isn't possible, my darling," and he rocked her gently. "Don't you see how desperately I want to make love to you, give you children of our own, grow old with you? I want you, Catherine," he groaned, and would have kissed her again, but she broke away from his embrace, hiding her face in her hands once more. Shame and guilt consumed her. She could hear the Holy Mother's words: "Treat this mission with reverence and respect . . . you can never doubt that God approves." Those words scorched her now.

"Dear God," was her anguished cry and she sank to the ground. Her body throbbed from Jeffrey's touch, his words. She looked up at him through tears and saw the love in his eyes. He was torn apart to see her in such torment, but he suffered as deeply as she did. He didn't want to add to her suffering, but he could not help himself.

"Catherine . . . Michael needs a mother," he

144

pressed. "No one knows that better than you. Who else on this blessed earth will he ever care about besides you? You've spoiled us for anyone else."

"Don't," she whispered. "Don't say any more," but she could see he wasn't listening.

"God spared the boy's life, twice, through you. Doesn't that tell you anything?"

"Yes," she wiped her eyes and stood up. "That I was there for him by God's will, because I had entered the sisterhood."

"But you haven't carried it to the next logical step," he broke in, his eyes blazing. "Has it occurred to you that God might have guided you to Michael, and him to you, because He knew there was another mission for you which included the union of the three of us? Can you honestly tell me you are certain that God didn't intend you to be my wife and Michael's mother by placing you at Our Lord of the Lamb?"

The Holy Mother's words came vividly to mind. The day Catherine left for Norwood, she had said, "God has sent you this test. Remember, we don't always see each step along the rocky way, but God sees the end from the beginning and there is work for you to do. You have to find out what that work is, and right now, your mission is one of an administering angel to a sick child." Catherine stood there, paralyzed, her mind in a quandary. What could she say to Jeffrey? Was it indeed God's will that she turn her back on the sisterhood to become the bride of this man? She honestly didn't know . . . perhaps in time the answer would manifest itself.

"Jeffrey . . . I love you very, very much . . . but I can't give you an answer now. I must go back to the convent. I must have time! This has shaken me." He could see her white face, but her words crushed him. He'd only just held her in his arms. She was his whole

145

life . . . to think of her leaving! He shook his head.

"I need you, Catherine. Leave the convent. Our love is holy, too."

She clasped her hands. "Jeffrey, you can't possibly know the ramifications of such a decision."

"What would you have to go through to leave the sisterhood?" The question jolted her to the quick. She paled even more. He realized that the very idea was unthinkable to her.

"I would have to lay my case before the Holy Mother," she answered, as if in a stupor. "Then I would have to go before the Bishop. He would present it to the Cardinal . . . who in turn would take it to the Mother General . . . then I would have to ask for a special dispensation from Pius the XII." It was much more complicated than he had ever suspected. Indeed, he knew nothing about such procedures.

"Would it be unbearable, darling?" he asked softly. She looked into his eyes and took a long time before answering.

"Not if I were certain it was the right thing to do. But you have to understand something, Jeffrey. If I were to leave the order before I had received confirmation that it was God's will, I would not make you a good wife . . . not ever," she explained. Jeffrey knew she was right. "But . . . if I should discover, after I return to Our Lord of the Lamb, that my place is at your side, and then stayed on in the sisterhood out of a sense of loyalty and guilt, I would offend God, for I would not bring a joyful heart to the altar any longer. That would be sacrilege."

He hung his head. Catherine was speaking the truth. He had to accept it. That was what made her the woman she was—her integrity. She had not refused him—she had confessed her love for him, but he knew what a devout person she was. How could he compete with the

146

Almighty? A sadness such as he had never known crept over him.

"Don't look like that," she begged. "Jeffrey, please . . ."

He raised pained eyes to her. "Catherine . . . I love you and I can't conceive of life without you. I don't think I could stand losing you."

"Don't say anymore."

"I must! You're going back to Castle Combe . . . away from me . . . and I have to go back to London on Monday with Michael. I'm going overseas soon. I don't know the exact date."

The news shook her to the depths. She drew closer. "Where?"

"Africa, probably, but nothing is confirmed. I can't tell you details."

"Will it be very dangerous?" She put her hand to her mouth. "That was a foolish question. I realize anything you do means risking your life. Holy Mother in Heaven!"

He was touched by her concern. "I'm not looking forward to leaving Michael again so soon."

"Who will look after him while you're away?" The thought of the boy with Elinore filled her with a strange foreboding.

"Millie. He prefers her to Elinore. I don't understand it. She and Connie were friends, spent time together. I assumed all along that having Elinore there would be a good thing . . . but it wasn't. That has hurt me and Philip, but it can't be helped." Catherine sighed with relief.

"Millie is good for Michael," she broke in.

"Yes . . . and I'm going to put him in school as soon as we get settled in at home. There will be other children for him to associate with. You see!" he caressed her

147

cheek with his hand very gently. "I'm following your advice." His smile was sad. "I think Michael is secure enough. I pray he is." Catherine suddenly remembered something. "The Holy Mother called several days ago."

He raised his eyebrows. "When?"

"While you were out riding. When I told her you were still worried about Michael's dependence on me, she made a suggestion. She said that Michael could come to the convent for visits, to see me and play with the children."

"I didn't know she allowed visitors at the convent." His mind was racing ahead.

"Michael is a special case. She has made an exception, just this once, because she, too, loves the boy and wants what is best for him."

Jeffrey looked elated at the prospect. Catherine knew what he was thinking.

"When I bring him, will you see me?" he asked.

Her mouth went dry. "Jeffrey, if you ever see me again . . . it will mean I am no longer a nun!"

His breath caught. He felt a dam bursting inside. "No, Catherine," and he cupped her face in his hands. "No . . . don't do this to me," he cried aloud. She reached up and put her hands on his, unwillingly forcing them away from her.

"What sense would it make if it were otherwise?" her voice shook with emotion. "You couldn't comprehend the shock this has been to me, to discover that I could form an attachment to a man," and she began to pace the ground. "I never thought it possible . . . not even in my dreams. Except for my father and brothers, I haven't had the slightest interest in men. I've never thought about marriage in terms of myself, until the day we went to visit your friend's widow. There are no

148

opportunities to come in contact with men at the convent. You see, in sublimating earthly pleasures for spiritual power, I had to sacrifice something of myself . . . my worldly possessions, my independence, my will. All this was given to God. But now, you have come into my life! These past weeks, even being in the same room with you has caused me excruciating pain. I've had no peace, and I've begun to respond to feelings I never knew existed, nor ever wanted to experience. Jeffrey, I've felt your lips touch me, your arms hold me. Under the circumstances, it would be an agony of body and soul to look upon you again, if I could not come to you, free to be your wife, to give my love wholeheartedly—free from all restraint. I would suffer beyond my ability to withstand . . . as I suffer right now." She paced the ground, then whirled around. "That is why I have to go back, now! I have to go back to the life I pledged myself to before I can make this tremendous decision. I love you, Jeffrey . . . but I love my life as a nun, too. I just don't know . . . can you understand that?"

He put his arms around her and drew her close. "I'm trying," he muttered against her soft skin. "Do you regret loving me, Catherine? I never wanted to hurt you."

She faced him and searched his eyes. "How can you ask such a question? You've become my other half, Jeffrey. Any woman would be privileged to become your wife. Don't you think I know that?" she cried out, tormented anew.

Her words gave him fresh hope. "Can I write to you while you're making up your mind?" he whispered.

"No . . . it is out of the question."

He closed his eyes tightly. "Will you write to me, or telephone me?"

"No."

149

He gripped her shoulders and held her from him. "Will you discuss this with the Holy Mother? Will you tell her I want you for my wife, that Michael and I can't live without you?"

"Oh, Jeffrey," she sighed . . . "Yes . . . yes . . ."

"Everything? That you love me, too?" he shook her.

"Yes," she moaned.

"How will I know when you've made your decision?"

"Jeffrey," she pleaded. "Give me time . . . I don't have answers yet . . . but I promise . . . I'll let you know . . . I promise."

"Will you give me something to remember you by?" he whispered.

"I have nothing to give," she sighed.

His hands dropped from her shoulders, his fists clenched. "I can't believe any of this is happening." He looked at her, his chest heaving. "Catherine!" He called her name and she came into his arms for the last time, unable to resist, unable to fight her own need and longing. Time passed and still they could not leave each other, clinging with a fierce desperation which wracked them both. Catherine found the strength to pull away, finally. Jeffrey cradled her head in his hands and examined every flawless detail of her face. "Make the right decision, my love," he begged and hungrily kissed her lips once more.

Her eyes shone as she looked up at him. "I love you and Michael . . . and I always will. Remember that . . . whatever happens." She wrenched free of his embrace and ran through the thicket.

Her last statement raised pure terror in his heart and he was rooted to the spot for many minutes.

IX

It was late afternoon. The sun's rays were low and slanting, bathing the sky in shades of pink and gold. Catherine had long since returned to the house. After telephoning the Holy Mother that she would be arriving at Castle Combe on the eleven-thirty p.m. train, she packed the few essentials she'd brought with her in her satchel. Jens had agreed to drive her to the station. There was only one thing left to do now . . .

She left her room, watching carefully to be sure no one was around. Then she hurried down the corridor and knocked on Michael's bedroom door. "Michael," she called out quietly. She knew he was there. She'd heard him running up the stairs earlier. Jeffrey opened the door. Her strength almost failed her. He stared at the satchel in her hand. "I—I want to talk to Michael for just a moment."

"Come in." She moved inside and he closed the door. "I had a long talk with him this afternoon," Jeffrey whispered. "He knows you are going away tomorrow." Catherine shivered . . . then saw Michael in the corner. He was busy sketching with charcoals and did not stop what he was doing.

"Michael, darling?" she spoke, her voice breaking, "do you understand why I have to go back?"

"Yes," he was still busy drawing. "Daddy says I can come and visit you whenever I want." The charcoal dropped on the floor. He looked over at her. "Sister?" he cried out and ran across the room, hugging her tightly. She picked him up and kissed him.

"Peter and Brock will be very happy to see you when you come."

He wiped his eyes. "I'm drawing a picture for Peter."

"Good, darling." The tears welled up in her eyes. "He will like that, I'm sure."

"Daddy says I can go with you when he drives you back tomorrow."

She bit her lip. "Michael . . . I'm afraid there has been a change of plans . . . that's why I've come in to see you now." The boy looked perplexed.

"What change?" Jeffrey demanded. The idea of her going was unthinkable to him still.

She swallowed hard. "I'm leaving Norwood in a few minutes. Jens is driving me to the station. It is all arranged," she stated as calmly as she could.

"No, Catherine," Jeffrey started to protest. He had planned to have some time with her driving back. He hadn't begun to tell her everything that was on his mind.

She put up her hand, unconsciously, as the Holy Mother would do when an audience was over. The gesture was intimidating. "It has to be this way . . . don't you understand?" she pleaded with him. "Jeffrey," she whispered so Michael could not hear. "Give me time. Let me work this out in my own way!"

"Dear God, Catherine . . . this is really it, then."

"Yes."

"At least let me thank you one last time for what you've done for Michael. If it weren't for you, I wouldn't have him now."

"Yes you would, Jeffrey. Perhaps for a time, after his mother died, you felt Michael had deserted you. You couldn't see the love he had for you. But little boys have feelings for their mothers. I've seen it over and over at the convent. When they are frightened, or worried about their parents, they inevitably cry out, 'is my London still there? Is my mummy all right?' It isn't their father they call for, even if they think he is the most wonderful person alive, and make no mistake," she spoke with conviction, "Michael idolizes you. At the time though, he was suffering the shock of losing her . . . it had nothing to do with you. Once he overcame his grief, he was there . . . loving you more than ever. You never lost him."

"Thanks to you." He looked at her with too much tenderness. "Catherine . . . come back to us . . . please come back!"

"Michael," she caught him up to her again. "Come and see me soon?" she rubbed his cheek. He nodded his golden head. "We won't say goodbye, will me?" Suddenly Jeffrey had his arms around both of them, hugging them. "I'll never say goodbye, my darling," Jeffrey murmured.

Catherine handed Michael to his father. Then she fled from his arms, from the room, only stopping long enough to take her satchel in hand. She ran down the stairs and out the front door, almost colliding with Philip.

"Mr. Norwood," she greeted him, out of breath. She looked about for the car. Jens was still in the garage.

"Where are you going?" asked Philip. She seemed to be in great distress. Her usually rosy complexion was white as alabaster.

"I'm leaving . . . I'm going back to the convent." Philip's eyes narrowed and he put down his briefcase.

"I thought you weren't going back till the end of the week.'

"There has been a change in plans."

He peered more closely at her. "Are you all right, Sister? Forgive me for asking, but you look as if you don't feel well."

"I'm not ill."

"Is Jeff going to drive you?" He knew something was wrong.

"No," she answered too abruptly. "Jens is driving me to the station. I'm taking the train back to Castle Combe. It is better this way . . . easier for Michael."

"Then allow me to drive you back. It's the least I can do after the way you put this family back together again. I don't have to tell you what your coming has meant to . . . to all of us. You're a remarkable woman, Sister," his eyes grew misty. "I shall never forget you."

"Thank you, Mr. Norwood," she murmured, overwhelmed. "But I've already made my arrangements. Please say goodby to your wife for me. I haven't seen her recently. She went to a great deal of trouble for me and I am very grateful."

"I'll convey the message, Sister . . . but it may be some time before I see her . . . she has left me!"

"Left you?" Catherine's eyes opened wide.

He nodded. "That's why she is in town today, consulting her solicitor."

Catherine's heart went out to him. "I'm so very sorry! How dreadful for you."

"No," he answered abstractly. "Things have not been right between us for a long time. Several years to be, in fact. In the beginning, I excused our differences on the grounds that we were newlyweds . . . then I began to think it was because of the differences in our nationalities . . ."

"She isn't English?" Catherine questioned.

"She was born in Germany. Her parents emigrated to

154

South Africa when she was in her teens and I met her just after she moved to London. She was a secretary for one of my colleagues when we became acquainted.''

Now Catherine began to understand what Michael had meant about the way Elinore spoke sometimes. It explained a lot of things.

"Sister, I don't know why I am telling you all this.''

"It's all right, Mr. Norwood.''

"I suppose I need someone to talk to and Jeff has enough on his mind right now.''

"Does your brother know?'' she asked quietly.

"No . . . I'll have to tell him tonight. He'll realize something is amiss when she doesn't return. She's gone back to our house in Ipswich. Oddly enough, your being here has had something to do with it.''

"What?'' her face had turned ashen.

"I think the only reason she stayed as long as she did was because of Michael . . . but when you came, she realized how much the boy loved and needed you. Elinore and I haven't had children. I think she wanted Michael to fill that need, but Michael has never taken to her. Seeing Michael so happy with you must have been the deciding factor. You're as much his mother as Connie ever was.'' Catherine bowed her head. "Sister, I haven't told you this to upset you. I'm sorry . . . please don't misunderstand. It was the best thing that could have happened. I'm grateful if your coming brought things to a head. When a marriage disintegrates, when one of the parties is no longer happy, the best thing is to dissolve it.'' Catherine heard his words and felt as though someone had just walked over her grave. She shivered, but the moment passed. "When we were first married, I thought I loved her. She was intelligent and rather challenging. I know now that she was never in love with me. There has been someone else all along

155

. . . I'm not saying she has been unfaithful to me. I have no proof . . . but I suspect that all these years, there has been someone else."

Catherine clutched at the folds of her skirt. Somehow she knew it was Jeffrey . . . she'd seen the signs. She wondered if Philip knew, but didn't say because he loved his brother too much. "What will you do?"

"What I've been doing for years . . . working! But now I will be free to pursue a new life. Who knows," he winked kindly at her, "maybe I'll find a real woman someday, with a heart and soul."

Philip was a kind, gentle man, so much like Jeffrey. It hurt her to think he had to go through such a traumatic experience and she wept inside for both men. "Goodby, Mr. Norwood. God bless you." She got into the back seat of the car and he closed the door, then leaned through the open window.

"I hope not forever. I would like very much to see you again one day. Goodbye," he said with a sober face. As the car pulled around the circular drive, she saw Jeffrey standing on the lawn. Michael was at his side. They waved. . . .

She felt like a drowning victim. Her whole life was passing before her eyes. She sank back against the seat, numbed almost to the point of unconsciousness.

On the ninth day after Catherine's return to Our Lord of the Lamb, the Holy Mother went into the chapel to converse with the young nun. They had not communicated since her arrival, for Catherine had gone immediately into retreat. The Holy Mother realized that the Sister wished to be left alone and felt it was wise for Catherine to have this time to commune with the Lord and get her spiritual values back into perspective. It did not surprise her when she received a phone call from

Commander Norwood the day following Catherine's return, wanting to know how she was. The Holy Mother could tell him nothing. Every day after that, she continued to receive a phone call, and every day she had the same message to give him. Sister Catherine was still in seclusion.

The Mother Superior grew alarmed when Catherine still refused to see anyone after an entire week of fasting and prayer. It was an indication that Catherine was still struggling with a problem she could not resolve. The Holy Mother knew what that problem was . . . she would not wait any longer before she confronted the Sister.

It was apparent Catherine had been fasting . . . she was much too thin and gaunt. The Holy Mother was shocked when she beheld her condition. She pulled on the nun's sleeve, and Catherine's head jerked around, her eyes sunken. There were no traces of the fresh vitality which had characterized her face a few short months ago. She seemed to have aged.

The holy woman bowed her head and made the sign of the cross. The test had been too difficult. This Sister was tortured by a new attachment. Here was a woman suffering for her beloved, just as the Commander was suffering. Yet, the Holy Mother was touched by Catherine's devout faith. Despite this new experience of earthly love, she did not doubt for a moment Catherine's spiritual sincerity. This Sister was in a spiritual abyss . . . something had to be done. . . .

Catherine made the sign and her burning lips kissed the Holy Mother's hands. She looked closely at Catherine. The girl was ill. Catherine's shoulders shook and she found herself sobbing at the feet of her guardian and mentor.

"Holy Mother," she cried aloud in anguish. "What

157

am I going to do?'' Her head came to rest against the holy woman's skirt.

"Do you love Michael's father, my child?"

"Yes . . . I love him very much."

"Does he know of your love?"

"Yes . . ."

She cupped Catherine's chin in her hand, lifted it till their eyes met. "He has expressed his love to you, hasn't he?"

"Yes," she whispered. "He has asked me to leave the Community." The older woman closed her eyes and nodded. It was as she had thought. Tears pressed against her closed lids.

"My child," she sighed, "we must talk. I've left you much too long, and you are feverish. I want you to go to the infirmary. I will come to you there."

"Yes, Mother." But as Catherine rose to leave, she fainted at the Holy Mother's feet.

An hour later, Catherine found herself on a cot in the infirmary. Sister Margaret had brought her broth and crackers. The Holy Mother had commanded that Catherine discontinue her fast. Catherine obeyed her orders without remonstration. She was in a state of despair in which nothing mattered.

She had been back at the convent for over a week, all of which time had been spent in retreat. During this time, she withdrew from the affairs of the Order for solitude, self-examination, prayer and amendment of life. She spoke to no one, not even the Holy Mother. How could she find words, when her mind was so confused? Many hours were spent in prostration before the altar. For Catherine, the aromatic smoke of the incense, ascending heavenward, symbolized the path of her prayers to God. But the divine office held no comfort for her now. The psalms, chants and prayers did not increase her faith as they heretofore had done. She selected scriptures which she'd always loved to read, but they gave no new insight into her dilemna. She turned frantically to the lives of the saints, and the works of preferred theological writers, praying she would find some earth-shaking passage which would set her soul on fire, and smother the flame of love that burned deeper and deeper in her soul for two mortals, but no such manifestation occurred. After nine days, she was no further on the road to recovery than at first. No amount of prayer or fasting could ease the conflict within. She loved God . . . that would never change. He was the Creator, the Giver of life . . . but she also loved a son of God, and she could not deny it. As each day passed, she could not prevent thoughts of him from creeping into her prayers and studies. Sometimes she almost felt his presence next to her. She would see his face and wonder where he was and what he was doing, and she would feel an emptiness that she wasn't sharing precious moments with him. And there was Michael . . . and Philip . . . She would reach for her breviary and begin another prayer, but in the middle of a Hail Mary, she would see Jeffrey's eyes, full of love and longing . . .

The Mother Superior's heart went out to the Sister lying on the bed. Her illness was of the spirit, much as the Norwood child's had been, and if something weren't done right away, she feared for Catherine's life. The eyes lacked lustre and stared vacantly at the ceiling. The face was no longer animated and happy, irradiated with holy joy.

"Sister," the Holy Mother drew up a chair alongside the bed.

"Yes, Mother?"

"I've known you since you were fifteen. I have never

known you to make a decision in haste. I've always felt that that quality made you a particularly fine nun . . . yet the situation presented now requires action."

"Yes," she answered listlessly.

"I can see that your feeling for this man is all-consumming. You have not found peace in your meditation, have you, my child?"

"No, Holy Mother. He is in my every thought and prayer." Hot tears trickled from the corners of her eyes and she turned to face the older nun. "I've never felt such emptiness. I love the Lord, Mother . . . that has never changed . . . but I cannot deceive myself any longer. Never to be in Jeffrey's company again is unthinkable to me. Even my love of God does not sustain me when I consider a permanent separation from Michael and his father." The Holy Mother sighed heavily.

"Mother," Catherine raised up and put a hand on the Holy Mother's arm. "He is so good and kind . . . so gentle . . . I have seen how he is with his son . . . with other people . . . his brother . . ." she lowered her eyes and released the woman's arm. "I didn't know a man could be so godly," she whispered, staring into space. The Holy Mother listened patiently as Catherine poured out her heart. "It didn't happen all at once . . . but we were in each other's company, night and day, for weeks. We talked for hours about everything. I tried to remain detached, but it was impossible, with the child always there to force us together. At first I found it only stimulating to be in his presence. Then the days passed by, and little by little, we grew more . . . aware of each other. I didn't want this to happen, Mother. I never thought it *could*. I've set my goals, made plans for my life's work. I've never wanted anything other than what the convent could offer. But now, nothing seems as important as being with him and Michael. It takes precedence over everything else. I thought that coming back here, away from both of them, would help me regain the peace and joy that I've always felt here at Our Lord of the Lamb. Instead, I feel like a wanderer in a desert wasteland. I don't love God or the sisters less . . . but a new dimension of love has come into my life. It's so powerful, Mother! I can't believe I'm saying this to you, but—but I want to be his wife and Michael's mother. I wouldn't be telling the truth if I didn't admit that to myself, to you and to God. Mother, you once said that if a sister was not an eager bride of Christ, then she would not make a good nun. I've searched my heart, and I know, now, that were I to labor the rest of my days here, in this part of the vineyard, it would not be productive. I can not survive without them'' she wept.

The Holy Mother stood up and walked slowly to the window. Her face held a deep sadness as she peered out. ''Sister . . . if you were any other Sister inside these walls, I would try to persuade you differently. I would counsel you that you were too young to know your own mind and heart. I would tell you that with the passing of time memories of this man and his son would fade . . . that you would find new challenges which would free you from this bondage; but you, Catherine, have a wisdom beyond your years and a capacity for love which makes me think you will go to your grave still loving this man and his son.'' She clasped her hands to her breast. ''The Bishop is coming to Our Lord of the Lamb tomorrow. I will arrange for you to talk to him, and I will lay your case before him. I have no idea how long it will take for the Pope to grant a dispensation . . . these things take time . . . but under the circumstances,

I think it will be granted.''

Catherine wiped her eyes and stared at the Holy Mother. Her words seemed to come from far away. Catherine could scarcely believe that the first step towards freeing herself to go to Jeffrey had actually been taken. A month ago she would have said it was an impossibility, but since she had returned from Norwood, she had been in a stupor. The answer to her prayers now lay in her leaving the sisterhood, the very vocation she thought she'd chosen for a lifetime. She loved Jeffrey and Michael more than life . . .

She closed her eyes and for the first time in weeks a feeling of peace and happiness began to permeate her being. She could see him . . . she could imagine the look on his face when she told him she was free. The feeling of happiness grew, and she knew beyond a doubt that she was receiving confirmation from above. One day in the future, she would become the bride of the man she loved. It was right and it was good.

So deep was her reverie, the Holy Mother sighed. She saw into Catherine's heart which was pure and undefiled. God's will was being accomplished. Before her very eyes she saw new life animate the lovely face once more. Catherine had been an exceptional nun. Soon she would be an exceptional wife and mother for the Norwoods. There was a part of the Holy Mother which could not be sad. Catherine was being called to a different mission, in its way just as holy. From the very start, when Commander Norwood had come to Our Lord of the Lamb, she'd had a premonition that Catherine's life would take a different turn. He was a fine man and a good one, and his little Michael was angelic. His gain would be the loss of many children in the world who would never have the opportunity of knowing Sister Catherine; however, other spirits would be born from their union and no child could ask for a better mother than Sister Catherine.

"Holy Mother," Catherine spoke again, but this time the eyes were no longer troubled. "God has answered my prayers."

Mother Angela walked over to her side and patted her hands. "Yes, my child. God has decreed it in his infinite wisdom . . . and you must feel no more remorse. You've always been able to love others as yourself. It is one of the greatest of God's commandments. Now it will be possible for you to share your love of God with this fine man and his son. I am happy for you, Catherine . . . and sad for us. Every day of your life here, you have served faithfully, and your devotion has been an inspiration to all. It may well be that in this marriage to come, there will be new ways to serve your Father in Heaven, which will bring joy and satisfaction to yourself as well as others. If your mother were alive, Catherine, this news would make her very happy."

"Yes, Holy Mother. Thank you." Catherine kissed her hands and sobbed quietly.

"Catherine, the procedure with nuns who wish to leave the sisterhood is to wait until they have received confirmation from the pope before going back into the world."

"Yes, Holy Mother. I desire to serve the Lord with all my heart until the Holy Father has given me a bill of divorcement and a benediction. I need the time to prepare myself for my new role. I told Jeffrey he would never see me again unless I were no longer a nun."

The Holy Mother smiled. Catherine was unique. Her level-headed maturity would always be one of her leading characteristics. Hers was a special spirit. Our Lord of the Lamb would miss her very much.

"Sister . . . could you see fit to accept an assignment away from the convent until your dispensation is made official?"

Catherine blinked. "Of course, Holy Mother. I will serve anywhere. Are you referring to the work we talked about on the phone, concerning the Mother General?"

She cleared her throat. "Yes. But before I explain the nature of this assignment, I want you to know that you do not have to accept it. It could be dangerous . . . and I would understand if you preferred to stay at Castle Combe till you were free."

"Go on, Holy Mother . . ." Catherine slid off the bed and stood on shaky legs. The food brought to her earlier had done a little to fortify her, but the earth-shaking decision to leave the sisterhood had all but drained her once more, and now the Holy Mother was about to discuss something which portended danger.

"The Holy Father is deeply grieved over the senseless killing which is taking its toll of humanity. There are many refugees fleeing the war zones, seeking temporary shelter in neighboring countries who are offering them succor. Whether they be Belgian, French, Pole, Italian, Austrian or Dutch, the pope is asking everyone to aid them in their plight. The Mother General has been out visiting the various communities to discover what the sisters can do to help these unfortunate victims.

"Our Mother General is very pleased about what is being done here at Our Lord of the Lamb, but some of our sister priories are in trouble." Catherine's blood turned cold as the Holy woman continued to explain.

164

X

"I'm referring particularly to the priory in Spain," the Holy Mother said, "and as you know, that country is on more than friendly terms with the Third Reich."

"Do you mean Saint Theresa's convent, in the Pyrenees?" Catherine questioned.

"Yes . . . that's the one, near the Spanish-French border. Recently it has been housing neighboring families, refugees from areas in France and beyond. Most of them are children, plagued with injury and illness. There are other problems as well which the Mother General did not go into, but one fact remains — there are not enough sisters to manage the convent. They are in need of help . . . dire need! The Mother General has petitioned the Church in Rome to send more sisters and medical supplies, but she has taken it upon herself in the meantime to recruit extra nuns for a temporary period of duty. It could mean two months or more. When she came here, asking my help, I told her you were the most qualified to go from our convent because of your gift for helping troubled children, and because of your background, which would automatically enable you to communicate with the French people: and that isn't all! She prefers that young nuns in good health be selected, for the trip will be rigorous, and the work exhausting. There are few nuns in the whole of Great Britain who have all of these qualifications. Naturally, it is not a requirement that one speak a foreign language . . . they would welcome help of any kind . . . but you can understand why I thought of you."

"Of course," Catherine answered in a daze.

"It would be a mercy mission, full of peril. Yet there are those sisters who still desire to make this sacrifice. But Catherine, I repeat, you do not have to go . . ."

Catherine pondered the Mother Superior's words. She had been completely honest with her. It would be dangerous, Catherine knew, but when she thought of the refugees who had nowhere to turn, the poor sisters who were understaffed and overworked, slaving around the clock giving comfort and medical attention to the little children, her heart filled with compassion, and she knew she had to go. It would be her last act of service to God before marrying Jeffrey. Perhaps there was another child like Michael who was crying out to be loved and made to feel secure again. The war did terrible things to people, and particularly to children. And it was true, her knowledge of French and Spanish would make it so much easier to communicate. Catherine had faith that in fulfilling this obligation, she would have a life with Michael and Jeffrey. She also had to admit to herself that it would be easier to labor away from Our Lord of the Lamb. The convent was a constant reminder of them. Once again, the Holy Mother was inspired. The next few months were going to be extremely difficult to get through, but now she would be too busy, too far away to think, and when it was over, she could go to Jeffrey. She turned a smiling face to the Holy Mother.

"I will go to Spain, Mother. I want to . . . for many reasons. I can not do otherwise."

The Holy Mother nodded with satisfaction. Catherine would never do anything other than that which was right and good. She was a dedicated soul, no matter what the circumstances. "Bless you, my child. This mission to the Pyrenees should not require any more time than the allotted waiting period for word from Rome. When you return to England, you will be free . . . but Catherine, remember, you will be entering hostile country and will need God's divine protection every step of the way. Do you fully understand what I'm saying?"

Catherine nodded. "Yes, Mother, but my mind is made up. It is God's will."

The Holy Mother patted Catherine's hands. If all the other sisters were like Catherine, God's will would prevail throughout the earth. "Sister, you have my permission to telephone the Commander and give him this news which he has been waiting for. He had called me every day inquiring about you. The man has been in agony, just as you have. It would not be kind to leave England without letting him know of this latest decision."

"Bless you, Holy Mother," she began, but a knock interrupted them. Sister Margaret appeared in the infirmary. The Holy Mother went over to her. The two conversed a few moments, then Sister Margaret left. The Holy woman turned to Catherine.

"It appears you have visitors. Mr. Norwood, Michael's uncle, has brought Michael to see you. Now you can tell the boy as well. But before we join Mr. Norwood, I would like to explain further about this mission to Spain. You will have to leave this week . . ."

Philip was standing near the desk, looking worried and preoccupied as Catherine and the Mother Superior stepped into the room. She remembered that Elinore had just recently left him. That would account for his

167

depression. As she studied his face, Jeffrey's image came sharply to mind and her body tingled with an excitement she need no longer suppress. She looked about for Michael, but he was nowhere in sight.

Philip glanced up when he heard footsteps and smiled at Catherine for a long moment. He'd missed her. His eyes took an immediate inventory. She was extremely pale, her face thinner than he remembered, but her eyes were radiant. He knew Jeff would give his right arm to be standing in his shoes right now. Perhaps she had found the answer to Jeff's question. His brother had broken down and told him everything the night Catherine had returned to Castle Combe. Jeff had been in love with her from the very beginning. He'd remembered the days when Jeff was courting Connie, and lovely as she had been, Jeff had never behaved as he did around the Sister. His love was written all over his face. They were beautifully matched. Sister Catherine had charm and warmth and beauty. Her spirituality only intensified her other qualities. That was the problem. Philip could see she was in love with Jeff, but he also knew she was a very devout woman. She wouldn't give up the sisterhood without a fight. Had the Lord won out after all? She no longer looked tortured as she had that afternoon in front of the house. Instead, she stood there in an almost serene beauty. Jeff would absolutely lose his hold on life if she decided to remain a nun.

Catherine drew closer, smiling her special, glorious smile. He breathed deeply. She had made her decision. He could tell . . . but if she had decided in Jeff's favor, surely his brother would have known by now. The Holy Mother would have said something. The poor devil had called the convent every morning since Catherine left. Philip broke out in perspiration. How could he tell his brother that she loved God too much to give up the religious life? He shuddered over the repercussions. Jeff wouldn't get over it. He knew is brother too well . . .

"Holy Mother . . . Sister," he greeted them.

"Where is Michael, Mr. Norwood?" Catherine inquired.

"We arrived a while ago, so one of the other sisters took him to play with his friends in the courtyard."

"You must forgive us, Mr. Norwood," the Holy Mother explained. "There have been some pressing matters. We came as soon as we could."

"I understand. I've enjoyed listening to the music. It is very beautiful." He was growing more and more uneasy. "Holy Mother, may I speak to Sister Catherine for a moment? If it weren't of vital importance, I would not ask. It concerns Michael's father." The two women exchanged glances.

"You may," she said quietly and left the room, closing the door behind her.

Suddenly Catherine was afraid. Something could have happened to Jeffrey during their separation. She leaned toward him. "What is it?" she asked in a tremulous voice.

"Jeff was called away on a secret mission last night." Catherine heard the words and could not move a muscle. The only sign of distress was in her eyes, which clouded immediately. Philip forced himself to go on. "It came sooner than he had expected or wanted, but his particular services could be rendered by no one else. He asked me to give you a message. He knew I would be seeing you today. He has written a letter, but he is afraid you will not read it. He has asked me to read it to you."

Catherine's mouth turned up at the corners, despite her anxiety. Her husband-to-be was a determined soul. How she loved him for it! "I will read it," she said softly. Philip was surprised, but he took the envelope from his coat pocket and handed it to her. She accepted it and he noticed that her hands shook. She clasped it to her bosom and walked to the end of the room, away from his gaze. She opened the letter. His handwriting was bold, the letters formed with straight, simple lines, like his drawings.

My darling Catherine,

Less than two weeks have gone by since you went away with my heart. I am the one languishing now, just like Michael. Every second without you has been utter agony. I've been on my knees many hours, pouring out my heart to God, begging him to let you spend the rest of your life with me. (She blinked back the tears.) *This will be my last chance to communicate with you before I leave London. What I told you the day of the picnic has come to pass. This new assignment will require several months, instead of days, to accomplish. I would not have taken it if Michael weren't so much better, and now that Phil is going to be there to watch after him, I can go away resting a little easier. The part that is so difficult to bear is knowing I'm going to be so far away from you. I love you, Catherine.*

She couldn't see the writing. It was all a blur. Now she would not be able to tell him for months. Dear God, what if something happened to him on the mission? What if she never saw him again? She finally continued to read.

I had to tell Phil, Catherine. He is probably reading this to you right now. Forgive me, my darling, for divulging matters between us, but I trust Phil with my life. He will continue to bring Michael to the convent till I can come back to do it myself. And Catherine, I will come to Our Lord of

170

the Lamb, and I'll convince the Holy Mother that I have to talk to you. I plan to make you my wife!

All my love,

Jeffrey

She folded the letter and put it back in the envelope, wondering how she was going to exist till she could feel his arms around her again. She turned back to Philip and returned the letter to him. He could tell nothing from her expression. Her face looked terribly sad. The luminous eyes were wet. She was fighting for composure. What was going on in her mind?

"Thank you," she whispered huskily. "I'll have Sister Margaret show you to the refectory. There will be food prepared for you. I will go and find Michael now."

"Thank you, Sister." He couldn't stand it any longer. "Sister Catherine?"

"Yes?" she turned and waited at the threshold.

"There is a chance that Jeff will contact me tonight. A slim one. I don't know where he is or how he can arrange it, but apparently he is still in England. He said he would try to phone and see how things went today. Please . . . is there any word I can give him from you? He has suffered so much since you left. You have no idea." There! He'd asked her, point blank, but he knew it was useless and didn't really expect any kind of an answer.

She didn't make a move. She seemed to be rooted to the spot. He probably shouldn't have asked, but suddenly she looked up and her face seemed to glow with a luminescence all its own. She walked back to the table, her eyes looking directly into his.

"Tell him," her voice caught, "tell him that I have laid my case before the Holy Mother. I am leaving the sisterhood."

Philip had been prepared to hear the very worst. He

stared at her. "What did you say?"

Catherine smiled. She could see the news had astounded him. "My love for Jeffrey is too strong to be denied. I plan to become his wife as soon as the Pope grants a dispensation."

"Are you serious?" His voice still sounded unbelieving.

"Completely," she smiled and put out a hand to touch his arm. His face lighted up.

"My brother is going to be the happiest man that ever lived, Sister! Jeff is a very lucky fellow," he whispered. "When will you be free to join him?"

"In several months. Tomorrow I have an interview with the Bishop. That is the first step. There are many things involved, you understand."

"Of course. Jeff won't be the same man when I tell him." He cleared his throat. "I don't have to tell you how I feel about you. You're the best thing that ever happened to any of us."

"Philip," she said his name for the first time with such sweetness. They looked at each other with love. "There is something else I want him to know," Catherine added. "Until he comes back from his mission, and my dispensation is official, I still have work to do for the Lord."

"I understand."

Catherine grew nervous. "I have accepted a special assignment which will take me away from Castle Combe for a few months. I will be leaving this week." Philip was listening, alert to the tension which had crept into her voice. "I'm being sent to Spain, to join our sisters at Saint Theresa's convent in the Pyrenees, near the French-Spanish border. It's one of our Benedictine priories."

"I don't understand."

Catherine licked her lips. "The priory is housing refugees from France . . . and it is severely under-staffed. I am going there to render service."

"But we're at war, Sister, and Spain will come into it officially at any moment. You will not be safe."

"Rest assured, our Heavenly Father will protect me. I am only one of many being asked to give aid. How can I refuse?"

Philip was flabbergasted. "If I tell Jeff about this, on top of the other news, it will tear him to pieces!" It was one of the few times in his life that Philip felt totally helpless. His legal mind had no answers. How was it possible that the Church would allow a young, innocent sister to travel to the war zone? It was inconceivable. He doubted he would tell Jeff the complete truth if he should call. It would kill him to be so close to having her now, and then hear she was going off for one last time. She might never come back! Philip experienced a new heaviness and he feared for Catherine. He loved her, too, and even if this adventure was sanctioned by the Vatican, Philip did not have her faith.

Catherine saw his reaction. What would the news do to Jeffrey? "Please don't be concerned for me," she pleaded with him. "I want to go. There are children who need help."

He bowed his head. "We will never stop praying for your safety. How will you get there?"

"By boat. The Mother General will be traveling with us."

He shook his head. Perhaps it was best after all if Jeff weren't able to reach him. Catherine could read his mind.

"Philip, it will turn out as God wills."

"You're right, Sister."

"I will go and find Michael now. He must be told as

173

well." Philip's lips broke into a tight smile. "He loves you so much. I wish I could see Michael's face when you tell him."

Catherine returned the smile. She cared a great deal for Philip. "When Michael and I have had our talk, we will come and find you."

"Very good . . . and Sister? . . . Catherine?" he said her name at last. "God bless you."

She bowed and left the room, walking as always with consummate grace. Jeffrey was a fortunate man, but Philip wondered if the two of them would survive the war, if they would ever see each other again . . .

Catherine found Michael playing with his best friends, Peter and Brock, out on the grassy slope behind the convent. They were involved in a game of "Doggie come running," but when Michael saw the figure of Catherine in her flowing white habit, he left his play and dashed up the hill into her outstretched arms. "Sister!" He hugged her.

"Michael, darling," she nuzzled her face in his neck to kiss the soft skin.

"I've missed you. Did you know Daddy went away last night?"

"Yes," and she finally put the boy down. They clasped hands and started walking toward the brook.

"I wish he didn't have to go away."

"I'm sure he didn't want to, but he has a job to do to protect our country, like King Richard, remember? And soon he will be back again."

"Uncle Phil is staying with me. Aunt Ellie has gone away. I'm glad."

Catherine was pensive. "It should make you very happy that your uncle is home with you."

"But I still wish you could come. I wanted to visit you last Sunday, but Daddy was sick."

Catherine slowed her pace. "What was the matter with him?"

"He couldn't sleep. Dr. Endicott came over." There was a pause. "Sister, why did you have to go away?"

Catherine knelt before the child, brushing the curls out of his blue eyes. "Michael . . . in a few months, I'm going to come and live with you and your daddy." Michael looked incredulous.

"For a visit?"

She shook her head. "Forever! I'm going to marry your father." It took a moment for the words to register. He cocked his head.

"Then you'll be my new mummy?" his eyes opened till they were round as saucers.

"Yes, darling."

"And you won't have to wear that long dress and funny hat anymore?"

"Oh, Michael," she crushed the boy to her, laughing and crying all at once. "No . . . I'll be just like all the other mummies," she whispered. He pressed himself against her and they clung for a long, long time. Words were unnecessary. She'd never known such happiness. Finally she let him go and stood up. "Michael, I want you to listen carefully to something else I have to tell you. Until I can come to live with you and your father, I, also, have work to do. There are some poor little children at another convent who need my help for a while. That means I won't be here at the convent. You won't be able to come and visit me . . . but you won't mind, will you darling? Pretty soon we're all going to be together, and I'll never leave you again."

He was very calm. "That's all right, Sister. You're going to be my new mummy," and he clapped his hands. "Can I tell Peter and Brock?" Catherine could see that the news brought a light to his eye. He didn't care about anything else, to her relief.

"Not yet . . . this will be our little secret. Just you and your Uncle Philip know."

"Daddy doesn't know?" he asked.

She enfolded him once more. "No . . . not yet. Your uncle is going to tell him tonight, if he should call."

His eyes danced. "Daddy said he was going to ring me up tonight. Can I tell him, Sister?"

"If you want to," she kissed him. "Now, let's go find your uncle. He will be anxious to get back to London."

The child ran on ahead of her in carefree delight. He was going to be her very own little boy soon. Another life was about to unfold for her. When she thought of being in Jeffrey's arms, of bearing him children, she couldn't breathe.

A few minutes later, Philip and Michael were in the car once more, traveling back to London. The child rattled on endlessly about the exciting news. Philip realized she had not told Michael any details about her new assignment. It was wise that she had spared him. He drove faster than usual, his mind in a fog. Michael finally fell asleep on the back seat, exhausted from the excitement. This left Philip with several hours to consider this new state of affairs. He prayed that it would all turn out right!

Coastal Command Headquarters were set up outside London in an immense mansion which could house several hundred men if necessary. Jeffrey had driven there with Lord Wyngate the night before. They had come from a special air ministry meeting and went directly to headquarters for further conferences. Jeffrey had been ordered to attend and to be prepared to brief the staff of dignitaries on his last intelligence gathering mission to the Mediterranean. The summons had come sooner than he would have liked, for Michael's sake as well as his own. He had planned to drive to Castle Combe that very Sunday and speak to the Holy Mother about Catherine. For nine days he had waited impatiently for some word, and every moment away from her had been excruciating. Then he was told to report to Headquarters and he had to go. He had no choice.

Jeffrey was ushered into the conference room and immediately recognized General Gort, Mr. Alexander, Mr. Lloyd and General Auchinleck, top men in the department. The meeting was even more important than he realized. When they were all seated, General Gort stood up.

"Gentlemen, good morning. I've asked you to assemble on a moment's notice so we can be briefed in detail on the situation around the Gibraltar Straits. Lord Harley sat in on the meeting we held with the Prime Minister, in Commander Norwood's place last week, and he advanced some of the theories written up in the Commander's dossier, but I felt that specific points brought up made it necessary for us to hear from him in person. His son has been seriously ill, so we've waited until now to hear from him. He has a real grasp of the problems, so without further ado, we'll hear from him now." He turned. "Go ahead, Commander."

Jeffrey nodded and took his place by the map which was an up-to-date picture of the enemy's air power throughout the Straits. "Gentlemen," he began, thinking that one bomb dropped on this building could wipe out the entire leadership of Britain's air power, "In March, I was asked to go on a mission to Gibraltar and ascertain our air strength as compared to the enemy's. As you know, since the outbreak of the war, we've used the London flying boats based on Gibraltar to ferry important dignitaries between England and the Mediterranean area. They've also had a workout escorting convoys passing southward. We haven't been too worried in the past about increasing our air power there because of the obvious reason that the fighting was centered elsewhere, but now the situation has changed drastically. The Bay of Biscay is crawling with Germans, here, here and here," he demonstrated on the chart. "The French fleet is in harbor, and our men are skirmishing with Luftwaffe at least three times a week." Some of the men raised skeptical eyebrows. "This, gentlemen, means that escalation of enemy air power has begun in this part of the world. I recommended in my reports that we triple our defense posts in West Africa or we're going to lose the fight in the Mediterranean. We cannot afford to leave Malta unprotected from this end. The Germans have grasped the entire coastline of Europe. Franco hasn't catapulted his country into the war yet, but Spain has become a stronghold of German bases, the extent of which is still unknown. Franco's December meeting with Mussolini was up to no good . . . we all know that. I don't think we even begin to know what we're up against. I'm not at all sure that tripling our air power in that region will be sufficient. We know Spain is mass producing ammo and parachutes for the Third Reich, but that is nothing compared to what is happening in their harbors. The area is inundated with U-boats from Lorient and Bordeaux, but they can't all be stationed in French ports alone. Those U-boats can turn up anywhere in the Atlantic and come after one of our convoys, and with our air power at current strength, we don't have the resources to stop them. And worse, there are pillboxes stretching from Algeciras to the Pyrenees.

"Establishing bases in West Africa is the answer, in

my opinion . . . and that is tricky as well with the Vichy French, but I see no other choice. I know that there has been some question about the necessity of extending the Coastal Command war zone further south into Africa, but I assure you, if we don't, we're in big trouble. The build up of the enemy in Spain has me worried. I took in a squadron in March and set up a base of Sunderlands. We camped on the edge of a mosquito swamp. That part of Africa is inhospitable at best, but we were able to manage it. Later, we put up another base at the mouth of a river. We got together the necessary ground staff and were in full operation within a week, and none too soon. Our men sank two U-boats within three days of being there.''

He stopped to allow the men to digest his words. "I have advised that we get more aircraft in there, and I've suggested the Hudson. It's a medium fast land-aircraft, capable of carrying a sufficiently heavy punch to deal with the U-boats . . . a few squadrons of those at newly erected bases will even up the odds down there. Again, that is assuming we can get the Hudsons. In the meantime, our Sunderlands are doing a Herculean job.''

Jeffrey sat down and the men conferred for a few more minutes. Finally General Gort stood up. "Commander, we'll get you those Hudsons and anything else you need. Tomorrow you can take off with as many squadrons as you can put together and set up bases. Think it is possible to do it in three weeks time?'' Jeffrey nodded. "An important convoy will be coming through the Straits then.''

One of the staff raised a question. "Commander, I overheard one of your crewmen saying that during your recent mission to Gibraltar, you improvised a very fine oil filter . . . what did you use?''

Jeffrey laughed quietly. "Toilet tissue, Sir.'' A roar

went up from the men, followed by applause.

"We're sorry you couldn't get those split pins and lubricants requested."

"They arrived, Sir, just a touch behind schedule, but it really didn't impede our progress. Squadron leader Dudley came up with a unique idea for the hydraulics . . . home made ground-nut oil. The men are resourceful."

"That's how we're making it through the war. Sounds like our boys, Commander. And now, to get to the heart of the matter. Your intelligence reports about Spain have given us a few more gray hairs. We need detailed information about enemy activity there. Commander, we are asking you to do some reconnaissance work for us on this mission. We want proof of what Franco is up to. We want you to tell us anything you can about the movement of neutral and enemy surface and underwater craft. We need reports indicating troop movement, construction of new aerodromes, the number and type of aircraft on existing aerodromes, and the location of new U-boat bases along the coast line. This hasn't been your usual line of work, Commander, but we need an expert and we know you can spot ship nationalities, recognize deck cargo, classify type. We need this information as soon as you can send it to us on the teleprinter. When you have established bases and things are in running order, we would like you to penetrate as deeply into Spain as you can, particularly the mountain areas. Use charts, camera pigeons, anything, but we need that information. I realize what we're asking of you. There's nothing the Jerries love more than taking on a British aircraft flying in low for a good look. I hope you've got a photographic memory . . . there will be times when you won't have a chance to jot down a note. Up to now, the information being fed to us has not been adequate, and I'm sad to report that some of the reconnaissance crews never made it back to base to report a few weeks ago." Jeffrey realized he had his work cut out for him. "You know that area better than anyone, Commander. You've lived out there. In anticipation of this mission, we've assembled the best wing commanders and reconnaissance pilots in the business. They are in the war room now. You can begin briefing them on the new tactics immediately . . . and good luck." They saluted.

Jeffrey shook hands with them before leaving the room. Lord Wyngate followed him out. "Excellent presentation . . . had them eating out of your hand. It's too bad you couldn't have talked to them last week. Those Hudsons would be on their way by now, but with Michael ill, that was impossible, I realize. Jeff, I'm sorry you have to leave with Michael barely back from the hospital."

"He'll be all right. Phil is there with him." He paused. "Elinore is divorcing him. Did you know?"

"Yes . . . she told me herself. Sorry for that. It won't be easy for Philip."

"He seems to be getting along amazingly well, actually."

"And you?" he looked at the young Commander and noticed his pale countenance.

"I'm all right."

"I've known you too long to believe that! If it isn't Michael, then it must be a woman. We've been friends for years . . . out with it!"

Jeffrey smiled tightly. "I'm in love."

"I thought so . . . and about time. Who is she?"

"Believe it or not, she's a nun."

Lord Wyngate was visibly shocked. "You don't mean the Sister that came to take care of Michael?"

"Yes . . . Sister Catherine."

"Is there any hope? Knowing you as I do, I can't imagine your failing to win her over."

Jeffrey sighed. "You don't know her. I'm not sure if she even wants to see me again, and she won't see me unless she is free."

His brows furrowed. "I'm deeply sorry about this, Jeff. Under the circumstances, this mission might be just the thing to get her off your mind."

"I doubt anything could do that. Phil took Michael to visit her at the convent today. He should be back in London tonight. I was hoping to talk to him before I left for Africa. Perhaps he'll have a message for me . . . I pray to God he does."

"Do you want to phone Philip from here?" Wyngate asked. It was against the rules, but he held Jeff in great affection and the man was obviously suffering.

"I was hoping you'd ask that," he grinned at his good friend.

"I'll arrange it now, before I leave for Whitehall. Just tell the man in communications to clear number four when you're ready. That's my line."

"Thank you very much. I won't forget your kindness!"

"Not at all, my boy. Affairs of the heart are top priority! And Jeff, good luck!" Lord Wyngate saluted and left.

Jeffrey went into the war room to brief the men who had been handpicked for this important mission, but his heart was not in any of it. He almost dreaded hearing what Phil might have to tell him. It had been ten days now, and there was still no news. The Holy Mother insisted Catherine was still in retreat and had told her nothing. What if she decided to remain there?

"Gentlemen, some of you who were with me in

March complained about the heavy action building up around the Gibraltar Straits. Well . . . now we're going to do something about it!" A cheer went up from the men and a few whistles.

"We're going to set up three new bases at strategic spots along the West African coast line. Some of you will still be carrying on escort duties and watching for U-boats in the Sunderlands, but the rest of you will go out on sorties with the Hudsons. Several squadrons of this American aircraft will build up our defense power appreciably, and we can penetrate even deeper south if necessary." Another rousing cheer broke forth from the men. "One hitch . . . they want these bases in working order in three weeks time. I say we can do it in a fortnight!" Again, the cheers.

"For the rest of the day we're going to get our ground staffs together, and make lists of supplies . . . the works. Then I want everyone of you to have steak and eggs before retiring. Get your sleep . . . you're going to need it. We take off at 0400 hours. There are only eight Hudsons available to us now, but more have been promised. You eight will have to refuel in Gibraltar. The rest of us in the Sunderlands will make the long stretch in one hop and commence setting up camp. I have the three locations for the base sites sketched out here. If there are no questions, let's get to work."

During the next six hours, an elite wing command force was being put together under Jeffrey's careful scrutiny. Despite the urgency of the business at hand, he was preoccupied and glanced every so often at the clock. He wondered if Phil had gotten back to Mayfair.

"Commander?" Someone had been calling him for the last few seconds, but his mind had been on Catherine. He reddened noticeably when one of the officers poked him in the ribs. "You've put a note here to remember pumps. What do you mean by that, Sir?"

"If you go down in your plane, you've got to get those dinghies inflated. If one pump goes, you'll have a hell of a time on your hands trying to inflate it. These are shark infested waters. I know because I played footsie with one a while back. I don't have to tell you that an inflated dinghy looks mighty good at such a time. I want every man equipped with a pump, just to make sure. It will save lives."

"Right, Sir."

"There's going to be some reconnaissance flying, men. I don't know how many of you have done much of that sort of thing, but there are times when you feel very alone once you're off that runway. You've got a long way to go before you feel good old terra firma again. You're on your own. Your strength is in yourselves and in the aircraft. Many times there will be no one to help you out of a tough spot. Sometimes you won't have any cloud cover for an entire mission, particularly now with summer upon us. If you have to ditch in the sea, don't let your hearts fail. That's what the dinghies are for. I've experienced it several times. I know you chaps feel your chances of survival are slim. In fact, it is a standing joke that our type of aircraft *might* float for thirty seconds, but the manufacturers won't guarantee it." The men laughed loudly. "Seriously, keep your minds off forced landings at sea. Don't think about it. That's the way to approach it. This work is a strain, and borrowed worries add to it. Just remember why you're out there, and what it is all about and you'll make it. It's been said that the heart of the air force is the spirit of its airmen. I believe that . . . but its limbs are its aircraft. We've got good planes, and we're expecting more. Take meticulous care of your planes, and they'll take care of you. I can testify that this is so. And remember something else

184

. . . God is on our side!"

There was a brief silence in the room. Then the men gave Jeffrey a standing ovation as he left the room. He went directly to the communications center, a massive jungle of electrical equipment, telephones, teleprinters and wireless sets. The man at the switchboard turned around as Jeffrey came through the doorway.

"Are you Commander Norwood?" Jeffrey nodded. "Okay, you can come in. I'll plug you in to the London operator."

"He told me to use number four."

"Correct, Sir. Over there on the end." Jeffrey went down the row of phones and picked up a receiver.

"Okay, Sir. You can put your call through. Take as long as you want. It's quiet tonight."

"Thank you."

XI

"Millie? We're back," Philip called to the housekeeper as they entered the Mayfair house. This was home now that he and Elinore had separated. Michael ran straight up to his room and Philip went into the parlor. He put the letter Jeffrey had written to Catherine on the table.

"Good evening, Sir. How was your trip?"

"Fine, Millie."

"And Sister? Was Michael pleased to see her?"

"Very!"

"You look upset, Sir. What is it? Michael isn't sick again?"

"No . . . nothing like that. Has Commander Norwood phoned?"

"No, Sir . . . no one."

"Very good then. I'm going to shower now. If there is a phone call, it will probably be the Commander and it will be important."

"Yes, Sir. I'll just go on up to Michael and get him into the bath."

"Fine." He went straightaway to his room to freshen up. A half hour later he walked back into the parlor and discovered, much to his surprise, that Elinore had come to see him. She was standing by the hall table. His eyes wandered to the letter. She had been reading it because the note was half out of the envelope, which was not the way he had left it earlier. Elinore had never made him as angry as he was right then.

"Elinore . . . I wasn't expecting you. What were you doing with that letter? It's against the law to tamper with other people's mail."

She looked up, her gray eyes almost black. "I didn't know it was tampering to be curious about a letter which I thought might be from my solicitor to you. I haven't heard from you in days. I was beginning to think you had never received the papers."

"You know I'd never keep legal papers lying about. I only received your papers three days ago. Did you find out what you wanted to know?"

Elinore eyed him and was surprised at his show of anger. Philip was generally rather phlegmatic. "He's in love with her! I knew it!" she hissed.

"That letter was private. Even I don't know what is in it."

She ignored him and sat down in the nearest chair. "When did Jeff leave? I thought you'd both be here this evening."

"He left last night."

"Where is he off to this time?"

"Really, Elinore, you're quite insufferable, you know? He never reveals details of a mission."

She stared at him. "Except to Sister Catherine."

Philip had never struck anyone in his life, but he was tempted to do it now. "What possible difference does any of it make to you?"

"It doesn't, actually. I came to talk about the details of the settlement. Since you're not even interested enough to answer your mail, I thought I'd save you a stamp. What shall we do with the house? I've taken a flat here in Mayfair."

He sighed and seated his weary body. "Let's put it on

the market. You take what you want to furnish the flat. It makes no difference to me.''

"Won't you be finding a place of your own?''

"Eventually . . . but for the time being, I've promised to look after Michael till Jeff gets back.''

"Do you know when that will be?''

He shook his head. "No idea whatsoever.''

"I see . . . well, I guess that about takes care of it. Tell me . . . how is our beloved Sister Catherine?''

"Do you really care? I always had the impression you kept your distance with her.''

Elinore didn't move an eyelash. "Is she going to stay in character, or will Jeff be expecting a house guest shortly?''

"Sister Catherine is going away,'' he said flatly. He had no intention of telling her anything under the circumstances.

"After Jeff?'' she smiled maliciously.

He closed his eyes. "No . . . she's being sent to another convent.''

"Looks as if they are punishing her for overstepping bounds. I expected as much. Where? In the Midlands?''

He just shook his head and wondered what it was he had ever seen in Elinore. He couldn't resist the temptation to bring her up short.

"No . . . actually she's taking on a very dangerous assignment, traveling to the Pyrenees. To Saint Theresa's priory, to be exact, to help take care of French refugees and children. The convent is understaffed and she is placing her life in jeopardy to go.

Elinore stared at him and her eyes grew larger. "I believe you're in love with her,'' she whispered.

He didn't move. Was he in love with the beautiful nun? Maybe he was . . . He watched Elinore for a moment. Neither of them spoke. There had been a time when he found her attractive. God, how could he have been so blind?

"Philip?" Elinore was vexed. "I asked you, when is Sister Catherine going to leave?"

"This week some time. I'm worried about her. It's suicide to go over there right now."

"I thought we all agreed that she had supernatural aid. Surely she'd be able to perform a miracle for herself." It was then that Philip began to see things for what they were. He'd wondered on and off if Elinore's feelings for Jeff were strictly platonic. Now there could be no mistaking her jealousy. It didn't really surprise him, and it didn't matter any more.

"That's enough, Elinore. You're very boring this evening."

She got up. "Well, I guess that's all, Philip. If you need to get in touch with me, you have the exchange of my solicitor." She opened the door and walked out. "Goodbye, Philip."

She was gone and Philip went to the kitchen, rummaging for something to eat, but nothing appealed to him. He wasn't capable of concentrating on anything this evening. His mind was conjuring up all kinds of dangerous situations in which Catherine might become involved. While he poured himself a cup of tea, Michael came bouncing into the kitchen, hair still damp from his bath.

"May I stay up, Uncle Phil? I want to talk to Daddy."

"He might not be able to phone, Michael, but you may sit with me for a while longer, just in case."

Michael bit into an apple and occupied himself with his hand puppet on the living room floor. When the phone rang, the boy had the receiver off the hook before the second ring. Philip rushed to his side.

"Hello . . . Daddy?" the blue eyes were bright with

anticipation. Jeffrey was surprised at the quick response.

"Hello, tiger. Have you been waiting right by the phone?"

"Yes . . . and guess what?" He sounded terribly excited, out of breath even. He'd been with Catherine, Jeffrey thought. That had to account for his jubilance.

"What is it, son? Did you see Sister Catherine?"

"Yes . . . and do you know what?"

"What?" He gripped the receiver more tightly.

"She's going to be my new mummy!" There was a long pause. Jeffrey wasn't sure he'd heard Michael correctly.

"What did you say?" His heart was pounding.

"Sister is going to come and live with us forever!" Another pause. "Daddy? Aren't you there?" Philip knew what Michael's words meant to Jeff. It had to be the supreme moment in his brother's life.

"Yes, son . . . I'm here," the voice was so choked up, Michael barely recognized it. "What else did she say, tiger?" Michael looked up at his uncle.

"I think Daddy is crying," he whispered. Philip put his arm around the boy's shoulder. Michael spoke into the phone once more. "She said she was going to marry you. Aren't you happy?" he called out in all seriousness.

Jeffrey had pulled out a handkerchief. "Very . . . Michael, put Uncle Phil on, will you, son?"

"Okay," he handed Philip the receiver and went back to playing with his puppet.

"Well, old chap?" Philip began. "I presume the news has made a new man of you?" There was no sound on the other end. He waited. "She's actually done it. She told the Holy Mother everything and has asked for a dispensation. Tomorrow she has an interview with the

190

Bishop. Her exact words were, 'My love for Jeffrey is too strong to be denied. I plan to become his wife.'"

"Thank God," came the low reply. "When will she be free?" Phil could feel his impatience.

"A couple of months."

"I can't believe it. She loves me, Phil! She's going to be my wife!" he shouted, pure joy rang in his voice. There was another pause. "She's told Michael . . . now I know she means it. I don't think I've ever been this happy in my life! Tell me everything. How is she?"

"She's fine, now. Thinner and paler . . . you could tell she's been through hell, Jeff. A nun of her caliber doesn't give up the religious life without a struggle. It was obvious that her life these last few weeks has been utter agony for her."

"Yes . . . I know the feeling."

"Well, old chap . . . she was worth fighting for." Philip had a lump in his throat.

"You don't have to tell me that. Did you read her my letter?"

"I didn't have to. She read it eagerly, and her face lit up when I told her I might be speaking to you tonight."

"Good," was the emotional reply. "I'd give anything if I didn't have to go on this mission right now. I've got plans to make. I'm going to take her away somewhere for a long honeymoon. Lord, I can't believe it . . . Phil, I'm going to ring off now. I've got to speak to her tonight and I don't know how much longer I'll be allowed to use the phone."

"I understand, but—"

"Phil?" Jeffrey broke in before Philip could begin to tell him about her new assignment. "Have I ever told you I rather like my older brother?"

"Yes . . . you have, and I have news. The feeling is mutual." Maybe it was best he heard the bad news from

Catherine. She had a way of expressing herself which would reach him, but Philip's heart was still heavy.

"Jeff . . . go get 'em, old chap."

"Right . . . tell Michael I'll be back soon and the three of us will be a real family."

"I'll tell him. God bless."

Catherine had just gone to the dormitory to prepare for bed when Sister Margaret tugged at her sleeve.

"Yes, Sister?"

"Holy Mother said you were to come to her office, immediately." Catherine bowed and went straight to the office. What could she want at this late hour? The Mother looked up when Catherine came in the room.

"Sister, you are wanted on the telephone." Catherine blinked. It was Jeffrey! She knew it. After Philip had driven away with Michael, she realized how much she wanted to tell Jeffrey the news herself. She experienced more torment, knowing they were both going off to parts unknown, with months of separation still ahead of them. She didn't know if she could bear it. Now she could hear his voice and tell him what was in her heart. The Holy Mother left the room and shut the door. Catherine reached for the receiver.

"Hello? Jeffrey?" she spoke softly.

"Catherine?" came his voice, full of love. "Catherine . . ." Her heart pounded outrageously.

"I love you," she cried. "I want to be your wife. These past weeks have been the most desolate I've ever known . . . but that's all behind me now. I adore you, Jeffrey," she whispered.

"You don't know what those words mean to me. I wish I had you in my arms right now. I'd show you how I feel, my love."

"I know. I feel the same way. I didn't know it was possible to love anyone as I love you. I surprised myself. Perhaps it is better that I can't see you just yet," she laughed in a low, husky voice. "I'd never let you out of my sight and you would grow tired of me."

It was difficult to believe that she was speaking to him this way. He was insanely happy. "Never," his voice shook. "I love you," he spoke with deliberation. "As soon as I can get back from this mission, I'll drive out to Castle Combe for you. Phil said your dispensation would be final in two months."

There was silence. Catherine realized his brother had said nothing about her plans to travel to Spain. She would have to choose her words carefully.

"Darling?" she said softly.

"Yes?"

"It is true that I should receive the dispensation in two months, but I may not be at Our Lord of the Lamb upon your return. If I'm free to come to you before you're back, I'll go to London and take care of Michael. We'll wait for you together. But . . . I have accepted another assignment until my dispensation is final, and though it is temporary, I don't know the exact date of my return. We will just have to wait and see."

Jeffrey listened very carefully and was instantly troubled by the hesitant tone in her voice. "What is this new assignment?"

"I'm leaving this week to go to another convent to help with some refugees, children mostly, who need food and care. The sisters there are overworked. The Mother General has been recruiting sisters all over Great Britain to give assistance. I have been chosen to go. I want to do this last act of service before leaving the order. It will help me to get through these months of

193

waiting for you. Here at the convent I'm plagued with thoughts of Michael and you. Over there I will be much too busy to think and the days will pass quickly. Then we will be together, forever."

Something was wrong. What did she mean, "over there"? She was talking too fast. He knew his darling Catherine too well, and a prickle of fear darted through him. "I wish we didn't have to wait for anything," came his low reply, "but you haven't told me where you are going. Where is 'over there'?" He was growing more nervous by the second. The perspiration broke out on his forehead.

She didn't know how to tell him. After Philip's reaction, she was almost frightened to say more.

"Catherine?" he prodded. Still, nothing.

"It's a mercy mission, Jeffrey. They need sisters who are young enough to—to withstand the journey, and my French background will be of tremendous help."

He had to bite his lip to keep from losing control. "Where are you going, my love?" he asked as calmly as he could.

"To Spain . . ."

This time it was his turn to be tongue-tied . . . speechless was a better word.

"Jeffrey, it's our sister priory in the Pyrenees. Saint Theresa's, near the French-Spanish border, high in the mountains. Please don't worry. I'll be safe. The Holy Father would never ask us to go if it weren't God's will, and I will be traveling to the convent with the Mother General and the other sisters who have elected to go."

"I don't believe it!" he muttered. Perhaps he would wake up to find this whole night a dream. "You can't go, Catherine! I won't let you! We're at war with Spain, unofficially. You don't know . . . you don't realize how dangerous it would be to go there now. The Nazis are

194

everywhere. What could the Church be thinking of?" His voice was really angry. Catherine was crying.

"Jeffrey . . . listen to me. The Mother General travels under the sacred seal and protection of the Papacy . . . her documents are honored in all countries. We will leave from Southampton and sail to Lisbon. Then we will take a train into Spain. It will be all right. Believe me," she implored.

It was the first time in his military career that he was tempted to break regulations and tell her about his intelligence mission to Spain, if only to warn her of the perils involved. Lord, she'd be going to the very area he was being sent to do reconnaissance! He put his head in his hands, trying to think. All it would take was one U-boat in the Atlantic, and she'd never make it to Portugal. Perhaps what she said about the protection of the Vatican was true, but getting to the Pyrenees was going to prove hazardous at best. In a few months she'd be his wife. It was bad enough knowing he had to leave her, but now . . . she'd be in a country torn apart by civil and world war. He'd never have a moment's peace.

"Jeffrey . . . I love you. Don't worry, darling. I know what you are thinking, but you must have no fear . . . not for me."

When he answered, his voice was so full of emotion, she did not recognize it. "I don't have your deep faith. I've been in hell these last weeks thinking I'd lost you. Now, when you've just told me what I've prayed to hear, I find you're leaving the safety of Castle Combe to go into the midst of war where I could really lose you. Catherine," he cried in pain, "don't go! Let someone else travel in your place. Only two more months . . . please . . ."

"Jeffrey . . . I'm needed. I can't refuse. You are

leaving to go on a dangerous mission as well. Don't you think I'd like to beg you to stay in London where I'd know you were relatively safe with Michael? You can't imagine what I'm feeling right now, knowing you're going so far away.''

"Catherine, it's different with me. I have to go! It's not the same thing at all,'' he stormed.

"I have to go, too. This is my chance to serve. I, too, want to feel that I'm doing my part for God and for England. Can't you understand that? The Lord says that he who loses his life for my sake shall find it. We'll find our lives, darling. We'll be together. I promise you. We will be married. Will you remember that?''

"Don't let anything happen to you, Catherine. For our sake, be careful. If something happened, I'm afraid I'd feel exactly like Michael. I wouldn't want to go on living.''

"Nothing is going to happen to me . . . to either one of us. We'll be together again. Do you believe me?''

"I'm going to have to,'' he answered so quietly she scarcely heard him. "You've never thought about yourself in your whole life. I guess that's part of why I love you so much. I'm depending on God to take care of you till I can do it myself. I'll pray for you every minute of the day and night, as it says on the plaque in the Holy Mother's office.''

Catherine could see the maxim in front of her. His words burned deeply inside her. "I will do the same, darling, till we can hold each other again.''

"No goodbyes . . .''

"No . . . I love you.''

"And I worship the very ground you walk on,'' came the tender response. "Till two months from now, Catherine.''

"Yes . . .'' and the phone clicked off.

Catherine put down the receiver and sank to her knees, too weak to stand. She was glad to be leaving Castle Combe now. The sooner the better. If she were to stay here and have time to think, she'd go mad.

Jeffrey hung up the receiver and bowed his head. He was remembering something his father had told him in his youth. "Faith can move mountains." Jeffrey didn't understand at the time . . . now he wanted to believe that faith was all-powerful, because Catherine was going to be his wife and her life had to be spared to that end. He found himself wondering what he'd ever done in his life to deserve such a blessing.

They'd work together and travel. They'd have other babies for her to love and raise as only she could. Perhaps she could teach at a school in Mayfair. There would be no more loneliness. When they went to Norwood on weekends, she'd play the piano and he'd sketch. There would be more picnics with Michael . . . hours to go riding into the countryside . . . swimming in the ocean . . . they'd go to the theater, concerts . . . he'd take her up in an airplane . . . and he'd have the rest of his life to make love to her, over and over again. Lord, when he really allowed himself to think, to really think of touching her, of lying next to her on cold winter nights, or warm summer mornings, before anyone else was about . . .

The young man at the communications desk had been watching the Commander for a solid ten minutes since he'd rung off, and he wondered what could possibly be causing that look of elation on his face. Something was brewing. Suddenly, the Commander dashed out of the room, and again the boy was astonished at the strange behavior.

Jeffrey went immediately to the conference room to find General Gort. If anyone knew anything about the transportation of VIP's to the war zone, he did . . . but to his disappointment, the meeting had ajourned and everyone had gone. He couldn't break radio silence once they left England to make any inquiries. At least he could find out the location of this convent in the Pyrenees. The statistics room would have books and maps. He headed in that direction. There were men busy filling out reports as he entered the room. One of them looked up. "Commander? Can we help you with something?"

"Yes. How would I go about finding the location of a Benedictine convent in the Pyrenees, Spanish side?"

"Well, we have books which list all public and private buildings in each country. It might be in one of those. Then we could locate it on a map."

"Good. Could I see the one of Spain?"

"Just a moment, sir," and he went over to a wall which held hundreds of important books and sources which needed to be at Air Command's finger tips. He pulled a fat book from the shelf. "Let's see," he began searching, running his fingers down each page. "What's the name?"

"Saint Theresa's."

The man continued the search. "I don't see it listed, Commander." Jeffrey's brow furrowed. "Look under priories."

"Right, sir," and he began again. "There it is, sir." Jeffrey took the book.

"Do you have the map?"

"Yes . . . it will take me a minute to find it." He went over to a rack from which hung dozens of maps. He filed through them till the portion on the Pyrenees came into view. He pulled it from the holder and laid it out on the desk. Jeffrey immediately began the search.

"Here it is, Commander. The map doesn't show the

name of the convent, but that would be the location. It looks like a town called 'Monte Jaizquibel,' whatever that means.''

"It's obviously a Basque name," Jeffrey muttered. It was a start, but he had to know more. "We wouldn't have anything on the Pyrenees, would we? Old travel brochures or such?"

"Afraid not, but the library in Maidstone isn't far from here and it's still open. It might have what you're looking for."

"Right, but I can't leave headquarters," he answered, defeated.

"I'll be off duty in a quarter of an hour. Can I look something up for you? I could pick up some books I've been wanting to read at the same time."

Jeffrey smiled. "I'm very much obliged."

"What exactly do you want me to look for?"

"A book describing that region . . . how close it is to the French border . . . anything." When he'd done the necessary reconnaissance work, he'd be able to write his own book on the area.

"Very good, Commander. I'll see what I can find."

"Thanks . . . you don't know how much I appreciate this. It's very important to me."

"Right, sir!"

Jeffrey left and went back to quarters. He lay on the bed with his hands behind his head and allowed himself to be bombarded with alternate thoughts of Catherine, and the mission he would begin in the morning. It struck him for the first time what an amazing coincidence it was that she was being sent to the Pyrenees, and his mission would be over those very mountains. She'd be so close, yet so far. If anything happened to her . . .

His mind gave way to thoughts of her once more. He'd never seen her in anything but her habit. Unconsciously he began undraping her body. For a fraction of a moment, he let his desires run rampant, then got to his feet. He could stand no more. There were reports which he needed to commit to memory before 0400. He forced himself to his desk, and an hour later there was a knock. He sprang to his feet.

"Commander? There wasn't much. This was the best I could do." Jeffrey looked at the thin book. "*A Wayfarer in the Pyrenees*. Thank you very much. It was decent of you. I'll try to think of some way to repay you."

"That's all right, sir. Good night."

"Good night." Jeffrey went over to the bed and began devouring the information. The book described the Pyrenees from a traveller's point of view. He began filing away pertinent facts which would be of value at a later date. He became engrossed in the account of one man's adventures in those magnificent mountains. It was a very beautiful area of the world. If there weren't a war on, he'd like to take Catherine there for a holiday. The index did not tell anything about Monte Jaizquibel. Maybe he would come across it as he read. He started with Biarritz, Bayonne and the French Basque coast . . . an hour later he came to a section on the fourth of the Spanish provinces, Guipuzcoa. It began with a description of San Sebastian, its capital. He read on and delighted in the description of Fuenterrabia, an ancient city and fortress during the time of Francis the First. The name recalled to mind Michael's little spaniel. He smiled, then his attention was drawn to the words, "hostal de Jaizquibel." It began, "by road, take the route of the Irun end of Fuenterrabia—it leads you around the outside of the city walls, past the bull ring, and then climbs steeply through rolling country that offers superb views of the mountains and the valley below. It climbs into a terrain of fir and pine, leaving behind the oaks and beech trees . . . after three miles, a turn to the left leads to the sanctuary of Nuestra Señora de Theresa, whose kindness to the victims of the siege of pirates during the reign of Philip I, in 1598, contributed to their survival. The priory is absolutely isolated and magnificently situated on top of the highest cliff overlooking the Atlantic. From its ancient courtyard can be seen a view of Irun, Fuenterabia, Hendaye, the Pyrenees, and along the French coast as far as Les Landes. Superb in their majesty, steep green hills rush headlong to the sea below . . . a series of rock headlands thrust out into the ocean.'' Jeffrey could imagine Catherine's ecstasy when she arrived there. It was her kind of setting . . . and his. The more he thought about it, the more he wished they could honeymoon there. Damn the war! He read on. ''There are patches of darker pine against the softer green of the precipitous meadows, and an occasional solitary white farmhouse glimpsed in the valleys or clinging dizzily to a peak. The country glows with a hundred shades of green and gold and russet . . . and always there are the Pyrenees and the ocean to enchant the eye.''

Jeffrey's eyes held a far-away look as he allowed himself to dream of the two of them alone, in that white farmhouse on the peak. He could have her all to himself. What heaven that would be! Jeffrey closed the book. To think the Nazis now had a stronghold in that beautiful paradise . . . it was beyond comprehension. He prayed the priory was just as isolated as when the book was written back in '28, but he knew better. There were Germans everywhere . . . and who knew what went on in the minds of those goose-stepping Huns? He got ready for bed and turned out the light. Then he sank to his knees to pray for Catherine's safety till he could hold her to him for good.

It was a Monday afternoon in June of 1941. Elinore Norwood was walking down a street in Mayfair, smartly dressed in a gray suit and hat. Her flat was not far from the house where Philip lived with Michael, but she had no intention of paying her ex-husband a visit . . . now, or any other time. There was a fairly new and posh tea salon which had just recently been established in the area. It catered to a better class of people than the salons of Soho. She found the address and went inside. The place was swarming with politicians, scientists, writers, actors, senior officers of the RAF. She went to a corner table and waited.

For two weeks now she had been frequenting the salon in hopes of running into Dirk. It was dangerous to meet out in the open this way. Not at all procedure for two agents of the same category, but she had no other choice. The GRU preferred to have their meetings in parks, on deserted benches, but for once, she had run onto something of importance and decided to break tradition. Once Dirk knew of the details, she might be spared the humiliation of being sent to Germany for a job less worthy of her. What she had to tell could not wait to be put in the mail drop and sent through usual channels to Abwer headquarters in Berlin. It would take too long. No, this was vital.

She'd thought the matter over very carefully. For the last six years, she had never been able to come up with anything of much significance. Jeffrey Norwood knew how to keep his secrets. Month after month, year after year, he never made a slip . . . it had looked all but hopeless that her entry into the household would ever bear fruit . . . until now. Only once, in all that time, had he finally made a mistake. She couldn't give Dirk proof.

He would have to take her word for it. But since this was the first time she'd sought him out, he'd have to realize it was important. She was counting on her past record to convince him that this time, it was worth the risk of a daylight meeting.

She ordered tea and lit a cigarette. Smoke was thick in the room. She recognized two of Philip's colleagues. They came to her table and asked about her health . . . the usual inane pleasantries, then left. Philip obviously hadn't told anyone about the divorce. He was like that. No fanfare, no emotion. God, she was glad to be out of it! Soon she'd go back to South Africa. Dirk could arrange it. There was a time when she was certain something would happen between her and Jeff, but no longer. If he had loved her, she would have given up her affiliation with the Secret Service. It had become routine and she often felt the strategems naïve . . . besides, she'd never been able to produce any worthwhile evidence until now. This time she might be able to contribute something of note, and Elinore was determined that Jeffrey and his saintly nun would pay a price! She could go to Capetown with that much satisfaction, at least!

Finally Dirk made his appearance. At forty-five, he was still attractive. He came from a patrician Hanseatic family and had been well educated. He was acknowledged a master in espionage circles. He'd had his day in the hot spots of Europe and South America. Then orders from Berlin set him up as leader of the Abwer in England. Settling first in Scotland, then London, he travelled under a Danish passport and organized the system. It was one of his agents from Capetown who had forwarded Elinore's name to London. Elinore Pook, formerly of Hanover . . . active in the Nazi youth corps, both in Germany and South Africa. Shrewd . . .

competent.

Dirk approached her, offered her the job after finding out she was the wife of a barrister who sat in the House and was sister-in-law to a pilot in the Coastal Command. She was in a very pretty situation. It might prove interesting. What did she have to lose? Elinore agreed.

Dirk saw Elinore and his eyes narrowed. He walked over to her table. "Hello, darling," he greeted her, with a kiss on the cheek. "This is highly unusual, to say the least." The hazel eyes were not smiling.

"Hello, Dirk." She felt panic, but her exterior betrayed nothing but cold, calculating determination. "I think I have something." Her large eyes focused intently on him.

"All right . . . Knightsbridge, South West 7, Philip's Road, Flat 3. Come after ten. Nice to see you again, my dear," and he went back to the bar, patting the hips of the hostess as he walked by.

At ten-fifteen, Elinore was ushered into a flat which served as one of the rendez-vous points for agents of the Abwer. It was the first time she'd been inside. There were five workers present, two of them women. No one spoke to her. Dirk motioned her into the living room and shut the double doors.

"All right. What do you have that has caused me to miss an important meeting this evening?"

She began to feel foolish. If she had misunderstood Jeff's message to Sister Catherine, it was all over. "You've wanted information about Commander Norwood, his whereabouts and secret missions for a long time. Two weeks ago he left on another mission, but this time, I know how we can find out where he was going, and I'm positive that the source I have in mind will give us details of his meetings involving Lord Wyngate and the Prime Minister! But I have to bring you up to date on

204

a few facts first. Then you'll see why I felt this could not wait to go through channels."

"Go on . . . I'm listening." He puffed on his cigar, his trademark to all those who knew him.

"As you know, Commander Norwood lost his wife last year, and then the boy got sick and was sent to a convent in Wiltshire. One of the sisters there nursed the boy back to health. Her name was Sister Catherine."

"Ja . . . Ja . . . so . . . get on with it. I've read most of that in your report," he prodded.

"The boy recovered, then became ill again when he returned to Norwood. His father sent for this same Sister because he thought she could help him again."

"Und?" his eyes glared.

"He regained his health, and for some time, this nun has been in Commander Norwood's company, day and night. They've fallen deeply in love."

Dirk slapped his leg and flicked his cigar. "Why are you telling me this idiotic love story? I have better things to do."

"I haven't finished," Elinore retorted. "She returned to the convent and he left to go on a secret mission."

"So, what is the point?"

"Dirk, do you want to hear this? Be patient."

"All right . . . go on."

"It's true that I don't know where he went, but the Sister does!" She watched him purse his lips. He put down his cigar.

"How would you know this?"

"Because she hadn't been out of his sight, day or night. She's lived under the same roof with him, having breakfast, lunch and dinner. One evening, two weeks ago, he'd been in meetings with Lord Harley and Lord Wyngate and then was with her for days after. I know this latest mission is a very important one. The signs have been building for weeks. He's had important calls . . . it is something big.''

"Ja . . . so, how do you think this Sister knows so much?''

"I'm coming to that. After she went back to the convent, he moved back into London with the boy. Philip, my husband, is there now, living with them, and recently he took the boy out to the convent to visit the Sister. I was at the house when they returned and I found something. Commander Norwood had written her a letter which Philip was to deliver. In it he said, "The things we talked about on the day of the picnic have come to pass. This new assignment may take months instead of days to accomplish. This will be my last chance to communicate with you.''

"So?'' he shrugged his shoulders. Elinore was exasperated.

"It means that he revealed to her the facts about this new mission. I'd stake my life on it. You can't tell me he hasn't confided in her. He trusts her, Dirk. When Michael was in the hospital, Commander Norwood barely put in an appearance at the house. He would have had to conduct business from the hospital . . . she would have been in on it. I know for a certainty that there isn't anything he wouldn't discuss or talk about with her.''

"What makes you think he'd tell her anything top secret when you haven't been able to discover one leak in all these years? I thought he trusted you completely.''

"He does trust me, but he loves her, and he was desperate not to lose her. I think he told her things to win her sympathy. You know, a little leverage . . . he wants her to leave the convent so he can marry her.''

Dirk was pensive. "Is she a postulant?"

"No . . . she has taken her vows. She's professed."

"And the love affair has gone that far?" he asked in surprise.

"Far enough that she is being sent to another convent. My guess is that she is being punished for breaking her vows and is on the verge of leaving the sisterhood. There's no question that she's in love with him. In his letter he said he intended to make her his wife. He's a very persuasive man. She won't be able to resist him."

"So . . . the Commander is as relentless in matters of love as war, eh?" he chuckled. Elinore paled.

"Does that distress you? I see that it does." He cleared his throat. "All right . . . suppose your theory is correct. Suppose she knows details which could be useful to headquarters. I must have proof. Did you bring the letter with you?"

"No . . . it's in Philip's possession and we are separated. I'm no longer welcome in his house."

"I know nothing of this," he raised his eyebrows.

"It was in my last report. You probably haven't had time to look at it. The only reason I married Philip in the first place was for security. I arrived in London with nothing . . . there is no love lost between us. Dirk, if I were to try to get that letter, he'd suspect something. As it was, he caught me reading it. I told him I thought it was a legal paper, and he bought it, I think. He was upset, but not for the reasons you're thinking. I'm positive he's in love with Sister Catherine as well, and has become very protective of her as well as his brother."

Dirk began walking about the room. "Then all I have is your intuition to go on."

"Yes . . . but I've never bothered you before. Believe me, I know what I'm talking about."

"All right . . . tell me more about this nun."

"She's young, maybe twenty, twenty-one. Beautiful, very loyal to England . . . talented, devoted to his son."

Dirk laughed. "She sounds too good to be true!"

"Jeffrey Norwood thinks so," she said bitterly.

"It couldn't be you have a personal vendetta against the nun, eh? All right, Elinore. You say she's back at the convent?"

"I'm not sure now. She was leaving for the other one soon."

"I don't know how we could get to her . . ." The wheels were beginning to turn inside Dirk's head and Elinore relaxed. He was starting to take her seriously.

"That part is easy, Dirk. The S.S. should have no trouble."

He blinked. "Go on."

"She's leaving to fulfill this penance in the Spanish Pyrenees. She'll be there for some time, according to Philip. We have German intelligence agents in Barcelona and Madrid. It shouldn't be too difficult to seek her out for interrogation, once she is away from England, from protection, if you follow me. She must be there by now. It's been two weeks since I read the letter."

"Ja . . ." he sounded far away. "What's the name of the convent?"

"Saint Teresa's . . . I presume it's in an isolated mountain region. She loves him, Dirk. If you were to apply the right kind of pressure, she'd talk. She's faithful to her principles. If any of her vows were put in jeopardy, she'd tell all rather than face God's punishment. I don't need to paint a picture, do I?"

"No . . . You know, Elinore? You make me think women can be more ruthless than men when it comes right down to it." Elinore stiffened. "I hope you're right about this, Elinore."

"What does that mean?"

"Berlin frowns on mistakes and the Fascists are not on the best terms with the Vatican. We'll have to handle this very carefully. There must be no embarrassment for us."

"I'm not wrong, Dirk. And when you have the information, you can thank me by sending me back to South Africa. I have friends there and I want to leave England."

"Why? There are many other spots in London where I could use someone like you."

"No. My marriage to Philip is finished. I've done what I can. I have no desire to stay here any longer. Now is a good time to go."

"Tell me something, Elinore. Why did you come to London at all?"

"I had a chance for a position with a secretarial agency. After Father died, I had no reason to stay on in Capetown. It was his idea to leave Germany in the first place, not mine . . . but once we left, I had to do something with my life."

"What about going back to Germany?"

"Not interested. I've grown accustomed to a few comforts, Dirk. Father was not looked upon with favor. I don't relish the thought of having to prove my loyalty in my own country. No . . . Capetown suits me fine."

"All right. If your lead is fruitful, I'll help you get back there. If not, I can do nothing. You will have to accept the consequences."

"I understand."

"Now . . . give me a complete description. I want to know everything there is to know about this Sister . . . any weaknesses . . . family background, education . . . I want to hear it all. Then I'll send it on to Berlin. It is going to take several weeks just to do the ground work . . ."

XII

Southampton was a dingy port town bustling with soldiers, ships and lorries. Catherine felt she had stepped into the heart of the war. Castle Combe was light years away. She stepped off the train to be greeted by the smiling face of the Mother General, an Italian woman of tiny proportions. She had an olive complexion and black eyes, small as raisins. There were five nuns beneath the parapet with her.

"Sister," the Mother General waved her hand. "I am so happy to meet you. God bless you for coming to the aid of your sisters in Spain. Sister Catherine, meet Sister Margareta from Edinburgh, Sister Luke from Leicester, Sister Maria from Wales, Sister Luisa from Shannon, and Sister Angelina from London."

Each inclined her head in greeting. Sister Angelina was no older than Catherine. Catherine bowed to each of them . . .

"We are going to sail to Lisbon by aircraft carrier. The captain has given us a room which is normally occupied by one of his officers. It will be our sanctuary for the next few days. I hope you won't suffer from the *mal de mer*. I have only experienced it once. Even during the war, it is the only discomfort I have had. I trust our Heavenly Father to guide us safely to our destination."

"Yes, Mother," they bowed.

Catherine had had no appetite since she had spoken to Jeffrey. At the Mother General's words, she felt seasick already. They drove to the dock in an old car. There were hundreds of men in uniform and everyone was busy. There were lorries with supplies, jeeps, tanks, ammunition in great piles ready to load. Catherine cringed at the sight of the instruments of war. The carrier was enormous. She felt a sinking feeling in her stomach. The smell of the sea and dead fish wafted past her nostrils. She knew she was going to be sick.

"This way, Sisters," and the Mother General hustled them into a crudely constructed building at the entrance gate. There were signs indicating only authorized personnel were able to pass beyond this point. They went inside the building and waited while the little woman produced many papers and documents. After some time they were cleared to board.

"Sister?" an officer opened the door. "We'll take you alongside in the jeep," and they followed him out. Catherine climbed into the back and sat on the edge, wedged between two sisters. The jeep took off and wound around the docks till it stopped in front of one of the gangplanks of the great carrier.

There was no canopy for the gang plank, and just the idea of having to traverse it put fear into each Sister. However, the men with duffle bags seemed to manage it with ease.

"Come along, Sisters." The Mother General started up the long wooden ramp which rose almost another story into the hold of the ship. Catherine placed her feet carefully and held on to the thin rope which served as a handrail. If she looked down, she felt dizzy. The water was a long way below. She kept her eyes straight ahead and managed to walk up and into the heart of the ship. Her heart was pounding so hard, she thought she would

211

faint, but soon it was over and they were shown to their quarters which were already hot and cramped. To think humans had to put up with such conditions for months on end! She felt increased compassion for all fighting men, whoever they were.

When Catherine's father died, she and her mother and brother had crossed the Channel to England on a ferry. It took the whole night, but then they could eat a meal and sit on deck chairs, and the crossing was gentle. The circumstances now were anything but pleasant or reassuring.

They were confined to their room for the remainder of the afternoon, and after several hours, they felt the movement of the ship as it began to inch its way out into the channel. The huge engines vibrated and the smell of disinfectant continued to nauseate Catherine. There was no port hole, only a small pipe which conducted air. Catherine felt claustrophobic and wished she could leave the room. They would all sleep in here together. There were six bunks and a cot. The bathroom facilities were in the adjoining room. The Holy Mother suggested a period of meditation, after which she would tell them more about this new and challenging assignment.

Catherine closed her eyes as she sat on the bunk. Several hours passed and her stomach churned more the farther out into the ocean they went. Finally, she could sit still no longer and ran into the bathroom, shutting the door. After retching, she emerged and two more sisters dashed inside. The movement was unpredictable. Just when she thought the ship should go up, it would swing sideways and her insides would lurch all over again. She hung on to the bunk with her hands and prayed that she would survive the next two days.

There was a galley for the officers, but none of the sisters was up to eating that first dinner. Catherine lay down on her bunk and continued to feel ill and queazy for the next twelve hours.

The next day she wasn't feeling much better, but there was nothing left in her stomach to lose. The Mother General, chipper as ever, began to tell them about conditions at Saint Theresa's and what they would be expected to do there. Catherine sat up and tried to pay attention. Besides refugees, Spanish Republicans were also being sheltered, and dysentery was a major problem. There was little milk and food was scarce. They would have to be frugal with money used to purchase supplies. All in all, the outlook was bleak. But Rome would be sending help in six to eight weeks.

Catherine caught bits and pieces of the explanations, but she was too sick to concentrate. Poor Sister Angelina hadn't moved her head from the pillow yet. Her face was absolutely green.

After a day and a half out at sea, however, the ocean began to grow calm. The swells were less mountainous, and Catherine was beginning to feel better. The Mother General suggested they take a walk on deck and take the air, but only three sisters, Catherine and two others, were up to it. They walked down a narrow corridor on unsteady legs, hugging the walls, and climbed the stairs to the next deck. When Catherine felt fresh air coming through the door which led to the flight deck, she drank it in and filled her lungs with the life-giving breeze. The sea was dark green, almost black, and clouds hovered close to the water. It was impossible to distinguish the horizon. One officer, short and blond, was on hand to greet them and show them about. There were many men doing their chores and the sight of the nuns on board caused quite a stir, for there were furtive glances from all the crew as the sisters moved about.

"I'm Officer Reginald, Sisters. The captain has asked

213

me to be your guide for the journey." The young man seemed to enjoy the added duty. It probably helped to take his mind off the danger lurking beneath the waters or behind the clouds. The sisters bowed to him. "What would you like to see? The planes, perhaps? We're delivering some to the Mediterranean." Catherine's face brightened. She turned to the sisters, but the other two did not feel up to it and declined the invitation. They went back to the room in a hurry, but Catherine couldn't resist this opportunity to get closer to Jeffrey. Being here brought him back to her.

"I'd be very much obliged if you would show me about," she replied to the officer.

"It would be a pleasure, Sister," he said briskly. "Follow me."

They walked to one end of the carrier. As they passed various crewmen, smiles appeared spontaneously on the men's faces. Catherine flushed from all the attention. The officer turned to her.

"Don't mind the men, Sister. They're not used to seeing such a pretty face on board this monster. We have to be content to look at each other most of the time, and the scenery isn't quite up to specifications, if you know what I mean," he winked. She smiled in spite of herself and lowered her head. She liked him and wondered how the men could seem so cheerful beneath the pall of war.

Finally they came to the area where the planes were lined up, wing to wing. She recognized them immediately. "These are Hudsons," she exclaimed. Jeffrey's drawings were exactly like them. With a flash of pain, she remembered those wonderful days they spent together with Michael. When he was asleep, she would watch him sketch and they would talk for hours . . .

"You're right, Sister," he replied in astonishment.

214

"How did you know that?"

"I've seen drawings, Officer Reginald." They proceeded down the row. "These aren't as big as the Sunderlands," she murmured. "I remember now . . ."

"No . . . these seat a crew of four . . . the Sunderland—"

"Seats a crew of seven," she finished his explanation.

"Right, Sister," he said, eyeing her almost suspiciously. "I have the feeling you know as much about airplanes as I do."

"No . . ." she blushed. "I've had an expert explaining various things to me. It fascinates me, that's all." She went over to inspect the low-wing monoplane. "What would be the reason for needing this type of craft as opposed to the Sunderland?"

"Well, the Hudson is not as manoeuverable in the air as a Sunderland, but it can take an extraordinary amount of punishment from anti-aircraft and enemy fighters. It's a real tough plane. I'd rather be in this if I had a Jerry on my tail." Catherine straightened up and her face sobered. She mustn't allow herself to think of Jeffrey out in one of these. She couldn't stand it.

"If you're ready, we can go out on the flight deck, Sister." She nodded, but he noticed that a shadow had crossed over her lovely face.

The wind was fierce, whipping Catherine's habit about her as they walked out on to the broad expanse of deck. It exhilarated her. The mighty ocean had a calming effect on her, and slowly the fear began to leave her. Portugal was closer now. They should be there in the morning. She had to admit she was excited to be traveling to another country, to be doing something new. She had always had an adventuresome spirit when she was young. Now, after knowing Jeffrey, she wanted to see and feel and experience everything. Her nausea was abating and she began to see this mission through new eyes. Time would fly now. It would make their separation easier to bear. She was glad the Holy Mother had selected her for this assignment. She was anxious to pitch in and be of some use until she was free to take on her responsibilities as mother and wife to the little boy and man she adored.

The tour was over and she went below deck, thanking the officer for his kindness. He stared after the beautiful nun and shook his head. "What an appalling waste!"

Catherine was actually hungry when she sat down to the evening meal. The walk on deck had rejuvenated her appetite as well as her spirit. She retired early and let the ship lull her to sleep with its regular rhythm. Her prayers were long and fervent. First and foremost was the hope that Jeffrey was safe and that Michael was well.

Morning came and the Mother General was once again giving instructions:

"Sisters, we are outside the port of Lisbon, but we will go in on a tender. Don't be frightened. I've done it dozens of times. It may be a little rocky, but I assure you it is very safe."

The sisters had learned through sad experience that the Mother General was somewhat inclined to under-emphasize discomfort and danger. So far, all of them had had difficulties, and it was with trepidation that they followed her to the hold of the ship. A metal door was opened from the top and a bridge suspended from the doorway over the water into a wooden boat which bobbed up and down like a cork. The wind was still strong enough to form whitecaps. When it was Catherine's turn, she gingerly placed a foot on the bridge and held on for dear life. Officer Reginald offered his hand in assistance, but she was thrown forward, out of his grasp, and fell into the tender. She laughed softly at her clumsiness, and the ability to laugh at herself brought smiles to the faces of the other sisters as well as the crewmen. It seemed to dispel the tension and fear which always lay beneath the surface. She righted herself, and when everyone was seated, the motor revved up and the tender pulled away from the giant carrier toward the land in the distance.

The sky was the color of pitch and the gulls which called from the distance stood out like white chalk marks on a new blackboard. It took forty minutes for the tender to maneuver itself to the buoys and finally into the harbor. There were fishing boats and large trawlers off shore. Some of the men on the little boats were hauling in their nets and stopped to wave and smile at this strange company of nuns who seemed to come out of nowhere. The carrier was already receding into the distance. Catherine's heart lurched again. It was on its way to the Gibraltar Straits and Jeffrey.

The tender rode up and down on the waves with an occasional sudden dip which took everyone's breath. Once they were inside the safety of the bay, the water became as glass and the tender shot ahead quickly toward the dock. There were sailors waiting to tie up the craft as it pulled into a slip. Hands reached out to help the sisters up the wooden ladder to the cement walkway. Catherine put her feet on land and sighed with relief. The first leg of the journey was over and so far, they were safe. But the motion of moving up and down was still upon her. She started to take a step and found herself falling forward. One of the sailors caught her arm.

"Be careful . . . the sea is still with you," he laughed aloud, several teeth missing in his grin. Catherine smiled back and tried to keep herself upright. Several of the other sisters were having the same problem.

"Sisters, soon that sensation will leave you. Walk slowly and take a deep breath."

"Yes, Mother," they sighed and began walking, trying to keep up with the spry Mother General. Their loss of equilibrium began to dissipate. Catherine turned for one last look at the carrier, but it was a mere speck, almost out of sight, and she heaved a deep sigh.

"Come, we must find a taxi and get to the station. There isn't a moment to lose. It will take two days to reach the priory, and knowing the Spanish, it could take much longer. They only run the trains three days a week because of the lack of coal," said the Mother General cheerfully. The sisters rolled their eyes Heavenward and prepared to follow. Two hours later they were on a train, headed north. The supplies brought along by the Holy Mother were piled high in the entrance of their car. Catherine was worn out and rested her head against the uncomfortable seat of the train, which was packed to overflowing with men, women and children. The smell of unwashed bodies was thick in the air, and it was warm. Her habit was sticking to her arms and legs. Everything was damp from being at sea. She longed to bathe in cool water.

It was evening when the train reached the Spanish border, and it was there they saw the first German soldiers of the trip. There were half a dozen of them at the lonely frontier station of Braganca where the nuns deborded. The sisters would have to wait an hour or so for the other train which would take them to Palencia, Burgos, and finally Bilbao. From there they would go by bus to the sanctuary in the mountains.

They sat in the station house and waited while the Mother General went through the tedious process of explaining their business and producing the proper documents and visas. The supplies were brought inside on a cart. The two German officers, boots gleaming and impeccably uniformed, were both tall and young and blond, looking remarkably healthy in comparison to the Latins. One began inspecting the supplies while the other walked over to the sisters and called each one by name, to make sure of the count. His eyes fastened on Catherine and he appraised her outrageously, before returning to the desk. She lowered her head and fidgeted with her rosary. Everything appeared to be in order, and the Mother General took her place among the sisters as casually as if she had just returned from market. The officers stayed in the room and both of them leaned against the wall and continued to stare at Catherine from time to time till the train pulled into the station. The nuns quickly boarded, anxious to be away from the soldiers. There were no incidents, to Catherine's relief, but as she stepped into the corridor, the officer of arrogant demeanor called to her, "Good journey," and saluted with a smile. She hastened inside, blushing.

The interior was worse than that of the Portuguese train. It was filthy. The smell of spoiled food and urine produced a nauseating stench. The remains of food littered the aisles, dirty children and peasants crowded the seats so there was barely room to stand or sit. To Catherine's horror, she saw ravenous toddlers putting the garbage they found on the floor in their mouths. Her eyes wandered from one person to the next, repulsed at the condition of their persons and their clothes. It was shocking to see such poverty. It sickened her. Her tender heart was wounded. For several hours, she was forced to stand in the aisles, hanging on to the railing above. When the train pulled into Palencia, many of the passengers got off. She wondered where they were going, what would happen to them . . . It was growing hotter and perspiration soaked her garments. Window panes were missing, yet the air was muggy and close. They rode on in silence, the train slowing down time and time again; once it was for cattle stranded on the tracks, another time there was an engine breakdown which it took three hours to repair, and the flies buzzing about Catherine's face drove her to distraction. She noticed bugs crawling on a child's arm and recoiled. She was certain they would never reach the Pyrenees.

Evening came and the Mother General broke off a portion of bread for each sister. Catherine discovered hungry eyes fastened upon her as she started to put a piece in her mouth. A mother with two youngsters was seated across the aisle, and none of them looked as if they had eaten for days. She took the bread and divided it between the three of them. She wasn't hungry, just thirsty, and there was no water. The children gobbled the bread as though they'd never seen food before and she sighed, wishing she had more to give them. The mother timidly gave Catherine a grateful smile. She bowed and decided to close her eyes and try to sleep. She would think about Michael and Jeffrey, and that would sustain her until they reached the mountains.

Night fell and still the air was sour. They came to Burgos, and welcomed the few minutes they were allowed to get off the train and buy mineral water. The Mother General complained loudly that they were being robbed for having to pay so many pesetas for the precious water, but it could not be helped. Then they were off once more and Catherine slept fitfully the rest of the night.

By noon of the next day, the city of Bilbao came into view and Catherine was encouraged, as were the rest of the sisters, that the long train ride was almost at an end. Bilbao seemed to be one big industrial complex crammed with traffic and humanity. She could see the harbor and the beaches. The sky was still dark, and the view reminded her a great deal of Liverpool and the Mersey river which ran through it. She had been there once on a visit with her mother. To Catherine, both cities looked somewhat the same. The sand on these beaches was a muddy gray, the scene as dreary as the docks of Southampton.

The train pulled into the busy station and once more the group of hungry, exhausted nuns waited in the lobby till a bus pulled up in front of the station. It was antique, and the driver smelled so of garlic and wine that Catherine was positive they'd never make it to Saint Theresa's alive. There were more Germans at the station, but now that the sisters were not in a border town, the sight of them did not cause a stir. They were hustled out of the station and onto the creaky bus along with families and farm workers, a few business men, even a policeman.

The Mother General had said they had an eighty kilometer ride ahead of them. It took four hours to reach the base of the mountains. They had stopped at every town and village along the way, even stopping once in the middle of the road with nothing in sight but fields. But eventually they were paralleling the coast line and Catherine saw that the sand turned a soft yellow color, as they neared the mountains. She noticed a drop in temperature, and the air was softer. Slowly the bus began rattling into the low hills and the sun, which she hadn't seen since leaving Castle Combe, made an appearance from behind the dark clouds, bathing briefly the lushness of the spring grass in golden light. Flocks of sheep covered the hillsides and the slopes were astonishingly green. Now and then, red and white Basque chalets which hugged the slopes came into sight. Suddenly, the jutting summits of the magnificent Pyrenees came into breathtaking view. There wasn't a sister who didn't gasp at the beautiful sight.

The small town of Irun was soon visible. To Catherine's eyes, it appeared to be badly damaged and of a gray color. The bus let out the other remaining passengers in the square and the driver turned around.

"We go up to the top of the mountain, now." The Mother General nodded, and he started up the motor which coughed and spit. Catherine closed her eyes in silent prayer. Again they followed the coastline along a winding dirt road which was so narrow in spots that the bushes scraped the sides of the bus. They came to the town of Fuenterrabia, and to Catherine, it looked like an English country garden. The houses were painted gay colors, and most outstanding of all was the profusion of flowers which clustered against the balconies of wood and wrought iron on every street. Below the houses in the harbor were the fleets of fishing boats whose sails were every color imaginable. They passed through the original town, entered by a gate of the city wall, and followed the cobbled Calle Mayor to the Plaza de Armes, an open square lined with tall, balconied houses. There was a massive castle built into the wall, and the sisters filled their eyes. They passed out of the walled city and the bus began to climb steeply through the rolling hills of the wooded country. Catherine caught her breath as the superb view of craggy mountains and green valleys came into view. Behind her was the heavenly panorama of the French Basque coast. They drove past the fort of San Telmo and wound higher and higher, where the pines were thick and dark. She could have feasted her eyes forever on the majesty of the steep hills which rose from the sea below. It was the most beautiful sight her eyes had ever beheld. She wished Jeffrey could be seeing it with her for the first time.

"We are almost there," the driver muttered. "I don't come up here very often," he called back. Catherine was enchanted with the various shades of green and gold which blended together so harmoniously. A few farm houses nestled beneath the trees lent a timeless peace to the scene. They felt they had left the war and civilization behind. Here, all was serene perfection. Here the air was pure where the mountain peaks reached toward Heaven. It was like being in a cathedral which had no roof but the sky. The mountains reached up to God. Finally, the walls of the priory of Saint Theresa's could be seen at the top of the mountain, and the sisters *oohed* and *ahhed*. It was a square structure of Moorish design, with few windows. It looked more like a fortress, very white and stark against the tall green trees surrounding it. It seemed to rest on a pinnacle, out of reach. The bus coughed and lurched its cumbersome way up the final steep ascent and came to a standstill before the wooden doors of the convent.

For a moment, none of the sisters spoke nor moved. The driver turned around and sobered as he saw seven heads bent in prayer. The Mother General stood up. "Sisters . . . we have arrived. The long ordeal is over and the Father above has protected us so we may begin His work. Let us be thankful for this supreme blessing," and she made the sign of the cross. Catherine's heart was full of thanksgiving. She wiped the tears from her eyes and studied the small, indomitable figure of the Mother General. She was a fearless, dedicated woman of God. She personified the selflessness of the ideal nun. Catherine's life could have been that way if she had not met Michael and Jeffrey. But God had another plan for her, and she rejoiced in it. She would never forget the sisterhood, the tremendous spiritual strength of the Holy Mother, the Mother General, and the other sisters whose goodness was truly Christ-like. Catherine loved both her lives and the thought occurred to her that she was a blessed human being indeed to have been privileged to taste of both ways of life. God had been abundantly kind to her, and she wept.

"Come, Sisters," the Mother General commanded, and they filed out of the bus. The Mother General jerked the bell-pull, and in a moment a portress, accompanied by the Mother Superior, opened the door. Her round brown eyes opened wide in happy surprise to see the group of English sisters in the company of the Mother General herself.

"Welcome," cried the Mother Superior. "Welcome! How we have prayed for this moment! The Blessed Father has been good to us," she whispered. They were ushered into a large hallway, of Moorish design, with pillars and alcoves of white sculptured wood. It was very beautiful. This would be Catherine's home for the next few months. The sisters were shown to the dormitory and then ate a Spartan meal of lentil soup and black bread. They bathed and went to bed. Catherine was asleep almost before she had time to finish her prayers.

XIII

In one grueling week, Jeffrey and the airmen whom he'd briefed at Coastal Command Headquarters had flown to West Africa and had begun setting up bases in the remote, undeveloped regions. To add to their problems, they had to put up with some of the worst climatic conditions known anywhere in the world. The mosquitos in the swamps carried malaria, and the drenching tropical rain storms which hit without a moment's notice had penetrated every piece of equipment, including the bedding.

On their second day, they were hit by a tornado. Jeffrey's heart swelled with pride when he saw how adaptable the men were to the change in weather conditions. Only months before, the men had battled the Icelandic climate, but that hardly compared to the incidents of dysentery, malaria, and fever the men encountered here.

Some of the natives had promised the crewmen use of their buildings, but they proved to be so inadequate that Jeffrey instructed the men to set up tents for temporary housing, and it was under these taxing conditions that the escorting of convoys began. When the first tornado hit, the rain literally washed the men right out of their tents, bedding and all. The rain had become an incredible nuisance, and Jeffrey decided to install the squadron in a local chapel in order to dry everything out. The housing was anything but satisfactory; however, he found the area to be the ideal place for aircraft. There were no heights around to hinder their approach, just a stretch of flat country consisting mostly of mangrove swamps and palm scrubs.

The ground staff encountered the most difficulty, owing to inadequate supplies. Much equipment required for servicing the Sunderlands was due to arrive on the next carrier from Southampton. The men had to come up with substitutions until the supplies arrived. Packing box nails were converted into usable split pins, and oil pipeline joints were packed with sheets of brown paper. Jeffrey conceived the ingenious idea of covering the absense of marine craft which were also due to arrive later. They needed tenders for the flying boats, so he told the pilots to remove the engines from some of the decrepit lorries and fit them into the dinghys, thus constructing makeshift motor boats. He recruited truck drivers and crews for the marine craft from the local labor who worked with great enthusiasm. In just a few days, Jeffrey decided to keep the natives on permanently. When word arrived over the radio that an aircraft carrier was docked at Gibraltar with 24 new Hudsons, a cheer went up from the men, and Jeffrey immediately dispatched a crew to pick up the new planes and equipment which were so sorely needed. Now the Coastal Command could join with the naval forces to protect the adjoining waters, and Jeffrey was pleased that things had happened so quickly.

"That's a beautiful sight, Commander," Officer Dudley exclaimed as the last group of Hudsons flew into base camp. "I thought you said we wouldn't be seeing them for some time yet."

"Headquarters must have pulled some strings. Things are going better and faster than I anticipated, despite the bloody rain."

"I never thought it possible to establish a camp here. When we flew over this route last week, all I could see was swamp and surf. How did you know about this spot?"

"In March, I flew over this area and scoured it thoroughly. I know it's inhospitable. Just clearing that eight foot high stretch of grass was something of a miracle, but you have to admit this is the ideal spot to station our aircraft. And then I spotted that old air field up the coast. We can use that for our aerodrome."

"It's amazing," he spoke with awe, and wiped his forehead, sweltering in the intense heat. "Did you know it got up to 130 degrees out there yesterday?"

Jeffrey squinted from the sun's rays as the last Hudson touched ground. "I thought as much. Quite a change from Iceland, isn't it?"

"Yes, sir," he slapped the bugs from his face. There were so many mosquitos and other insects infesting the area that it drove the men to distraction. The plane taxied in and Jeffrey walked over to speak to the pilot. His eyes fastened on the Hudson. By tonight, they would be going on regular patrols.

"Commander," the pilot saluted as he jumped down.

"Captain . . . how does she handle?"

"The landing speed is a little high . . . it's rough coming in, on that swamp. Had to use all the flaps."

"Right, but you'll be glad you're in this when you've got a Dornier on your tail."

"Yes, sir," he grinned.

"What's it like out there? Any news from Gibraltar?"

"The carrier saw no action this trip. I know because I have a buddy who was working flight deck duty. He said it was a peaceful crossing."

"No U-boats?" Jeffrey's eyes narrowed. He couldn't help thinking about Catherine and the possible danger to her. He didn't know where she was, or if she'd even left England, for that matter. It tore him apart.

"Not a one, sir. Too much bad weather. Even the Jerries wouldn't venture out in it."

"That's unusual," he muttered.

"It was fortunate, since they had an unusual group of VIP's on board."

"Oh?" Jeffrey answered abstractly, his thoughts far away.

"Yes . . . a group of sisters . . . you know . . . nuns!"

"What in the hell were nuns doing on board a carrier?" Captain Howard blurted out.

"I don't know."

"Are you absolutely sure?" Jeffrey questioned.

"I'm certain, Commander. Reggie, that's my buddy, got acquainted with one of the sisters. Apparently she was a looker. He said she was the only one who wasn't sick, and he also said she knew more about airplanes than he did. Couldn't figure it out. Just when he was getting to know her, the nuns left the ship at Lisbon. He said it was the damndest sight you ever saw. Never did know why they were there, or where they were going." But when he looked closely at the Commander for a reaction, Jeffrey's head was bent and his eyes were closed. Howard had been on several missions with Jeffrey, as his adjutant, but this trip he'd noticed a difference in the man. He was more preoccupied, more tense than usual. Generally the Commander was calm and steady. Something was wrong, probably of a personal nature, but Commander Norwood never discussed his private life with the crew, not even with Howard.

So, thought Jeffrey, Catherine had arrived in Portugal. Thank God! That was three days ago. Possibly she was installed at the priory by now. In less than

228

two months they'd be together, but the waiting was unbearable. He looked up and shook the Captain's hand fervently.

"Thank you, Captain," the husky voice spoke softly.

"Sure, Commander," and Howard watched the tall figure walk across the field seemingly in a daze. Something was up, that was for sure, the young captain remarked to himself, and busied himself unloading supplies.

Later in the day, Jeffrey made stops at the other bases located further south to be sure things were getting on. At the third camp he discovered that one of the Sunderlands on routine patrol had spotted a torpedoed ship and picked up twenty-three survivors suffering from burns received during the explosion. They were all but dead. Twelve others had perished in the explosion, and a team of medics was busy setting up a hospital when Jeffrey flew in. He assessed the situation and radioed Gibraltar for special supplies. The word was out that things were getting hot in the South Atlantic, as he had predicted at his meeting with the Air Command. What if the Sunderland hadn't been out cruising? Every day there was more Luftwaffe crowding the sky from here to Sicily, and more and more U-boats appearing as if by magic. They were in for it. From here on out, it was going to get sticky. The place was a hot box in more ways than one, he muttered, cursing the blazing sun which mercilessly scorched everything as soon as the rains stopped.

In another week he'd begin vital reconnaissance work over Spain. They'd go out in a Hudson. There'd be Dudley, Doherty and Friedling, the best navigator in the business. He could find anything blindfolded. Sometime soon, they'd fly over the Pyrenees and take a good look, and he had every intention of including Saint

229

Theresa's in his flight plan.

The first morning after the arrival of the sisters from England, Catherine was summoned along with the other nuns to the office of the Mother Superior, as soon as Matins had been celebrated, and was surprised to see a dark, handsome young man of about her own age seated near the Holy Mother's desk. His eyes were black as obsidian and his hair was long and straight. His skin was the color of coffee. When Catherine came into the room, he stood up. They were the same height, she and this dark eyed Basque. Most of the men she'd met on the journey were shorter than those of Anglo-Saxon background. The Mother General was not present. She had probably left the convent, after a much needed night's sleep, to be about her business, on her way to Rome. Catherine's eyes strayed about the small room and she noticed the absence of pictures and statuary. Only one niche in the wall held a madonna and child. Like the office at Our Lord of the Lamb, the room was somber, owing to just two small windows placed high up in the wall. Little light could filter through.

Sister Angelina gave Catherine a timid smile. They all felt uncomfortable in these foreign surroundings. Finally the Mother Superior made her appearance in her flowing black robes. The head nun was an attractive, fresh-faced woman of about sixty, Catherine surmised. She was graceful in her movements as she took small, unhurried steps to her desk, bestowing a warm smile on each sister. She was small, with white skin and brown eyes the color of rich loam. Catherine liked her immediately . . . she'd been too tired the night before to notice much of anything.

"Sisters, I hope you have been refreshed with your night's sleep and I hope the food was not too unpalatable. I don't have to tell you that we are in the middle of a famine which has grown worse over the last month. Bless you for making this sacrifice . . . for leaving your mother houses to come to the aid of a war-torn land. Whatever our nationality, we are all one family beneath this roof. This is a house of God, and all are welcome who work here, or find refuge here.

"I don't know how much the Mother General has explained to you. This country has been in the throes of a violent civil war for many years. The casualties have reached the one million mark." The sisters eyed one another in disbelief. "There isn't a family which hasn't lost a relative or a loved one. Death has touched everyone one way or another. Our country continues to be pulled apart by political factions and it grows worse day by day, threatening our very civilization. We not only look after the French refugees who are sick and wounded and come to us for aid and sanctuary, but we care for our own people in the low lying villages and in the mountains, for typhus and dysentery are running rampant and there is no help from any other source. We also open our doors to the Basque and Catalan men who would otherwise be imprisoned by the Franco regime in the larger cities. There were, at last count, approximately 300,000 men who fled the country last year to escape prison or death." Catherine paled. "These men are political outcasts and have a difficult time finding work. Many come to our doorstep daily, seeking refuge, food and comfort. They stay a few days, then must move on. You can't possibly comprehend what this country has been going through, nor what it has yet to face. Franco intends to be a Gauleiter to Hitler, and there are eighty thousand Germans or more within our boundaries at the present time. I fear civil war has only been a prelude to what is going to happen. We must

231

depend on God for courage and strength. He is our only salvation," she said fervently.

"I am saddened to report," the Holy Mother went on, "that many of our own sisters have fallen ill from exhaustion and are unable, themselves, to be of assistance. That is why the Mother General brought you here. The sisters from priories on the continent would have a much more difficult time than you from Great Britain in obtaining traveling papers. The borders are so heavily guarded that even the Mother General has difficulty passing through. We are thankful you have arrived here safely, and without incident. We are not a large convent. We house forty sisters, but at the present time, only half that number are carrying the load. You see, the majority of our sisters are elderly, and too weak in body for the work here. We simply cannot handle all that needs to be done on our own. Those who can help have been running the hospital we've set up in the back of the convent. The children need constant supervision, and that is the area where most of you are needed.

"But our duties extend beyond these walls, as I have pointed out. There are many more refugees who have been given temporary shelter by the Basque people up in the mountains, some of whom are too ill or wounded to come down to the convent. We must go to them. I've asked you to meet this morning so I can introduce you to Dr. D'Avezedo. He will decide which of you will work with him."

Catherine looked at the dark young man and blinked in disbelief. He seemed so young to have such heavy responsibilities. She admired him instantly for being willing to sacrifice everything for the good of mankind. Then she remembered that Jeffrey had told her the same thing when she explained about her life's work, and she smiled in understanding.

"Dr. D'Avezedo lives here at the convent and divides his work between the priory and outside our walls. He makes daily trips into the villages and mountains. Recently, Sister Nina, who assisted him, passed away, and now he needs another helper. There is one problem. He does not speak English; therefore, he needs an assistant who is fluent in both Spanish and French. He assumes that all of you have had some medical training, but he's particularly concerned about the language problem. The people here do no look kindly on foreigners at this point, and since you come from across the Channel, I fear your presence will only add to their suspicions. Some of our people trust no one. Which one of you feels most qualified to help him?"

Catherine looked at the other five sisters, but it was apparent that none of them felt equal to the task, and certainly Catherine was not qualified. Not only was she untrained in medical matters, but her Spanish was limited to book study alone.

The Holy Mother spoke in Basque to the young doctor. The conversation was lengthy. The doctor seemed to have a great deal to say. Finally, she turned to the sisters. "How many of you are trained nurses?"

Sister Maria raised her hand. "I have worked in a hospital this last year, Holy Mother."

"Do you speak French or Spanish?"

"No, Holy Mother. Not a word."

She looked perplexed. "Sister Margareta, you have no nursing experience?"

"No, Holy Mother. When the Mother General came to the convent, I was the only one who volunteered . . . pardon me, Mother, but the ones who would have been qualified were concerned about coming to Spain at this time," and she lowered her head.

"I see . . . is that true of the rest of you? Were you all

233

chosen because you, alone, were not afraid? If that is true, it is very commendable."

The sisters said nothing, but their eyes betrayed their thoughts. She turned to the doctor and said something else. Finally she looked at Catherine. "I see from the Mother General's report that French is your native tongue, Sister Catherine."

"Yes, Holy Mother, however, I've had no medical training. My work has been in history and languages . . . literature . . . in preparation for becoming a teacher. I would be of no value to the doctor," she said and avoided his eyes.

"The doctor says you can learn, Sister." Catherine looked up, startled.

"But Holy Mother . . . he needs a trained nurse!" It was the first time in Catherine's life that she had actually taken exception to anything said by a superior.

"The doctor will help you. Your record indicates you've studied Spanish extensively as well."

"But I have no *speaking* knowledge, Mother." Catherine could see that her arguments were going nowhere. She didn't like hospital work, and worse, she didn't feel comfortable with the young man watching her so intently.

"Sister . . ." there was warning in the Holy Mother's voice. Catherine bowed her head submissively.

"Yes, Mother."

The young doctor spoke in French. It had been a long time since anyone had conversed with her in her native tongue. He spoke with a charming Basque accent. "Sister, I will teach you," he smiled, his black eyes alive. "Sister Nina was not a nurse, either, but she could communicate with the people. Sometimes that is more important. The war broadens your education amazingly

234

fast." Catherine had no more arguments. She nodded.

"Good," he turned to the Holy Mother. "We will go down into the village now. We should be back at noon. Sister?" he turned to Catherine. She rose reluctantly and glanced at Sister Angelina, whose face was still peaked. Then she followed him out the door with some misgivings. This was going to be a hard test. Medical work had never appealed to her. She wondered if she had the strength. The Holy Mother smiled encouragingly at her once more and the door shut behind them.

Dr. D'Avezedo walked quickly out the front doors of the convent, and she had to almost run to keep up with him. They soon came upon a mule-drawn cart, piled high with straw.

"When we get back tonight," he began, "we will fashion that straw into mattresses. We do not have enough beds at present for the sick children and babies." Catherine nodded. He climbed into the cart and indicated she was to sit at his side.

"We have not been properly introduced," he smiled broadly. His white teeth were a surprise. Generally the men she'd seen in this country were minus a few, and the ones remaining were stained by years of tobacco. "I'm Miguel de Lorca D'Avezedo."

"How do you do. I'm Sister Catherine." He studied her exquisite face and was lost for a moment in the depths of her violet-blue eyes. He sighed inwardly. Never had he seen such great beauty. She was so young to have given herself to God!

"I'm not really a doctor, so you can call me Miguel. The Holy Mother introduces me that way so the sisters will not lose heart," he laughed. Catherine's eyes opened wide with surprise. "Actually, I've had two years of medical study at the University in San Sebastian, but when the civil war broke out, I escaped to France for a year with other Basque students. When I returned six months ago, I was put into prison with hundreds of others. A guard became ill one night and I told him what to do to get better. I was released after that to work for him." He paused. "With a little money, many of my friends could be out of prison, now, because the guards accept bribes like candy. I came to Saint Theresa's and began helping the sisters. They gave me food and shelter. It is the work I like best. After the war I will become a doctor, I hope . . . if it ever ends," he spoke passionately. "I have no right to do half the things I do, but there is no one else qualified in the area. Many people would die if I did not help them. The Holy Mother is so thankful for any assistance, she just calls me Doctor, but I wanted you to understand before you started to work with me. You see?" he winked. "It's almost the blind leading the blind," and he urged the mule on to a walk. Catherine admired his honesty and dedication, but she was so surprised by his revelation she had nothing to say for a minute. "Sister?" he asked. "Have I shocked you?"

"No . . ." she shook her head, deep in thought. "I realize war makes everything different. It changes people and lives," she answered slowly. "I will do all I can to help, but you will have to be patient with me. My work has been with ideas, books . . . not illness, except for one little boy. I did spend some time with him in a hospital in England, when he was very ill with pneumonia." She fell silent and he noticed how far removed she was from him right then. He was intrigued . . . she had an unusual sweetness and maturity.

"I'm sure that any experience you've had will be of help. If there were just enough food . . . but there isn't!" he sighed, as the little cart moved down the treacherously steep mountain road. The sky was full of broken clouds and the sun was shining sporadically, warming the air about them. The scenery was even more magnificent in the morning light. It didn't seem possible that a war was going on. In fact, Catherine could not believe she was here at all, sitting next to this young man, high in the Pyrenees.

"I want to look in on Señora Alba. She had her fifth baby last month. Word has come from the village that her husband has died in the prison. There is no money or food. I always keep some supplies and food beneath the straw in the cart. We will go by and see if there is something to be done."

"The Holy Mother at my convent in Wiltshire told me there was a shortage of food, but I had no idea of the magnitude of the famine here. It is incredible. On the train, the children were eating the left-over food in the aisles," and her face contorted. He gave her a sharp glance and was troubled. This sister was in for many such shocks.

"That is nothing, Sister! Do you realize there is no garbage anymore, anywhere?"

She stared at him and her eyes filled with tears.

"Last week I found some children down in the valley eating locust pods . . . the hunger of these people has turned them into walking skeletons." Catherine shuddered. He spoke on. "In the last few years over a third of the livestock have been lost. And the bread . . . I wish you could see . . . it is made of sawdust. Only the privileged classes eat white flour," and he spit to show his disgust. "Señora Caracas showed me the sack of potatoes she stood in line to get with her ration book. It was half full of stones. Either the Fascist pigs or the army take it all. There is nothing left to eat. We are more fortunate here in the mountains because we have gardens. We could not live without it. Sister, be thankful you are not in Madrid at this moment. The bodies are heaped in the streets.''

Catherine hugged her arms to her. Miguel was right! She was not prepared for what was going on here. This would be difficult for her.

''Sister, we are lucky to be here in the mountains. At least we can keep each other alive. That is something!''

They continued on the road down through the trees till they came to the little town of Irun once more. He turned the cart on to a side road and presently pulled up in front of a tenement whose front had collapsed. The beams which had once supported the floors were splintered. The windows had been covered with paper where there was no more glass. There were gaping holes in the walls. Catherine did not understand. ''Does she live *here*?''

He nodded with a grim expression. ''Last year a delayed action bomb penetrated to the basement before exploding. They live down below. I have not been here since the baby came. Step carefully, Sister,'' and he brought along a canvas bag which he pulled from beneath the straw.

They descended amid the debris and entered a hallway. A child of four or five, whether boy or girl, she could not tell, stretched out an emaciated hand to Miguel. The wretched little creature's skin was like parchment and death seemed to hover like a spectre behind the child. Miguel gave the child some bread and it disappeared. They went on till they came to a room reeking with the odor of human feces and vomit. Catherine grimaced in horror as she saw a woman and four children lying stark naked on a bed. Their bodies were mere bones, the skin stretched taut on their gaunt frames. The new baby was screaming hysterically at the mother's breast, which obviously had no milk. One child was lying face down, not moving.

"Sister," Miguel called out when he had examined the bodies. "Go out to the cart. There is a blanket beneath the straw. One of the children is dead. We must remove the body and then clothe the family. See what you can find to wrap them in. Anything will do. I have milk in my bag to feed the baby. We will put this family in the cart and take them to the convent."

Catherine heard him, but she couldn't move. Miguel turned around. The sister was retching violently in a corner. His heart went out to her. Such scenes were not for so tender a soul. He was used to it and had to remember that this was her first day.

"Here, Sister. You wrap the baby in this and I'll go out to the cart." He handed Catherine a filthy rag which lay at the side of the bed. There was human excrement on the floor. She had to step carefully. It was all she could do to draw closer to the bed. Her body was still shaking from her attack of nausea. Finally she leaned over to take the screaming infant from his mother's breast. The woman lay there, her large, vacant eyes watching Catherine without a flicker. She was beyond the point of caring, Catherine thought. The baby continued its incessant cries. With tears streaming down her cheeks she folded the baby inside the cloth and hugged it to her. Miguel came in and one by one carried the children who were in a catatonic state out to the cart, covered by the blanket. Finally he covered the mother and lifted her emaciated body from the bed. They left the tenement, once the family was put upon the straw, and started up the road again. Suddenly Catherine told Miguel to wait and handed him the baby. She ran back to find the child to whom he'd fed the bread. Catherine found the child hiding in a doorway with a blank look on its face. She picked it up tenderly and carried it to the straw, laying it down with the others. Then, feeling ill, she cradled the baby in her arms and they went back to the convent. She tried unsuccessfully to stifle her sobs. She was horrified by the suffering she had observed.

"How can the government let this happen?" she cried out at last. "Why isn't something being done to help? It's criminal . . . it's worse than that!" she muttered angrily.

"The Relief Agency of the Phalanx Party, the Fascist regime, has soup lines for those who can get to them. But families like the Albas are not even capable of rising from their sick beds. The government only helps those who can to some degree help themselves. The rest are left to die."

"But what if we had not come by here today, Miguel?"

"Now you understand why I must help," he murmured.

"Dear God . . . the cruelty . . . the inhumanity!" she moaned. There was God's work to be performed here . . . now she was beginning to understand.

"Yes," he said quietly. "My father, sisters and two uncles were shot to death in front of our home in Fuenterrabia two years ago. Their blood ran down the street . . . no one came near the bodies for two days."

"Why?" Catherine was horrified once more.

"My father was accused of being a Red separatist. I don't suppose you know much about what has happened in our country since the civil war broke out. Franco wants to subject all of Spain to Castile . . . to make us one nation. General Rivera tried to bring Basque and Catalan home rule down. He wants Madrid to have all the power. We Basques and Catalans naturally

240

sided with the republicans. We had lived in peaceful coexistence till Franco came to power. He wants to do away with our own language, strike it from our liturgies and abolish our ancient rights and *fueros*. This was something my father could not accept, nor could hundreds of thousands of others. That is why so many fled to the mountains, to France . . . until the Germans took over their land. That forced us back. You see, Franco has been punishing our provinces. He withholds money from our factories, causing unemployment. He has labeled everyone who was a liberal, socialist, or communist a traitor. He keeps a list of those Basques and Catalans who have not contributed to the war effort. He rounds them up and puts them into prison or has them shot. Those of us who escaped and came back later were barred from working and we've had to find jobs with foreigners. And none of us of military age is allowed to emigrate. It is insufferable. I have friends in the mountains whose farm was confiscated for christening their baby in the Church and giving it a Basque name. The father was hauled off to prison. He is still there awaiting trial because there are no interpreters to plead his case and Franco denies the Basques that privilege. Sister, you do not begin to know what it is like! Our children die of hunger in the meantime. I do not plan to marry till the war is over. Something could happen to me at any time. I could not bear to leave a wife and child as my friend had to do, wondering if they were dead or alive."

"No," Catherine agreed. "It would be too horrible." She thought of Jeffrey and Michael and thanked God silently that at least she knew Michael was not suffering. As for Jeffrey . . .

They rode on in silence until they reached the convent. The sisters hurriedly took the stricken family inside and began the seemingly impossible process of restoring them to some semblance of health. Sister Angelina took one look at the Alba family and fainted dead away.

Catherine's work had only begun. As soon as the Alba family had been taken care of, Miguel indicated they would drive up into the mountains. It would be a longer trip this time. There was a French refugee family being housed with a Basque couple and the children had broken out in painful boils. He was taking them a supply of milk which he had managed to secure by bribing an official at the Nestle depot in Santander. He would also take them a ration of flour. Their diet was being depleted of vital proteins. Catherine could learn to dress boils, which were prevalent everywhere. Again they climbed into the cart and began their journey into the glorious mountains. The ride offered temporary respite from the appalling scenes Catherine had just witnessed. She needed to get her second wind. They sat side by side in quiet thought. Finally he spoke.

"Sister . . . I must tell you something else. I am still a political exile. The Fascists could throw me into prison at any time. I tell you this to warn you. I have stayed away from the large cities, and so far, no one has noticed me. I have not caused trouble and so I am not worth bothering about, for the time being. And I have friends in the villages below who get word to me if there is trouble."

"Were you involved politically before?"

"At the beginning I listened to the Fascist youth groups like everyone did. In fact, I attended a student's organization which met in a basement room of the Escoril, and I listened as they poured out their hatred of the republican system. But I am a Catholic, and I could not support their logic. Madame Franco may be a Cath-

olic too, but Fascism is too aligned with Naziism . . .
the Fascists do not honor the Catholic traditions, no
matter what is said to the contrary. I went away from
that meeting feeling very disillusioned and sad. My
country has been torn apart. I cannot see where all of it
is going to end. Do you know that my distant relatives in
the Pontevideo province were persuaded to surrender
to Franco? They were republicans but they had been
promised amnesty. As soon as they surrendered, they
were shot!'' Catherine shook her head in dismay.
''There is no freedom anywhere, for if the Fascists and
Nazis don't get you, hunger will. I don't know why
anyone goes on living, or even wants to.''

''It is because we all have hope of a better world,
someday. Someday, somehow, this tyranny has to
stop, Miguel. If we don't fight it with God's help, there
will be nothing left!''

Her outburst gave him courage. ''You're right, Sister. So we go on . . . each in his own way.'' He glanced
at her. ''What is it like in England? I've always wanted
to go there.'' His question surprised her.

''It is not like this, Miguel. Everything is rationed.
We have very little, but we are not starving to death, nor
do we have civil war. We've gone through our own kind
of hell with the bombing raids, and we've lost many men
and women. I—I lost my brother last year, but our
conditions are not yours. What I see here is utter misery. What monsters these Nazis and Fascists are! But I
am wrong to say that. We are all God's children. But
how can some defy God so completely? So expertly?''
He felt a kinship with her, for she echoed his feelings
exactly.

''No one knows, Sister, and part of the tragedy is that
our young people grow old without enjoying the de-
lights of youth. Our old people die of heartache instead

243

of old age. The war leaves us with no time to live. We must seize any precious moments of happiness we can to make any of it worth while."

Catherine saw Jeffrey's face then, and Michael's. To seize happiness . . . yes . . . that was what she intended to do one day soon. An ache passed through her, so intense that she moaned. Thus the first day of life in the Pyrenees continued for her, the first of many such days. As the weeks passed, she learned how to set broken limbs, pull teeth, clean festering boils and wounds, even deliver babies . . . and contrary to her earlier opinions, she found that taking care of people's physical needs was just as fulfilling as nurturing their minds and souls. The results of her effort was more immediately apparent, and the look of gratitude in the eyes of those whom she helped gave her the reason to praise God and go on working.

Four weeks passed and Catherine grew accustomed to the light meals and lack of sleep. All the sisters had fallen into the rigorous routine without complaint. There was so much to do, there were not enough hours in the day to care for all the sick and the hungry. She fell upon her straw mat at night, exhausted. Many evenings she forgot to eat the thin soup and bread prepared in the refectory. Important matters needed her attention, and they helped to take away the sting of separation from her beloved.

XIV

For over a month Jeffrey and his crew had been making routine reconnaissance flights from the Balearic Islands, to the northernmost frontiers of Spain, teleprinting data back to England which set the Air Command Headquarters buzzing. From the outset, it was apparent that every tank or plane from England had to pass within a few miles of Franco's naval and air bases, and he controlled every foot of territory on both sides of the narrow straits. The pocket-sized airfield at Gibraltar couldn't accommodate fighters or heavy bombers. It was just an old race track. It was providential that the Hudsons and Sunderlands had home bases in West Africa. One German cannon at La Linea could seriously impair the naval base at Gibraltar. The Rock required constant surveillance.

Jeffrey mapped out flight plans, and each week his crew covered a different sector. Day after day, information poured back to England, confirming Jeffrey's worst fears. One of their more important finds was the number of U-boat and sub bases up and down the Galacia coast. They counted thirty-five merchant marine boats of German make and two tankers. This coastline had many fine natural harbors and was fully occupied by German troops. The ports were stockpiled with diesel fuel. The relief crews of U-boats stayed aboard tankers while others kept the subs at sea. Hit-

ler's work was being made easy by Spanish coopera-
tion. Jeffrey even spotted lighters outside Spanish ports
which did a lot of refueling.

After another week they went inland. Franco's navy
consisted of six cruisers, a dozen destroyers, six subs
and three to four hundred obsolete Italian or German
aircraft, but they did not notice any new German
planes, nor any factories. The famous ship building
facility, El Ferrol, was full of subs and German tankers
in for repairs. Old aerodromes were beehives of activity
supplying mercury, wolfram, pyrites, and manganese
to the Nazis. It was apparent that the Germans had
taken over Spain as thoroughly as they had done the
helpless countries ahead of them; however, Jeffrey
thought with bitterness, Franco had handed Spain to
Hitler on a silver platter when it was defeated from
within.

In all those weeks, they'd had Messerschmidts, Dor-
niers, and Glenn Martins hunting them down, and in
some circumstances, chasing them half way back to
Africa, but so far so good. The early summer weather
had cooperated with them. There had been more rain
than usual, and the cloud cover had allowed them to
take daring scans which they might not otherwise have
done. their reconnaissance work was almost finished,
except for a scan of the Pyrenees. All month Jeffrey had
been waiting for the time when they could pass over
Monte Jaizquibel. He wanted to get a good look at the
convent. There were times when he wondered if
Catherine were not just a figment of his imagination . . .
but then he remembered holding her in his arms. They
were going to be a family one day, the three of them. It
wouldn't be much longer now.

Officer Dudley went over the flight plan with Jeffrey
the night before they were to take off. Friedling was ill

and was confined to base, but Doherty would be along. The three of them would manage this flight alone. It was decided they'd make a sweep over Irun, the border town between France and Spain where it was rumored that the majority of German troops passed through. Then they'd fly east, into the mountains, and make as thorough a search as possible before winging back to Africa. It would be the longest and most dangerous of all their missions to date. Once it was accomplished, Jeffrey would fly back to London and report to headquarters. If Catherine wasn't there, he'd go to Spain and bring her back himself. He'd waited long enough!

They took off at 0300 hours, after checking their equipment thoroughly. On impulse Jeffrey had them double check their seat packs. He had a premonition that this mission was particularly significant, but he couldn't nail it down to any one factor. Doherty was pilot for the first leg of the journey and Jeffrey used the time to study the notes he'd jotted down the night he'd had to remain in quarters. As they flew over the southern tip of Spain, the right engine sputtered twice. They checked it out, but nothing seemed to be wrong. Perhaps a bird had flown into the propeller. Since it didn't sputter again, they thought no more of it. Six hours passed and they had the accompaniment of heavy clouds to hide them. As they approached the Irun area, they flew into a violent cloudburst. Lightning was flashing off the wings.

"Hang on, everybody . . ." Doherty called out. "We're going for a ride!" They were knocked around mercilessly for the next half hour.

"We're approaching Irun now, Commander," Doherty said, consulting his charts. "I don't think we're going to be able to see a damn thing down there. It's one solid wall of rain."

247

Jeffrey nodded quietly. This was bad luck! And it didn't look as if there were going to be any let-up. They continued east, hoping to find a hole in the clouds, but there was none. They tried to fly above the clouds but the soup was everywhere. They climbed higher.

"Commander, we'd better turn around and head back. This rain is here to stay."

"You're right. Let's go home. We'll come back tomorrow," he spoke with disappointment. Catherine was somewhere down there. "I'll take over now."

Jeffrey seated himself in the cockpit, his jaw set. It was then that the right engine began to sputter again. They flew on for a minute and it sputtered once more before going out.

"Damn!" Jeffrey muttered, watching the air speed. "Well, we've just lost our right engine. "We're down to half power, just under 100 m.p.h. We're right over the mountains. I don't like it. If the other engine goes, and it could in this weather, we'll have to jump. Just pray this baby holds till we reach the water."

The three men were quiet as they watched the control panel. The plane was losing altitude and they were still being tossed about like leaves in the wind. The strain on the other cyclone engine was building. Jeffrey could hear a distinct clattering noise coming from within. He tried to stabilize the plane at present altitude, but he knew the engine was going. His eyes were riveted to the motor. He watched in horror as the cowling peeled back and the propeller came to an abrupt standstill. His heart almost failed him as he saw flames shoot out. It had caught fire from the fuel line.

"God, we just lost our left engine," Howard whispered, ashen faced.

"Right . . . I don't know what I hate more. Ditching at sea or bailing out into God knows what. Engine trouble—" he said disbelievingly, "after all the Jerries we've had chasing us these past weeks!" Jeffrey had a knot in his stomach now. This time they probably wouldn't get out alive. They had descended as low as they could.

"All right . . . bail out!"

The two airmen wasted no time following each other out the hatch. Jeffrey remained at the controls till they were out, then undid his seat strap, leaped to the hatch opening and tumbled into the black wetness. The freezing cold of the slip stream came as a tremendous shock. He'd bailed out before, but it had been over the desert and mild temperatures of the ocean. He wasn't prepared for the lonely, icy experience which hit him now. The violence of the elements took his breath. One flash of lightning seemed to last much longer than usual and he realized that the plane had crashed. The wind carried his chute in an easterly direction, but the tremendous up and down drafts kept him air born for close to half an hour before setting him down roughly in an alpine pasture approximately fifteen kilometers from Saint Theresa's priory, high up on a mountainside. Dudley came down in a pine tree, and Doherty was lying in a ditch some eight kilometers from Jeffrey, lower down the same mountain.

As his feet touched earth, the powerful momentum sent him rolling and his body became entangled in the chute lines so that when he finally came to an abrupt stop against a low stone retaining wall, he lost consciousness from the impact.

It was in this condition that old Luis Ortega came upon him. He'd been out to the barn and heard the sound of an engine in trouble. Then he heard the explosion and ran into the pasture in time to see the burst of bright orange flame in the next valley. He shook his head sadly . . . he had no taste for war. Either someone was inside the plane and burned to death, or someone had bailed out, and the old sheep herder didn't think much of a person's chances for survival in these rugged mountains. It had happened before, just last month. Four English flyers had been shot down over by Gazula's farm.

The old man stood scanning the black sky with the rain beating against his weathered face, and he thought he heard a thud, but it was so soft a sound, he disregarded it. He stood a moment longer, then started back to the barn when he heard a groan. Someone was out there in his pasture. Maybe it was a German pig, and he spit. But his conscience would not let him leave the poor wretch to die in agony. He would go down and take a look. If the airman was German, he could rot in hell!

The old Basque hurried down the hill, taking small leaps to reach the wall. He came upon Jeffrey and leaned over to inspect him. The entangled body wore the uniform of a British airman. He snorted with a smile. Now, he would help. He reached down and began extricating Jeffrey from the chute and harness. The driving rain did little to expedite matters, but the man was used to the violent elements of these mountains and was oblivious to everything except helping this man who was still groaning with closed eyelids. A quick appraisal told him the airman's left leg was at an unnatural angle, but everything else appeared to be all right. He would get him inside the hut, then he could make an inspection. As soon as possible he would send the boy, Rodrigo, from the Gazula farm down to the convent for Miguel.

Jeffrey was still unconscious. The sheepherder lumbered back up the pasture to get the hay wagon. He hitched up his mule and brought the wagon to within a

250

few feet of the body. Then he climbed out and hoisted the dead weight up into the hay, taking as much care as an old man could not to injure the leg further. The wounded man was beginning to come to. The Basque muttered under his breath as he tugged to get the long limbs up into the hay. He sighed heavily when that had been accomplished, and quickly gathered up the chute and stashed it in the hay. Then he went round to the front of the wagon and started the mule on its way. The storm had no intention of letting up. He would put the airman to bed and get him into dry clothes. Miguel had not been up for a visit in over two months. It would be good to see him, to hear news from the village. Now they would have much to discuss. Plans would have to be made with some of the others of the underground to get the flyer out of the country, and the Boche were everywhere, but it could be done. The rugged old man had helped before, and would again.

By the time the cart pulled up to the front of the stone hut, Jeffrey was opening his eyes, but the pain from his lower extremities was so intense, he could not think of anything else, and the freezing rain caused him to shiver uncontrollably. He tried to sit up, but lost consciousness once more. His head settled back into the soft hay and all went black. The old man lifted him from the hay and dragged him by the armpits into the hut. It was an ordeal and the man cursed under his breath that the Englishman was so tall. He wiped the perspiration from his face, wondering how he would get the body up to the loft. He eyed the ladder, then looked at the man lying prostrate on the floor. It was far too damp and cold to let him stay there. The Basque took a deep breath and hoisted the airman over his shoulder, almost buckling from the weight, but he had sinews of iron and a strong heart. He'd carried logs which were heavier . . .

He grunted and groaned and rested on each rung of the ladder, but soon he had him flat on the bed, taking as much care with the affected leg as possible. He hurried down to the fireplace and stoked the dying embers, adding more kindling to build it up again. The old man felt snow in his bones . . . it often happened on June nights. This kind of weather went right through to one's insides.

He rummaged in an old trunk for some work clothes and found a black sweater and brown leather pants. He doubted they were big enough, but any dry clothes were better than nothing. He reached for another blanket and some long wool socks, then went back upstairs. The airman was still unconscious as the old man carefully stripped him to the skin, cutting away the pant leg of his uniform with his knife. He would burn the uniform in the fire. The Germans might come sniffing around. All traces of the flyer would have to be gone, even his underwear. He lighted a candle at the bedside table and began looking for other signs of injury. There was a large bruise on the right cheek and temple, and several cuts on his arm, but they had stopped bleeding. He seemed to be in fairly good shape. His eyes rested briefly on the golden, curly hair. The good Lord made men in all sizes and colors, he mused. Then his gaze went to the bad leg. It seemed swollen around the knee. Probably buckled under when he touched ground. The old man crossed himself when he thought of the brave flyer tumbling out of a plane into the night. He was lucky. He might have landed in the river, or in a crevasse.

The old man set to work, dressing the body in the clothes. The pants were too short and the sweater too small. It stretched tightly across the broad chest. He pulled the socks over the big feet. He had no shoes to fit feet that size. Pedro might have some. He would find out in the morning.

With the man dressed, and covered with blankets, there wasn't much else the old man could see to do. The flyer was still in shock. He might be that way for hours. Luis would warm up some *paille* so that when he awakened, there would be hot food. But now, he must get rid of the chute and clothes. Anything that would not burn he would take out to the root cellar and hide in the floor under the potato sacks. Even the German swine would not think to look there.

His chores attended to, the old man climbed the ladder carrying the bowl of stew and took it over to the table. Jeffrey was moaning and thrashing about on the bed. He clutched at his bad leg. The old man pulled up a chair and watched until the eyes opened. The airman was still in a daze but Luis began feeding him the broth, spoonful by spoonful. The man swallowed what was given him, then sank back on the mattress once more. The Basque blew out the candle and hurried out the front door to find his friend Pedro. Rodrigo would have to go immediately for Miguel. Then the old man would come back and sleep on a mat in front of the fire.

Morning brought more drenching rain and thunder. The clouds seemed to envelop the mountains with their heavy mist. Some of the old sisters, the ones who had been there many years, muttered that it was unusual to have so much wet weather this time of year. Catherine listened to their talk as they worked in the infirmary, giving the hungry children the skimpy breakfast of watered down milk and fish . . . not very appetizing, but supplies had run dangerously low. When she finished that chore, there were dressings to change.

Catherine worked quickly, for Miguel would be back

253

from the village at any moment and they would leave for their afternoon rounds. Even though she would be soaked to the skin by the time they were outside the convent walls, she welcomed the change of scene. The atmosphere was dismal inside the priory walls. She longed to be active outside, where she would not think about Jeffrey and Michael. It had been a month now, and the agony of not knowing or hearing anything about them was beginning to wear on her nerves. She felt she was a hundred years older and wiser, and there were moments when she thought Jeffrey and England were part of a beautiful, unattainable dream. It was as if she had spent her whole life here on the mountain with Miguel, and this morning she had little taste for it.

Footsteps approached. Catherine looked up. It was Miguel. He did not smile this morning, and Catherine knew something was amiss. They had spent every day together for the last four weeks. She was acquainted with his various moods and now she ascertained he had something vitally important on his mind.

"Good morning, Miguel," she spoke in English, expecting him to answer in kind. She had endeavored to teach him two or three new English expressions every day, and he in turn was giving her lessons in the fundamentals of Basque, but now he slipped back into French which told her immediately that he was all business and wanted to get to the heart of the matter immediately.

"Sister," he nodded. "Can you manage things alone if I should be gone overnight?"

She raised her eyebrows. They'd never worked separately before, but she saw no reason why his being away should make things any more difficult than they already were. Something was wrong, though.

"I can try, Miguel. What is it? Is Madame Créancy's baby ready to come too soon?"

He shook his head. "If I tell you something, Sister, you must swear that you will not reveal anything of our conversation to another soul . . . not even the Holy Mother. It could put everyone at Saint Theresa's in the gravest danger."

"I will tell no one, Miguel. What is the matter?" Her face had paled considerably. He took her elbow and ushered her into the supply closet. His eyes darted about the room, but the other sisters were busy with the patients and took no notice of them. He turned so no one could see his lips moving.

"Sister, I have just received word from a trusted friend that a British aircraft crashed high up on the mountain to the east of us, last night. One of the flyers bailed out and landed in my friend's pasture. He was tangled up in his chute and was found unconscious. My friend thinks the man has a broken leg and possible head injuries. I must go to him immediately.

Catherine's body went rigid. "Don't you want me to come with you to help? I can talk to him, find out if there were others. Does your friend speak English?"

"No . . . none of my friends can converse in anything but Basque. I will have a great deal of trouble trying to communicate, myself, but it would not be safe for you to accompany me right now. The German pigs will ccome snooping around, there is no question of that! When a plane goes down in these mountains, the swine conduct a very thorough search. But in this case, we have time on our side. My friend acted quickly. If I can get back to the injured man and take care of him, then he can be hidden till the search is called off, and we can start making arrangements to help him escape. If you were to be at the hut and the Germans came looking, it might not be easy to explain your presence, and it would cast suspicion on all the rest of us. You must stay here in

255

the safety of these walls with the other English sisters. You can be sure the Germans know of your arrival here in Spain and have monitored your activities. As long as you stay out of sight, it will not cause trouble. I would feel better knowing you are here to take charge. Later, when the coast is clear, I will take you up to the hut and you can translate for us. Please tell no one, Sister."

"No, of course not, Miguel." Catherine had listened carefully to every word. "Do you think the Germans will come to the convent to look as well?" Her heart began to pound with fear.

"Possibly, if the flyer does not turn up elsewhere. That is why no one must know anything. Then there is no reason to worry. If one is truly innocent of knowledge, there can be no betrayal of secrets. You understand?"

"Yes . . . and you must go. The poor, poor man! He must be in a great deal of pain. I cannot imagine having to jump out of a plane. It would be too frightening. You say it happened last night?" He nodded. "Then it was during the thunder storm."

"Yes . . . he is lucky to be alive."

"Miguel . . . I could write him a note, explain that we wish to help him."

"No, Sister. If I should be apprehended, and they find a paper like that on me, it could mean the end for him, for all of us. My friends would be found out and our operation would fold."

"What are you saying? What operation?"

He smiled strangely. "I belong to an underground group called the 'Friends of Liberty.' I thought perhaps I'd never have to tell you. There are hundreds of us scattered throughout these mountains. We have pledged our lives to helping others escape from political tyranny. That includes RAF flyers. We helped two to

256

get back to England just three weeks ago."

Catherine gazed at him. She remembered how odd his behavior was then, but not knowing him well, she had dismissed it at the time. "I didn't know," she spoke softly and her head fell. There were facets to Miguel she was only beginning to understand. She put a hand on his arm. "You are an exceptional person. God must love you very much."

He shook his head and covered her hand with his. "It's you who are exceptional, Sister."

She smiled. "What can I do to help you, Miguel?"

"Prepare a bag with splints and wrappers. I will gather up medical supplies and food. Then I will be on my way. If all goes well, I will return tomorrow."

"How did you find out about the crash?" She was intrigued at their unique spy system.

He was rummaging through the shelves. "My friend's son was sent down from the mountain last night to fetch me. I was just returning from town when he trotted into the back courtyard on his mule. He gave me the message and left. It would not do for the two of us to be seen talking together. There are Germans everywhere. We have to be careful every moment. It cannot appear that anything unusual is going on."

Catherine bit her lip. Her thoughts were with the injured flyer, but they were also with the brave mountain people who were risking their lives for a total stranger. There were many ways to serve God in the world, she mused, and that thought gave her new comfort.

XV

Luis Ortega heard noises outside. Was it possible that Miguel had arrived from the convent? Rodrigo must have gone very fast. The old man reached above the stone fireplace for his gun. He always locked his door these days, as a precaution, and went up to the loft for a look. He would look out through the shutter and see who was about. The rain was still coming down but he could see Miguel's cart. He scratched his fuzzy head, wondering how Miguel could have made it up the mountain so quickly in all this rain. The flier was moaning again. The pain in his leg was worse. He'd awakened once in the morning and the old man had tried to explain with gestures that he was a friend, that he knew about the plane crash. The airman stared at him and sipped the broth, even ate some of the bread, but the Basque couldn't tell if he understood or not. The rest of the morning he had slept and continued to shiver beneath the blanket. Luis sighed. Now Miguel could take over.

He hurried below, undid the bolt and opened the door to greet his young friend. Miguel saw Luis in the doorway and rushed to embrace him. They slapped each other on the back, kissing on both cheeks. Then they engaged in a long conversation. The old man's eyes shone and the soft Basque language flowed between them as Miguel stepped inside to warm up in front of the ire.

"Where did you put the Englishman?"

"He's still upstairs in the loft. I know it is dangerous to leave him up there, in case they come, but I was afraid to take him out to the root cellar until you examined him."

"Tell me about him."

"I think it is only his leg that is broken. I wrapped him in blankets because he shivers and there is a big mark on the side of his face. I found him next to the stone wall."

"He must have hit hard when he landed. Let's take a look."

"I think he is asleep right now. He has been dozing most of the time. He woke up earlier and ate some soup, but mostly he just lies there and moans." The old man sighed. "I will warm up the stew for you."

Miguel nodded and started up the ladder. The loft smelled strongly of pine. He could hear the even breathing of the injured man, and made a mental note that that was a good sign. He was turned on his side, and his body faced the wall. He was still shivering uncontrollably. It made Miguel shiver, despite the new found warmth. The blanket was pulled up around his ears, but the blond, curly hair was plainly visible. The boy, Rodigo, had called the man a golden god . . . a giant . . . and he was right! Miguel leaned over and put a hand on the man's shoulder. There was no response.

"Hello," he whispered in his best English. "Hello." The man muttered but did not move. The face was totally hidden by his arms. He felt for the forehead. It was hot and clammy.

"How is he?" Luis whispered, coming up the ladder.

"I don't know, yet. He's still feverish and trembling. I'll take a look at his leg while he's still asleep." Miguel pulled up the blanket and began examining the long

259

limbs, one at a time.

"He has a fracture right above the knee. I will go downstairs and get my supplies. Sit with him, Luis, and do not let him move that leg." The old man put a sunburned hand on the flyer's ankle, just in case.

In a few minutes Miguel was back with the bandages and splints. Luis watched with fatherly pride as Miguel treated the leg, as expertly as any doctor. His own father would have been proud to see his son work so quickly. It was good to see this skill in Miguel, who was like a son to him. When Miguel had finished, he glanced at the old man and they smiled with mutual respect. The flyer moaned several times, but still did not awaken.

"Now," Miguel said, "Let's get him flat on his back. I want to check his head for injuries. I'll move the bed away from the wall," and he slid the straw mattress held up on slats to the middle of the floor. He went around to the other side. "All right. I'll put my hands underneath his shoulders. You support his head. Ready?" The old man did as he was instructed and they started to turn him. It was then the man cried out so loudly that Miguel almost lost his grip. The Englishman began babbling the same words over and over again. Both men stared and Miguel tried to make them out, but they were too garbled. He finally became silent as soon as they had him flat on his back. Miguel examined the long, lean body the blond head. There was a large bruise already turning black running from his temple to the lower part of his face. He was probably suffering from a concussion. If his head hit that wall as hard as he imagined, the flyer was in for a bad headache, possibly worse. But there was no way to test him for skull injuries.

"Has he vomited?"

"No."

"Well, this is good news. We will just keep him warm
260

and calm. I'll clean the wounds on his arm, then we'll just wait and see."

"What did he say just now?"

"I don't know. It sounded like a name. The new sister has been teaching me English, but I do not know enough yet, to understand him."

"Ah . . . you have a nurse to replace Sister Nina since I last saw you?"

"Yes . . . the most beautiful sister in the world, Luis. I love her."

The old man crossed himself. "Holy Mother of God, what insanity is this? A nun? You love a *nun*?"

"Don't worry, Luis. I love her the way one adores a saint. There will never be anyone but her for me . . . not ever."

"You talk foolish, Miguel. It is good you are here. We must have a long conversation. Come and eat," he grunted, then added, "and tell me all about this holy love in your life."

"All right, and after that, I will help you hide the airman."

"I've been thinking the root cellar should be a safe place, underneath the wooden bin at the back."

"Good. Have you destroyed his uniform?"

"Yes, I burned everything but the harness and the wallet. They are in the cellar."

They began eating the stew. "Have you ever seen hair that color, Miguel?"

"No . . ." he mumbled around his food.

"You must bring black dye the next time you come." Miguel nodded. Suddenly the airman began muttering again. Luis' eyes darted to the loft. Miguel put down his bowl and climbed up the ladder. Perhaps now the Englishman was waking up. The blanket was on the floor and the man was thrashing about on the bed. There

261

was perspiration on his upper lip and forehead. Miguel pulled a chair to the side and watched as the man started to come out of his deep sleep. The Englishman had been many days in hot sun. His skin was tanned the color of leather. The same word was repeated over and over. Finally, the man sighed and his eyes slowly fluttered open. Miguel leaned forward to get a good look. Their color was like the clear sky on a summer's day. Miguel had never seen a blue so intense.

Jeffrey tried to focus. The wooden beams of the ceiling came into view. One hand was resting on his chest and his fingers rubbed the sweater . . . the fibers felt foreign to him, and he was lying in a bed. He vaguely remembered the little hut from the night before. It was impossible to move his leg, which felt heavy and stiff. He changed positions and winced from the pain. He carefully moved his aching head to the side, anxious to survey his surroundings, and then he blinked. His eyes met Miguel's, and their blackness came as a great surprise. The last thing Jeffrey remembered was the kindly face of an old man. Jeffrey rubbed his eyes and stared hard at the dark, handsome young Basque.

"Hello," Miguel spoke first, in the best English he could muster. "My name is Miguel. A friend," he smiled broadly. Jeffrey appraised the man, surprised beyond belief that he was hearing English.

"Hello," he answered back with a faint smile, and held out his bronzed hand which Miguel shook with enthusiasm. "Where am I?"

Miguel thought he understood. "House of Luis, my friend," he pointed to his chest. Jeffrey fell back against the pillow. He felt for his leg and discovered a splint had been applied and expertly wrapped. He pulled up the trouser leg. "You did this for me?"

"I," Miguel smiled.

"Are you a doctor?" How could it be that he had run into such a godsend!

"No," he shook his head emphatically. "A friend."

"Thank you. Thank you very much," Jeffrey replied, and grabbed Miguel's hand to shake it firmly.

"Is nothing," Miguel grinned. They he put his hand to his head. "It hurts?"

Jeffrey winced. "Yes."

"Are you hungry?"

Jeffrey's eyes opened wider. "Yes . . ." he flashed a grateful smile.

"Good. You eat now."

Jeffrey smiled and expelled a heavy sigh, but the exertion of trying to make himself understood caused the eyelids to close and he was once more in a light sleep. Miguel had seen enough to satisfy himself that the Englishman was not suffering a severe head injury. He went down the ladder and told Luis to come up and help him get the flyer down the stairs.

Miguel tapped Jeffrey on the arm. The eyes opened, instantly alert. That was another good sign. "We help you down," he pointed to the floor. Jeffrey wasn't sure what Miguel meant but he tried to sit up and do their bidding. Luis went around the side and together they got him to his feet and over to the ladder. In a moment, they had him downstairs and lying on a mat in front of the fire. The fire felt deliciously warm to Jeffrey.

Miguel spooned out some stew in a bowl and placed it in front of him. "*Paille*," he said and pointed to the stew. "Eat!"

Jeffrey needed no second invitation. His hands shook so, he had trouble holding the spoon. He was offered bread and goat milk which he ate and drank with equal relish. The more he ate, the better he felt. There was nothing wrong with the Englishman's appetite. When he was full, he looked over at Luis and smiled. "Thank you for the food . . . for your house." Luis did not understand the words, but he saw the look of gratitude on the bronzed face. He nodded back and his smile stretched from ear to ear. It was that face Jeffrey remembered in his muddled dreams. Miguel took the bowl away. Then he squatted in front of him, staring. "Your name?" he pointed to him.

"Jeffrey Norwood."

"Jeffrey?" Miguel repeated, stressing the last syllable. The Englishman nodded. Miguel reached for his hand. "Jeffrey, Luis and I, we hide you . . ." He looked around as if he were afraid. "The Boches . . . they come."

Jeffrey concentrated on his words. Boches . . . he knew that word well enough. Now he understood and squeezed Miguel's hand.

"Come," Miguel spoke with authority. "We go outside." Luis went for more blankets and together they helped him around the back of the hut and into the root cellar. They pulled away a long bin half full of vegetables and spread out a blanket on the floor where he would lie down. "You stay here," Miguel explained and helped him to lie down. Once he was flat on his back, Miguel put the other blanket over him. Then the bin was wedged up against him as tightly as possible and the boards over the hole were put back in place.

"Okay?" Miguel called out.

"Okay," came the muffled reply. The footsteps went away and he was sealed in the cool darkness. The sudden movement had caused his leg to ache and he cursed the fact that he had so little mobility. It smelled of onions in the damp space, and it suddenly struck him how unbelievable it was that he was lying in a hole, utterly alone, somewhere in the Pyrenees. He was wide

264

awake now and the reality of his precarious situation assailed him. It was a miracle he was alive. His thoughts wandered to the other two who had jumped ahead of him. How long ago? He'd lost all track of time. The poor devils . . . By rights, he should be dead. He sighed again. How was it possible he'd been found in that storm and taken care of? It appeared he'd come out of this with nothing worse than a broken leg and a few bruises. He touched his cheek, aware for the first time of the puffiness at his temple. It hurt if he applied even the slightest pressure.

There were a hundred questions he wanted to ask, but he'd have to be patient. They might leave him in the hole for days. The Basque men had thought of everything. They had risked their lives for him. There was literally nothing to do at the moment but think, and it was then that memories of Catherine and Michael swept over him, till his face was wet with tears. He had to get out of this alive so they could be together! She had promised him they'd be married. Would it ever really happen? Right now he could only pray that the Germans would not discover his hiding place.

He had no idea how long he lay there before he was oblivious to his world. His thoughts were back in England with Catherine and Michael, and the remembrance was so sweet and poignant, it erased the pain and the uncertainty of his present situation. He slept on and off till nightfall.

Miguel and Luis had just finished their evening meal when there was a loud banging on the hut door. Someone was trying to force it open. Miguel's black eyes darted to Luis and he got to his feet.

"Who is it? What do you want?"

"Open up in the name of the Third Reich, and be quick about it," the gutteral words reached his ears.

The urge to kill was foremost in Miguel's thoughts just then. He reluctantly undid the bolt and three soldiers burst in, almost knocking him over. One motioned for the two of them to get over against the wall, waving a gun in their faces. The other two began a very thorough search of the hut, starting with the kitchen cupboard, the fireplace and finally the loft. When nothing in the hut looked suspicious, they helped themselves to the rest of the stew and stuffed their pockets with cheese and vegetables they found on the counter. Finally, they all went outside and the two Basques were forced to watch as the soldiers sifted through the hay with a pitchfork. Still they found nothing. One of them over-turned Miguel's cart and set fire to it. Miguel's face was livid as he watched this insanity, helpless to stop it. Never had he been so close to taking a human life.

The soldiers walked through every inch of the upper and lower pasture, breaking into the upper hut. A few minutes later and they were reassembled, trying to decide where to go next. Miguel understood German fairly well, and picked up enough to realize that the soldiers were satisfied that no one was here. Apparently they had searched the entire area surrounding the plane crash and had come up with nothing. The pilot and crew must have burned to death. They started walking off, but one of the men caught the metallic gleam of the handle of the root cellar door and called to his friends in a loud voice. They rushed over and pulled the boards away. Jeffrey was awake and heard the noise. His heart stopped beating. Outside Miguel stood poised for a struggle. If the soldiers discovered the airman, Miguel was prepared to fight, hand to hand. Luis had similar feelings and girded himself up for a fight he figured was imminent.

The soldiers rummaged through the bin, taking their

time. There was a lot of conversation. With famine still plaguing the land, the sight of vegetables was difficult even for the German soldiers to resist. They stuffed their coats with potatoes and onions. Jeffrey guessed what was happening and praised the Lord that their desire to fill their bellies was greater than their desire to conduct a further search. The men finally stood up and walked off without replacing the board. Jeffrey could feel fresh air on his face. The footsteps grew fainter. After a minute there was total silence.

"Thank God," he muttered to himself.

"Jeffrey," a familiar voice whispered. "The Boches . . . gone!"

"Yes," the exultant voice replied. In a moment, all three were back in the hut, but Jeffrey hadn't failed to notice the charred remains of Miguel's cart, nor failed to smell the smoke which filled the air. His hand gripped Miguel's shoulder.

"I'm sorry . . . it is my fault."

"No," Miguel shook his head. "It is nothing."

"Thank you for helping me."

"You—do—same—for—me?"

"Yes," Jeffrey nodded, and cursed again that he could not communicate. The goodness of these mountain men would never be forgotten. His thoughts returned to his two crewmen who could be lying dead anywhere. What was their fate by now? He shuddered to think. By some miracle he had landed in a pasture. The perspiration poured off him and his leg began to buckle from weakness. Miguel felt the dead weight and tightened his grip on the airman's arm. They got him into bed immediately and took him more food.

Jeffrey sat in the bed, deep in thought, weary from the tension. Miguel handed him a plate of bread and cheese. "Thank you," was all he could say. It was not enough.

Because of him, Miguel had lost his wagon, and the two men had risked everything. Lord, what a mess! Jeffrey had no way to repay them, but when and if he got back to England, it would be a different story. He gobbled his food. Miguel could not help but smile at the ravenous airman. "You—stay here now." Jeffrey hesitated, then answered with a broad smile.

"Good," Miguel replied and they shook hands.

"Now, you sleep!" Jeffrey nodded. The urge to sleep was overwhelming . . . how did Miguel know? The close call with the soldiers had depleted him of his last ounce of strength. He closed his eyes and it wasn't till the following morning that he awoke and looked into the warm, dark eyes of the old man. This morning his head was clear and the bed felt warm and comfortable. The pain was not as bad in his leg.

"Good morning."

The old man nodded.

"Where is Miguel?"

The other one shook his head, not understanding.

"Miguel?" Jeffrey said the name distinctly.

Luis stood up and gestured . . . apparently Miguel was not here. Then the man pointed to the hot milk and cheese on the table. Jeffrey ate in silence and felt the man's eyes on him. When he finished eating, he tried to work himself over to the edge of the bed. If only he could stand up. Lying around in bed would not help him to recover, but when he tried to stand, the pain shot through him like a hot poker. He could not put any weight on his leg.

Suddenly Luis pushed Jeffrey gently back against the mattress and held out his hands for him to wait. He went downstairs and out of the hut. Jeffrey shook his head, not comprehending, and had to be content to lie there, utterly helpless. If Philip and Michael could see him now! And Catherine—there was always Catherine to think about. Was she still in Spain? Was it possible the convent was anywhere near where he lay at this moment? To see her face, to hear her voice and feel her lips on his again . . . he'd give his life for such an opportunity!

He had to find out his location! If Catherine were still at Saint Theresa's, he could get word to her. When the old man came back, he would try to make himself understood. He needed paper and pencil. He could draw a map. He grew more and more excited. It was not beyond the realm of possibility that his darling Catherine was closer to him than he ever dreamed. His thoughts were flying so hard and fast, he felt feverish. He slept a little and finally heard the hut door open and shut. The old man climbed the rungs of the ladder carrying two long wooden sticks beneath his arm. He stood them on end. Crutches! The Old Basque had actually fashioned him a pair of crutches! A broad smile stole across Jeffrey's face. Luis held them out. Jeffrey clasped the strong hand. "Thank you, Luis!"

The crutches were awkward to handle, but after ten minutes, they served him perfectly well. Jeffrey smiled again at his friend, then sat down on the bed, exhausted. He put the crutches on the floor at the side of the bed. "Luis? Do you have paper, pencils?" He pretended he was writing in the air. Luis watched and tried to make it out, but he did not understand. Jeffrey thought some more. Then an idea leaped out at him. There would be charcoal in the fireplace. He could use that to write with. He grew more excited and reached for the crutches. In no time he was on his feet and over to the ladder. He indicated to Luis that he wished to go downstairs. With the old man's help, he made it to the ground floor, and Jeffrey, out of breath, worked his way

269

to the fireplace and felt about for a piece of charred wood. When he found a small one he sat down on the floor and began to make marks on the hearth. Luis watched, fascinated.

"*Papier*," Jeffrey said the word in French, hoping it might ring a bell. The old man scratched his head and finally nodded. He rushed over to the cupboard at the end of the hut and rummaged through a drawer. He came back to the hearth with an old section of newspaper. It was better than nothing. Jeffrey spread it out over the wood floor and began sketching the outlines of a map of the Pyrenees. He drew the shape of the Basque coast line and filled in the towns of Fuenterrabia and Irun, putting in several mountain ranges that he remembered from the map he saw in the little book. He drew a plane and a chute. Luis nodded and smiled. Then Jeffrey offered him the charcoal.

"Your home," he pointed to the man and Luis looked carefully at the drawing. Finally he put an x near the town of Irun. Jeffrey's eyes opened wide. If that was so, then the convent was close. He took the charcoal and drew a cross and the word Theresa below it, then gave the charcoal back to Luis. The old man's eyes lit up and he made sounds. He put another x on the paper, right next to the previous one. "Senora Theresa," he called out excitedly.

"How many kilometers?" Jeffrey questioned. "Ki-lo-me-ters?" he held up his fingers, one at a time. The old man's face beamed with comprehension. He held up ten fingers, then five more.

"Good Lord," Jeffrey thought. Saint Theresa's was just fifteen kilometers from here, if he understood Luis properly. Where was Miguel and when would he be back? If Jeffrey didn't have a broken leg, he'd set out immediately to find Catherine. Was she still there? Was

270

she safe? It just wasn't possible that she could be so close to him after all this time! It was as if the hand of God had again reached out and gently guided him to the right spot. His emotions were at fever pitch.

Luis too, felt frustrated that the language problem prevented them from communicating. Apparently the convent meant something important to the Englishman. Luis would try to find out what it was that caused the man to appear so excited all at once. He patted Jeffrey's arm.

"Miguel," he said the name and then pointed to the convent. "Miguel."

Jeffrey concentrated hard to discover what the old man was trying to convey. Something about Miguel and the convent. Maybe he meant Miguel had gone there for help. He couldn't make any other sense out of it. If that were true . . .

The old man put his palms together and laid them against the side of his cheek, closing his eyes in a semblance of going to sleep. "Miguel," he repeated the name.

"He sleeps there?" Jeffrey mimicked the gesture. Luis clapped his hands and nodded. That was it! Miguel slept there. That meant he had to know Catherine! Why did Miguel live there? What would he be doing at a convent? Then Jeffrey remembered his leg. Miguel wasn't a doctor, that's what he said, but maybe he helped the sisters. Was that the explanation? He took another look at his leg. It was a professional job of splinting and he had little pain now. The medics couldn't have done a better job. Jeffrey's mind was full of questions and ideas. Again, Luis could see the look of eagerness and frustration cross over the airman's face. Well, in a few days, Miguel would come back. Then the Englishman could get the answers to his questions.

XVI

As it turned out, a week passed before Miguel could return to the hut of Luis with the Sister. New cases of typhoid had been reported in Fuenterrabia and the surrounding area. Sister Catherine, along with the other sisters, was kept busy day and night, looking after the poor families whose members had fallen victim to the dread disease, while Miguel waited on the sick and drove himself mercilessly till the early hours of the morning. Scarcely a word passed between the two of them. During that time, the Holy Mother had received an unprecented visit from two German soldiers demanding to see every room. Catherine was in the supply closet when they marched into the infirmary. Miguel was down in the village at the time, much to her relief. She shook like a leaf as they walked about the room, looking over each patient with ruthless scrutiny. The sisters on duty kept their wimpled heads lowered and tended to business as if the soldiers were not there at all. Catherine kept her back to them and continued to fold bandages. One of the soldiers came to the doorway of the closet. It was obvious to see no one could be hiding in there and he grunted an obscenity. Then they were gone. Ever since Miguel had told her about the plane crash, Catherine had harbored secret fears that the Germans would come to the convent. She had imagined many horrors, but now, they had gone. She was thankful that Miguel was away at the time and praised his wisdom in not telling anyone about the flyer. There was no curiosity on the sisters' part, no discussion once the soldiers went away, for the sisters knew nothing.

Miguel returned from town that evening and she told him in detail about the surprise visit. He broke out in a cold sweat when he realized for whom the search must have been instigated. His mind was on the Englishman once more.

"Sister . . . I think it is safe now for us to go up to the mountains. It is set for the day after tomorrow. We will leave as we usually do for our afternoon rounds. No one will know our destination. I must see how the man's leg is getting along." He sighed, his eyes holding a far away look. "But even more important, pray that Señor Polila in the village will have some milk for us tomorrow. I plan to take fresh vegetables from the convent garden to bribe him. I think God will forgive me for a little subterfuge . . ."

Catherine smiled sadly. "I have been praying for days now, Miguel. The supply is running low. If the Alba children do not get more milk, they will die as surely as their mother is going to die." Miguel stared at the lovely face and realized the young sister was a changed person from a month before. Her idealism had been replaced by a more down-to-earth approach. In a way, it was sad that her foundation of high hopes had been shaken, but it made her a more useful, productive Sister of God, more capable of rendering the kind of service needed in such difficult times.

"I will use all the influence I can to get us more milk, believe me, Sister," he responded in great sobriety.

"It isn't just milk, Miguel. It is everything. We cannot exist much longer without help from the outside."

"I know . . . oblivion is not a state one looks forward

273

to." She shook her head. Her compassion and fear for the welfare of these sick people was too great for tears.

A new day dawned once more and the sun was warm, even in the early hours of the morning. It felt like a real summer day at last. Catherine saw Miguel off to the village with a prayer on her lips that he would come back with the precious milk. He was to see about another wagon as well.

She hurried through her duties in the kitchen, then went to the infirmary to make rounds of dressing changes. There was a restlessness upon her, brought on by weeks of toil and strain. She was near the point of exhaustion, and always in the secret chambers of her heart was her aching love for Jeffrey and Michael and the fear that something might prevent them from being reunited. This last mission was truly a test of faith and she feared inwardly that she was not passing it. Then shame would consume her for her lack of faith and optimism, and she would repent and pray anew.

Catherine bathed the babies and wrapped them in clean linens, all the while feeling the pressure of her burdens more heavily than usual. It was in this depressed state that the Holy Mother came upon her in the infirmary. She was followed by a large congregation of olive-skinned dark-eyed, healthy-looking nuns whom Catherine had never laid eyes on before. She turned in their direction when she heard the shuffle of many feet on the hardwood floors. Her face registered shock. She put the Sauvaget baby down and stood up to gaze at this vision of holy sisters. They looked like angels. It could mean only one thing and her heart leaped with joy and thanksgiving. Help had come at last! Catherine blinked back the tears and bowed before the sisters, overcome with happiness that God had heard their prayers. He had not forsaken the little priory! She raised her head to

274

peer into the eyes of the Holy Mother. The older woman read the joy in the nun's face. She, too, was in a state of bliss, that the Lord had seen fit to bless them at this moment.

"Sister Catherine, Our Mother General has arrived from Rome, and these are the new sisters. God be praised!"

"Amen, Holy Mother," Catherine replied. "Welcome, sisters," she beamed. "You are truly welcome," and she greeted them with her special smile. It was almost impossible to remain composed under the circumstances. She wanted to hug each of them. They smiled, then began looking about the room, and Catherine noticed from their expressions that they were horrified with what they saw. Disbelief and shock registered in many pairs of eyes. Catherine, too, had experienced just such feelings on the day of her arrival. The memory of the Alba family, lying naked in that filthy hole, literally starving to death, would haunt her forever; however, the sisters would soon get used to the conditions. They would have no choice!

"Where is Miguel, Sister? I wish to introduce the sisters to him."

"In town, Holy Mother. He should be back shortly. He was afraid it was futile, but he is making one more attempt to find milk for the children."

Her eyes lit up. "Sister, our prayers have been answered once again. The Mother General has brought many supplies with her . . . milk included. The Lord has seen our need. Is it not a great testimony of His goodness and power?"

"Indeed it is, Holy Mother," Catherine whispered reverently.

"Sister, I would like you to spend the rest of the morning showing the sisters around. Let them become acquainted with your routine. Miguel will be pleased to find that half of them are trained nurses. This should mean a great deal to him.''

"Nurses?" she mouthed the words. When the Lord distributed blessings, there was always an abundance. The Holy Mother drew closer and lowered her voice. "Before you begin, the Mother General would like to speak to you . . . alone. She is waiting in my office. Go to her now . . . I will complete the tour of the convent with the new sisters. When you are through, report back here, Sister.''

"Yes, Holy Mother." She left the room and hurried to the office at the front of the convent. She was filled with conflicting emotions of happiness on one hand, and confusion on the other. Why would the Mother General wish to speak to her? It was very strange. It obviously had nothing to do with the other English sisters or they would all have been summoned.

"Holy Mother?" Catherine called softly as she stepped inside, shutting the door. The tiny Mother General looked up. Her dark eyes appraised Catherine for a long time. She did not look happy. Something was wrong. Catherine waited hesitantly for her to speak.

"Sister, come closer and sit down."

Catherine bowed and hurried to a chair near the desk. She was totally perplexed by the Mother General's demeanor, which was usually sunny and optomistic. Catherine looked upon her spiritual leader as a saint whose selflessness was the personification of the Father's. She had to speak. "We are so thankful you have come, Holy Mother. It is an answer to many prayers.''

"Yes," she spoke as if troubled by a great problem. "We were able to get back to Spain sooner than I had imagined, and the officials in Barcelona were unexpect edly gracious to us, allowing us to bring our supplies instead of confiscating everything. There is no question that it was God's will. But Sister, there is another matter of which I must speak and it grieves my soul. It overshadows my happiness. In fact, Sister, I confess to you that in all my days in the service of God, I have never sustained so personal a sorrow."

Catherine blanched, totally at a loss for words. What was this terrible thing? The Holy Mother pursed her lips.

"I have here a paper . . . a document . . . signed by the pope himself, stamped with the sacred seal of the Papacy," her voice shook. "It is your dispensation, Sister!"

They stared at each other and neither of them spoke. Catherine's thoughts these past weeks had been so far removed from the matter of the dispensation, that the shock of the news reduced her to a state of complete disbelief and wonder. The Pope had actually granted the dispensation. She was free! The paper was the proof. She was no longer a nun!

She stood up and paced the floor to stem the tide of feelings that raced through her. The realization of what the news meant assailed her. She could go back to England . . . to Michael and Jeffrey. "Jeffrey," she whispered his name, forgetting the Holy Mother was in the room. Dear God in heaven . . . her life of a religious had come to a close. It was unbelievable! The Mother General watched all of this from her seat at the desk. Her shoulders were hunched over as if she carried a heavy burden.

"Sister," she spoke at last. "Apparently you requested to leave the Order before you accompanied me here to Spain."

Catherine heard her words and returned to her seat,

nodding soberly.

The woman felt the Sister's absolute sincerity. "You puzzle me, Catherine. You showed no signs of wanting to leave the Order during the voyage over here, and the Holy Mother has had nothing but the highest praise for your work. You've driven yourself unceasingly, I'm told, without complaint of any kind. You must forgive me, but none of this sounds like an oblate who wants to be free to go back into the world."

Catherine lowered her head and prayed she'd be able to find the right words. "Didn't the Holy Mother at Our Lord of the Lamb tell you I had laid my case before her, while you were still in London?"

She shook her head. "No, Sister . . . and I think I know why." She stood up and walked around to the front of the desk, clasping her rosary. "When I was in Wiltshire, recruiting sisters to come to Spain, we had a long talk and went over the qualifications of each sister housed at the convent. It was apparent from the very beginning that the Holy Mother held you in the highest esteem. She remarked on your deep spirituality . . . your dedication. I have never heard higher praise given a sister."

Catherine kneaded her hands, and listened as the Holy Mother continued.

"It is possible she hoped you'd have a change of heart in your new surroundings . . . that you would see things differently and decide to remain a bride of Christ. I can understand that she would wish to say nothing to me, in case you desired to rescind your earlier decision. To lose a nun like you would cause her much heartache and sadness, as it has all of us." She paused. "Is there any chance that while you have labored here, you've had time to reflect and reconsider? It is not too late, my child. I'm fully aware of the unique circumstances involved here. I reviewed your case with the Cardinal and read very carefully the long explanation from the Holy Mother. We went over it in detail. The love between a woman and a man is very powerful. I had to choose between a man and God when I was young. I had to pass through the same way that you are now passing. It was difficult. You see, the man I loved was a childhood sweetheart. We were engaged to be married. The banns were posted . . . and then a very strange and marvelous thing happened to me . . . too sacred to reveal to anyone . . . but the Lord had spoken and there was no doubt in my mind what I had to do. I gave up the man, and to this day, I have never regretted it. Catherine, it is not too late for you, either! I realize this love of yours for this man and his son is powerful. But a daughter of God as noble as you, as talented and as spiritual, has so much to give to the world. Yours is a rare gift. Can you not see this?"

This was the difficult part, after all. Catherine stood up once more. She felt pain, not because she feared she'd made the wrong decision, but because she didn't know how to explain to the Mother General so she would really understand.

"Holy Mother, I'm sorry that you were not informed of my case before you left England. I thought of course that you knew. I meant in no way to deceive you."

"I understand that, my child," she spoke with kindness. "I have no intention of upsetting you, Catherine. I just had to be absolutely certain that you were firm in your decision.

May God grant you happiness, my child, and a blessed life with this man and his son. He must be very special to have won your love."

"He's the most wonderful person I've ever known. He too loves the Lord. I think it is this, above all else, which caused me even to consider marriage to him. I love him very much," her voice trembled with emotion.

The Mother General handed Catherine the dispensation. She hugged the parchment to her breast. The waiting was over. She could go back to Castle Combe, remove her habit, and then travel to London to look after Michael, to feel his little arms around her neck.

The Mother General saw the look of joy sweep over her face. "Catherine, you are free; however, I suggest you retain your habit till you're back in England. It has been my experience that our habit offers protection during these destructive times. We are always in danger. It would be foolish to think otherwise. A ship will be outside the harbor at Lisbon in eight days to take you sisters back to England. I will accompany you there and see you safely aboard the ship."

"Bless you, Holy Mother. I do not intend to leave the Order or remove my habit till I've returned to Our Lord of the Lamb. I must say goodbye to the Holy Mother there. She took me in when I was fifteen. She is like a mother to me. I owe her so much," Catherine bowed her head. "I will tell no one about this dispensation. No one knows except the Holy Mother in England, and you."

"That is very wise," the dark eyes softened. "The others care for you very much. It could hurt them deeply. I will say nothing, either."

"Thank you, Holy Mother. There is a part of me that will always be with the sisters. They will forever be in my thoughts and prayers."

"It could not be otherwise, could it, Catherine?" she smiled sadly. "You have other work to do which cannot be done inside these hallowed walls. God go with you, my child. I think Commander Norwood is a very blessed man. I pray that he knows this, too."

Catherine rushed to her side and knelt before the Mother General, kissing her hands and ring. Then she arose and walked quietly from the office. She headed for the chapel, wanting to be alone for a while, to commune with God.

Miguel returned from Fuenterrabia empty-handed. There was no more milk to be had in the village or the province. When he reached the infirmary, he stopped dead in his tracks and crossed himself in disbelief. The presence of twenty new Italian sister, already tending to the needs of the sick, filled his grateful heart to overflowing and he could not find words.

He worked with the new nuns for over an hour, shaking his head every so often at this outpouring of goodness from above. Some of the sisters were conversant in French as well as Spanish. It would make their training so much easier . . . he sighed with relief, but always lurking in the background was this great new fear for Sister Catherine. Finally, she made an appearance. He saw the regal white figure in the doorway. Her face was radiant. He swallowed hard when he thought of what he must do. It would be difficult to convince her . . . she had a strong will and a mind of her own. She would not like it, but she had no choice. He had to make her see that! He waved and she hurried across the room.

"Miguel . . . we're witnessing a miracle!" Her eyes sparkled with happiness. There was a new glow about her. He wondered if it were only the presence of the sisters from Rome that caused it.

"Yes, Sister. Your prayers must be powerful," his eyes remained fixed on her. "God has heard your pleas and has answered you tenfold."

"He has answered *all* our prayers," she discreetly corrected him. "The sisters have brought milk, chocolate, flour, fresh oranges . . . even sugar," she stated joyfully. "And look, Miguel! Medical supplies!" She pointed to the supply closet.

"Yes . . . it is hard to believe," he nodded but the smile on his face was forced. "Sister, I must talk to you alone."

She saw the shadow creep over his face. What could possibly have produced that look on such a joyous occasion? "Very well, Miguel. Just as soon as I finish my rounds with the new sisters. It should not take more than an hour."

"No, Sister," his voice was firm. "Now! This cannot wait."

"What is the matter, Miguel? Has it something to do with the flyer?"

"No," he shook his head. "Sister . . . why would the Boches be looking for you?"

She stared at him. "The Boches?" she mouthed the hideous word.

He nodded. "There is talk in the village. I have friends . . . contacts. Two German agents from Gestapo headquarters in Madrid were in town yesterday, asking questions about you."

Catherine blinked and the blood drained from her cheeks. "Surely not me?" she cried. "You must be mistaken, Miguel."

"No," he shook his head again. "There's no mistake. They wanted to know if any of the villagers had seen the English sister from the convent. The tall one, with the white habit and the beautiful face. They knew a group of you came over from England last month. They have made many inquiries already, Sister. They wanted to know if you had been in town, making contact with someone."

"I don't understand," she whispered.

"You are in some kind of trouble, Sister. I want to

help you. I have a plan," he offered seriously.

She bit her lip. "Miguel, I'm not in any trouble. Why would I be? I've been a professed nun for over three years. I've done nothing but live the life of an oblate all this time. This has to be some misunderstanding."

"Think, Sister," he almost shouted at her. "Do you possess any information they might need to have?" She shook her head. "Do you know someone important to them?" Again, she shook her head.

"I know a lot of people. The sisters, the Holy Mother, the sick people we've been caring for."

"What about back in England?"

"This is ridiculous. My life is the same there. I work with the children at the convent, the Holy Mother there. Do you suppose they want to know how I came to Spain? By what means? Something of that nature?"

"No," he muttered. "Otherwise you'd have been questioned thoroughly when the soldiers came to the convent the other day. That would have been simple enough, and they could have picked any one of you. No! This definitely has to do with you, and only you. I'm asking you one more time. Believe me, I know how the pigs work. You must know something of vital importance, even if you're not aware of it."

"But what?" she demanded, her consternation growing.

"They think you are trying to get in touch with someone, or that someone is trying to make contact with you. Who would that be, Sister?" His face was white. "Do you have a friend, or a relative, someone close to you who might be trying to reach you, who could be of interest to the Gestapo?"

She thought the question through. "Jeffrey!" she murmured so softly he could not hear.

"You *do* know someone!" he shouted.

She paced the floor. Could it be that Jeffrey was trying to get in touch with her and the Germans had found out about it? She thought back over previous conversations with him in the hospital and at Norwood. He'd never told her anything about his top-secret work in the Coastal Command. She remembered the meetings with Lord Wyngate, and others he attended. They were highly confidential. He had never so much as breathed a word about his business. Besides, he was in Africa. He wouldn't be trying to reach her now. How could he? He didn't even know the location of the convent, and the two months were almost over. Perhaps he was already back in England.

Miguel was at the end of his patience.

"Sister, you whispered a name just now. For your sake, tell me anything you know. These men are from the S.S. They are ruthless monsters and would torture you without so much as thinking about it. They could drag you away from Saint Theresa's this very day, and I'd never see you again. Your habit . . . your vocation would not protect you. The jails are full of prisoners who've been there for years . . . rotting . . . they'll be there till they die. You could be taken to the women's prison at Figuras. I have seen it—incredibly sordid, full of vermin and filth. They could take you back to Madrid, to their own headquarters." Catherine turned terror-filled eyes to him. She knew the Nazis did not respect the sanctity of human life.

"I know a man, Miguel . . . a Commander in the RAF who is stationed in Africa right now. He does important work for the British Air Ministry, and on occasion has been in consultation with the Prime Minister." Miguel shook his head. Catherine went on. "If anyone is trying to reach me, it would be this man. I know no other."

"Is he a relative, Sister?"

She bit her lip.

He saw her hesitation and grabbed her shoulders with forceful hands. He began to shake her. "Tell me everything you know! Your life could depend on it. Do you understand?"

She pulled herself from his firm grasp and haltingly began telling her story from the very beginning. She began with the arrival of Michael at the convent and ended with the fact that she had just received her dispensation, that she was free. When she finished her tale, he stood there in a daze. He didn't speak. There was so much to absorb, he could not collect his thoughts at once. He gazed at her, unable to believe that she was no longer a nun, that she was in love, that she planned to return to England to marry. This new revelation momentarily blinded him to the situation at hand. All this time he'd thought her unattainable . . . he'd put her on a pedestal above all other women. But she was human, like the rest of the world; she belonged to another man. What irony that he had assumed he could not have her, dared not think of his love, when another man had already claimed her heart. She was a prize. There was no one else like her.

Catherine was not fully aware of the impact of her words on Miguel. She had no doubt that what she told him had damaged her character in his eyes. She had been a nun, a bride of Christ, and now she had given all that up to do something very ordinary in the eyes of the world. She sighed heavily and closed her eyes. It was then Miguel started talking.

"It won't be safe for you to remain here. You may not know anything about the whereabouts of Commander Norwood, or the details of his missions, but the Gestapo thinks you do. Perhaps he has been trying to contact you. I have no way of knowing. Somehow they have information about the two of you and are looking for you, Sister. You are going to have to leave here. My friends will arrange for you to get back to England along with the injured flyer. It is your only chance to get out of Spain alive."

"Surely not?" she cried.

"They will come to the convent for you. Now that you have told me this, I have no doubts whatsoever. Even if you had nothing to tell them, and it is obvious that you do not, you would not be safe. Forgive me for being so blunt, Sister, but you are much too beautiful." He realized he still called her "Sister." That was a habit that would be difficult, if not impossible to break, despite everything he knew. "They would use you in any manner they desired, and believe me, you would pray for death when they finished with you. Besides, they might make reprisals against the other sisters for giving you refuge. It is not only your well-being that is at stake. Think of the others."

Catherine hung her head, wracked with guilt.

"Sister, the Gestapo will have to move carefully where a nun is concerned, but mark my words, it is just a matter of time till they come to the priory for you. God is with you . . . we have been warned in time, and the arrival of the sisters from Italy has come just in time. On the way back from the village this morning, I had decided that I would take you to Ortega's hut. That is exactly what I intend to do, but we will leave now instead of waiting until tomorrow."

"But I can't just leave, Miguel. The Holy Mother would not understand."

"Leave that to me. I will speak to her. I will explain everything. You are no longer a nun. You are free to leave. When I tell her everything, she will wish for you to escape. Do not worry. Sister, there is much to do and we have to be away from here within the hour. I want you to listen carefully to what I have to say." She looked up, alert to his business-like tone. "I want you to change out of your habit immediately." She went white once more. "Don't be so shocked. The Gestapo is looking for a nun in white, not a peasant girl. By the way, is your hair dark?" She nooded in a daze. "Good, that will help. Later, we will stain your skin with wild berries . . . your coloring is much too fair for a Basque. And while you are changing, I will pack food and supplies to take to the hut, and I will tell the Holy Mother everything. Go out to the cart in back when you are ready."

"Miguel, I will do as you say, but are you certain the sisters will be in no danger? What if the Germans should retaliate and do something terrible to them?"

"Do not worry. You have received your dispensation. Leave the paper with your habit so that the Holy Mother has proof that you have left the sisterhood. They will recognize the official seal of the Papacy. The Holy Mother can honestly tell them that you have gone away, and she knows nothing. They will have to believe her."

"I hope you're right," she sighed. "But what about you? The Germans know we have worked together. They will be watching you."

"Possibly. That is why I am going to stay at the hut for a time, completely out of sight, with you. It will be like a vacation. We deserve one, don't you think?" he smiled for the first time.

"Yes," she rejoined warmly. "You are a very godly man, Miguel. I do not deserve such help and kindness."

"Enough of that talk. Now hurry . . . and remember, Sister. Change *everything* you have on!" She blushed crimson when she realized what he meant. They exchanged glances and she left the classroom, heading for the dormitory. There was a closet full of old clothes which had been washed and put away for those patients who were in rags. For the first time in years, it occurred to her that she had no clothes of her own, no worldly possessions of any kind . . . nothing . . . only the habit which she was about to discard. It was a new feeling to know that in a few minutes she would walk away from these walls in ordinary clothes, never to return.

She almost ran to the dormitory, her mind in turmoil, and then cold fear took over. Her hands shook as she rummaged through the folded clothing. She pulled out some dresses, but most were too small. At the bottom of the pile was a faded blue dress, longer than most of the others. Perhaps it would fit. She reached for the largest pair of shoes she could find, work shoes with thick soles. She gathered up a petticoat and stockings, and went to her room to undress. Her fingers would not stop shaking as she removed the wimple from her head. She unfastened the scapular, then the habit. They dropped to her feet. She removed the heavy black boots and stockings, finally her undergarments. It didn't seem possible that this was really happening. She quickly dressed in the borrowed clothes. The dress had a square cut neck and puffy sleeves which reached to her elbows. The bodice hugged her rib cage and revealed the outline of her round, firm breasts. She felt as naked as a new born babe, but there was nothing to be done. There were no other clothes.

She trembled as she sat on the edge of the straw mattress and pulled on the stockings. The shoes were too small, she had to work to get them on. Still, they were better than no shoes at all.

When she was ready, she folded everything neatly, placing the crucifix and dispensation on top of the habit and headed for the chapel. It was early afternoon. The sisters would be about their duties. She hoped that no one was in the chapel. She tiptoed inside and went to the rail. Her eyes fastened on the altar. Catherine sank slowly to her knees and laid the clothes at the feet of the Mother of God. Her hand rested briefly on the crucifix, and suddenly she found herself dissolved in tears.

She poured out her heart to God, asking for His blessing at this trying period of her life, and that he be with her during these times of danger and peril. She prayed the Father to preserve Jeffrey's life until they could be together, to watch over the Holy Mother and the sisters at the convent, to take care of Miguel, to keep Michael well, to help all the unfortunates of the world who needed the aid of the Divine Comforter. As she spoke to the Lord, she was aware that someone had entered the chapel and was kneeling at her side. Catherine finished her prayer and looked around. It was the Mother General and at her side was the Holy Mother. Their eyes shone with love and kindness. The Mother General made the sign of the cross over Catherine's head, then bowed her head in prayer. The Holy Mother did likewise. Catherine stood up, slipped the ring from her finger, placed it at the feet of the Mother General and hurried out of the chapel.

Another wagon, much like the one that had been burned, was sitting beneath a tree. The mule turned to look at her. She climbed numbly into the seat and sat there in a daze, pulling her skimpy skirt over her knees. The sun was shining overhead. Never had there been a more beautiful day in the mountains, but she was not thinking of the weather. Her emotions were in turmoil . . . everything had happened too fast. She was not prepared to be catapulted back into the world like this.

Miguel appeared with a basket heaped with supplies and they were off. Neither of them spoke for over an hour. Miguel sensed that Catherine was distressed. He could only imagine her feelings at such a moment. It would not be easy to walk away from her former life, even if she had requested her freedom. He chanced a look at her from time to time. He'd often wondered what she would look like without her habit, but he wasn't prepared for what he saw now. Her hair was black as night and hugged her head in soft, short curls which framed her beautiful face. Her arms were long and tapered. She looked even taller without the billowing habit. Her body was voluptuous and ripe as a peach. He stared at her, unable to pull his eyes away. "Holy Mother of the Sepulchre," he muttered beneath his breath and crossed himself. "Ai, ai, ai!" he sighed. There was no woman anywhere in the Pyrenees who looked like that!

Catherine felt his eyes on her. It was hard enough discarding the habit without feeling his disturbing gaze. She wrapped her arms around her in an effort to hide her exposed flesh but it was no use.

"You are very, very beautiful," he spoke boldly. Catherine crimsoned. She looked down at herself. She'd never given any thought to her body, but now she blushed. She looked up at the sky and then closed her eyes. This was what it meant to be out in the world. To be constantly aware of one's self, the way one looked, the way one fixed one's hair, the clothes one wore. It was an experience for which she was not prepared. She felt like an unveiled statue on display for the first time. Miguel's eyes did not leave her.

"Miguel," she finally whispered. "Must you stare?"

"I'm sorry, Sister," he blurted out and fixed his eyes on the road ahead. It was difficult to concentrate on anything else. Seeing her this way made him think many forbidden thoughts, yet there was an inner purity which still radiated from her. She was still untouchable. The mixture of saint and woman was tantalizing.

Catherine returned to her thoughts. She truly was being watched over, her path was prepared before her, and though she was frightened, she had the deep-seated assurance that God had her in his care. Strange, that her faith seemed suddenly even stronger. Her mind wandered to the injured flyer. What must his thoughts be, alone in a shepherd's hut with no one to talk to? She'd almost forgotten about him.

"Miguel, you never did tell me about your talk with the Englishman. Am I a good English teacher or not?"

"You are, but I'm a poor student. I think I made myself understood. Of course, it was all very basic. He is an intelligent man and very grateful for our help."

"I can imagine how thankful he must be, for I feel the same way now. Is he young?"

"I think he is in his early thirties. There is a maturity about him. He is no boy."

"The poor man . . . probably has a family somewhere and no one knows if he is dead or alive."

"I would like to see the look on his face when you appear on the doorstep, speaking English no less. That should help him to recover in a great hurry." Catherine bowed her head. "And if he is normal, he will fall in love with you right away." Catherine sighed. "Forgive me, Sister, I should not say such things."

"Miguel, I am no longer a nun. Do not ask my forgiveness any more. There is nothing to forgive. You can say what you think in front of me. I must get used to such talk. You have no idea how strange it is for me to be re-entering society after seven years among the sisters. I have to readjust my thinking. It will take time, but it is a fact of life, and I will need your help," she smiled.

"You can depend on that Sis—" he stopped. "May I

call you Catherine?''

"Please do, from now on."

"I might forget . . . in a way, you will always be Sister Catherine to me."

"I shall never forget that I was once Sister Catherine," she said quietly, and they rode on in silence, their bodies swaying as the cart bumped roughly over the mountain road. Evening came on and the pines cast long shadows over the landscape. Miguel broke the long silence.

"It is getting chilly now that the sun has slipped below the horizon. There is a blanket in the back. I'll get it for you."

"Thank you, Miguel."

Once she was wrapped in the covering, he began thinking out loud. "If you and the airman were to pose as a farm couple from Northern Spain, my friends and I could outfit you with a mule and wagon, and you could travel the back roads to Portugal, hiding out at night in the huts of trusted friends. Eventually you would reach the coast and we could get you out of the country on a fishing trawler. Some of our boats have radios and you could be picked up by one of your English ships. I think it is a good plan. If you travel as a married couple, with forged identification papers, there should be no trouble. I have brought black dye with me to disguise the hair of the flyer. But he will not be ready to travel for several weeks. He must not go anywhere till I can remove the splint. A broken leg would be a dead give-away to the pigs."

Catherine listened to his ideas, but she couldn't imagine how any of it would work out. She shook her head in amazement, then sadness. If she had to wait several more weeks before they could leave the Pyrenees, it would make the separation from Jeffrey that much harder to bear. She didn't think she could stand it. Always she had pictured herself discarding her habit and driving back to London, seated at Jeffrey's side with Michael on her lap. She was helpless now, dependent on the goodness and generosity of Miguel. He was her only hope. Jeffrey would suffer when she did not return to England at the expected time. And Michael . . . it could upset him all over again. Dear Father in Heaven, how would it all be resolved?

XVII

The stars were twinkling in the heavens as the cart drew closer. Jeffrey had been gazing out the window of the loft, studying the constellations and breathing deeply of the invigorating mountain air. For over a week now, he'd been confined to the hut. He was more than grateful for the food and shelter provided by Luis and Miguel, but he was not used to such inactivity. He'd done some sketching until he'd run out of old newspaper. He didn't dare venture outside for fear of being spotted. He had to remain patient and wait for Miguel's return. The idea that Catherine was only fifteen kilometers away haunted him endlessly. There was no way to get in touch with her until he could maneuver better, and that wouldn't be for some time. And there was always the possibility that she had returned to England. His leg was still far from being healed enough to withstand the long walk to the priory. The last few nights a restlessness had come upon him so disturbing he could not sleep. He ached for Catherine and for his son. Suddenly he caught sight of the mule-drawn cart slowly making its way up to the doorway of the hut. He strained to make out faces. It was Miguel, and there was someone seated at his side, but the figure was huddled under a covering. It was impossible to distinguish details from this distance.

"Thank God he has come back," he murmured aloud

and hurriedly reached for his crutches. He hobbled over to the ladder and edged down to the ground floor. Luis had been sitting in a chair before the fire, deep in concentration. He was worried because it had been a week now and Miguel had not yet come back. He heard the crutches and looked up to see the Englishman's happy face looking down at him.

"Miguel!" Jeffrey pointed to the door. Luis stood up and cocked his head to listen. Sure enough, there was the unmistakable sound of hooves outside. Luis smiled back and flung wide the door before Miguel could knock, and the surprised young Basque stepped inside to hug the old man affectionately. Jeffrey extended his hand in greeting. Miguel grabbed hold of it and shook it vigorously, noticing with satisfaction that the flyer seemed healthy and fit. Then the two Basques began a lengthy conversation, much to Jeffrey's consternation, for he had many questions to ask. For a moment Jeffrey's eyes strayed outside. He saw the other figure descending from the cart, still enveloped in a blanket.

Catherine gathered up the basket in her arms and slid off the seat on to the ground. She worked her way around to the end of the cart. For a brief moment, Jeffrey caught a glimpse of the lower half of her face. It was only the merest glance, but the proud thrust of chin, the fullness of the wide mouth were unmistakable even from this distance. There was a hammering in his ears. He pushed past the two men and hurried out into the darkness. Catherine was just coming around the other side of the cart, her head lowered. Had he been mistaken? Was his mind playing tricks on him? That had to be it! He wanted her so badly, his mind had conjured her up. Still . . . The figure moved closer. He called her name. She stopped where she was, frozen to the spot. Her eyes traveled from the work boots, the bandaged leg, up the lean body clad in Basque clothing, and came to rest on the handsome bronzed face, the golden hair.

"Jeffrey," she whispered in disbelief, and suddenly the basket was on the ground, the contents spilling out in all directions. The blanket slid from her head down her shoulders and fell to the earth in a heap. The light from the doorway illuminated her exquisite face turned momentarily white from the shock of seeing him. He was instantly reminded of a description from an old fairy tale: "Lips as red as blood, skin as white as snow, hair as black as ebony." That described his fair Catherine. His eyes took in the curves of her magnificent body. He could scarcely breathe.

Suddenly the crutches went crashing to the ground and he drew her into his arms, repeating her name over and over again, burying his face in the warmth of her neck and hair. Nothing existed but their closeness. She wrapped hungry arms around his body and he hugged her until her ribs ached. His neck was wet with her tears. She clung to him, sobbing uncontrollably in the warmth of his arms. "Jeffrey," she gasped over and over again. He couldn't speak, the thickness in his throat was too great. He ran trembling fingers through her short, glossy black hair, and finally his mouth found hers and he kissed her until they were caught up in a dizzying vortex of ecstasy.

"Catherine," he moaned her name, and the thrill of each other's nearness consumed them both. Her fragrant, soft body was intoxicating. "Dear God, I don't believe it," he murmured into the silky hair he had never seen before, much less touched. She had no words, only love to give him, and her eager lips sought his again as if she could never get her fill. Time passed, and they were oblivious to everything except each other. He gently forced her head back and looked

296

quietly into her shining eyes. He shook his head as if she were a heavenly apparition.

"Lord, you're beautiful!"

"So are you," she replied in a husky voice. She said it in all seriousness. For the second time since she'd known him, he blushed.

"Catherine, men aren't beautiful."

"You are . . . I've always thought so."

His mouth fell upon hers and he kissed her with an aching tenderness that left her limp. "I love you . . . there have been times when I thought I'd never see you again," he cried out softly.

"I know . . . I love you too, Jeffrey," and her fingers gripped his arms. "I had no idea it was you up here . . . I didn't know! Thank God you're alive!" She looked up at him, stroking his curls with her hand. "You've been here all this time . . . alone . . . in pain . . . and I've been at the priory, thinking that you were back in England or in Africa. Oh, my love," she closed her eyes tightly. He hugged her to him.

"Then by what miracle are you here now?"

"It's a long story, darling . . . but I'll never stop thanking the Lord that I came with Miguel today!" She stopped talking, eager to feel his mouth on hers once more, and they were caught up in a new intimacy that set their bodies on fire. He crushed her to him and the joy he felt at having her safely in his arms at last erased the months of loneliness and frustration. Catherine felt his heart beating wildly against her breast through the rough sweater. This was where she had longed to be. He was all she ever wanted. Words were unnecessary as they delighted in the wonder of being united at last.

Miguel and Luis had long since gone inside the hut and closed the door. When Miguel stepped outside to help Catherine with the basket and saw the two lovers, he thought he'd lost his mind completely. Then he began putting the pieces of the puzzle together and realized that the injured Englishman was her beloved. There was no other explanation. Such a coincidence as the two of them meeting at this remote hut hardly seemed possible. The expressions of joy and desire on their faces was enough to make Miguel green with envy, and he went back inside the hut, pulling the dazed old man along with him. There was much to explain to Luis, who stood in awe over what was transpiring before his very eyes. In fact, Miguel wasn't exactly certain how he was going to tell Luis everything, for he didn't understand it all himself. The only thing he knew was that he had an aching sadness in his breast caused by seeing Catherine in the arms of the flyer.

The moon started its upward journey over the top of the mountain behind the hut, spreading its light on the landscape below, bathing the lovers in its pale glow.

"You're not wearing your habit," he finally whispered in her ear.

"No. Just this morning I received my dispensation from the Pope. The Mother General gave it to me in person, instead of sending it on to Our Lord of the Lamb. All day I've been wondering why . . . but now I know, my love. It is as if I have been set free just so I could come to you now."

"Catherine," he pressed her more tightly to him. "I can't believe my eyes or my ears," and he swung her up off the ground, kissing her with wild abandon. He could never get enough of her. When he put her down again, she felt his body trembling. It occurred to her that he'd been standing on his bad leg all this time, without any support. If he were in pain, he'd never admit it. She raised her head.

"Let's go inside, Jeffrey. It's chilly out here and you

298

mustn't stand on your leg. I know you're uncomfortable. I can feel you tremble."

He smiled down at her, loving her the more intensely for her concern. "That's not why I'm trembling, darling." How he adored her! "We'll go back in, but not until I've kissed you once more."

It was some time later that he reluctantly let her go. She knelt down and picked up his crutches. He put them under either arm while she gathered up the contents of the basket. Then with the blanket and basket firmly secured, they went into the hut, holding tightly to each other in spite of the crutches.

Miguel looked up as they came inside. He'd never seen two such radiantly beautiful people.

"Miguel," she addressed him in French, "I don't know how to explain it, but this man is the man I am going to marry. It seems to be a day of miracles. I want you two to become the best of friends."

"We're well on our way," Miguel responded. "Luis!" he called to the old man. "This is the sister from the priory who intends to marry the Englishman." Luis smiled broadly and put out his hand to shake hers. In her best Basque, she thanked him profusely for taking care of Jeffrey, for allowing her to come and for giving them refuge. It pleased him that she knew some phrases in his native tongue and he told her that she and her man were welcome to stay as long as they liked. Miguel looked on and noticed that the flyer was in pain. In his excitement to greet Catherine, he had forgotten his leg and was suffering the consequences. Under the circumstances Miguel understood.

"You, Jeffrey . . ." he spoke in English. "Get off that leg, now!" he pointed and shook his head as if he were chastising a naughty child.

Catherine immediately agreed. "He's right, darling.

299

You must rest." Jeffrey nodded. She looked around the room so sparsely furnished and tidily kept. "But where do you sleep?"

"Up in the loft. Luis has given up his only bed. And he's risking his life for me," he muttered.

"I'm discovering that there are many godly people in the world, like Luis and Miguel. We are so blessed!" Jeffrey eyed Catherine and realized just how blessed he really was.

"Catherine," he motioned for her to come over to the ladder. She took his crutches while he propelled himself up the rungs. She handed them back to him and as she did so he caught hold of her hand. "Come up here, darling." His eyes were dark with desire and she felt a sensation not unlike a current of electricity flow through her body as she drew closer. When she reached the loft he pulled her away from the edge and together they went over to the bed in the corner, opposite the window. It was nothing more than a straw mattress covered with several blankets. There were pieces of newspaper on the floor by the bed covered with his sketches. Her eyes smarted as she watched him sit down and rub his thigh above the break.

"We shouldn't have stayed outside so long, Jeffrey." There was alarm in her voice. For answer he drew her down into his lap. One arm went around her shoulders, the other gently forced her head to lie on his arm. "It's a small price to pay," he whispered and began kissing her eyes and nose. Suddenly he was covering her mouth and throat. His touch sent chills through her body till she felt drugged.

Miguel poked his head into the loft and waited till he felt he could intrude, but no such moment seemed to present itself. He cleared his throat noisily. "Excuse, please."

300

Catherine crimsoned that Miguel had come upon them so unexpectedly. She swayed visibly after getting to her feet. Jeffrey lay back against the pillow and grimaced as Miguel lifted the bad leg on top of the bed and began unwrapping it. Catherine watched in rapt attention, anxious to see if his leg were mending properly. She raised soft eyes to Jeffrey from time to time. They gazed at each other and spoke silent words of love. Miguel examined everything carefully, then rebandaged the leg. He stood up and patted Jeffrey's shoulder. "Your leg is good," he said in perfect English. Then in French to Catherine, "It is coming along well, but he must stay off it as much as possible . . . and he most definitely cannot expect to travel for another six weeks or longer. You will both stay here till he is better."

"But we cannot do this to Luis, Miguel."

"Luis wants you to stay. You will be safe here."

"Thank you, Miguel. We will never forget your kindness. Please tell Luis again how grateful we are."

He nodded. "I think I am safe in assuming that it will not be lonely for either one of you," he winked. "It is the best plan. In a month or so, the pigs will have stopped actively looking for you."

"Yes," she answered excitedly. "I will keep house and do the cooking. I want to be of as much help as possible." Miguel flashed her a broad smile.

"Catherine?" Jeffrey called to her. She went quickly to his side and he took her hand. "What are you two talking about?" He felt an uncontrollable jealousy of her attentions to the handsome Basque who spoke only in French so Jeffrey couldn't understand. Miguel noticed the Commander's possessive manner and chuckled. He didn't blame him. The Englishman was hopelessly in love with her. That much was obvious.

And no wonder . . .

"Darling, your leg is getting better, but Miguel says you are not to leave here for at least another six weeks. After that, you will be able to travel without the splint. He has worked out a plan for our escape, but you must be totally recovered first."

"Is Luis willing to let us stay here?"

Catherine nodded. He bent his head in concentration. For a moment it took her back to the morning she first laid eyes on him at the convent. He had looked just like that . . . it seemed so long ago. Jeffrey's head came up and his arm reached around her waist and drew her down to him. "Ask Miguel if there is a priest in the area who could marry us right away. If we are going to be living under this roof for the next month or so, I will have to make you my wife. I couldn't stand it otherwise."

She looked longingly at him. "I couldn't either," was her fervant reply. His hand reached for hers.

"Catherine, you don't mind if we're not married in England? If you'd rather wait so Michael and Philip can be with us, I'll understand. And you have an aunt as well. I'm being impatient again. It's one of my worst faults. Since I've met you, I'm worse than ever."

"Darling," she whispered. "Do you honestly think I care where we are married? Do you think I want to wait?" she squeezed his hand. "You don't know me very well. Nothing matters except that we are together, permanently. I can't wait to belong to you," and she kissed his lips lightly. His arm tightened around her waist. She finally turned to Miguel, translating Jeffrey's request into French. Miguel eyed the Englishman enviously. Putting himself in the Commander's place, he understood the urgency of his request. He called down to Luis and they talked it over. In a moment he

302

was making explanations to Catherine. Jeffrey was once again exasperated that he could not understand their words, and something Miguel said caused Catherine to blush. He nuzzled next to her. "Darling?"

"Miguel says that Luis is friends with the priest and will speak to him in the morning. His house is just down the mountainside. Luis says it will be too dangerous for us to be seen at the Church, so the Father will have to come here to perform the ceremony."

Jeffrey beamed. "What else did he say?"

Catherine's mouth broke into a half smile. "That Luis will tell the Holy Father it is an emergency!"

Jeffrey laughed quietly. "It is . . . tell Miguel to tell Luis that he is a man after my own heart."

Catherine translated and soon everyone was smiling, but Jeffrey was still concerned for her feelings. "Darling, I realize this isn't the way either of us visualized things. You at least deserve to be married in a house of God."

"Hush," she put her fingers to his lips. "God is everywhere . . . even in this humble loft. We're together now. Could anything else matter?"

"No," he caressed her cheek with his hand, then extended his hand to Miguel. "Thank you, friend."

"It is nothing," Miguel grinned and turned to leave.

"Miguel, thank you for everything."

"You must stop thanking us all the time, Sister." He stopped talking, realizing what he'd just said. It slipped out so easily. "You can sleep up here, or down by the fire. Whatever you choose. Luis has more blankets in the dresser below, and there is hot stew in the pot when you wish to eat."

"Thank you . . ." She felt a tug at her side once more.

"What did he say?"

303

"He was discussing the . . . sleeping arrangements." She felt suddenly shy. "I can go down by the fire."

His nostrils flared as he took her hand and kissed the palm. "No, Catherine," he shook his head. "You'll stay right here with me tonight, and every night, for the rest of our lives," the husky voice commanded in a tone which excited her. It was what she wanted, too. After finding him at last, she couldn't bear to be apart from him, even for one hour.

"I will stay up here with Jeffrey from now on, Miguel."

"Be happy then." His smile spoke volumes.

"I've never been so happy. Good night," and suddenly she was at his side, hugging him. "You're very special. So is Luis," and by force of habit she made the sign of the cross over him. "Bless you, Miguel." Jeffrey watched the graceful gesture. There was a part of her that would always be a nun, he knew that. Perhaps it was that part he loved best.

Catherine watched Miguel go downstairs. The two men prepared for bed and doused the candles. The hut was still. Miguel was truly a saint, though he would scoff at the title. She would never forgive herself if anything happened to him because of her.

Jeffrey felt Catherine had withdrawn from him and it hurt. He wanted to share her every thought. He got up off the bed and hobbled over to the ladder, slipping his arms around her waist, drawing her up against him. "What is it?"

She turned in his arms. "Miguel is a very dear friend, Jeffrey. I don't want anything to go wrong for him or Luis."

Jeffrey pressed her head to his chest. "He's in love with you. I can see it in his eyes every time he looks at you. I can't blame him."

304

She lifted her head and cupped his face in her hands. "There is so much to tell you . . . so much you must tell me."

"Yes," he whispered, silencing her words with his lips. They went back to the bed. Catherine helped him to a sitting position. He rubbed his leg again. She stood helpless before him, wanting to ease his suffering. He raised up and caught her around the waist with his arms, pressing his head against her warm body. "I've had so many dreams about you," he began quietly. "Don't ever leave me, Catherine," his voice shook.

"Jeffrey," she said, gently forcing him to lie back, smoothing the damp locks from his forehead. The exertion of getting up again had caused the perspiration to break out on his brow. "I'll never leave you," and she rubbed her cheek against his. She realized just how fragile this apparently strong man was, and it made her love him all the more. He clung to her with an intensity that spoke of his deep need.

"I love you, Catherine," he sighed and kissed her long and hard, pulling her down so their bodies touched.

"When I think you had to jump out of a plane into—into *nothing*," she cried. "How many were with you, Jeffrey?

"Dudley and Doherty. God knows what has happened to them. Luis and Miguel have searched, but they found no traces of them, poor devils."

"Are you really all right?"

"I've never been better, now that you're here. I'll never know by what stroke of Providence we're together again like this, but right now, that isn't important. You and Michael are all I've ever cared about." They gazed at each other, examining every line and feature. He shook his head. "I still can't believe you're real." His fingers traced lightly over her arched brow,

305

down the slightly upturned nose, along the lovely lips. She kissed his fingers. Her touch was electric. He urgently wanted to feel those lips on his, as if he had never tasted their sweetness before.

"Jeffrey? I thought you were in Africa? Were you trying to reach me when your plane crashed?"

"Lord knows I wanted to, Catherine. It's a long story. I'm stationed in Africa."

"Tell me everything," she begged. "Right from the beginning. Don't leave anything out."

"When I called you at the convent, I had just been in heavy briefing sessions at Coastal Command Headquarters outside London. We flew out the next morning to set up new bases in West Africa, but that was only part of the mission. The other part was to do surveillance over Spain. That's all I've been doing for the last few weeks. Three of us were out in the Hudson last week, taking a scan over the mountains and we ran into a bad electrical storm."

"I remember . . . that was the night the Perignon child passed away. Go on, darling."

"Our engines iced up . . . one caught fire. We had to bail out. I had hoped to catch a glimpse of the priory, but there was too much rain.

Catherine sat up. "You knew I was here?" she questioned incredulously.

"Catherine," he pulled her back down and kissed her. "You don't think I'd just say goodbye to you on the phone and then wonder for months where you were. No . . . I did a little homework so I could picture you in your new surroundings. You can't possibly imagine my horror when you told me you were going to travel over here, knowing what I knew about the state of affairs between Berlin and Madrid. It was all I could do not to break regulations. I didn't want you to come over here.

306

I've hardly slept since we talked on the phone.''

His concern for her was overwhelming. She nestled closer. ''And I lay awake every night for the last few months trying to picture you someplace in Africa. Some nights I thought I'd die from the suspense of not knowing.''

''I was sure I'd seen the last of you when I tumbled out that hatch!''

''My poor, poor darling,'' she wrapped her arms around him. ''Oh Jeffrey,'' she cried out with love. He put his hand under her chin and forced her face to his.

''You still haven't told me how you happened to come to this hut with Miguel, and why he means so much to you. I could be jealous,'' his eyes narrowed.

''No,'' she put fingers to his lips. ''I was assigned to work with him the day I arrived here. His assistant had passed away and he needed someone to replace her. Miguel is not a doctor yet, but he will be some day. He's had two years of medical training. He's the finest man I've ever known, next to you. He's dedicated and unselfish . . . fearless, like you.''

He tousled her hair to cover his emotions.

''We worked together every day, sometimes all night. You can't imagine what conditions are like here,'' her voice caught. ''Sometime I will tell you . . . anyway . . . Miguel and I grew close to one another. I knew his every thought, almost, and he knew many of mine. He belongs to an underground organization that helps people like you to escape. He's a political outcast in his own country, yet he stays on to help his people. His devotion is Christlike.'' Jeffrey listened, totally caught up in what she was saying. ''Just this morning he was in town and discovered, while he was trying to find milk for our starving babies, that two men from Gestapo headquarters in Madrid had been in town, asking questions about—about me.''

Jeffrey's blood ran cold. He sat straight up and stared down at her. ''The Gestapo?''

''Yes . . . it sounds incredible, but apparently they wanted to know if I had been making contact with someone from the outside, or vice-versa. Miguel was convinced that my life was in danger, and persuaded me to come to this hut where I would be safe. He felt that my connection with you was the reason for their inquiries. Miguel knew nothing about us, till I broke down and told him everything this morning. I had to! The pictures he painted of what could happen if they came to the priory for an interrogation . . .'' she shuddered. ''Anyway, darling, do you think Miguel was right?''

''Yes . . . definitely, but I have no idea how their intelligence traced you over here, Catherine. Only a handful of people know about us.''

''I know. When I told Miguel everything, he thought that perhaps you had been trying to reach me and I had to admit that it was a possibility. I was so frightened!''

''Oh, Catherine,'' he drew her up into his arms. ''To think my loving you has brought you to this . . .''

''I'm thankful that it has, Jeffrey . . . We *are* together, aren't we? It's not just a dream?''

''Yes,'' he blurted out. ''Yes, yes, yes,'' and they fell back to embrace each other again. Later, Catherine stirred.

''Who could possibly know about us and inform German intelligence?''

''I don't know, Catherine. There must be someone in England who thought you knew important information about me. Someone who knew we had been together at the hospital and at the house.'' He paused, ''There have been rumors that a Nazi spy ring has infiltrated the RAF in London. I've been reluctant to place much credence

308

in the story, until now.''

"I don't know how these things work, but Miguel said that even though I knew nothing, that wouldn't stop them from taking me off to prison, or worse . . ." her voice trembled. "He's been through terrible ordeals with his own family. I had to believe him."

"And he was so right," Jeffrey cried out violently. "Thank God you listened to him."

"I've already thanked Him. He brought me to you."

"I'll be indebted to your Miguel for the rest of my days for preserving both our lives. Someday we'll repay him for this sacrifice when we get back to England. We're far from home and safety, but after finding you again, I believe everything is going to be quite perfect. Now, no more talk," he whispered, finding her soft lips to caress. He kissed her again and again. They clung as one flesh. A new feeling of love for her swept over him. "I can hardly believe I have you in my arms at last," he buried his face in her bosom.

"I know," she murmured in his hair. "I love you," and tears fell on his cheek in the dark intimacy of the loft.

"If Michael were here," he finally spoke, "he'd ask why you were crying." Catherine laughed quietly and wiped her eyes. "And he'd pester us with questions we haven't even begun to ask each other yet," she said, kissing his chin. They sighed. He looked at her, still wondering how the miracle had happened. Again she mirrored his thoughts. "It is a miracle that we're together."

"Yes," he put her hand to his lips. "But you promised me over the phone that we'd be married, and I never doubted you'd keep your promise. I worship you! Tell me I'm not dreaming this."

"Look at your leg, my love. I'm afraid it is very

309

real." The too-short leather pants emphasized his long legs and big feet, which hung out over the end of the little mattress, as did hers. He laughed out loud and she laughed with him. They fell back staring at each other in absolute awe that this night had brought them together.

Catherine was a woman in every sense of the word, thought Jeffrey. She loved like a woman . . . could be provocative one moment, saintly the next . . . and soon she would be his wife. He closed his eyes tightly, anticipating the wedding night to come, the days and nights of loving her.

She lay next to him and her body throbbed with wanting him. She prayed the priest would come soon and turned her head to discover he was looking at her, probably reading her mind. She smiled quietly and then they began to talk once more, about everything that had happened in their lives since that painful day of parting back at Norwood. They laughed and cried as they recounted adventures to each other. They'd both lived several lifetimes since then. Another hour passed and still they were relating experiences, describing situations, helping each other to live the lapses in time when they had been apart. Catherine finally fell asleep, her head against his shoulder. Jeffrey reached for the blanket, pulling it up over them. He watched her in sleep, marveling that this angelic woman, so beautiful in every way, was to be his lifetime companion. Finally his eyelids closed.

Luis heard them talking. He did not understand their words, but he didn't have to. He smiled and felt a stab of envy for their youth and the years of life still ahead of them. Miguel had told him about their great love. Even in his old age, the thought of love took him back to those years with Maria. His eyes dimmed at the memory and fell asleep.

Miguel did not fall asleep till early morning. He was suffering torment that he was not that fortunate man upstairs holding Heaven in his arms.

Morning came and Catherine woke before Jeffrey. It was a strange, marvelous feeling to wake up in this man's arms. She felt a twinge of pity for the sisters who would never experience this dimension of life. Catherine would never have known of its joys had it not been for Michael. How she ached for the child! Being with Jeffrey brought him back so forcefully. She watched Jeffrey, memorizing every feature. Her heart swelled with love for him. Her eyes strayed to the window. She sky was still a lavender pink. It was very early. She was in the habit of waking before the sun was up to go to chapel. Now that would no longer be part of her daily ritual. Instead she would be fixing breakfast for her husband and son, seeing him off to work, and Michael off to school, then welcoming them home at the ene of the day. Her thoughts went back to that night at Norwood when Jeffrey had begged her to go outside walking with him. Thank God she had resisted that temptation. The waiting period had been long and difficult since that night, but she had no regrets, only fond, sacred memories of her life among the sisters, and now . . . she could come to him unashamed, unfettered by guilt of any kind. Her eyes still on the dawn sky, Catherine repeated her morning prayers with a full and grateful heart. She nestled closer to him and found he was awake, watching her. His face showed concern. "Catherine, darling? What's wrong?"

"Oh, nothing," she sighed and hugged him hard. "Everything is so right! That's all."

He smiled and marveled anew at her flawless skin, the perfection of her features. He leaned over and kissed her. She impulsively put an arm around his neck and responded with an urgency that made him want to forget all about the rules of propriety . . . but just as quickly, she slid away from his grasp and stood up, shaking out her skirt.

"Where are you going?" he demanded, still reeling from the impact of her passionate embrace.

"To fix you breakfast."

"How did you know I'm always ravenous first thing in the morning?"

"Are you?" she winked saucily. "I'll have to remember that. And have you forgotten that I already know a great deal about you, Commander?" Her half smile tugged at him. Lord, they would have to become man and wife soon! He couldn't stand much more.

"Don't be long," he murmured. Just before her head disappeared over the edge of the loft, she blew him a kiss. "I love you!" She was gone and he was dizzy with happiness.

Catherine found Miguel out in the barn, loading hay. Apparently Luis had already left. "Bonjour," she called to him. He waved a greeting. "I was just coming to find Luis and tell him I will fix all the meals from here on out."

"He will like that arrangement, but he had gone to get the priest. He said to tell you that he would not return without him."

"He's a wonder," she smiled. "Miguel, could you tell me if Luis has a tub big enough for bathing?"

"Yes . . . there is one in the barn. After breakfast, we can heat water."

"Thank you."

"Luis told me to tell you something else. The hut in the upper pasture is not as large or as clean as this one, but with some minor repairs, you and the Commander can sleep there until you leave the mountains. It has no

312

pump, so you will have to eat your meals with us, here, but at least you can have privacy."

"And Luis can have his bedroom back," she answered with gratitude, then went inside, humming happily to herself. After acquainting herself with the primitive kitchen, she commenced to prepare breakfast. There were eggs, cheese and oranges. Fresh citrus fruit was hard to come by in Spain right now. She blessed the name of the Mother General. When everything was ready, she called Miguel, then took two full plates up to the loft. Jeffrey was sitting up in bed, his head against the wall, arms folded. He flashed her the dazzling smile which always had the power to take her breath away.

"Here, my love," she put the plates on a low table. "Eat all you can. These oranges are straight from Italy." Jeffrey didn't need to be coaxed, but waited till she said grace before eating his breakfast. Never had food tasted as good to him as it did now. She sat by and watched, occasionally eating something from her own plate. She could feel his happiness. Everything he said and did fascinated her. He was terribly handsome. To think she was going to belong to him!

"It's almost like a honeymoon," she said with a little smile.

"Almost," he replied, pinching her cheek playfully as he popped another orange section in his mouth. "Of course, we're not exactly alone."

"Miguel told me that there is another hut in the upper pasture. They are going to fix it up for us to stay in." He stopped eating and stared at her. "It will be our first home as man and wife. No one has the right to be this happy!" she burst out.

He nodded. "Everyone has the right, but since there's only one of *you*, I'm the only man alive privileged to experience that kind of joy."

313

"Jeffrey," she blushed. He put the empty plate back on the table and pulled her down on the bed. He felt wonderful. He could have ten broken legs and it wouldn't matter. The love of his life was tucked safely away in his arms. Their lips met again and he began smothering her with kisses till she called out for help.

"There's nobody around to rescue you," his eyes flashed. "I have you in my clutches, me proud beauty," and he began tickling her ribs till her rich laughter rippled in the air. He loved it . . . he loved her!

"Stop, Jeffrey, please," she finally begged him, and the laughter ceased. His hands still spanned the slender waist. "I love you so much, Catherine."

Later, she insisted he take a nap while she busied herself with a few domestic chores. Miguel was out in the pasture. He'd eaten and gone out very quickly. She took advantage of her time alone and took a bath, washing her hair and pampering herself to make herself as attractive as possible for Jeffrey.

Later still, the smell of fresh bread wafted into the two men's nostrils. She made omelettes from the eggs and hot chocolate with the milk and chocolate she'd found in the basket. When the three of them gathered around the table for the afternoon meal, the compliments were unending. Jeffrey realized his wife-to-be was a spectacular cook, besides everything else. She never ceased to amaze him. In his whole life, he could never remember being so happy.

As Catherine said grace, suddenly she saw before her the faces of Señora Alba and her children. Catherine realized that she was being showered with untold blessings. Miguel's "amen" resounded in the small room. She had a feeling his thoughts were on the Alba family as well, and that he, like herself, was inwardly thanking God that they were on the road to recovery at last.

314

Jeffrey was content to watch her in silence as she waited on them; so was Miguel. All her movements were graceful. She sparkled . . . her freshly washed hair framed her face in swirling black curls and each time she passed near him, a sweet fragrance was noticeable.

After lunch, she washed the dishes and acted as translator for the two men who discussed everything from airplanes to politics. Still later she went to the loft while Miguel helped Jeffrey to bathe and shave. A feeling of well-being permeated the little hut. It was hard to believe there was a war on, that people were starving to death, that even they in their little world were living on borrowed time.

Miguel was laying a fire and Catherine was sweeping the floor when the sound of hooves on the hard-packed earth outside the hut reached their ears. Jeffrey went over to the loft window to look out. His eyes beheld two figures. He went over to the railing. "Luis is back." Catherine looked up at him. "The priest is with him!"

Miguel opened the door. There was a commotion as the three men greeted one another. They talked rapidly, their voices animated. The priest walked briskly inside and nodded to Catherine, who quickly put the broom away, suddenly nervous. She bowed. He was short and heavy set, with a great deal of fuzzy gray-black hair, and his eyes were the same black as Miguel's. Miguel introduced Catherine first, then Jeffrey, who was still up in the loft. Miguel forbid him to come back downstairs just then.

"Sister," Miguel began, then laughed and started again. "The Holy Father says he is delighted to make your acquaintances and that he is happy to perform the ceremony. Never in all these years has he been called upon to do anything quite so romantic. He says he does not blame the Englishman for being anxious."

Catherine smiled and shook her head, her cheeks flushing.

The two old men seated themselves in chairs by the fire and spread their short legs apart. Luis puffed on his pipe and they began chattering back and forth like two old women. Miguel emptied the basket Luis had brought into the house. "Look, Catherine! Wine for the occasion!" There were other things as well. Three candles appeared. They must have come from the church. Finally Miguel held up a mantilla. It was yellow with age and delicate. The priest indicated that she should wear it for a veil. Then Luis produced a little leather pouch from his trunk in the corner. He handed it to Miguel with an explanation, which Miguel translated.

"This was Luis's wife's wedding ring. Now he wants you to have it. Theirs was a very happy marriage. He knows it will bring you luck, but he thinks you won't need that." Catherine quietly bent down to kiss the old man's weathered cheek.

"Father Joachim must get back to his house tonight, Catherine. If you are ready, he would like to begin."

Catherine nodded. Miguel reached for the cups, fit the wine bottle and candles in his arms, and one by one they went up to the loft. Catherine clutched the mantilla tightly. She felt she was suffocating from happiness.

Jeffrey was dressed in clothes Miguel had brought, a dark blue sweater and brown trousers. He was leaning up against the wall, in bed.

"It's time, Jeffrey. The priest must get back to his home tonight, so he is going to marry us now." The Father went over and shook his hand. His eyes traveled from the man to the woman. Never had the old priest seen such a handsome couple. Catherine slowly raised the mantilla and placed it on her head. It felt very natural after wearing her wimple all these years. Jeffrey

316

was instantly reminded of Sister Catherine as he had first seen her. The priest took her hand and led her to Jeffrey's side. Miguel lighted the three candles. Then he took the small gold ring and handed it to Jeffrey, who stared, not comprehending. "For her," he pointed to Catherine. Now Jeffrey understood. He felt for her hand and clung to it.

When everyone was ready, the two witnesses in their places on the other side of the bed, the priest cleared his throat, pulled out his breviary, and began the ceremony in Latin heavily accented in Basque. The soft, slurring sounds were music to their ears. Jeffrey had wanted this for so long . . . it didn't seem possible he was finally going to have his heart's desire. He, like Catherine, felt the sacred solemnity of the ceremony.

When the proper moment came, the priest pointed to the ring and Jeffrey tried to place it on her finger, but it was too small. Catherine was forcibly reminded of that other ring she'd left behind at the altar of St. Theresa's. Jeffrey's hands shook. She let out a nervous laugh, then put out her least finger so he could slip it on. He smiled up at her in gratitude. The priest pronounced the benediction and made the sign of the cross above their heads. Catherine Rosine Prouet and Jeffrey Alen Norwood were now man and wife. There was a silence. The priest made a gesture.

"Catherine," Jeffrey whispered. "Bend down so I can kiss you," he laughed quietly. She leaned over and he tenderly bestowed a kiss on her lips. The priest smiled and slapped Jeffrey on the back, the wine was poured, and everyone began toasting the health and long life of the English couple. Father Joachim said something to Miguel, who in turn translated for Catherine.

"He says it is a pity there cannot be music and danc-

317

ing which is what our people love to do so well. He says never has he seen such a beautiful bride." Miguel's eyes were sparkling. "I agree," he added, and exercising his right as best man and honored guest, he pulled Catherine into his arms and kissed her warmly. The old men laughed heartily. For a little while no one had a care in the world. Jeffrey looked into the faces of these remarkable people. It was probably the most unusual wedding ceremony that had ever taken place, and he loved it! Every second of it. His eyes fastened on his adorable Catherine. Tonight she had a radiance about her he'd never seen before. He was almost in awe of her. She made his blood pound with desire; at the same time, he wanted to worship at her feet. She was laughing and talking modestly, completely at home with the others. He would have to be content for a little while longer to share her with them. His thoughts took him back across the ocean to England, to Michael and Philip. There would be so much to talk about when they went home. Yet he felt almost as much at home in this mountain hut among these dark-eyed men as he did at Norwood. Catherine was here. Nothing else mattered. He closed his eyes and tried to quell the violent beating of his heart.

When all the wine was consumed and everyone had kissed the bride, the priest bowed and said he must be going. Catherine and Jeffrey signed the marriage document which he witnessed, then he shook hands with Jeffrey once more before descending the ladder. Luis followed. Miguel turned to Catherine.

"Luis and I will stay at the other hut for two days. Then we will come back and you and your husband can move up there. Bolt the door after us and do not build any fires till we return. Do not light any candles. If the pigs come snooping, they will think the hut is deserted.

There is a gun over the fireplace. Tell the Commander it is loaded.'' He finally smiled. ''May you always be as happy as you are tonight.''

''Bless you, Miguel.'' She followed him down the ladder and fastened the bolt after him. The sounds of the mule's hooves grew faint. There were embers smoldering in the fireplace. She looked all about her in the last dying light of the fire, then took the mantilla from her head and slipped out of her clothes. Miguel had found an old robe of Maria's for her to wear. She slipped into it and fastened the belt, marveling at the intricate embroidery with which Maria had embellished it. Catherine folded her clothes and put them in the trunk. Her hand lingered on the worn blue dress she'd taken from the priory . . . was it only yesterday? Crossing herself, she sank to her knees.

Jeffrey sat up in the bed, and waited for her to come to him. Time passed and still there was no sign of his new bride. He knew without being told that she would be praying.

''Jeffrey,'' she whispered. He turned his head and watched her approach. She was wearing a black robe which came barely to her knees, held together by a simple belt. It revealed her long, slender legs. In the candlelight her skin gleamed like satin and the flush on her cheeks and throat was like the dusky pink tint on a half-opened rose. She came over to the side of the bed. ''Ours has to be the most unique of wedding nights, my darling,'' she smiled. He stared as if he had never truly seen her before. His hand reached out and rested on her hip. The soft skin was warm beneath the thin material. She felt his touch and gazed at him with loving eyes. There was a thickness in his throat. For a moment, he could not think. His hand passed down her leg. Catherine knelt beside him.

"Here, let me help you," she said, easing his pant leg over the cast. His hand cupped her chin. "I should be helping you, not the other way around." She gazed at him through the heavy black lashes. Her eyes were purple in the dying light and they shone with a lustre that rivaled the stars he could see through the open window.

"Everything about us has been different right from the very beginning," she answered in a tremulous voice. "Perhaps—perhaps it isn't proper for me to be saying this to you, but I've longed so for this moment."

"Catherine," his brilliant blue gaze fused with hers. "You gave up a whole other life to become my wife. I pray you'll never regret that decision."

"How could I regret what was destined to be from the very beginning? I'm your wife now . . . forever. I want nothing else." Her voice broke. They looked with love and longing deep into each other's eyes. Jeffrey blew out the candles. She came to him then. They reached out to each other with that eagerness and joy only those who truly love can experience, and the passion which had been kindled over the passing months now burst into glorious flame. They sought only to bring each other happiness, and in this total giving of themselves, a deeper union was created that would withstand all the trials that still awaited them. One day soon they'd go back home to England, to Michael, to begin their new life as a family, the three of them bound together inextricably by the silken bonds of love.